Praise for Carole Nelson Douglas and the Midnight Louie feline PI series

"Midnight Louie's contributions to the book are insightful, humorous, and imaginative... Along with all these wonderful offbeat characters, Douglas has an interesting plot, good story, and an intriguing mystery. If you are looking for something fun to read, this is the book for you."
—*Affaire de Coeur* on *Cat in an Alphabet Soup*

"...just about everything you might want in a mystery: glitzy Las Vegas, real characters, suspense, a tough puzzle. On top of it all, it has a fine sense of humor and some illuminating social commentary."
—**The Prime Suspect** on *Cat in an Aqua Storm*

"Midnight Louie sniffs through plenty of plausible red herrings...before pointing a claw at the killer in this brisk tail that even mystery readers who don't love cats will relish."
—*Publishers Weekly* on *Cat on a Blue Monday*

"...the best Louie adventure yet, full of intricate plotting and sharp characterization. And Louie? Nine lives wouldn't be nearly enough for this dude."
—*Publishers Weekly* on *Cat in a Crimson Haze*

"Once again Ms. Douglas lights up the skies with a dazzling blend of witty prose, clever plotting and just plain old good fun. No wonder Midnight Louie is everyone's cat's meow"
—*RT Book Reviews* on *Cat in a Flamingo Fedora*

"Feline PI Midnight Louie prowls the alleys of Las Vegas, solving crimes and romancing runaways like a furry Sam Spade. This time out, the always engaging Louie stalks a serial killer."
—*People* magazine on *Cat in an Indigo Mood*

ALSO BY CAROLE NELSON DOUGLAS

Midnight Louie Mysteries

CAT in a ZEBRA ZOOT SUIT

The Twenty-seventh Midnight Louie Mystery

by Carole Nelson Douglas

"Snaps and glitters like the town that inspired it."
—*NORA ROBERTS*

WISHLIST BOOKS

CAT IN A ZEBRA ZOOT SUIT:
A MIDNIGHT LOUIE MYSTERY
Copyright 2015© Carole Nelson Douglas.

Published in the United States by Wishlist Publishing

Copy Editor: Mary Moran

Formatting by Dan Keilen

Images Copyright © iStock.com

Author photo Copyright © Sam Douglas

Cover and book interior design by Carole Nelson Douglas

Printed in the United States of America

Library of Congress Control Number: 2015910881

ISBN 978-1-943175-01-7

Digital ISBN 978-1-943175-03-1

Audio book ISBN 9781681413785

www.wishlistpublishing.com

FIRST EDITION

For Betty Willis, neon designer, 1923-2015
She will shine forever for her iconic Vegas signs.
1955 Moulin Rouge Hotel and Casino
1956 Blue Angel Motel (just saved)
1959 "Welcome to Fabulous Las Vegas"

TABLE OF CONTENTS

Previously in
Midnight Louie's
Lives and Times...

What is a humble hotshot PI to do?

Here I sit in Las Vegas, a city that has been a Capital of Crime for seventy-five years. I have an inkling that my nearest and dearest clients have scattered or are ready to scatter to the wind's four corners.

(Why the wind has corners, I do not know. I have four corners myself...right front and rear shiv holders and left front and rear shiv holders.)

Anyway, shivs aside, how am I supposed to keep an eye on those who need it if they are planning on leaving me at home alone?

Although we just successfully concluded the case of Murder Most Rock 'n' Roll and the music show is a hit performing nightly at the Crystal Phoenix, I have not forgotten the messy, ragged ends of the previous adventure.

Not long ago, my posse—both human and feline members—had their lives on the line, but the Las Vegas Cat Pack came through the confrontation with snaggle-tooth and ragged nail mostly intact. The outcome is that all of my human associates are concealing the facts of what went down from the police, and, like the Cat Pack, the offending psycho is nowhere to be found.

I was not the only one among the wounded—if you count broken nails as a wound, and I do. Mr. Matt Devine was shot in the side, not seriously only because I launched my twenty fully-packed

2 CAROLE NELSON DOUGLAS

pounds at the perp's weapon as the gun fired. He is recovering nicely under the ministrations of my doughty roommate, Miss Temple Barr.

Mr. Max Kinsella received another blow to his already banged-up head. Who knows what setbacks his recovering AWOL memory may encounter?

The Cat Pack acted only as intimidating muscle, under my direction. However, their usual leader and my esteemed streetwise mother, Ma Barker, performed a banshee howl as I jumped the gun and I then administered a four-shiv slash to the assailant's face as a *coup de claw.*

This "coup de claw" is a classic finishing move in the art of cat fighting, a swipe across the kisser. Since our opponent is a female of her species, she will see my handsome white-whiskered black face and razor-sharp stilettos every time she looks in a mirror.

Perhaps I should formally introduce myself as founder and CEO of Midnight Investigations, Inc. I plied the mean streets of Las Vegas for many years as a bachelor about town, and then moved into PI work. I now have my own condo with my Titian-haired, live-in PR woman and amateur detective (thanks to me), Miss Temple Barr.

She may not be a Miss much longer if she weds Mr. Matt Devine as planned, alas. Our cozy condo does not need interlopers, especially on the California king-size bed, which is perfect for the two of us right now, with my curl-upable twenty pounds and her one hundred.

Yes, she is a tiny thing as humans go, but she has the heart of a mountain lion and the relentless investigative instincts of a bloodhound. Actually, she is much more attractive in human terms than this characterization sounds.

So back to me again. Yes, the neon-lit Strip is my beat.

For a Vegas institution, I have always kept a low profile. I like my nightlife shaken, not stirred. Being short, dark, and handsome... really short...gets me overlooked and underestimated, which is what the savvy operative wants anyway. I am your perfect undercover guy. Miss Temple Barr and I make ideal roomies. I like to hunker down under the covers with my little doll, but she also tolerates my wandering ways.

Call me Muscle in Midnight Black. I play bodyguard without getting in her way. We share a well-honed sense of justice and long, sharp fingernails and have cracked some cases too tough for the local fuzz. She is, after all, a freelance public relations specialist, and Las Vegas is full of public and private relations of all stripes and legalities.

So, there is much private investigative work left for me to do, as usual.

Then you get into the area of private lives. I say *you* get into that area. I do not. I remain aloof from these alien matters among humans. I will not give away the more intimate details of my roomie's lifestyle. Let me just say that everything it seemed you could bet on is now up for grabs and my Miss Temple may be in the lose-lose situation of her life and times.

Since Las Vegas is littered with guidebooks as well as bodies, I here provide a rundown of the local landmarks on my particular map of the world. A cast of characters, so to speak:

To wit, the current status of who we are and where we are all at:

MIDNIGHT LOUIE, PI

None can deny that the Las Vegas crime scene is big time, and I have been treading these mean neon streets for twenty-seven books now. I am an "alpha cat". Since my foundation volume, *Cat in an Alphabet Soup* (formerly *Catnap*) debuted, the title sequence features an alphabetical "color" word from A to Z. So, *Cat in an Aqua Storm* (formerly *Pussyfoot*) comes next, followed by *Cat on a Blue Monday* and *Cat in a Crimson Haze*, etc. until we reach the, ahem, current volume, *Cat in a Zebra Zoot Suit*. I assure you that no cats were actually forced to wear a zebra-striped zoot suit during the events of this book. Not to my knowledge.

MISS TEMPLE BARR, PR

A freelance public relations ace, my lovely roommate is Miss Nancy Drew all grown up and wearing killer spikes. She had come to Las Vegas with her soon-to-be elusive ex-significant other…

MR. MAX KINSELLA, aka The Mystifying Max

They were a marriage-minded couple until he disappeared without a word to Miss Temple shortly after the Vegas move. This sometimes missing-in-action magician has good reason for invisibility. After his cousin Sean died in an Irish Republican Army bomb attack during a post high school jaunt to Ireland, Mr. Max joined the man who became his mentor, Garry Randolph, aka magician Gandolph the Great, in undercover counterterrorism work all over Europe.

Miss Temple's elusive ex-significant other has also been sought—on suspicion of murder, no less—by a hard-nosed dame...

LIEUTENANT C. R. MOLINA

This Las Vegas homicide detective and single mother of teenage Mariah is also the good friend of Miss Temple's freshly minted new fiancé...

MR. MATT DEVINE

Mr. Matt, aka Mr. Midnight, is a radio talk show shrink on *The Midnight Hour*. The former Roman Catholic priest came to Vegas to track down his abusive stepfather and ended up a syndicated celebrity now in line for hosting a national talk show.

MR. RAFI NADIR

After blowing his career at the LAPD when Miss Lt. C. R. Molina mysteriously left him, and for years the unsuspecting father of Mariah, he is moving up in Vegas hotel security jobs. Miss Lieutenant Carmen Regina Molina is not thrilled that her former flame now knows what is what and who is whose...since she told Mariah that her dad was a dead hero-cop.

MISS KATHLEEN O'CONNOR

Deservedly nicknamed "Kitty the Cutter" by my Miss Temple, she is the local lass that Max and his cousin Sean boyishly competed for in long-ago Northern Ireland but now has turned embittered stalker. Finding Mr. Max as impossible to trace as Lieutenant Molina has, Kitty the C settled for harassing with tooth and claw the nearest innocent bystander, primarily Mr. Matt Devine.

Miss Kathleen O'Connor's popping up again like Jill the Ripper has been raising hell for we who reside at a vintage round apartment building called the Circle Ritz, owned by seventy-something free spirit, Miss Electra Lark.

Someone arranged for Mr. Max Kinsella to hit the wall of the Neon Nightmare club with lethal impact while undercover. His traumatic memory loss means he knows he and my roommate were once a committed couple, but he recalls none of the emotional and, ahem, spicy details. So far. And now Mr. Max has vanished again, no doubt making himself a target who will take Kathleen home again to Ireland, where they can lay to rest her ghosts, and his. And maybe make ghosts of each other for eternity.

All this human sex and violence makes me glad that I have a simpler social life, such as just trying to get along with my unacknowledged daughter...

MISS MIDNIGHT LOUISE
This streetwise minx insinuated herself into my cases until I was forced to set up shop with her as Midnight Investigations, Inc. She alleges that I am her deadbeat dad, but I will never cop to that charge.

That is how things stand today, full of danger, angst, and confusion. However, things are seldom what they seem, and almost never that way in Las Vegas. So any surprising developments do not surprise me. Everything in Sin City is always up for grabs 24/7 — guilt, innocence, money, power, love, loss, death, and significant others.

Like Las Vegas, the City That Never Sleeps, Midnight Louie, private eye, also has a sobriquet: the Kitty That Never Sleeps.

With this crew, who could?

1
Off-Black

In every relationship, there are times when polite illusions must not only be tolerated, but embraced.

At least, that is what I tell myself as I sneak out of my Miss Temple's rooms long after my namesake midnight hour, dragging a white plastic Albertson's grocery bag over the walnut parquet condo floor to the ajar patio door, and outside.

With a powerful swing of my neck and shoulder muscles, I cast the bag and its ghastly contents over the balcony's low railing. The bag plummets through the night like a suicide victim in a nightshirt. It lands one story below with a sickening crunch on the asphalt, barely missing the rooftop of Mr. Matt Devine's freebie silver Jaguar. Car, that is, not the Big Cat.

I breathe deeply at my narrow escape from inadvertent automotive vandalism. Then I scan the parking lot below for witnesses. None but the moon. I swing over the railing and climb down, landing lightly on my feet.

Okay. I do not land so lightly, being a muscular dude with a lot of bone mass.

Twigs and leaves rustle in the tall oleander bushes ringing the lot, warning me of possible unseen eyes. Las Vegas never sleeps, nor does Midnight Louie when he is on a mission.

My teeth snag the white bag and I continue to drag its broken contents away from the Circle Ritz condominium and apartment building. The black marble circular façade gleams in the moonlight like a giant chocolate icing-frosted doughnut. Wait. My home, sweet home is classier than that. It shines like the Coliseum in Rome magically made whole again and enameled Punk Black.

A guilty twinge assails me. These plastic bags are intended to be recycled at the grocery store. I am contributing to unauthorized littering. Yet I must remove the evidence of my crime from the premises and into other custody. I can only hope my contacts are the ones shaking the oleander branches. Every bit of that plant is poisonous, but not as vile to me as the contents of my bag.

A piece of shadow separates itself from the trembling leaves.

"Have you got the goods?" a rough voice asks. Similar shadow figures bunch behind it. I am now confronting a gang.

"Right," I answer. "Primo stuff, freshly imported." I flick the bag lying between us open with a razor-sharp nail. "You can do a sniff and taste test, if you like."

"I like," Gravel Voice responds, edging near to do just that.

"Hey," I cannot help noting, "this is Family business. One would think you would trust your own son."

"*Hah!*" answers Ma Barker, Cat Pack clowder leader and my long-lost mama. I sometimes wish had remained long lost. A clowder is the feline equivalent of a street gang-cum-extended family, and you do not want to mess with the leader of the pack. So I remain mute as Ma Barker admonishes me as if I were an ignorant kit. "You are sneaking around on your Miss Temple Barr like some craven domestic slave. Why would you be straight with me?"

"I am not *owned*," I say. "I am a free and independent roommate."

"Who freely rips off this expensive domestic-slave gourmet food."

"For the Cat Pack, Ma. I do not see you turning up your whiskers at my, er, donations."

"Whadda my whiskers have to do with it?" Ma advances with a growl.

I shrink back slightly. Whiskers are a sore point with Ma. Hers are not only grizzled, but more prominent on her chin than her muzzle now that she has reached a certain age. She is still the only female clowder chief in Vegas, maybe the world, for that matter.

"Punk," she sniffs. Then the yellows of her eyes narrow as she gazes over my shoulder. "It looks like your roommate is entertaining a gentleman caller. No wonder you snuck out."

Behind the glass French doors, a pinpoint of bobbling light tailed by a tall, black shadow passes by.

My eyes widen as the Front Four shivs on my limbs curve into asphalt for traction. My brain processes several facts. Mr. Max Kinsella, my Miss Temple's ex, has headed to Ireland on secret agent business. Mr. Matt Devine, her current and closest, not only works nights, he never sleeps overnight in her condo on religious grounds, although Miss Temple's religion allows her to visit his quarters on overnights.

"You need backup?" Ma's harsh voice asks behind me.

"Not hardly." I yowl. I rake my claws into the nearest oleander trunk for a dose of poison. I am already halfway to the leaning palm tree that is my ladder to our balcony.

I am twenty pounds—give or take sixteen ounces here and there—of snarling defensive fury. If my dereliction of duty tonight causes one glorious red-gold hair on my Miss Temple's head to acquire a split end, somebody's epidermis is getting a bone-deep massage.

I am up the palm tree's rough trunk like a Singer sewing machine set on "Gather". I bound to the railing, then to the balcony floor, and shoulder the door wide open. It hits the wall loud enough to wake Miss Temple and cause a thumping and shrieking in the bedroom. I hesitate momentarily.

Ma is right, human bedroom activities can be...er, confusing to those of our persuasion. Has Mr. Matt come home early from his *Midnight Hour* radio gig and paid an amorous visit, despite past restraint? Is this assault or ecstasy? I am sure humans ask the same thing of my own kind's activities of that nature.

Yet this is no time for inter-species sensibilities to hold me back. With a banshee battle cry (or one of my own courtship wails) I charge into the darkened bedroom.

2
Off-Guard

Temple awoke to a ray of light streaking across her vaulted bedroom ceiling.

Then something like the weight of a dead body fell crosswise onto her bed, pinning her hundred pounds to the mat. Uh, to the mattress.

Was this a nightmare? Was she really awake?

Her heart went into a chorus line of rapid-fire beating, and not because of a welcome but unprecedented surprise post-midnight visit from her fiancé Matt Devine.

A glimpse of the red LED letters on her bedside clock showed 2:15 a.m., too early for Matt to be home from work. So…

Not. A. Dream.

She screamed, bucking and kicking to free any and all limbs. At least the dead weight wasn't a "corpse". It jammed an elbow into her side, gave a basso groan, and thrashed across the covers to leave the bed. A California king-size mattress offered a lot of wallowing, mushy territory to leave.

Apparently the invading big lug hadn't expected a super-long bed and had tripped. Some klutzy cat burglar he was.

Temple's cries of "Help, fire!" echoed from the ceiling while her churning legs pushed her upright against the upholstered headboard, where Midnight Louie perched atop the tufted-linen, cussing out the intruder. Their combined outraged yowls passed through the—what? Open? How?—French doors to pierce the night silence.

Louie's infuriated lethal weapon—tail switches—slapped Temple across the face as she lunged for the only defensive weapon available on the bedside table...her red plastic phone shaped like a high-heeled shoe. At least she'd had practice swinging a spike heel like a bludgeon in the past...

Meanwhile, the burglar's flashlight had fallen onto the bed, casting a narrow beam at no one and nothing.

Someone was in the hall, pounding on her front door.

"Temple, Temple!" Electra Lark, the landlady, shouted while brutalizing the metal lock with frantic scrapes of her passkey.

Temple sensed out-of-place arrangements in her usual nighttime landscape, the most obvious being the large, moving shadow of a man far from dead through the open door to the balcony. Beside her, Louie's bristled tail gave her one last kisser swipe as he jumped to the mattress foot ready to spring atop the intruder's vanishing shoulders.

"Louie, Louie!" Temple hollered in counterpoint to Electra's screams of, "Temple, Temple!"

If the invader had not known the names of the occupant and purported pet by then, he sure did now. At least "Louie" sounded like a resident (and presumably formidable) male instead of only being the resident male...cat.

"He's getting away!" Temple shouted to whoever might hear or care. She hoped the light illuminating her ceiling was on a police cruiser already arrived outside, although it was not the carousel of flashing red and true blue she'd welcome.

The escaping man growled a dirty word even Midnight Louie's full-range of feline invective couldn't match, and shrugged off the cat's pounce. Temple had clawed her way to the bed's foot by then, hoping to cushion Louie's fall. Silly her. She spotted the reflective greens of his eyes already atop the bureau near the open balcony door.

The departing shadow met a like form swinging down from above like Spider-Man. Then the two figures blended into one.

By then, Electra had managed a panting entrance and turned on the living room lights. "I have a gun," she shouted, rather shocking coming from a plump older lady in a pineapple-patterned muumuu. "Temple! Which one should I shoot?"

The landlady's breathless threat alarmed Temple more than it did the two men. From the heavy breathing and scuffling sounds on the small triangular balcony, the women were hearing a serious fist fight. "Shoot nobody, Electra," Temple said. "We have the intruder on the run."

Electra's wide, bright flashlight beam grew to spotlight the men dwarfing the open doorway and rocking the terra cotta pots. Then one ducked unexpectedly. The other catapulted over his bent back… and the railing, to fall onto the parking lot one story below with a raw cry of pain. Electra reached Temple, her big, square flashlight trained on the last man standing…on the balcony, at least.

"Max," Electra mouthed with the tiniest breath of surprise. And hope.

"No. *Matt!*" Temple said, just as surprised. She ran to him. "How did you know I was being home-invaded? Did he hurt you? Are your stitches all right?"

"I think you should ask if I hurt him." Matt clasped her in a bare-chested embrace, so romance-novel coverlike she was inclined to swoon instead of follow her first instinct, which had been to throw plant pots down on the vanquished intruder. She settled for leaning over the edge in Matt's firm custody to view the perp.

A shambling black form was up and loping apelike to the shrubbery edging the parking lot, right into the oleander hedges. Screams and curses ensued, along with yowls and curses. This was a feeding station for the Las Vegas Cat Pack, not a one of them declawed, and they deeply and effectively resented trespassers.

That left the deserted couple in the full beam of Electra's flashlight, clinging breathlessly and asking if each other was all right.

"Golly, kids," Electra said. "That was scary."

Matt frowned. "Not as scary as the sight of a presumably loaded gun aimed at us."

"Um, oh. Sorry." Electra lowered the flashlight beam, then the gun barrel. "Sure it's loaded. It's for protection. You two better get away from the window. I'm going to drop off the hardware at my penthouse and then go downstairs to call the police. A squad car can at least check the lot." She headed through the unit door into the hall.

"The intruder is gone," Temple called after her. "And probably marked for life," she muttered. "Those oleanders are crawling with feral cats."

Matt stepped inside to get them out of the public view, if any public other than alley cats lurked to view them.

Midnight Louie meowed indignantly from the floor, stalking inside before Matt swept the French doors closed and locked them. The cat jumped atop the bureau to wash his jet-black gloves.

"I think we were more alarmed than Electra." Matt pulled Temple close again. "When I realized the screams were coming from your room—"

She allowed herself a delicate shiver as he pulled her down beside him on the living room sofa. "I glimpsed the clock when the intruder pounced, but didn't think you were home yet."

"Left early and made good time. I should have checked in with you, but didn't want to wake you."

"You should have." Temple burrowed into his arms. "I didn't know you slept topless," she said, "or I would have been upstairs to wake *you*."

"That's a big problem and we've got to put a stop to it," Matt answered.

"You sleeping topless or my not knowing that?"

"Both."

"You can easily get rid of these martial arts bottoms," Temple said, toying with the waist string. "I'm so impressed by my Tarzan, swooping down to rescue me."

They were snuggling on her sofa like sleepover teenagers, both too revved to go back to sleep. Midnight Louie stalked away to make periodic prowls from the bedroom to the office bathroom where his always-open escape hatch window was, yowling at anything possibly still lurking in the darkness outside.

"I woke up hearing you screaming," Matt said, "and I could have scaled the Paris Hotel Eiffel Tower to get to you."

"So…you're more King Kong than Tarzan?"

"Don't joke, Temple. You must have been terrified."

"Too scared to be terrified. I turned into the Little Engine That Went into Overdrive. I screamed, I kicked, I clawed, but I think the guy was as startled as I was. He seemed to be struggling to get away from me as much as I was intent on eluding him. Then Louie came flying, all claws so not in, and they are like Ginsu knives… then Electra was at the door shouting, pounding, and scraping her key in the lock.

"Bottom line"—she pulled the waist strings again—"I think he was a burglar, not a rapist."

"I'm serious." Matt quieted her teasing fingers. "I don't know what that intruder was after, but it's crazy for us to be apart nights at this stage, even if I have night-owl work hours. First thing tomorrow morning, I'm telling Tony Valentine to amp up negotiations with the TV talk show people in Chicago. We're either going to relocate or get more secure quarters here."

"Telling your agent to call Chicago? Matt, that's wonderful." Temple sat up, recharged. "I've hated that you put off your career opportunity trying to protect me from Kathleen O'Connor. If you'd asked me, I'd have said let her eat eggroll."

"More like corned beef and cabbage, given her Irish heritage," Matt said with a smile. "And I hated not telling you. Thanks to her blackmailing me into 'counseling' her after my two a.m. show sign-off, I've spent more night hours with her than you lately."

"Oooh! Finding that out had me steaming—or not steaming—but she's gone now. When she returned the stolen mate to my shoe I got the message that she was done tormenting us. She has her real target in her sights now. I'm sure Max has lured her into following him to the Old World."

"So if she's gone, who's breaking into your rooms in the middle of the night now? And why?"

"I don't know. Maybe just a garden-variety thief. After having a psycho stalker, that would be refreshing."

"Don't even kid about it, Temple. Changes have to be made. We're going to sleep in the same unit."

"And not sleep there too?"

"And not sleep there too. But you'll still be alone from eleven p.m. to almost three a.m. And don't tell me Midnight Louie is adequate protection."

"Whose unit are we moving into? All my clothes and shoes are down here and that's a lot of stuff compared to your sparse closet."

Matt considered. Temple knew he probably felt her bedroom held too many memories of Max.

"We could use this pull-out sofa in my place if the big bed in the bedroom has too many cat hairs for you," Temple suggested. "And here is cozier."

He laughed and pulled her closer. "You're not mentioning the elephant in the other room, but I think I'm over that."

"I'm sure the Fontana brothers can give us private security."

"That's not good enough in the long run, and I don't want our nighttime whereabouts public knowledge. There's one thing we urgently need to do, though."

"What?" she asked, getting cuddly again.

"Temple, we're going up to Minnesota to do the family meet thing ASAP."

Temple threw her arms around his neck. "Oh, Matt, I can't wait to get you up to Minnesota, where you will knock my family's socks off! It's time. I'm so glad we're finally free to live our lives without any monsters from the past messing with our future."

"Amen." He answered her with a long, breathless kiss that morphed into more. "Enough with business from the past. Still, where do you keep your maps and notes from the Synth magicians' plan for a major magical heist, the Ophiuchus star map and all the Effinger Chicago lockbox leavings?"

"You don't think someone was after that?"

"Not likely. Who knew about it but you and me and Mr. Magic Kinsella? Better let me keep it, though. Danny Dove put a hidden safe in my rooms."

"Good thinking. Especially if we're making a quick trip out of town. Oh, you are so smart."

"Thanks."

"And handsome."

"Thanks."

"And hot."

The only answer to that required no further dialogue.

3
Off the Map

Midnight Investigations, Inc., is having a meeting of the board, and all I can conclude is that we are both bored by a—heh-heh...pawcity—of evidence. (I do know how to spell "paucity" but cannot resist an occasional pun for fun.) What we are dealing with is not fun.

The two principle partners, Miss Midnight Louise and I, have finished scouring the Strip from the Downtown Experience to the Excalibur Hotel and the lower Strip luxury hotels like the Luxor and the Mandalay Bay.

We have then zigzagged our paws east and west of the Strip like berserk sewing machines.

Three days, and not a trace.

Mr. Max Kinsella and Miss Kathleen O'Connor have left not a trace or track of themselves in this whole town that is not seventy-two hours old.

Even Miss Louise's fluffier-than-mine tail is dragging. She curls it around her sharply manicured toes and gives the terminal hairs a listless lick.

My own agile, whip-thin appendage just lies there like a dead snake. Well, maybe a sleeping Black Mambo, because I am always armed and dangerous, even when I am discouraged.

Discouraged! That word is banned from Midnight Louie's vocabulary.

"They are gone," Miss Midnight Louise says. "Really and most clearly gone."

"Most clearly and most sincerely gone," I agree. "Even Nose E, the drug and bomb sniffing Maltese dog, could not inhale one recently shed skin cell from either of them."

"At least it was not a violent departure," she says. "We could not find a blood trail either."

"That is even worse. Now we are not only totally in the dark as to whether the departure was forced or voluntary, but whether they went off separately, or"—here I shudder—"together, Bast forbid."

Miss Louise's head seems to nod morosely as she tongue-lashes her long black bib. "It is like sitting through the endless battles of the first two *Lord of the Rings* movies and never seeing that miserable ring go over the cliff into the fire in the third one. Who knows what epic battle of good and evil between Mr. Max and Miss Kathleen is even now occurring offstage?"

"And we shall never know what disposition has been made of our own local favorite magician, Gandolph the Gray," I add, "or in what forgotten plot of the Old Sod his body may lie."

"Oh, quit wailing like a Dublin pub band," she snaps. I mean literally snaps.

I back off, pretty literally too.

"And," she adds, "Garry Randolph's stage name was Gandolph the *Great*, not Gray. You are confusing him with the fictional inspiration for his performance persona."

"Same difference. Dead and gone is dead and gone."

"Gandalf the Gray came back from the dead to Middle Earth," she points out. "But no one is likely to fight to return to this glittering bit of High-end Earth. Listen to me, Da."

I roll my eyes at her using the Irish version of "Dad".

"We can be sure," she goes on, "Mr. Max Kinsella is capable of charming news of his late mentor's final resting place out of a four-leaf clover, but perhaps not if Miss Kitty the Cutter has lit out after him, as it seems."

"He wants to lead that Hibernian headcase a merry chase away from our favorite people," I say. "And the scene here is much more serene without him here, the awkward 'X' as in X-Acto knife, not to mention being a leftover leg of a romantic triangle."

Miss Louise growls.

"Oh, I forgot, Louise. Your favorite person *is* Mr. Max, and now he has left you lovelorn and forlorn in dull olde Las Vegas while he engages in a deadly game with Miss Kitty in Ireland."

"And that is yet another thing. Your Miss Temple was clever to nickname her 'Kitty the Cutter' for her lethal ways with a straight razor, but I am beginning to resent a pet name for our breed being constantly associated with a psychopath."

"This is old business, Louise, and we avoid the main issue here. If Miss Kathleen O'Connor is gone, who has perpetrated the latest outrage on my Miss Temple? I was indeed farsighted to have the Cat Pack move a sizeable presence from the police substation to the Circle Ritz grounds."

"You? It was *I* who convinced Ma Barker she needed to expand her territory."

"Me, you. Schmee, schmoo. What are we going to do about it?"

"Obviously your duty lies with Miss Temple. The Cat Pack got a generous sampling of the intruder's DNA, but we do not have an inside operative at the crime lab to process it."

"Much less a *CSI* with the skill and stones to remove the evidence from the claws of a pack of ferals. Besides, I think the last thing this poor excuse for a housebreaker wanted was an encounter with Miss Temple."

"Why?"

"She leaves a night-light on in the second bathroom to facilitate my coming and going through the open narrow 'eyebrow' window. This is an example of her tender regard, for we know I do not need any night vision amplification. The intruder could have thought the resident was sleeping on the other side of the unit."

"Seeing you eel your expanding midsection through an eyebrow window sounds like an entertainment I could sell tickets to. What was he after, then?"

"She has a bad habit of sticking genuine and costume jewelry in her bedroom scarf drawer. I have fished out an amusing string of freshwater pearls for my own entertainment a time or two."

"*Hmpfft.* Besides the flash on her ring finger that Mr. Matt gave her, she has not much in the way of fine jewelry to interest a thief."

"Or…" Here I pause, to build suspense. It does not work.

Louise merely rolls her eyes and yawns. "Senior moment, Daddy dude?"

"No! Or…someone is after the secret map of Vegas Miss Temple put together for where Miss Kitty's secret stash of big-time money and guns for the IRA might be hidden in town, or hunting remnants of the Synth conspiracy to continue their aim to stage the Vegas heist of heists."

Miss Midnight Louise is still yawning. "Those scheming magicians are dead or scattered. Nobody who ever looked for that 'buried treasure' saw more trace of it than a rat-chewed, crumpled bearer bond. The underground tunnels between the Crystal Phoenix, Neon Nightmare nightclub, and the Fontana brothers' Gangsters hotel have now been remodeled into entertainment entities so popular and crowded you could not hide a mouse whisker in there."

"Still, there is the Ophiuchus connection between several of the deaths our associates have investigated."

"Ophiuchus is a constellation of a man battling an improbably big serpent. The ancient myth-tellers and modern comics purveyors are fond of that notion. I know this 'forgotten thirteenth sign of the Zodiac' appeals to conspiracy nuts, like those UFO freaks that recently descended on the city. I would hope that superior and sensible species like ours are not so gullible as the human one. If one cannot see, hear, or eat it, it is likely to be a hallucination."

Well, I have been told off! I guess I will not remind Louise that a drawing of Ophiuchus was found only a couple of weeks ago in an old lockbox the late Mr. Clifford Effinger left with Mr. Matt's mother in Chicago. Vegas is as full of lost treasure tales as Oak Island is on cable TV. At least Vegas has had seventy years of mob shenanigans to make it a more likely spot for harboring such mythical things.

"Very well, Louise," I say. "I will keep an eye and ear on Miss Temple. You will have to tail Mr. Matt."

She sighs. "The hours are lousy and it is a long midnight trek back and forth from his radio station, but the Jaguar has a splendid sound system, at least. I will have to monitor his show. His call-ins do nothing but caterwaul about their personal woes. And then I must put in a full day as Crystal Phoenix house detective. It will be a taxing, boring assignment, but someone must do it, and you cannot be in two places at one time."

"Yet," I say. "You are whining like a Weimaraner dog. Except for the occasional intruder, I predict it will be a snoozer around the Circle Ritz too. I must agree that Mr. Max and Miss Kitty enlivened the neighborhood a good deal."

4
Off-Base

"I come bearing Pecan Sandies," Electra told Temple the next morning when her summons on the unit doorbell was answered. "If you have the coffee."

"I love Pecan Sandies. Stand and deliver."

Electra presented the box and followed Temple into the kitchen. The arched white ceilings reflected the sun rays flooding in from the balcony as Temple poured a stream of dark-chocolate-rich coffee into two mugs.

"*Ooh.*" Electra pored over a selection of individual flavored creamers while Temple arranged the cookies onto a plate.

"What can I do for you?" Temple asked after their mini-feast had been transferred to the living room coffee table.

"Get outa town fast," Electra said in a blissful cookie-crunching mumble.

"Which I'm planning on doing as of now." Temple sipped a double dose of caramel mocha coffee, then leaned forward to add yet another creamer. "Matt and I are flying to the Twin Cities ASAP. He's a major frequent flyer because of his talk-show guest appearances in Chicago, so he got tickets for Saturday morning."

"And a lucky thing." Electra had concentrated on the cookies first and was shaking more out of the box onto the plate. "Is Matt beside himself because of last night?"

"He wasn't pleased that some clumsy ninja broke in. The police patrol car didn't find anyone suspicious lurking in the neighborhood. We weren't planning to move in together until we got married, but—"

"Excuse me, dear. You know I never pry..." Electra's beringed right hand, free of cookie crumbs, patted her temporary hair-coloring choice du jour, magenta and purple. Electra used her snow-white hair as a canvas, and her mode was avant-garde.

Temple politely didn't contradict her.

"But..." Electra went on. "Matt doesn't, er, cohabit here nights, does he? I mean, we all know these are modern times. And he *is* right above you every night. Maybe I should rephrase that."

"You know we'd talked about Matt buying his unit and combining it with mine."

"I'm not averse to a two-story unit, but I don't understand what keeps you two kids living like a couple in a fifties sitcom."

"Matt is too considerate to wake me up when he gets home from his midnight gig at *WCOO*."

"'Considerate'?" Electra repeated. She cocked a gray eyebrow. "Oh, wait. I suppose Max's California king-size bed might have issues for him."

Temple glanced through the bedroom's open door. "It certainly doesn't for Midnight Louie."

Electra half-rose from her chair to peer in. Temple had spotted Louie's four limbs and signature tail sprawled like a big furry Rorschach blot on the zebra-pattern comforter with red piping.

Electra sat back to sip coffee. "You're not taking Louie with you to Minnesota? Or is he still snubbing your new carrier?"

Temple glanced at the red-lined, zebra-striped canvas cat carrier with its door open like a protruding tongue. Inside lounged catnip mice and other goodies. "So far he's boycotting his new travel carrier. I'd hoped the zebra pattern would remind him of his favorite snoozing spot, but you know cats."

"Contrary," Electra said, nodding.

"I did just get something amazing for the trip, and I'll wear it whether Louie and his new carrier are on board, literally. Wanta see it?"

Electra eyed the unlabeled shopping bag leaning against the sofa. "I'm always ready to be amazed by your doings, dear."

The rattling of the paper bag brought Louie racing in from the bedroom to investigate.

Some people, like magicians, were good at pulling amazing things out of hats, but Temple excelled at pulling amazing hats out of bags. Now she had an audience of two for her latest score at her fave vintage shop, Leopard Lady, only it was a horse of a different color.

Her landlady, Electra Lark, perched on one arm of her off-white living room sofa. Midnight Louie had jumped up to pose on the other arm. Both stared unblinking at what Temple whisked out of the bag.

"*Voila!*"

"Oh my word," Electra said. "In my wild youth I had a hat just like that in leopard print. Fuzzy like real fur too."

"This is definitely fabric, and not politically incorrect hide." Temple lifted the zebra-print pillbox hat atop her wavy cascade of red-gold hair.

"A pillbox hat," Electra mused. "Like Jackie Kennedy wore. We smart young things all had to have one in my day, with a "birdcage" veil, no less. Women were still slaves to fashion, and it was not a casual age."

"Yours or the times?" Temple asked mischievously. "Aren't these tiny combs sewn inside the lining to anchor the hat to your hair just the cutest things?"

"Adorable, like you." Electra glanced at her fellow panel member, the cat. "And your new hat goes with Mr. Midnight Louie's new zebra-print carrying case. Too bad the party pooper is staying home."

"Just as well this time."

"Louie accompanied you to Chicago to meet Matt's family. You don't want your family to meet the grandcat when you and Matt visit?"

"We're not thinking of relocating to Minneapolis," Temple said.

"Don't worry. Louie and I will hold the fort while you and Matt are gone," Electra promised. Then she frowned. "You seem a bit hyper or nervous, Temple. Surely you're not afraid of going home?"

Temple lowered the hat and then dialed back her smile.

"I *am* nervous," she admitted. "My first candidate for a serious partner was not popular. It'll be Matt's debut for meeting the whole family, which means my four strapping brothers who *only* speak Sports and who *only* have sons among their sets of offspring. They're threatening to out-populate the Fontana brothers, only louder. Testosterone is an air freshener in my parents' house."

"You're the lone girl?"

"Except for my mother."

"No wonder you're such a feminine woman. Somebody had to bear the flag for the kinder, gentler, smarter gender."

"Maybe. And, thanks to looking fourteen, I've never been given credit for growing up."

"You'll thank your lucky stars for 'looking fourteen' a few decades ahead."

"And then, oh, Electra, there's the terrible gaffe I just realized I made with my mom, now that I need to call her again to tell our arrival plans."

"You? Made a gaffe? You're Miss Smooth PR lady."

"Not with her."

"I met your folks just to nod at during the dinner before Kit's wedding. They didn't seem at all like ogres."

Temple groaned and cast herself down on the couch, sitting with her hands over her eyes. "Of course you 'met them just to nod at' during the big Crystal Phoenix dinner. Of course they'd flown in one day for the dinner and out after the wedding the next day. Of course you were there because you were going to officiate for Aunt Kit and Aldo Fontana's wedding the next day. Of course you're only forty-some years older than I am, and you still have a memory."

"Temple." Electra sat beside her to pry the fingers away from her face without getting grazed by a long strong fingernail, all as natural as Louie's. No fakes for Temple. "Tell me what's troubling you. It can't be as bad as you think."

"It is. I got up my nerve to call Mom a while ago, before that crazy Area 54 project caused major havoc in my work life. I picked a Saturday noonish, when Dad and the boys were off pestering fish or something, to prepare her for Matt and me making a quick trip up to meet the whole Barr mob and discuss wedding possibilities."

"Which will include a lovely civil ceremony at the Lovers' Knot Chapel as a possibility."

"Yes, you're still in the running. Electra. As Unitarian Universalists, my folks wouldn't blink at a non-church wedding, unlike Matt's relatives in Chicago, who'd go ballistic."

"All in-laws fight for custody of the cross-country wedding locale, although the bride's family has the edge. We can have a secret, private ceremony here, if you like."

"Secret and private sounds just the ticket right now."

"So, dear girl, what did you do when you called your mother that has gone down in history as a Gaffe. Where did that word come from anyway?"

"It's from the French for 'blunder'. To me it's a combination of 'ghastly' and a self-*effacing* social error. In other words, you want to crawl under the bathroom throw rug and never come out. And maybe throw up for good measure."

"What could you do that's so awful?"

Temple cringed, delicately. "I forgot."

"What?"

"Everybody."

"Everybody who?"

"My parents."

"Oh. Bad."

"And…Matt."

"Worse. And this happened at the wedding banquet for Kit and Aldo?"

Temple nodded solemnly. "When I called Mom recently, I forgot that Matt and Aldo had joined my folks and Kit and me for dinner, and we announced my engagement. So I 'broke the news' to Mom all over again, and she played dumb and went along as if this were the first she'd ever heard of it. I only realized, duh, I was in the world's worst rerun when I was talking to Kit about my wedding arrangements.

"And Kit says, 'Thank God you ran Matt past them at that huge Crystal Phoenix dinner. So wise to confine the first meeting to such a short and chaotic visit. I was happy my big wedding hoopla provided cover. I don't think what happened really sank in with Roger. When you and I brought out our engagement and wedding rings, I think Roger took Matt for a jewelry salesmen, rather than a fiancé.'"

"So your dad thinks you're marrying some kind of jewelry distributor, like Avon but only via Tiffany?"

"Maybe. But my mom must think I'm nuts. Or, worse, flighty."

"You do seem to have a hang-up about going home. You haven't in two years."

"It was major trauma and family dramatics when I met Max at the Guthrie Theater and relocated to Las Vegas to live with him. You'd think it was a crime, the Barrs' 'baby girl', running off with a traveling magician without any visible signs of commitment."

"Bosh. Not criminal, but wonderfully romantic," Electra said. "I eloped with my first and third husbands."

"Eloping implies you get married right away. Max and I didn't."

"You were thinking about it, though."

"Sure, seriously. When thugs from Max's counterterrorism past forced him to 'disappear' without a word, I especially couldn't 'phone home' then. My judgment would really look Missing in Action."

"Poor thing." Electra patted Temple's shoulders. "But Max came back several months later. All's well that ends well. Thugs will never come for Matt and make him 'disappear on you'. Your mother seems to have been more amused than alarmed by your 'gaffe'. She may understand your being flustered more than you think. My goodness, I'd be flustered if I had just *one* of your two very eligible beaux buzzing around me."

"How will I explain my temporary amnesia, though, to my mother?"

"I have a great idea!"

Temple sat up, ready for redemption.

"Make it a game, and re-announce your engagement again, then say you hope the family won't make a big deal of it. Just sound very coy, like you're giving her the pleasure of hearing the news an extra time. You know how to spin it better than I do."

Temple sat up even straighter. "Yeah. I could do that. I could say she only has one daughter, so I'm giving her rerun engagement announcements so it feels like more."

"And then move on quickly to trip arrangements."

"Electra, you are brilliant! That's just what I'll do. I can't thank you enough."

"I'm not brilliant," Electra said into Temple's hair and heartfelt hug. "I just have a lot of experience with weddings, and marriage and mothers and daughters and nerves and all. And I'd be proud to call you my daughter no matter what you forgot, or ever could forget."

Somebody sniffled. Maybe two somebodies.

Midnight Louie yawned, and sat down on his haunches. He eyed the bag, hat reinstalled. Anybody who had been watching would see he had some mid-night romping plans for them.

"So," said Electra a while later, nibbling on a Pecan Sandie, "when you're gone, I'll have Ernesto and some other Fontana boys over for lunch and a security evaluation. With particular attention paid to your unit."

"The Fontana brothers are doing private security now?"

"Honey, if you are on their A list, the Fontana boys will do *anything* to help you out. Although, if Max still lived here, it'd be even safer."

"I'm not so sure." Temple frowned. "There's only so much you can do with an old building like this," she added. "All these cute balconies are a liability. That's how my would-be thief got in."

"What about that crazy stalker who was bedeviling you all?"

Temple shook her head. "Can't be her. Last I've heard, she was going so far away she's practically off the planet."

"I'm sorry to hear that."

"Sorry? Electra, why?"

The landlady made a sheepish face. "She'd be a good scapegoat for some recent disturbing events. Now I *really* have to worry about the locals. I didn't want to alarm the tenants, but the Fontana boys were going to upgrade security here before your break-in last night. There's been some exterior vandalism."

"Here?" Temple looked over her shoulder and walked toward the balcony to view the residents' parking lot below. "On cars, or what? Matt's Jag and my Miata might be tempting targets. Vandals are usually jealous and mean."

"Oh, the cars. Another thing to worry about. I'll have Ernesto see to that too."

"Where else would the vandalism happen?"

"If you want to take a stroll, I'll show you."

Her appetite dampened, Electra put down her half-eaten cookie, although Temple had not yet snagged a one, and they left their coffee mugs cooling on the kitchen counter. Temple was getting alarmed again. She grabbed her tote bag on the way out, for the keys and cell phone inside.

They only had to go down a floor in the tiny elevator. Once in the charming but small foyer, Electra turned right into a part of the building Temple rarely visited.

"The wedding chapel hasn't been harmed?" she asked, concerned. Matt's mother had recently been married there and it was on Temple's long list of possible wedding sites.

When Electra unlocked the door, they entered, then stopped. The space was airy and bright, a bower of green and gold with rows of white pews inhabited here and there by a gentle company of mute attendees. Temple picked out her favorite soft sculpture figures, elegantly hatted ladies with painted cloth features tricked out in estate sale clothing, so many decades were represented. The gentlemen were fewer, and not as colorfully attired. Of course, a jumpsuited Elvis was the glittering exception. She also glanced at the Lowery organ, where her then brand-new neighbor, Matt Devine, had played an unexpected wedding march, a Bob Dylan song.

"It's strange," Electra said, her fond glance on the organ too. "Strange that we never suspected the new tenant, who could play a wedding march from memory and was so at home at a chapel organ keyboard, was a former clergyman."

"'Love Minus Zero—No Limit'," Temple said, smiling.

"What?"

"That's the title of the song he played that day."

"What on earth does it mean?"

"Unconditional love, I think. Look up the lyrics online. They're another side of Bob Dylan. A classic love song."

"That's more my generation than yours, dear. I hope Matt will find someone else to play it when you two get married here."

Temple opened her mouth, but Electra forestalled her. "I know, I know. You both have families likely to pressure you about where you should get married, but I hope I'm family enough to be in the running."

"You sure are." Temple gave her another hug. She was beginning to realize she'd found a mother figure in her home away from home. "I may be in desperate need of neutral ground on that issue." She rolled her eyes. "Maybe the decision will be clearer after my trip north."

"But you and Matt are definitely getting married?"

"Definitely, finally, and sincerely getting married." Temple felt a familiar velvet brush on her bare calves and looked down.

Mr. Slugabed had roused himself to join them.

"Where'd Louie come from?" Temple said, laughing.

"Oh, he's a fast one, getting down here ahead of us. He often sleeps in the pews," Electra said. "Usually in Elvis's lap. He likes to commune with the King."

"Maybe, but he probably showed up now because he's angling for a replay of his earlier starring role here. Ring bearer for Matt's mother's wedding."

"He was so cute in his white bow tie," Electra reminisced, "with the ring box dangling from it."

Temple had noticed that the word "cute" was as annoying to Louie as to her. Being little didn't mean one couldn't be smart and, when occasion called, fierce.

Louie was not shy of the spotlight. All cats gravitated to basking in natural or artificial rays. But now he gave a restless *merow* and moved away.

"So," Temple asked her landlady, "everything looks great here. What's the vandalism?"

"Just you wait."

Electra led Temple, again joined by Louie, where Temple at least had never gone before. They walked through the chapel and out to the exterior entrance, which featured a drive-by window for the "marry in haste" crowd and parking for those who opted for more ceremony inside.

"How gorgeous. I've never driven around to this side," Temple said. "I love the twin shirred chiffon awnings for both the drive-up and walk-in areas. Flamingo instead of pale pink. Classy and kicky at the same time. You're a savvy marketer, Electra."

"And the awnings are made of microfiber fabric, so they're easy to clean." Her tone flattened. "Not so much now."

Temple looked closer, then walked under an arched awning. Black spray-painted graffiti of crude, even x-rated, language covered the interior.

"How horrible! Luckily," Temple added, looking for an upside and finding a literal one, "people in love tend to gaze at each other, instead of up at the undersides of awnings."

"Still, Miss Optimist, this will take a cleaning service to eradicate," Electra said. "I used the garden hose to lighten the stuff on the walls."

Louie had leaped atop a long, low concrete planter box, his head bowed to sniff the dirt. The lumpy, empty dirt. Temple looked at Electra.

She nodded. "Yup. The flowering plants were ripped out. And someone's taken a hammer to the decorative friezes."

Now that Temple looked more intently, she spotted scattered stone chips, evidence that Electra had cleared out a big mess. "Who would do this and why?"

Electra sighed and nodded to the street. "If you take a drive about a hundred yards down, you'll find a big empty building with a sign almost as big. A new business is going in."

"Huh." Temple was surprised. "This is an old strip shopping neighborhood, pretty isolated, but the Strip is always reaching out tendrils to new land like an octopus. Maybe some Strip enterprises got the zoning changed for future expansion. That can't be all bad."

"Your optimism is no help to the Lovers' Knot. The news *is* all bad."

"And—?"

"It's an offshoot business of Pornucopia, an Adult Wearhouse," Electra intoned.

"A porn shop?"

"A porn department store with a movie balcony. Yes. So I naturally looked up a what new business they were spinning off in the neighborhood. And now I'm considering a neighborhood protest. Whoever owns that operation does not play nice."

"And you think scaring your residents, like me, is part of a campaign to shut you up?"

"And shut me down."

Temple considered what she'd heard. "Max and I invested in the Circle Ritz condo because it was so near the Strip without being part of it. We didn't realize that cheesy adult businesses could ever fill the holes in-between the two locations, though."

"Me neither, kiddo." Electra's gray eyes broadcast steely determination. "Vegas got hard hit during the Great Recession. A lot of the innocuous surrounding businesses like dry cleaners and sandwich shops that CR residents found convenient have closed, with nothing to take their places."

"Except the demand for ever-expanding sleaze. I don't suppose there's a school nearby," Temple asked hopefully.

"No. My first thought. That would drive out any porn."

"Too bad."

Electra's eyes suddenly widened. "For sure…if Pornucopia's spin-off gets going strong, it'll attract more associated businesses."

"And your investment in the Circle Ritz goes up in smoke. I'm so sorry, Electra. Maybe you can move the building to someplace better."

"Howard Hughes could have afforded to do that. Can't you see him towing it away with the Spruce Goose? You want to walk along with me to the building site?" She glanced down at Temple's red suede pumps with gray steel spike heels. "Or do you need to change into flats?"

"Me, in flats? Only when I want to be completely invisible and have everyone looking over my head. My high heels are my edge, Electra. I wouldn't leave home without them, any more than Dorothy would have left the ruby slippers behind in Oz."

"Gee, what did Dorothy do with her ruby slippers after she got back to the farm in Kansas anyway?"

"Put 'em away for a rainy day. Let's hoof it to this new atrocity on the block."

5
Off-Beat

Temple attacked in *her bed at the Circle Ritz.*

Matt woke up late the next morning, that thought circling in his brain like the nightly intro music to his midnight radio show. Both were nagging noises he would never escape. Oh, sure, he was free for the day until showtime called him to *WCOO* a half hour before the magic moment of going live on talk radio with *The Midnight Hour.*

Now he was at loose ends, with Temple packing for their weekend trip north, always a mini-production of a road show. He was pre-packed from his quick trips to Chicago to guest on *The Amanda Show*, and guys with their small color range—khaki, black, and blue—pack light anyway. No matching shoes involved. He needed to do something…something useful, with all this daylight free time. Max was gone, as Matt had wished for months, leaving Vegas as a moving target with Kitty the Cutter hot on his trail to Ireland.

Now Matt would wish Max straight back if it would help find out why Temple and her Circle Ritz condo had been some intruder's target. Matt wasn't an undercover agent. He was an ex-priest turned radio shrink turned fiancé.

The attack. Coincidence? Maybe.

Lieutenant Molina had referred him to Woodrow Wetherly, a retired cop in his weathered eighties, echoing his surname. The man knew Las Vegas crime history like his long lifeline, going back to the founding mobs. Maybe Woody could clue him in why his nasty stepfather, Cliff Effinger, seemed to haunt Matt's own history in both Chicago, where he grew up, and here in Vegas, where Matt had moved for the exclusive reason of tracking down Effinger. When he was still alive.

So he called the old guy on the phone, cell to landline, and requested an audience. Woodrow was a character. Crude, gruff, and savvy in a pre-Netflix way you couldn't find or buy nowadays.

Matt ended up back in the fifties-vintage house by noon, regarding Woody ensconced in his worn recliner. Who had something not nice to say.

"Huh. You don't look like a liar. But it seems you weren't straight with me first time we talked, kid."

"Not straight? About what, Mr. Wetherly?"

"Your radio show. *The Midnight Hour.* It's not a crime show at all. It's the midnight soap opera." Wetherly's tone was scoffing.

"Okay, the title may sound hokey, but it *is* my show. That's true."

"Yeah, but you made it sound like one of those hard crime reality shows, like John Walsh with the dead kid hosts. Instead, it's people cryin' in their banana daiquiris or some chi-chi cocktail about their personal problems."

Matt opened his mouth to answer that charge as Wetherly waved him silent. "I know whinin' in public is what entertainment comes down to these days. You have a nice-sounding voice and, uh, bedside manner, but doesn't it drive you nuts to be talking to all these losers?"

Matt opened his mouth again. The old man waited this time. "I'm thinking of moving on from the show."

"*Aha!* So you're like some headline-happy reporter. You want a big juicy story to break." He nodded sagely. Ambition he understood.

"Yeah."

"So what's gonna be your ticket out of Sobsville?"

"This unsolved murder. Grisly murder."

"The best kind."

"Not in John Walsh's league, but nasty. Guy was apparently tortured and tied to the sinking pirate ship bowsprit like a mummified figurehead to drown one night."

Woodrow Wetherly grinned, showing his yellowed teeth. A certain generation hadn't heard about bleaching white strips and didn't care. "Yeah. That was a corker. Retired badge like me noticed the Metro cops went mum real quick on that case."

"That's why I was asking about mob activity in Vegas nowadays. That sounds like something Bugsy Siegel would have done."

"Bugsy? Naw. Bugsy got done *to* at the end, although he did a lot of doing *in*. He wanted to be a celebrity impresario, and forgot the bottom line is the bottom line."

"Or this Italian 'Jack the Hammer' guy you told me about. Giaccomo Petrocelli."

Woodrow's gnarled, sun-spotted knuckles made a leprous fist in front of Matt's chin while the retired cop considered it. "That ship killing was a retro-style hit, wasn't it, kid? And what passes for police now got quiet fast about that death too. That's what they do when there's no leads. Or. When there's leads they don't want to follow."

His hands parted to slap his palms against his knees. "But you want to follow up on who would do such a thing? Maybe you got some spine, after all. I might be interested myself in just what Creepy Cliffie Effinger was up to that merited an old-style slo-mo capping."

Matt tried to rustle up a grateful look, but failed.

"What makes you think there's any story left?" the old man asked in his raspy voice. "That these old-school mobsters didn't get what they wanted outa him and that's that?"

"For one thing, a lookalike corpse with Effinger's ID on him had fallen onto a craps table at the Crystal Phoenix before Effinger was actually killed. It's like someone wanted people to think he was dead before he really was."

Wetherly roared with laughter until it died off in coughing and wheezes. "That's a good one. Classy place like the Phoenix gets a low-end corpse stowed in its Eye-in-the Sky crawl space? No wonder that was hushed up."

"I guess it *was* 'hushed up'. It's still unsolved." Matt leaned forward. "And Effinger had a Chicago background."

"Everybody from Chitown isn't connected with what's left of the Chicago Outfit."

"But a couple local mob guys were, ah, looking into Effinger's connections there just recently. After he was dead."

"That's right. The bastard had some sweet set-up in Chicago, I heard. Good-looking wife, a two-flat bringing in rental money. Only the wife's brat soured the deal."

Matt had been that "brat" and his mother the woman Effinger had used and abused. The anger surge almost choked him, but rage would ruin his plan to investigate and overheat his cool.

"Chicago can't have anything to do with Effinger's death here," Woody declared.

Matt kept his voice even. "It would if Effinger had kept some… evidence there about things going on here."

"What kind of evidence?"

"I don't know. A map, maybe."

"A treasure map?" Woody wheezed with laughter. "There's been rumors about buried treasure around Vegas since the railroad came through. Only treasure is in the casino money carts and they're better guarded than Fort Knox."

"Effinger must have been into something that involved a huge payoff, to get killed in a gruesome way like that. That was warning someone off."

"That's just supposition, isn't it? If it was real, the cops would be all over it."

Matt was getting sick of the old man shooting down his ideas, yet he'd said as much as he'd dared about Effinger "having something" others might want. This old guy would never imagine Matt was seeking clues to a missing IRA hoard. That was such a Max quest. WWMD right now? What Would Max Do? Keep extracting information from the retired cop.

Wetherly was frowning now. "How do you know this stuff about what Cliff Effinger did or did not do in Chicago before his death?"

"I, ah, interviewed a local detective about the case."

"Private or police?"

"Police."

"Which asshole is that?"

Matt quelled a defensive retort. "Molina."

"*Hmph.* Lieutenant. Woman. That ain't gonna do you no good."

"She's extremely competent."

"If you say so, but she's from L.A. Whadda she know about Vegas mob history, the stuff that's not in all the new mob 'museums' around town? That stuff is all for show. For Chrissake, they're now doing weddings at the downtown mob 'attraction'. And the Fontana brothers are keeping their pretty suits pressed more than they're tending to their Gangsters limo service or Gangsters hotel."

"I guess I've come to the right person here, then," Matt said.

"That's damn right, sonny."

"And you can stop calling me 'kid' and 'sonny'. I answer to Matt, or Mr. Devine if you want to keep it formal, Mr. Wetherly."

"Speaking up, are we? I told you last time to call me Woody. And, Matt, do you answer to Father Devine too?"

Matt reared back as if punched.

"You find out about Chicago," Woodrow said. "I find out about *you.* You're not pulling the smooth cashmere sports coat over these old eyes. I wanta know who I'm dealing with. So you're right. You've come to the right person, Mr. Matt. You can call me a no bullshitter."

He braced his misshapen hands on the recliner arms and pushed himself up with a grunt. Matt rushed to support a forearm until the old man seemed balanced.

"Yup, young Matt. Ignore appearances, I am just the man for your job. We're gonna go where what's left of mob operators meet now."

"When?" Matt asked, alarmed. His hours weren't his own.

"Tonight. Don't worry. We start at ten and you'll be at the radio station soothing losers by midnight, Cinderfella. Get it?"

"Mobsters don't meet on the Strip?"

"Well, in a way they do." Woody chuckled and winked. "We're goin' to one of them nudie bars."

"Nudie," Matt repeated warily.

"That's right." Woody leaned near to impart a confidentially. "May be something *new*—get it? 'Nudie' may be new—to you, but old to me. I advise you to look like you like it so you ain't mistaken for a pansy. In fact, I advise you to look all your fill, 'cuz I'm bettin' you never imagined these places existed."

Matt imagined he was right.

6
Off-Campus

I, of course, escort the ladies. Unlike Miss Temple, I savor my short stature and being overlooked. The canny investigator does his best work under those circumstances.

As I take up my discreet rear guard position to watch the Circle Ritz ladies wonder and wander, I muse on the fact that my Miss Temple needs a foot system like mine, whereby I can retract my hidden shivs in a nanosecond. I would look ridiculous if I tottered along on extended tippy-claws. I am not sure why my Miss Temple does not when she is doing so, but if her fancy shoes had retractable heels, she could have it both ways, as I do.

Like Miss Temple, I am used to entering and exiting the Circle Ritz by the parking lot. I had never strolled around to the building's side entrance to view all that wedding chapel traffic. Now I notice the block of shops opposite the wedding chapel entrance. Many are empty, rental signs in their blank glass windows, but others cater to the marriage enterprise. The window of Making Marry showcases wedding cakes and champagne glasses, fresh floral bouquets and "instant engraved" napkins.

"Oh, look," commands my Miss Temple as we pass another going establishment.

So I do, then nearly bite off my tongue in shock.

"I did not know," Miss Temple is telling Miss Electra, "a bookshop was so nearby."

Neither did I.

She goes on. "I would have dashed over for the latest Anne Perry and Elizabeth George novels."

I would have dashed over to find out when Miss Maeveleen Pearl's Thrill 'n' Quill bookstore relocated here, next to *my* stomping grounds, with Ingram, that snooty tiger-stripe, still in residence.

The women have stopped to study the window, so I am forced to pause and be IDed by its resident alien.

"Look," Miss Temple says. "A cat in the window. How charming."

What a lazy, lay-a-book dude he is! Just because I consulted Ingram on a matter or two in the past and he lies around all day on the likes of Dostoevsky's *Crime and Punishment*, he considers himself my intellectual superior. Even now his acid-yellow eyes descend to half-mast as he spots me. Then he yawns and fans his prized six toes against his lower jaw in a most condescending manner.

If he were human, he would wear a bow tie, in plaid, like they put on Scottish terriers, which breed happened to be involved in my last case. Ingram is reclining near a magnifying glass in the display, but I would not put it past him to affect a monocle, should he ever get his paws on one.

"Look at Louie," Miss Electra chortles. "His tail is bristled up like a tumbleweed."

She should talk. Her hairdo is puffed up like a plate of pastel-tinted marshmallows.

We resume walking, thank Bast. I give Ingram a quick nod over my shoulder, but he has curled up into ball resembling a very large pair of rolled-up striped socks. I must admit that his camouflage options are impressive.

"You know," my Miss Temple is saying, "this is such a cute little shopping area, but it needs some sharp PR to get the word out on it. Then the area would attract new shops."

"I know," Miss Electra says as grimly as a bouncy personality like hers ever manages. "I own the whole kit and caboodle, but the Great Recession hit Las Vegas so hard I lost a lot of renters."

Miss Temple has stopped abruptly, causing me to smash my tender nose into her calf. I may have been distracted by giving Ingram a dirty look over my shoulder.

"Louie! Are you still with us?" she asks.

I should hope so.

However, she is more interested in Miss Electra's revelation than my stubbed nose at the moment.

"Why did you not tell me, Electra, that you owned some nearby commercial sites too? Drumming up business is my, well, business."

"The rent was welcome, but these shops mostly cater to wedding chapel customers. The newest one is the bookshop, which got priced out of its old location and lease after clinging on through the worst of the recession. Maeveleen Pearl, the owner, tells me independent bookstores are making a comeback. But when Vegas 'comes back' it is with more topless pools at the big hotels and more blue businesses in offbeat corners."

"Blue businesses?" Miss Temple asks my question for me.

Miss Electra laughs, patting the naturally white part of her coiffure. "In the old days, in the very old days, anything that was a bit smutty was called 'blue'. Blue humor is a satire on the bawdy ways of the world."

"Which are major in Las Vegas," Miss Temple notes.

"Yeah. When it comes to commercial ventures, I guess we are all ragtag hangers-on about to be drowned in Las Vegas sleaze."

"Electra! That is no way to think." Miss Temple paces back and forth in a two-foot range like a caged Big Cat, only she is a little cat. "You own the block of shops across from the wedding chapel. Anything else?"

"A few lots here and there. Most everything here was razed when the Strip expanded south years ago and this area is not on any main drag. You know the Vegas Strip still has odd pieces of property beside and behind and be-shadowed by the huge hotel spreads. That is where tacky tourist shops spring up."

We are all walking again, but Miss Temple has not walked back her pep talk.

"A smaller commercial space does not *have* to be tacky, Electra. It can be charming. It can be an urban village. You already have a bookstore and wedding accessory shop that complement the Lovers' Knot. You are halfway there."

"Urban village?"

"Yes! A destination inside the biggest destination city in the country, Vegas. A laid-back shopping and eating area within an encompassing metropolis."

"The only people who could see and patronize these few shops are my wedding chapel clients. And with even the Mob Museum downtown doing elaborate weddings, my place is not splashy enough, and I am losing customers. I was thinking of closing down."

"Closing down the Lovers' Knot? *Not!* You do not *want* splashy, Electra. You want charming. Trust me."

"Well, *you* are charming, so I suppose I gotta trust you."

"Urban villages are popping up in San Francisco, Seattle, out east."

"Las Vegas is not really a metropolis, Temple. It is a super-duper commercial roller coaster ride from a very small Downtown 'Experience' that has a very long and narrow tail, the Strip, thronged with a massive array of adult Disneyland 'attractions'. I do not see how you plant a viable 'village' in some forgotten corner here."

My Miss Temple sighs. This means she is sure she is right, but is going to have trouble proving it. When she thinks she will have trouble proving something, whether it is a commercial venture or a murder case, she will only work harder to do just that.

"Vegas already supports one super successful urban village, Electra."

"You are kidding. I have not seen one."

"Think. It is north of the Stratosphere but south of Downtown."

"That area is a kind of No Man's Land, Temple, with a hodge-podge of small downscale enterprises."

"Not the *Pawn Star* development."

"Oh, that freaky reality TV pawnshop show?" Electra pinched her nose in a gesture of disgust. "Way too low-brow to be considered a normal business."

"That is why it is popular. So popular they have four thousand tourist visitors a day and are putting in restaurants and shops to hold them as fast as they can."

"The title of the show has pre-cheapened the concept, Temple. So. You think a Pornucopia offshoot coming in down here will provide that *Pawn Star* draw? Lord knows what they will call that, and, on second thought, I am sure He would not want to know. Are you saying we should get aboard the X-rated sleaze train?"

"No. The opposite. I am saying we need to close that family-unfriendly puppy down so you can build your own urban village. You said you want to get a protest group going. That is a start."

"Temple." Now Miss Electra has stopped walking to pace in her cushion-soled flat-heeled shoes. She does not make a sound, whereas my Miss Temple always sounds mucho macho, brisk and businesslike, like say, a rattlesnake, when she gets her low-riding castanets clicking. "We do not have a reality TV show gone viral to draw fans."

"Not yet," says my Miss Temple. She likes mowing down obstacles the way a tsunami would if it had red hair. "Now. Let us see what is what with those would-be 'Porn Stars' down the block."

She turns to make sure I am bringing up the rear of our little party, my own rear member held high, supple, and handsome. Of course I am.

"From what you are telling me of this new kid on the block," she tells Miss Electra Lark, "I am not sure Louie should tail along. He is underage."

"I am sure he should," Miss Electra insisted. "I believe is it several human years to every cat year. At that rate, Louie should last—"

"Too much information, Electra." My Miss Temple plants her heels in place and holds up a traffic-cop palm. "I refuse to hear that Louie has an expiration date." She shudders dramatically in a manner I find most personally satisfying.

Miss Electra shrugs. "I was about to say I think if anything reincarnated, it would be cats. Especially Louie."

"Even worse. I do not want a retread. I want the real and original."

"In Vegas? You *are* an optimist, Temple. But maybe you are right. Maybe we *can* turn X-rated into X-iled."

7
Off-Color

Temple took in the huge, level dirt lot. It looked like a cheesy chessboard with yellow surveyor's flags deployed everywhere like pawns. Pawn Stars.

Smack-dab in the middle of the property sat a two-story brick hulk with windows only on the second floor and big double doors like a barn on the first-floor entrance. A forty-foot RV clung to its side like a cub. That must operate as an onsite office and night guard station, although the building was clearly absent any tenant, bare of signage on any side at any level.

There was, however, a huge construction sign on one corner Temple hotfooted over to inspect. "This billboard is big enough to advertise an entire housing development," she told Electra as they came around to view its message.

By now the landlady was breathing down her neck, heavily.

"Gosh, Temple, you sure walk fast for a petite person. Don't even think about an adult housing development going up on this land. What would they call it, Hootchy-Cootchy Condos?"

"Here it is. I'm reading the fine print. They have a pair of managers, Punch Adcock and Katt Zydeco."

"Great. They've got the strip club biz covered from A to Z. The guy sounds like a thug or boxer and the woman a hooker."

"Don't sound so glum. 'Zydecko' is a Cajun dance. I bet 'Katt' was born just plain Katherine Smith and this is her performance name."

"So I'm somehow relieved that one manager may be a stripper?"

"Remember way back when I solved the Stripper Killer case? Believe it or not, it's a step forward that some women now own and manage strip clubs. Less exploitive that way."

"Somehow I don't see the redeeming social value." Electra pointed to the big-type teaser line at the billboard's top.

Temple read, "Coming soon...and we mean it literally."

She groaned in disgust at the bawdy pun. "Cheesy." No class.

The pitch went on: *You know Lust 'n' Lace downtown as an multiplex playground of toys and joys, lingerie and latex, you name it, you get it. Now opening soon, Lust 'n' Lace Live on Stage!, Vegas's latest and lustiest and de-lace-iest gentleman's club. We'll have packages to suit every type and size of party. VIP, Bachelor, Bachelorette, Birthday, Couples, Corporate or Divorce Party. Each party package includes limo transport, liquor, admission, etc.*

It was that "etc." that Temple suspected covered a mega-lot of sins and extra charges.

"What was the building before someone decided to make it a gentlemen's club?" Temple asked Electra.

"I think it was a garage back in the forties. Driving to Vegas in the early days was hard on cars. Rumor was Bugsy Siegel parked his cars there."

Temple sighed. "Another 'surviving trace of Bugsy' claim. If he did all he was purported to do, and been everywhere he has been purported to be around Vegas, he'd have needed to live to a hundred...not be down, out, and dead at forty-one."

"True. He's among the soft sculpture people in the Lovers' pews."

"Really? I never noticed him."

"Well, he's slumped down and missing an eye under his gangster fedora, but otherwise nattily dressed, as always."

Temple winced. The blast of bullets that had ended Bugsy's life had shot out one eye. "I didn't know your artistic streak had such a macabre bent."

"There's a lot you don't know about me," Electra intoned mysteriously, making Temple laugh.

"I certainly don't know what color or colors your hair will be from day to day," Temple said. "Your rainbow hair was ahead of all the young pop stars."

Electra grinned. "At my advanced age, being ahead in anything is a triumph."

"So we're looking at Bugsy's garage, and what else?"

"I know the building was a nightclub back in the fifties when the mob was running the Strip hotels, then empty for a while, and then a big five-and-dime. Its last retail life was as an antique mall, with individual dealers having side-by-side booths."

"Oh, I *love* those places. Any vintage clothing and jewelry sold there?"

"Down, girl. That's long gone, and it was more used than vintage."

"So the old place is returning to its nightlife stage." Temple ambled closer to the gaudy billboard. The panoramic illustration portrayed a nightly naughty Strip show, with circus-tent poles and chorus girls wearing feathers and rhinestones and not much else. Showgirls had starred in the typical Vegas advertising image since Bugsy had pushed up roses in L.A.

Beside her, Electra sighed deeply. Louie stalked over until he sat right under the sign. In the next second he'd ratcheted up a rear wood support post to leap atop the three-inch-wide frame. He stretched a long forelimb down to paw a giant feathered headdress.

"I bet this outfit will carry a lot of 'toys' that might tickle Louie's fancy," Temple said, rolling her eyes.

"Sure. The traitor. Flash a feather at a cat and he doesn't ask if it's socially redeeming or not. Listen, Temple, Vegas was built on bad, and I don't turn up my nose at other people's preferences in anything. Seeing the size of this building, I know any PR makeover you might do for my miserable few acres will be hopeless in the face of that."

"Picketing would only publicize the place," Temple conceded.

They stood in glum silence, Temple was out of bright ideas as they viewed the sheer size of the project. It was bigger than Pornucopia and the two-story Adult Superstore south of Downtown. Once the exterior was wrapped in female body parts and neon, it would turn Electra's wedding chapel into an also-ran.

"You ladies can't wait for the Grand Opening, huh?" said a smirking voice behind them.

Temple turned faster than a whipsnake. "Crawford Buchanan? You're repping this project?"

"No, I'm just reporting on it." His smarmy grin widened as he looked Temple over like she was one of the sex objects on the billboard.

"Send that smirk to the Snark Hall of Fame, Crawford," she said. "I can see why some of the neighboring businesses are ready to picket this humongous expansion of down-market enterprise."

Buchanan, the local Napoleon of nasty gossip media, seemed oddly taller. In addition to the usual shoe lifts, his graying dark hair had now been gelled into an impressive peak atop his head.

That "look" would soon be the laughing stock of the 2010s, the way the 1980s brassy gold bathroom faucets were despised on Home and Garden Decor TV today. Temple couldn't wait until actors and other media men unloaded the "anthill" hairdo so fashionable and so unbecoming. At least Matt wasn't about to join the mob on that.

"Picketing," Buchanan said, "would just stir up publicity for Lust 'n' Lace, as you noted, T. B."

Temple also loathed his using her initials as a nickname. The implied intimacy made her skin crawl. At least he didn't know her middle name was the also-loathed "Ursula". Crawford could sure make hay with T.U.B.

"Seriously," she told Buchanan, "who or what corporation is bankrolling this project? Isn't it risky to put a Vegas Downtown-type business so far south?"

"Yeah, but there's not much land left anywhere now. I heard some out-of-town owner is getting older and ready to unload investments. And Vegas has finally come back from the biggest real estate dive in the country."

Telling Temple how much inside info he knew gave Crawford a superior glow. She just smiled politely and let him yammer on. "This will be a huge deal. The managers are a colorful couple."

She eyed the billboard. "I'll bet. Who are Punch Adcock and Katt Zydeco?"

"Each of them has run sex entertainment businesses, but they're hooking up to expand into this game."

"There are, what, thirty sex shops in Vegas, not even counting strip joints?" Temple noted.

"You're not saying you can ever get enough sex, are you, T.B.?" The smirk was back.

"I'm saying no matter how much the economy has bounced back, a big investment in an off location like this is iffy. I find it... puzzling."

By now Midnight Louie had tired of two-dimensional billboard feathers and had hopped down to stalk over and sniff Crawford's pointy-toed ankle boots. His nose reared back as his furry black belly swayed to the sidewalk, stretching to display his three-foot length from nose to tail-tip.

Then Louie strolled over to twine himself around Temple's ankles, offering a flash of fangs and a snakelike hiss.

"That animal looks rabid." Buchanan pulled out his cell phone and contemplated its face with faux regret. "Animal Control would snatch him up in a minute if they happened by."

Electra gasped. "That's a threat if I ever heard one."

"A fact," Buchanan told her, basking in her shock.

Temple was unfazed. "Louie has gotten into, and out of, worse dangers. And if you try anything like that, I will restyle your stupid hair with my steel-heeled shoes."

Buchanan glanced down in alarm. "You have steel-heeled shoes? By God, you do. Do you have a license for those things, T.B.?"

"Just a sales receipt, C.B. You don't have to register shoes as deadly weapons, even if they are."

Temple was glad she'd worn the vintage Stuart Weitzman spikes she'd bought as much for self-defense as style.

"Just watch you don't impale your cat on one of them someday." Buchanan finally moved away to photograph the billboard with his cell phone.

Electra edged close to Temple and Louie. "You've said he was a creep, but he outdoes your opinion. Is that the kind of person this new adult emporium is going to attract?"

"The business is legal, Electra, and many tourists come to Vegas for a walk on the wild side. A lot of mainstream couples patronize businesses like these. The biggest audience for *Fifty Shades of Gray*, the film of the kinky bondage novels, came from the South and Heartland. Folks who'd be gun-shy about being seen entering a strip club in their hometowns, know that here…nobody cares."

"Buchanan," a rough male voice yelled from fifty feet away.

The owner of it advanced on them fast. His mai-tai fruity Hawaiian shirt was louder than his hacksaw voice, but he was built like an aging bull. Brillo pad curls of iron-gray hair covered his head and poked out of the shirt's v-neck.

He stopped beside Temple and Electra. "These girls want work at the new place? The redhead is scrawny, but the blue-hair could help the girls with the wardrobe, such as it is."

The women's jaws dropped and then shut in unison.

Buchanan quashed a nasty giggle.

"So," Temple said, nudging Electra silent with a genteel tap of a steel heel on her instep. "You're the owner of this forthcoming enterprise, sir?"

"One of 'em. I don't rule out scrawny, mind you. It's the customers."

"I *would* like to work for you, but in my capacity as a PR manager." Temple whipped out her card, which read TEMPLE BARR, P.R.

"Heh," he said, punching the beefy hand that held her card forward in a thumbs-up position. "Like *Magnum, P.I.* Clever."

"My chief client is the Crystal Phoenix."

"The Phoenix." He savored the name, nodding appreciatively. "Classy Strip hotel-casino. I could use a little class. But very little, if you know what I mean."

She smiled sweetly. "I do, Mr.—"

"Nemo. Leon Nemo." His gazed narrowed. "The Phoenix. The Fontana boys are all over that operation, and others around town."

"Indeed they are. But you're, um, sponsored by the Lust 'n' Lace. They're a long-standing Vegas tradition too."

Leon's hands, beefy and hairy but expressive, pantomimed playing an iffy piano. "Just as a familiar introduction of a new tune. My people are an indie operation."

"I'm an independent operator too."

"I bet you are, Red." He leaned away to look down. "Nice ankles. You planning on doing some jack-hammering in those heels?"

"If needed."

Louie began weaving defensively around her ankles. Nemo looked away, back to her face. "So what brings you to my site?"

"Curiosity."

Leon looked down again. "That the name of your cat?"

"It could be."

"I like cats. You never know what they're thinking and you can't hear 'em coming. That's the way people should be. No useless yapping."

"Speaking of useless yapping," Temple jerked her head over her shoulder, indicating Crawford Buchanan eagerly eating up their conversation.

Nemo got the message. "Thanks for the run-by, Buchanan. I'll call you later. I got another fish to fry now." He looked down at the cat as Buchanan departed with a sour look.

"His name is Midnight Louie," Temple said.

"Yeah, he's a Louie, all right." Nemo squatted down, showcasing bare knees and hairy calves. "Big fellah. Put 'er there, Louie."

Louie sat back on his haunches, then patted the back of Nemo's hand. Like your average harmless Curious Kitty.

"Nice baby claws, Louie." Nemo grunted as he stood again and laughed. "He was holding back until he decides about me. I like cats. Velvet when you meet 'em, but steel like your heels when you cross 'em. So," he asked Temple. "Why are you here in this dead neighborhood eyeballing a sign for a live X–rated adult show?"

"I like to keep track of new business opportunities in Vegas. What does puzzle me is the zoning restrictions. This neighborhood is zoned residential, mixed use, which covers small businesses. Not so sure that covers an adult business."

"Zoning regulations?" Nemo slapped the rear of his khaki Bermuda shorts. "Right here in my back pocket."

Temple nodded. He seemed confident, and she knew adult enterprises were part of the city's bread and butter…and influence was peddled freely.

Electra finally unleashed her pent-up questions. "So who sold you this land? I heard it was an out-of-town owner."

"And how did you know that, Grandma?" Leon raised furry eyebrows. Temple thought of the Caterpillar in *Alice in Wonderland*.

"Well, sonny," Electra said in no-nonsense tones, "I was married to the man. He swore never to sell it without telling me. I can't believe Jay would sell out to an adult entertainment club. He was brought up Baptist."

"Oh, ma'am." Nemo waved gently placating palms. "This is not an extension of Vegas's second biggest X-rated store since the Adult Superstore. No tawdry warehouse operation like that."

"No?" Electra asked hopefully.

"No, no no. This is a small and intimate place, fitting for the neighborhood."

Electra took a deep, earnest breath. "So it's a done deal."

"Good as Fool's Gold. Don't worry. No X-rated movies or walls full of you-know-whats," Leon explained. "This will be just a nice, quiet, neighborhood topless stripper bar on a major scale." He turned to Temple. "Nothing you couldn't promote with the same classy style you'd use for the Crystal Phoenix, Miss Temple Barr, P.R."

His self-satisfied, somehow dirty smile made Temple think of someone who knew more about her than she'd like. Someone who'd been pawing through her underwear drawer for a prank. Someone who thought all women were alike, and lying if they said they didn't live up to his slutty expectations.

Someone Temple would like to kick down a flight of stairs. She probably was staring daggers at him, to no effect, when Electra grabbed her elbow.

"Maybe it'd be all right if we looked over the building," she suggested.

"Sure. Be my guests." He gestured to the shabby structure and then headed to a Lexus SUV parked suspiciously far down the block.

Temple was reluctant to leave Nemo with the last word, and a smirk to boot, but Electra had pulled her off balance, so she spun around on one steel heel to watch him leave.

"We can inspect the property, thanks to Nemo," Electra said, "but you don't have time to worry about him. You and Matt are leaving for an important family reunion. I'll ask Ernesto and his brothers about this Leon Nemo. The Fontanas know the sleazy operators in town. And they'd know about zoning and such, given all their business interests."

"That's a great idea, Electra. And what they don't know, the guys' uncle, Macho Mario Fontana does. He has true mob associations from his distant past to call on."

The prolific Fontana family exploited a vague aura of faded "mob", but was most noted for its crew of sleek, mostly bachelor men-about-town. Besides Nicky, the youngest brother who operated the Crystal Phoenix, the other nine brothers ran a mob-themed hotel and custom limo service, both called Gangsters. You need to go for a ride in Vegas? Fontana Inc. will provide with panache. It was all a harmless take on family history.

Electra turned to eye the diminished billboard, too distant to read now. "I have to check my files too. I'm foggy on where my property ends, since I left a bunch of it undeveloped."

"You mean that outfit may not have all the rights they're claiming?"

Electra's custodial hand squeezed Temple's forearm.

"I mean I do have some hidden resources." Electra winked. "Don't worry about me now. It's a good thing you're slated for a family visit in Minnesota so you young folks can settle where you need to be once you're married. You've given me an idea or two."

"Really? I *am* distracted with this trip coming up so fast. Our Mr. Leon Nemo was more than vague on the zoning question. Even if this was a sealed deal, I'm sure you'll find a way to make Lust 'n' Lace's excursion into live entertainment…history." Temple gazed around again. "Say. Where's Louie?"

"I saw him snooping around the construction office in the RV after Nemo left. I'm thinking he's smelled something fishy about that outfit too."

"Especially under that aluminum temporary foundation surrounding the RV," Temple said. "So if the cat's away, maybe we mice should play."

Electra stared at the abandoned hulk. "I'm dying to see what Nemo and his silent partners think is so valuable about this building Jay owns. Let's explore."

8
Off Market

"**What a dump,**" Temple said once they were through the double entrance doors, using an iconic Bette Davis line from an old movie.

"*Beyond the Forest,*" Electra said.

"What?"

"The name of the movie Bette Davis said that 'dump' line in. I saw it."

"In first run?"

"No, on *Turner Classic Movies,* silly. I'd have to be a zillion years old to have seen the first run." Electra looked around and bit her lip. "The building does look awful stripped down and empty."

"Dump" was too good a word for the interior space.

The exterior looked like an abandoned factory, but they hadn't realized the second-story windows had been painted over. They stood inside a dim, gray cube divided into smaller dim gray interior cubes facing onto a wide central aisle.

Temple gazed up the central staircase to the second floor and the dust-dulled giant glass chandelier overhanging. The U-shaped second-story balcony overlooked the wide central aisle downstairs. Most of the temporary walls that divided vendor spaces were still up, creating an impression of ticky-tacky one-room housing units in endless rows on two stories, like jail cells.

"So sad." Electra shook her head, her fanciful hair the only vivid color in a place of concrete floors and naked cinder-block walls. "All the dealers gave their spaces and the dividers so much personality when it was an antique mall. Cornelia used a folding screen with fabric panels to suspend her vintage hats, all velvet and feathers. Georgia kept a huge stuffed black panther over there. It was studded with a rainbow of rhinestone pins. Hank used stackable cubes to hold his old chrome toasters and other quaint appliances. Everything shone and sparkled and radiated new life for old things."

"What's the story on the ten-foot-long chandelier?" Temple turned her neck back as far as it would go to take in the tower of dusty glass that hung over the top of the stairs, and over her and Electra, like an elegant unused guillotine.

"It was from some old movie. George never sold it because he wanted four thousand dollars for it."

"He just left it here when the mall closed down?"

"I think he made a deal with the woman who rented the building after that. It would be murderously hard to move."

"All these funky items were a hop-scotch jump away from the Circle Ritz, and a vintage-hound like me never got a whiff of its existence? I must be losing my touch."

"You've been a little busy, dear, with your job and the occasional diverting murder and the always diverting two beaux." Electra sighed. "I once needed to juggle boyfriends myself."

"Well, one of them has diverted himself out of the country, so I'm finally and inexorably and permanently a one-man woman."

"I find that a bit…boring, to be honest."

"You had—what?—five husbands. That was more than diverting, Electra, it smacks of being hooked on weddings."

"I finally did find a way to have as many weddings as I wanted without all the messy men-stuff involved." Electra winked and patted her hair. "I've told you before that some of my generation had Elizabeth Taylor disease."

Temple's wrinkled brow prompted an explanation. "If we liked a man and he liked us, we married him, to avoid any example of wrong-doing."

"Even if the man was married to someone else first, I suppose. Did you know Elizabeth Taylor quoted that Bette Davis 'dump' line in *Who's Afraid of Virginia Woolf?*"

"No, but I'm sure that Elizabeth Taylor wasn't afraid of any wolf in Hollywood. Anyway, the antique mall went under before you gifted Las Vegas with your presence. A woman who provided Strip shows with costumes and wigs then used this place as a storage facility for a short while."

"Even worse!" Temple exclaimed. "I'd have *loved* to see her collection of all that glittery stuff. The costume department was my drug of choice when I did PR for the Guthrie Theater in Minneapolis. Ah, the scent of the grease paint and rhinestone glue, the roar of the crowd and the rustle of the costumes."

"I guess that Vegas was your cup of cake, then, even though your family felt that Max had 'dragged' you away with him to Sin City."

"My family was more than a smidge overprotective of the only girl, and I was also the youngest. I needed an escape clause and Max—"

"You don't have to explain yourself to me. I'd sign on the dotted line with him in a heartbeat. Poor boy. Aced out now. If you and Matt move to Chicago, it'd be nice to have him back at the Circle Ritz."

"I don't even want to *think* about that! What I need to think about is Matt and my looming trip to Minnesota. My family has been beastly to any boy who's been involved with me since Terrence Schulenberger as a maple leaf danced around my daisy face in the kindergarten program."

"You'd make an adorable daisy! I don't see Matt, or Max, as a maple leaf, though."

"Electra! I'm asking advice here, since you've gone through the engagement process five times. Should I wear this Art Deco engagement ring Matt bought me from Fred Leighton's at the Bellagio? Maybe I should slip on a more modest Midwestern ring for the trip."

Electra grabbed Temple's left hand to study the scintillating flash of dueling diamonds and rubies, of ice and fire. "Fred Leighton? That's where the movie stars shop. How much did it cost?"

Temple retrieved her hand. "More than you should know, or I should wear without carrying a gun. Just think. This from the man who talked his talent agent into committing a portion of his commission along with Matt's assigning ten percent of his fees to charitable causes. I don't know what he was thinking when he splurged on this."

"That he knows you love vintage things, and, like the Clairol ads say, you're worth it. Or do the ads still say that? I fear my decades are showing."

"Here in Vegas flash is common, and often taken for a good fake. I put it on for that disastrous dinner, but my folks seemed too dazed to much notice it. So what should I say about the ring if they comment on how expensive it is?"

"That Matt picked it out for you and you love it and it's both something old and something new for the wedding."

"That's the perfect answer. Thank you, Electra!" Temple embraced her, then withdrew, shaking out her red-gold waves of hair. "I don't know why I'm so nervous about this meet-the-fiancé ritual."

"They didn't approve of the last one, did they? But you've been independent and away on your own now for a couple years. You don't answer to anyone but yourself."

Temple nodded. "Why do the people who want only the best for you become the last to admit that you know what you're doing?"

"It's the parent thing. It's hard to let go of feeling responsible. That's why I do this." Electra swirled one hand over her wildly color-enhanced hair. "If old Mom can be an unconventional free spirit, there's nothing my grown children can do to shock me. Right?"

"Right." Temple looked around the forlorn space. "Why would anyone buy this sad mess for a strip club? The defunct Neon Nightmare club building. I can see that. But this? I don't get it."

Footsteps interrupted her monologue.

"Excuse us," a woman's voice said, "but what are you doing here?"

"I might ask the same thing," Electra said, stepping forward.

The man answered. "We'll be managing this new joint."

Temple jumped into the awkward moment of this standoff. "You must be Mr. Adcock and Miss Zydeco. So glad you dropped by. I talked with Mr. Nemo just now. Your plans for the building and site are wonderfully intriguing."

While laying down her PR patter, Temple did a fast read of the managerial couple.

Katt Zydeco was showgirl tall, wearing the riding habit look so popular: skintight jeggings and high boots. Her long hair was frankly dyed jet black. Pancake makeup couldn't disguise the badly pitted complexion some unlucky teenagers carry for life. Katt must be in her late thirties.

Punch Adcock. Hard to say if he was chubby or beefy, but his expression was petulant, and his lips pursed like a rather nasty Cupid's. His eyes were too close together and his huge shoulders hunched. All in all an unappetizing actor, as the cops might say.

Challenge radiated off both figures. *Who are you? Why are you here? We'll handle you, toots, don't worry.*

Temple had immediately dropped Nemo's name, sure he was the boss of the operation. Now she had to patty-cake these two unforgiving characters into pretending to be the professional managers they could never be.

Piece of angel-food cake.

"I'm Temple Barr. I do public relations for several on-Strip businesses."

"Well, we're in the public relations business ourselves," Punch said with a smirk at Katt. "We have to beat our customers off with a stick. Like what do you rep?" Punch asked, unconvinced.

"Like Gangsters, both the limo service and hotel-casino, and the Crystal Phoenix Hotel."

"Sniffs like all Fontana operations. Pure bottled spaghetti sauce." Punch snorted in distaste. His nose did indeed look hard used from his boxing days.

"It's true Mama Fontana's Italian sauce empire underwrote most of the family businesses," Temple said. "Still, it's one of the most profitable brands along the Strip, and this project, being a bit off-Strip, could use extra PR promotion."

"So you're sneaking around here looking for a job." Katt Zydeco put one booted foot before the other as she stalked toward the two women.

Electra gave a little mewl of warning and grabbed Temple's arm.

Temple agreed. These were tough customers. Time to show them a bit of T as in Teflon.

She stepped out on her steel-heeled Weitzman's to match Katt Zydeco step for step and meet her in the middle.

"Nice boots," Temple said.

"Nice booties," Katt said. "I do like the ankle accessory."

Temple didn't wear ankle bracelets. Then she felt the velvet brush. She looked down. Midnight Louie, of course, putting one sleek black velvet foot ahead of the other at a pace that had matched the two women's.

"Something I picked up in a dark alley some time," Temple said, stopped and shrugging.

"Hope it didn't require medication," Katt said. "Nemo is interested in your services?"

"He likes my pedigree." Temple cocked an eyebrow.

Katt Zydeco stopped her catwalk advance and shrugged in her turn. "If you're good enough for Nemo, you're good enough for me."

"Hey," Punch said. "What just happened here? We okayed Nemo hiring this little clueless redheaded dame and her cat and her grandmother? Or what?"

Temple flashed one of her cards at him. "Looks like it. Expect to see a lot more of us as the Lust 'n' Lace empire expands. We are the total package when it comes to viral social media expansion."

Punch's jaw remained dropped at hearing Temple's jargon, as if hit by a heavyweight. Temple turned Electra around and they left.

She hoped Midnight Louie had followed suit and left with them (but she didn't look back because it would ruin their exit), so Punch would really be confused.

She was sure Louie's chronic curiosity would not allow him to leave such a mysterious building unexplored.

9
Girls Club

"Well, Electra," Temple said on returning to the Circle Ritz lobby, "I guess we're back in the strip club business."

"What do you mean?"

"We need to pay Les Girls a visit."

"Why would we want to visit a strip club," Electra asked glumly, "when we'll soon have a new one so conveniently located in our backyard?"

"We're visiting Lindy Lukas."

"Lindy Lukas? I don't know—oh, yeah, the ex-stripper. We met her during the G-string murder case, when I made my stripping debut on Max's Hesketh Vampire motorcycle."

"I think the motorcycle stripped more than you did on that occasion, Electra." Temple's smile grew sad. "I have one of the stripper's extra pair of black-cat design spikes, but I've never worn them. It's hard to walk in a murder victim's shoes."

"No kidding, but why are we seeing Lindy?"

"I'm guessing if Katt Zydeco was a stripper, Lindy would know her."

"That's right. Lindy is head of WHOOPE, the professional strippers organization. What did it stand for again?"

"It was an unforgettably labored group acronym. Not my work. Let's see. We Have an Organization Of Professional Ecdysiasts."

"Ecdysiasts describes snakes shedding their skins, right?"

"*Uh-huh.*"

"That doesn't seem fair," Electra said. "From what you learned at the stripping contest, some of them are from abusive backgrounds. They're hardly snakes."

"And some of them are savvy self-employed businesswomen. You can't stereotype them, so let's see what Lindy knows about the new game in town."

Visiting a strip club in Las Vegas meant mingling with a crowd, even in the middle of the afternoon.

Neon sandwiched Les Girls inside and out. Its several stages fostered a sense of intimacy over the space of a football field of skimpily clad flesh. Acts were mostly aimed at men, but women and couples populated the milling audience.

The Frenchified name invoked *Les Miz*, the nickname of the smash musical made from Victor Hugo's downer novel *Les Miserables*, "Les" being the French for "the". "The Girls" were the consortium of strippers and ex-strippers who owned it.

When Temple asked to see Lindy, she and Electra were escorted to the office by a tanned hunk wearing only a black satin posing pouch and bow tie. They skirted what looked like a Roman orgy scene featuring rock-hard pecs both female and male. Temple found women's naked breast implants, all equally round and hard, as sexy as pink rubber duckies, but she wasn't a man. She was also a 32A, so might be prejudiced.

"It's so plastic," Electra commented. "Having something like this attracting crowds and parking and noise twenty-four-seven would drive out my tenants and kill my wedding clientele. The battle's lost."

"Hang in there," Temple said, regretting the expression at once, given their escort.

Lindy's office reeked of twice the cigarette smoke in the performing area outside, but when the door shut, the raunchy music and din died.

"Hey." Lindy rose from behind her huge, paper-covered desk. "It's the gals from the stripper contest, Miss Nancy Drew, Jr., and

Ms. Motorcycle Mama. Is that killer cat of yours still smokin' and tokin'? Miss…Tempe as in Arizona, isn't it?"

"Temple as in Acropolis. No, Midnight Louie never inhales anything but his food, as long as it isn't Free-to-Be Feline."

"Say, my Chauncey loves that Free-to-Be stuff, but he's just a 'found' cat, nothing Fancy Feasty."

"The best kind, like Louie."

"Have a seat, if you can shovel 'em off."

They followed her advice, heaping more papers on the desk.

"I see," Temple said, "you have a desktop computer. Haven't you gone paperless yet?"

"No," said Lindy, "and I haven't quit smoking yet either."

Temple had judged Lindy as a plain speaker from the first time she met her, which was why they'd come here. Lindy's T-shirt and jeans covered a buxom frame that hinted at a previous life as a Nature's Best hourglass figure, back when she was performing stripper.

Whatever she had been then, she liked total absence of artifice now. Her frankly dyed hair was a dull dead black. No plastic surgery had touched an unmade-up face puckered at the lips and eyes from a merciless nicotine habit. Las Vegas was the capital of "Smoking Allowed".

Lindy lit a thin Virginia Slim cigarette, and spun her office chair so she could put her feet in well-worn, no-name brand sneakers atop it. No more spikes for her. "I assume I can do something for you?"

Electra shared Temple's confidence in Lindy. She pored out her woes about the traitorous ex-husband and the imminent degrading of her livelihood property.

Lindy's already crumpled features squinched farther with thought. "So you want to know about the possible new owners? I can tell you about the so-called managers. Punch Adcock was a minor heavyweight boxer, born William Adcock. Didn't throw enough fights to keep going, so he did some muscle work for loan sharks, bookies, any surviving mob elements in town. I know about him because he hassled some of my girls, and I had to hire my own muscle to teach him to play nice around my place of business."

"*Ooh*," said Electra, looking at Temple. "That doesn't look good for getting nice new neighbors."

"What about Katt Zydeco?" Temple asked Lindy.

"Long-time stripper. Knows the biz. Has an R-rated dominatrix website. Lucrative at the right venue. More upscale than my joint."

"Whips and chains are 'upscale'?" Electra asked.

Lindy nodded and so did Temple. "Powerful men," Lindy said, "crave to relieve the pressure by being helpless at the orders and whip-hands of a dominant woman. Most of it is strictly ordered role playing."

"And after they pay a pretty penny they go back to their offices and underpay all their women workers." Temple snorted. "Poor guys. Fifty shades of freaked out."

"Vegas draws a lot of macho-challenged men with money," Lindy pointed out.

Temple nodded. "The brief, shining moment when all Vegas went family friendly in the nineties is forgotten history. Now, all the major hotels offer topless swimming pools, and Vegas hotel-clubs like the Cosmopolitan aggressively market 'Just the right amount of wrong', a campaign that started out with implied crush videos, the worst kind of porn."

"Oh, my gosh," Electra said, "what is that?"

"If you don't know, Electra, you don't want to know. Let's just say I hope PETA got on their tails for that ad."

Temple frowned. No doubt Punch and Katt were an unsavory couple. If they were just the managers, who were the owners? She asked Lindy for a guess on that.

"Anything goes in Vegas," Lindy said, "so you could be dealing with a huge multi-hotel corporation, or, if you're really unlucky, some remnant of the mob cutting itself in for a piece of the action."

Electra was even more discouraged by the forces leveled against her business. "The Mob. I thought it was just a tourist attraction these days."

"'If it plays in Vegas, it stays in Vegas,'" Lindy said on a dragon's breath of exhaled smoke and cynicism.

When Temple and Electra got up to leave, Lindy, cigarette in hand, ushered them through the crowded bars and performance areas that were as deliberately confusing as any major hotel casino layout. Vegas had built labyrinths long before home furnishings giant IKEA did it, designed so you could never leave (like at the Hotel California of song), and so you just kept spending money.

"Wait." Temple stopped dead, frowning toward a line of men lined up before one stage to push bills down the strippers' G-strings.

"What?" Electra asked.

"One of those guys looks familiar." Temple frowned with distaste.

Lindy laughed. "Of course you think you recognize someone. Every guy in Vegas ends up feeding slot machines and pushing bills under G-strings like they were clotheslines."

"Not the men we know," Electra said.

Lindy rolled her eyes with doubt. "Which guy is it?"

Temple strained to follow the figure through a crowd mostly taller than she was. "The skinny but slumped one wearing low-slung jeans and a soul patch and gimme cap. A scruffy thirty-something."

"I've seen about fifty guys like him just this week," Lindy said. "Definitely a resident, not a tourist. Dollar-bill-only guy, killing time on an electrician's or plumber's lunch hour."

Electra was indignant. "You wouldn't know someone like that, Temple."

"I just had a memory flash, a weird sense of familiarity, but I can't say from where or when. On the other hand, Las Vegas is my beat. I get around town a lot, and must see some people in passing more than once."

"That guy sounds like someone you'd never want to see again." Electra wrinkled her nose. "I'm so depressed to think that losers like him infest Vegas, and will be congregating in my neighborhood once that strip club gets going."

Temple put her arm through Electra's as they left Les Girls and were brought to a standstill by the bright light of day outside the club's eternal interior dark, all glitter and grind.

They paused as their eyes adjusted.

"We need to know if the buyers have mob connections," Temple said. "When we sic the Fontana brothers on them, the boys will know who the current players are. That kind of iffy backing could jinx any deal. So cheer up!" Temple shook Electra's forearm playfully. "I don't want you worrying while Matt and I are out of town, all right?"

"I wish you weren't leaving right now." Electra sounded truly forlorn.

Temple realized her landlady's upbeat, funky image and personality obscured the fact that she was an aging woman alone in a rapidly changing world. And her livelihood might become a casualty any minute.

Temple tightened her grip on Electra's arm with an encouraging squeeze. "Matt and I will only be gone one night and two days, Electra."

"I wish Max still lived at the Circle Ritz."

Temple felt stunned. Surely Electra knew the place couldn't hold both of Temple's…well, lovers, at once.

"You have the Fontana Brothers to keep watch over you," Temple said, only then realizing they had recently "adopted" the Circle Ritz as a hangout. Because…they saw what Temple hadn't realized until today.

"I've let Nicky and Van know we'll be gone for a short while," Temple said. And maybe forever if Matt's Chicago job came through. "This trip is only two days, Electra. A lightning raid on the relatives. What can go wrong in forty-eight hours?"

10
Off-Strip Joint

"I gotta talk to some people," Woodrow Wetherly had said that morning. "You better come to my place around nine thirty tonight and drive with me. That fancy car of yours can go in my garage instead of my beater. It just screams *Steal Me*. What were you thinking?"

"It was a gift."

"From who? Your worst enemy?"

Woody huffed and puffed to open the rickety garage door with a hand-hold at the bottom. Matt rushed to take over the job, overwhelmed by the scent of gas and oil. Wetherly's place didn't say much for the retirement pensions in law enforcement. Matt wondered what Molina would get.

Apparently the aging Dodge's air-conditioning didn't work, because Woody lowered the windows. As darkness crept over the western Spring Mountains, Woody steered them through the tangle of settled Las Vegas valley real estate where Interstate highway 93-95 intersected Highway 15, called the Spaghetti Bowl. These were tangled, dimming streets far from the bright lights and glitter of the Strip's artificial neon sunburst.

Just as the Manhattan theater scene supported Off-Broadway and Off-Off-Broadway venues, Las Vegas had its Off-Strip and Off-Off Strip drinking establishments.

By the time you got to Off-Off, the bars would be more accurately described as dives.

Matt had explored these places when he'd first come to Vegas searching for his no-good stepfather, Cliff Effinger. This time he was looking for old cops and old crooks who might belly up to the same bars together even though they were presumably out of the game. This time, he'd come prepared to fade into the foreground.

He'd visited one of Temple's beloved vintage shops to nab banged-up jeans, scuffed motorcycle boots, and a faded Grateful Dead T-shirt topped with a plaid long-sleeved work shirt. He even messed up his altar-boy smooth blond hair with some drugstore gel goop, teased into a point at the top. The effect was still too tidy, but would have to do.

Tired swirls of neon lettering indicated the bars among the lingerie, tattoo, head shops and Vegas T-shirt emporiums in these shabby, one-story strip shopping areas.

Tired girls and women anchored darker street corners, one leg cocked to rest a hooker high-heel against the wall. Matt saw the sheen of their neon-tinted eye-whites as their gazes followed him. Some shifted their weight onto two feet, ready to approach him through the open car window, but he didn't look, didn't stare, just gazed listlessly ahead like a hopeless drunk out of beer money.

LUCKY STARS the nearest neon sign announced in a meteor shower of gold, green and blue stars. Cars and motorcycles kept lurching company in the front parking strip, but Woody found an empty, if tight, slot for his ponderous old Dodge sedan.

"Here we are, Mr. Midnight. Slots and jukebox in the front, pool table and hookers in the back. Tabletop nudie entertainment, everywhere."

Woody nudged Matt through the door first. Matt's pushing palm encountered a stickiness that could be any unclean bodily fluid he'd care to imagine. He wiped his hand on the jeans. They'd be in the Circle Ritz Dumpster tomorrow.

Smoke haze was even thicker here than in the Strip casinos. Wetherly bulled through broad-shouldered guys wearing biker leather and jeans jackets to a large, empty corner booth. The old man sat with a fervent *oomph,* then pushed himself grunting along the curved vinyl seat until he sat in the center, back to the wall.

A jerk of his head had Matt sliding in beside him.

The cigarette smoke and pot fumes made Matt's vision blur, but he could see both sides of the oval bar and most of the room on either side.

"You have an in with the maître d'?" he asked Woody.

An elbow jabbed Matt's side, the one with the bullet wound, and Woody wheezed out a pained breath. "That's a good one. Yeah, Mr. Midnight, I have an in with the maître d'. Been coming here fifty-five years. You could say I'm married to the joint."

"Have you ever been?" Matt asked.

"I've been a lot of things. What?"

"Married, I mean."

"Oh, hell. I don't remember. I do remember some wedding chapel, so I was either a justice of the peace, a bridegroom, or Elvis assisting at a ceremony. You never been married." He leaned forward with a piercing look.

"Not yet," Matt said.

"Bet you got a girlfriend who would be shocked, shocked, if she knew you were here."

"I won't take that bet." Matt glanced at surrounding bar tops to glimpse a lot of luridly lit topless and maybe bottomless flesh, but the array of lights, particularly black light that turned skin an eerie spoiled skim milk purple-white, was so exotic it dampened the impression of wall-to-wall nudity. Oddly, half of the customers were favoring drinks over ogling.

"Boilermakers."

"Huh?" Matt said, startled, but as he looked back, he saw Wetherly was addressing a waitress, topless, who'd appeared at their table, and whose mascara looked older than she was.

"How many, sir?" she asked, holding up her pad with newbie importance and obscuring her personal scenery.

"Two." Wetherly raised stubby fingers.

Matt tried not to react. Topless waitresses and boilermakers were not his socializing style. And mixing beer and booze seemed redundant.

Wetherly waggled the fingers. "Each."

Matt tried not to choke. He needed a clear head, so he had to be either a slow or sloppy drinker tonight.

"This is how you do it." The old guy leaned close, the stale cigar breath coming through teeth riper than a rotten fish head. "Bull your way in. Establish a presence. Then wait."

"For what?"

"You look like you came right off the set of *The Bachelor.* I will stop calling you 'kid', but guys in here won't. Clean-cut, that's a gutsy thing to be in this part of town. They'll want to settle their curiosity, but then maybe we can satisfy some of yours about Cliffie Effinger. You gotta give a little to get something."

"I have a feeling I'm like…bait."

Wetherly grinned and slapped Matt on the back. "That's the spirit."

When the boilermakers arrived, crowding the round brown tray no gin joint in all of the world was ever without, Matt decided that was just what he needed.

Wetherly dropped the shot glass of whiskey down inside his pint glass of beer, but Matt already distrusted the cleanliness in this place. So he downed the whiskey in one go, like in the movies, and hoped the high-octane bolt wouldn't make him cough. That would be way too clean-cut for this place.

Wetherly chuckled. "That'll make your eyes cross. Don't look left. We got a customer."

Customer. As in the expression "bad customer". The guy who was swaggering over to their table was tame enough to have only a couple visible tattoos on his biceps and wrist. He also looked to be about sixty. The late Effinger's generation.

The guy screeched a heavy wooden captain's chair over to their booth. "Woody, my man," he greeted Matt's escort. "You got a long-lost grandson?"

Wetherly's wheezing laugh turned into a cough, but on a grizzled veteran it didn't sound weak.

"Naw. This here's Matthew from Chicago." Wetherly spoke slowly, as if spelling unsaid things out…not to Matt, but to his pal.

Matt was beginning to feel like a marked man, or a shill. Why had he trusted the retired cop? Because Molina knew of him? She was relatively new in town. "Woody" could have been as crooked as a scarecrow in his day. Matt sipped the beer and studied the bar, repelled by tattoo-clothed muscleman arms and a greasy ponytail snaking down a jeans jacket back. Narrow-eyed glances eeled over leather jacket shoulders toward the banquette and away so fast you'd wonder if you'd imaged the attention. This place was one step lower than a biker bar. Beyond the bar, Matt could only glimpse a supernaturally high-kicking chorus-girl leg over the crowded circles of hooting men. Nudie pole dancing.

Wetherly leaned forward over the huge table, and lowered his voice. "You know, Ox, I got some kin up there and said I'd help him out."

"With what?"

"Post-mortem report on a former brother of the coast."

Matt recognized the phrase "brother of the coast". That was old-time talk for pirates. Anybody who'd seen Johnny Depp Jack Sparrow movies knew that.

Not everybody knew Cliff Effinger had died tied to the figurehead of the pirate ship attraction far up the Strip from this place. Had died tied. Tie-dyed in water. A horrible death Matt wouldn't wish on his worst nightmare, which Effinger had been when he was a kid.

The newcomer named "Ox" laughed. "You old buccaneer. I think I see where you're sailing. What's to ask about that? Old business." He suddenly eyed Matt with suspicion. "You the law? Why no mustache?"

Matt was flummoxed. Then he recalled all the bicycle cops around town—tanned, fit, hair bleached blond from the sun, and their mustaches too. "I'm a—"

Wetherly took control. "Crime buff broadcaster."

"Well, he's buff enough," Ox said sourly. "We'll never be that again."

"Too true. You know how that mob museum craze Downtown and on the Strip stirred up the media and the tourists. Our checkered pasts here in Vegas are a big-time money machine nowadays for everybody but the mob, which was always a myth anyway."

"Yeah, a myth. Mythconception." Ox eyed Matt. "I can see this guy on TV. So what'd we owe him a story for?"

"I told you. He hails from Chicago, ain't that right, Matthew?"

He hated being called "Matthew" when his baptismal name was Matthias, after a Disciple, but Matt knew he should keep quiet, and had to anyway. He'd been sipping the beer to quell the hard liquor hit to his stomach and was unable to answer right away. If Wetherly's elbow jabbed him in the bullet wound once more, he wouldn't answer for his reaction. This charade was useless. He could never swim with the barracudas.

Matt nodded like a Howdy Doody puppet.

Wetherly lowered his voice even more. "Freaking Effinger."

The other guy regarded Matt with awe. "How'd someone like you ever know anyone like freaking Effinger?"

"My mother's cousin married him."

"Oh, gawd. Was she institutionalized at the time? Oh, hey. Kid. Just...like, uh, kidding." He'd noticed Matt's hands fisting on the table and probably felt the whiskey fire in his eyes.

Wetherly put an apparently restraining hand on Matt's well-muscled forearm. "I'd be obliged, Ox, if you would put my young friend's questions to rest as to the fate of said Effinger. If some bad actor we are all very grateful to hadn't of offed him, my boy here might be facing thirty years to life on a homicide charge. He's going back to Chicago soon, and would like to have some peace of mind about the guy."

"Yeah. I can see he's touchier than he looks. You really going back to Chicago?"

Matt nodded. He was going to Minneapolis, for sure, and maybe not to Chicago if the talk-show gig didn't come through, but he figured nodding was not really a lie...and that whiskey shot had hit him harder than he'd like if he was doing this confession dance in his head, worrying about lying to someone who was the scum of the earth, although it was wrong to judge...

"Okay, Matthew...whatcha need to know for your peace of mind's sake?"

Matt knew he needed to do this just right. St. Jude, the saint of the Impossible came to his rescue with the words that came out of his mouth, just the right thing to elicit what he wanted/needed to know.

Matt leaned over the table like his mentor, and lowered his voice. "You see, I'm afraid the bastard isn't really dead."

"Oh, man." Ox looked from Matt to Wetherly. "Isn't really dead? I tell you. We—um, he…the police *(poe-lease,* he said*),* they found him wrapped up like a mummy, you know about that?"

Matt nodded quickly to keep Ox's words and shock flowing.

"Well, only not dry as a mummy from some pyramid like at the Luxor but wet, drowned, and not in any good shape when he hit the water. You cannot get more dead than Cliffie Effinger in this city. At least, not since the Chicago outfit got pushed out by the FBI in the eighties. You, ah, have connections in Chicago?"

"Sure thing, but my generation is bit behind on current protocol in Vegas."

"Current protocol?"

"Yeah, uh, they sent me to college. When I was back in Chicago recently, a couple of made men searched his widow's apartment, not on any orders we knew about. Maybe these freelancers were Effinger's ex-associates and were looking for something valuable he might have left there a long time ago. What bothers me, see, is the way Effinger was offed, seemed kinda…I'm not being critical here…but kinda an old-fashioned hit. If you know what I mean."

Wetherly intervened. "A message was being sent. My question is, was it the right message?"

Both men stared at Matt, who explained, "Here's the thing. Before Effinger sailed off into the sunset, I learned a body with his ID on it, get this, fell to a craps tabletop at the Crystal Phoenix and was taken for, uh, Cliffie, by the *poe*-lease."

Matt glanced at Wetherly, and lifted his beer glass. "Any more of these? Ox might need a hit."

Three fingers shot up.

Ox commandeered what was left of Matt's beer and downed it. "I don't know nothin' about that. That was…nobody I know is doing Strip hotel whack jobs. I don't know any hit man could pass going into the Crystal Phoenix's front lobby, or back stairwell, not with that wall-to-wall Fontana muscle all over the place. It's also like they've got some secret robot surveillance unit on duty there. Why, some grifters with a sweet party pickpocket game got IDed there by a freaking black cat. Who needs K-9 mastiffs when you have undercover vermin? Whoever dumped a body in the Eye-in-the-Sky system at the Phoenix has balls."

"Robot surveillance." Matt, who'd been present at that very pickpocket targeted event, had to tap his lips with his fist to hide a smile. Luckily, that gesture read like impatience. And by then the returning round brown tray had been emptied of three beer pints and accompanying shot glasses.

This time Matt poured the shot glass contents into the beer. "That's interesting. Could Effinger himself do that? Dump his double's remains in the Phoenix spy areas?"

"I said 'balls'. Does that word mean something else these post-college days in Chicago?"

Matt made an apologetic face. "I haven't been quite honest, guys," he said.

"Oh?" the word, spoken in tandem, sounded ominous.

"I need to know who offed both guys, Effinger and Effinger clone. Chicago doesn't like muddy waters, even in the pirate ship attraction. Chicago wants to know what Effinger knew that a minor rat fink like him killed someone else to cover his tracks, or *who* did it *for* him. Chicago wants to know what results any enhanced interrogations on Effinger himself produced. It's like before with Bugsy Siegel. Chicago wants to know. And what Chicago wants to know, Chicago gets. It's a toddlin' town, not a coddlin' town. *Capiche?*"

Meanwhile half the bar had gathered around, drawn by the words "Chicago" and "Effinger". Matt sensed a noose pulling tight around the circular booth.

"Hey," Wetherly shouted, because Ox was up on his feet along with six other heavy-muscled guys who moved when he did.

"So 'Chicago' is critical of hits on our turf?" Ox demanded. "And sends an errand boy to slap our wrists? We had our reasons and we're not done with what got Effinger killed—the bastard never squeaked—and we don't like accountants from Chicago coming around to crunch our numbers 'cuz we'll crunch his nuts first."

The Vegas nutcrackers leaned in, fists looking as big as boxing gloves moving toward Matt.

Uh-oh, he figured, go big or go home. He stood, overturning the huge round table, then crouched behind it, using it as a giant shield. Glass shattered, waitresses screamed, men cursed. Woody had dived to the floor off to the side.

Matt spun the bulky table onto its edge.

Matt half-stood to see the six guys grabbing for the table. He stood all the way up, pushing the heavy table's single stainless steel support pillar into their midsections. They were the bowling pins and he was the ball. They clutched their guts in a chorus of grunts. Onlookers showed jaw-dropping disbelief as Matt rushed for the door, the six guys from behind recovering enough to lunge for him, tightening like a noose.

"Watch out, kid!" Wetherly shouted from somewhere faint and far away.

He busted through the exit door after smashing a waitress's tray to the floor, now wet and paved with glass shards. More curses and thumps and chaos behind him.

Barely through the door, he hesitated to gulp in the hot, stale air.

"And away we go," said someone outside, someone much too close, who grabbed the back of Matt's plaid shirt and slung him out down along the sidewalk like sack of garbage. Gasping, Matt felt himself flung around a corner out of sight, against a dark wall by tall guy with a lot of moxie, muscle, and hair darker than the night around them. A half block away, the roar the Strip was again dominant.

Matt hauled back an arm and fist that meant business. "Dammit, Kinsella, if you really aren't out of the country, I'll knock you right over the border into Mexico myself."

But the dark-haired man wasn't tall enough to be Max Kinsella. It couldn't be… "Frank"?

"*Adios, amigo,*" the man said, and slammed him hard in the jaw.

11
Off Leash

It has been a long night.

Alas, I did not turn tail and publicly snub Punch Sullivan and all his works by stalking off after my Circle Ritz ladies this morning. Frankly, I wanted to explore this unlikely site for serious contemporary reconstruction by myself.

The clod called Punch Adcock took some misplaced comfort in my remaining with him on-site.

"See. This cat knows where the action is going to be," he tells Miss Katt Zydeco.

She, bearing a feline name, is much more realistic. "Forget it, Punch. It is not our job to deal with that ditsy dame crew or the cat they came in with from up the street. We have more important duties tonight."

Wonderful. By then I am out of sight underneath the temporary "skirt" of the forty-foot RV. What a perfect eavesdropping site and base of operations.

Perfect, that is, until Miss Midnight Louise slithers in beside me.

"Ideal observation post, Pops. Guess your years as a homeless street person were good training for a useful life, now that you are living *La Vida* Gigolo at the Circle Ritz."

Miss Midnight Louise is adept at making statements that one answers at one's peril, because no way can I come out a winner on that set of implications.

"You can stay," I announce, magnanimous, because I cannot dislodge her without a lot of sound and fury of the cat kind that will give away our surveillance. "Our role here is to wait and watch. It is like *Star Trek*. No interference with the alien species and their alien actions."

"Sure, fine. I see you are still stuck in the milieu of your second-to-last case, where reported UFOs got the Strip in a furor. The aging individual must beware of living in the past."

"If I were living in the past, I would certainly see that you had remained a mote in Bast's eye."

For once a comment of mine has puzzled my alarmingly obstreperous maybe-offspring.

Her furry forehead furrows. "I must confess, although the older generation may be horrified, that I do not believe in Bast."

"Certainly that is your choice, Louise," I reply. "Bast has endured for five thousand years, almost as long as our kind. Unfortunately, there is very little else for us to believe in these days. Unless it is Free-to-Be-Feline."

"That is a scientifically vetted healthful and planet-friendly food source," she says. "You are short-sighted, but inadvertently generous, to share your bottomless supply with Ma Barker's clowder."

I see we are treading delicately around each other so as not to widen the generation gap. It is at times like this I wish I had Karma, Miss Electra's supposedly psychic Birman cat, to kick around. "If you insist on horning in on my investigation, Louise, I will ask you to remain silent and to follow my instructions. I am expecting mind-blowing revelations later this night."

Miss Midnight Louise sighs. "You sound like some of my most annoying suitors before I was mercifully made indifferent to the reproductive imperative. However, since you are the best your benighted generation has produced, I will do my best to help you, Daddy-o."

I am touched. I am also convinced that I will need some decent backup before this night is over. Or, at the least, a witness.

I have lived in Las Vegas since I was spit out onto the street to make my way.

In that respect, I am not unlike the average tourist who visits this town. It is all a matter of luck, good and bad, and luck is a matter of self-esteem.

I have seen many things, good and bad, and have experienced both...the touching charity of a homeless person offering me a pinch of cold, abandoned fast-food burger. The rib-kick of a drunken casino winner, swaggering out of a Strip hotel. The tears on my shoulder-blades from a fifteen-year-old hooker on the notorious Minnesota Strip, who believes for a precious moment that I have it worse than she does.

In all of this, I have grown philosophical. I have also learned a bunch.

So I hunker down, as dudes of my breed, size and color can and have done for many decades and centuries, and wait to see what will transpire. Luckily, I can wait with my eyes closed. I shift into daydreaming mode. And then it is night.

Am I knocked back!

Louise curls sharp shivs into my shoulder. (I prefer tears, no matter how poignant. In that Minnesota Strip instance, I managed to find a nearby undercover policewoman and intrigued her to follow me back to the young girl and get my tearful hookup off the streets, at least for a while.)

Anyway, I needed a wake-up pinprick. This deserted lot is suddenly Ringling Brothers Central.

An hour after the sun goes down, an old Volkswagen van covered in wild psychedelic artwork from the sixties lurches into the parking lot and backs up to the rear door. *Power to the People* is written on its side. The passenger opens the back doors to reveal one big mama of a generator. The driver comes around to Dumpster dive in the metal container next to the door and pulls out a mess of heavy cables he starts laying out in the parking lot.

Then a plain white van pulls up with a flashing neon sign on its side:

POP-UP CASINO
$$ VIDEO POKER $$
DUSK TO DAWN
LAY YOUR BETS AND WALK AWAY
WITH LUCKY LOOT

From our lowly observation positions, Miss Midnight Louise and I keep our peepers set on wide VistaVision focus.

Speechless (our normal condition, actually), we watch men pour out of the van and wheel dollies into the depths of the abandoned building. In minutes, the basement door disgorges crews of the same men wheeling huge video poker machines onto the dirt, crushing the few straggly weeds.

Usually seen in long rows in huge hotel casinos, gaming machines look like the innocuous wall of video games they are. One by one, at night, wheeled out of an abandoned hulk, they resemble invading cyber-aliens.

Soon, a couple dozen slot machines have rolled out from the central building into ragged rows on the sandy lot.

"Some of those machines are antique one-armed bandits," Louise points out.

Yeah, they are. Folks used to have to pull a lever to make the cherries wheel around or the poker hands show up card by card on an animated, colorful screen. Now, instead of feeding quarters or even nickels into slots, player use five, ten and twenty-dollar bills and push one big square button.

At least a while back you could lose a few calories as well as your paycheck at a casino slot machine. Now you lose "long green" in the time it takes a bill, courtesy of Uncle Sam, to be automatically sucked through a slot. And your forefinger can wrack up losses faster than a thoroughbred springs out of a Kentucky Derby gate.

Before our eyes, more cars are wheeling onto the lot in front of the trailer. People from nowhere are screeching in on new and old wheels, setting up shop as an outdoor gaming parlor.

"This," I declare, "is weird, even for Vegas. 'Dusk to Dawn.' That is like eight p.m. to five thirty a.m. I never knew this secret gambling stuff was going on."

"This is more than weird," Louise whispers back. "Those are vampire hours. Could something supernatural be occurring?"

Before I can answer, I hear the screech of speeding automobiles hitting the brakes. This unlit side street is suddenly illuminated by headlights that quickly go dark and is lined by parked vehicles, from which clots of four to seven people pour out. Wait. Not just people. Guy people. Of course the male of the species is the most hardened gambler. The female favors better odds than mere chance.

"Oh, my mama's lumbago," Louise hisses under her breath. "This has turned into a secret betting parlor under the stars. Even though gaming is legal in Las Vegas, licenses are still required. What the Havana Brown is happening here?"

Normally I know everything, but must confess to ignorance in the current instance. This nighttime carnival must have a rhyme or reason, but I am without a clue in this case.

Although the sun has slinked out of sight for the day, I am not surprised to see some usual suspects strolling onto the frantic scene.

Punch Adcock and Katt Zydeco, who would be dressed to the nine lives were they feline, play hosts, and escort the imported gamblers to various slot machines. Leon Nemo cruises the chaos, his eye on his Rolex wristwatch.

Louise and I watch a few dozen gamers argue about the house rules (only cash and gone by 5:00 a.m.), but the house, well... rules. Even more suspicious, Adcock, Zydeco and Nemo's cell phone cameras record all the frenetic doings of this elite few on the night crew.

After weary hours of crouching on my fore and aft limbs alongside my far more limber associate, I see the bettors shuffle toward the curbs to depart. Nemo counts out a paltry few bucks, which are pushed into gamblers' pants pockets as they leave.

Vehicle engines rev at the curbs. The pack of gamblers vanish in a herd of red taillights. Leon Nemo adds to the fan of bills representing the night's slim "take", and distributes them among the musclemen scooping up the slot machines on dollies and returning them to the unplumbed depths beneath the ex-antique mall.

He is left with empty hands and a grin we can see even from under the RV.

"This is the most bizarre event I have ever witnessed in Las Vegas," I impart to Louise's petite ear, which twitches. "And that is saying something given the over-the-top entertainment on the Strip."

"That is indeed a first," she admits. "Oh, I am tired of serving as a stock-still vermin attraction. Tell me we can fold our tents for the night."

"Agreed. I need time to think on this startling event, which," I proclaim, "is even odder than when UFOs were reported buzzing the Las Vegas Strip. What is most wrong here, is that I do not see anyone profiting in any way from this night's events. That is just plain unnatural in Las Vegas."

"Agreed. An absence of greed is hard to stomach. Oh, my aching pads!"

On Louise's last comment, we scratch our heads literally and simultaneously, and depart for our separate home, sweet homes.

12
Guardian Angle

Matt was jostled awake by a vehicle speeding over pockmarked roads.

His head ached, his side stitches from the bullet-wound burned, and his jaw felt dislocated. He kept his eyes closed to take inventory. All right. Semi-upright in a car seat, but not buckled in.

Yeah, mobsters dumping a body-to-be would worry about traffic rules.

The rough ride felt like an SUV, not Woodrow Wetherly's old sedan. Matt guessed he could have been out cold for three minutes, or a quarter of an hour. Would he make his showtime like Woody had promised? Not his worst problem. His closed eyelids sensed the regular rhythm of passing streetlights, intermixed with some vagrant neon, he'd bet.

The driver was exceeding the speed limit for this old, bumpy part of town. In Chicago, winter snow and distributed salt made for spring potholes. In the desert southwest, the summer sun did the same job on the asphalt in its own searing way.

It didn't sound like the vehicle was on its paved-highway path to a sandy grave in the litter box of the Mojave desert, where all the mobsters hits lay undiscovered.

"You can stop playing dead to the world," the driver said.

The man's voice was deep, but he wasn't Kinsella or Frank Bucek, Matt's mentor from the seminary. Matt must have hopefully hallucinated someone from his past coming to his rescue.

Yet this voice was so vaguely familiar… It could have belonged to the last guy at a gas station pay booth or an actor on a recent TV commercial.

It rumbled on. "Sorry for the 'light's out' tactic, but a fistful of bad actors were about to clean your clock, so I'm taking the inner workings home for patching up and some necessary adjustments."

Matt blinked his eyes open and struggled to focus on the driver's profile. The dark hair was thick and wavy, the nose beaked. He recognized the least likely person he'd expected to hear or see, but the guy talked like a cop.

Matt's voice came out a dry croak. "Mariah's new *singing coach* knocked me out? Why was an ex-cop like you at a dive like that?"

"That's *my* line, choir boy."

"But you *will* answer it." Matt made the sentence a demand. "What's your angle?"

"Lucky for you, I'm up for the head security job at the Goliath Hotel. I was doing some extra-curricular tailing of a guy I thought was sizing up the hotel for a hit. The Lucky Stars bar is a cesspool of what passes for organized crime in this city, which now finds street gangs the biggest policing problem. And who do I see raising a ruckus with six guys but Mariah's fave candidate for her freshman Dad-Daughter dance escort. Can't allow the kid's crush to get a broken nose."

"A broken jaw is better?"

"That shot hurts *you* more than it will your looks. We're heading for your Circle Ritz digs. I always wanted to see the inside of that infamous building."

"No! I need to pick up my car." Matt checked the street signs. "It's not far. I'll direct you. I guess I should say thanks, Rafi… Nadir, isn't it? Yeah. I got in over my head."

"So what'd you do to rile the Lucky Stars' Silver Senior crook crowd?"

"Those guys really go back on the Vegas crimeline, don't they?"

"And they are so out-of-date, but not out of cold criminal intent."

"I'm trying to figure out why my stepfather from Chicago came to Vegas and got himself offed in a dramatic way Bugsy Siegel would envy."

"Oh, yeah. That Effinger goof."

"You know about his murder? More gory than goofy."

"There are some extreme Las Vegas mob-style hits, but, dude, that drowning in the dark of night on a major Vegas attraction is infamous."

"Really? You say 'dude'? Man, you must be forty years old."

"A well-worn thirty-eight, like the caliber of my favorite gun. The 'dude' is from hanging out with the kid."

Matt wondered what else in Rafi Nadir's life might "be from hanging out" with Mariah's mother hen, all-pro homicide lieutenant C. R. Molina. A guy with major hotel security responsibility playing singing coach? Was this a way to edge Mariah's secret father into her life? Because Molina was well qualified to tutor her daughter herself, given her own fantastic vocal talents.

"If you have any influence, I wish you could persuade her mother to get back to performing," Matt said, hardly realizing he'd spoken aloud.

Rafi refused to share his status with the lieutenant or her family, just saying, "Carmen's torch singing was a classy act. And nobody persuades Molina to do anything," Rafi added, probably unaware of the naked bitterness Matt detected in his tone.

He went on. "The kid gig is because I used to be a…what you'd call an amateur 'talent developer'. Don't judge her mother. She has a huge job responsibility as a woman on the rise in law enforcement. Puttin' on the ritz now and then at the Blue Dahlia can't be on her agenda these days."

"She has a great voice, though. I'd want her to sing at my wedding any day."

"Wedding. That in the cards soon?"

"Yeah."

"Then you don't want to be offed in a free-for-all fight at the Lucky Stars nudie bar, do you? Might annoy the bride-to-be."

"No. But I don't want to make that big a step without knowing what my rotten stepfather was up to in Chicago and then here that was so bad it, thankfully, widowed my mother. That has got to be linked to something big."

"Stubborn, aren't you?" Nadir swung the steering wheel ninety degrees. Matt looked around to see Woody's house. "I guess if you're going to live long enough to get married, you should creep into the home place unnoticed tonight."

"I'm not staying. I've got to clean up and get to work for the night shift at the radio station. What have you done to me? I'm leaving early tomorrow morning with my fiancée for Minneapolis. My jaw will be a dead giveaway."

"Sleep on an ice pack and you'll be normal by morning. Say, I'd still sure love to see a condo or apartment at the Circle Ritz. Let me know if you and the lucky little woman are going to leave a vacancy."

Matt sighed and opened the SUV door, trying not to land hard on the asphalt. Every little move he made right now was not magic. *Ouch.*

Rafi leaned over the passenger seat to pull the door closed after Matt. "Remember. 'You've got a friend.' Carole King. 'I'll Be Watching You.' The Police."

"Babysitting not appreciated," Matt said. "I don't know if you're my guardian angel or worst nightmare."

"Sometimes, dude, they are the same thing." Rafi Nadir winked and pulled the door shut with a nerve-shattering bang, at least for Matt's nerves at the moment.

Being hauled away from his first serious investigative move like a delinquent teenager could be considered humiliating.

He didn't humiliate, though; he persevered. For Matt, the evening's debacle was proof that Clifford Effinger was gone, but not forgotten, and was still of deep interest to both the crime and punishment sides of Las Vegas. How could Matt marry Temple with that kind of threat from his past hovering over them?

He couldn't.

So the only way forward was to ID and eliminate the threat.

Matt groaned. He was beginning to sympathize with Max Kinsella.

First, he had to get the Jag out of Wetherly's garage before the old guy came back. The ramshackle door didn't have a lock. Woody must consider himself theft-proof for some reason and would know who had taken it.

Then Matt had to get home to ice his jaw for a while, drive to his radio talk-show gig, and rise and shine early tomorrow to look fine and accompany Temple to Minneapolis to meet his future in-laws.

Right now, he might prefer to be Max Kinsella on the run from Kitty the Cutter.

13
Call Girls Inc.

"I've found the visiting house louse. Are you game for some vermin extermination?"

Temple blinked to hear her cell phone's rude but mystifying announcement this late in the evening. The gritty voice didn't even sound like Electra's. Her watch showed 11:06 p.m. She'd just finished packing. She and Matt could nap on the plane, but Temple was eager to get some sleep now.

"What kind of vermin? Something creepy invaded the Circle Ritz?"

"Just my dirty rat ex-husband, who hasn't been in town for years, and who swore he wouldn't sell his land without telling me first."

"He's here? Now?" Temple's adrenaline was kicking into overdrive.

"No. In town, hiding out. At the Araby Motel."

"Oh."

"Yes, that dump. He must have needed money fast."

"How'd you find him?"

"I called his latest ex-wife, Diane, and she wasn't surprised he hadn't told me he was in town. His recliner furniture business in St. Louis hit the skids in the Great Recession. Jay has been gambling again to get back on his feet, which means he's only losing more money."

"You certainly have colorful exes."

"Look who's talking? And that's why they're exes."

"So what do you need me for?"

"I'm not dumb enough to go to the Araby Motel at this hour. Alone."

"And little me would be a witness and protection? Matt's already left for his midnight show, but I could call—"

"No. I want as few people as possible to know my business."

"So a Fontana brother or two—?"

"Out of the question. This is women's work. I'm not afraid of Jay. It's just that the Araby Motel is a two cell-phone destination. One with a 9-1-1 autodial for me, and one with a 9-1-1 autodial for you, if I have to resort to violence. That's how the hookers work it, in pairs."

"Oh, great."

"Great witnesses, though, if something goes wrong."

"This is crazy, Electra. It's late, and Matt and I are leaving early in the morning."

"I have to talk to Jay, and he's liable to move around, dodging people he doesn't want to see, like creditors or ex-wives. Listen. Jay is really a pussycat. I just need to do some instant lion taming. There's got to be a way out of this deal he supposedly wrangled. We split the Circle Ritz and some surrounding acres in the divorce, with him agreeing to give me right of first refusal on a deal for his acreage. I can't imagine him reneging like this. Please!"

"Okay, Electra. I'll go with you, but you're forcing me to do the unthinkable."

"What is that?"

"Wear jeans and my ugly running sneakers. At least it's dark out."

Temple had slipped her cell phone into a wrist case so she could use it fast.

They drove Electra's old Probe. Temple rebelled at her landlady's suggestion of them riding the Hesketh Vampire motorcycle that had originally been Max Kinsella's. It was fast but noisy at high speed (hence the screaming vampire reference), and not low profile. For the same reason, Temple was not about to take her Miata convertible.

Sixty years ago, the motel had been a chi-chi little motor lodge, the latest thing in Western Accommodations for travelers wishing to see the U.S.A. in their Chevrolets. Today it was someplace Bette Davis could loathe. Dump Central. Not many cars littered the asphalt, but they all were missing something—paint, various windows, wheel rims.

It wasn't that the Araby Motel didn't have the usual Vegas vibe, including a snazzy neon sign. The Araby Motel was laid out like an exclamation point: a long, low one-story string of rooms stretching out from a registration office that sat under a tower of tired neon. Earthworm-pink neon cursives spelled out *ARABY MOTEL* above a sputtering green minaret and a huge purple genie wafting up from a blue bottle.

Every entertainment Mecca has its low-rent areas where the offbeat, the broke and broken, and the slightly criminal congregate. Temple remembered Matt visiting places like this when he first came to town hunting his stepfather.

"Room 16," Electra said as the Probe turned into the motel courtyard. That proved to be one of the few units where the light above the door hadn't failed, or been turned off by the occupant.

As Electra knocked at the metal door, Temple couldn't decide if standing in the light was a good or a bad thing. She'd glimpsed shadowy women along the street, and men in cars cruising slowly.

"Don't worry. I'm armed," Electra whispered, worrying her again. Again? You bet.

"Jay. Jay." Electra leaned out to knock on the picture window glass instead of wearing her knuckles out on steel. "I know you're there. We've got to talk."

The dust-stained lining of the window curtains edged back at one edge.

"Jeesh. How'd *you* find me?" a man exclaimed through the glass.

"Diane."

The pinch of lifted curtain fell back into place.

Temple turned to face the parking lot as a low-rider grumbled through. When she turned back, the steel door was opening.

"Jeesh, Electra." The man stepped back with the half-open door as a buttress. "You and Diane in cahoots. Makes my blood run cold. Who's the kid?"

Temple was used to being cut down to her petite size.

"My bodyguard," Electra retorted.

Jay's jaw dropped. "Funeee. You girls better come in. This can be a rough neighborhood."

Inside the room, by the insipid light of a floor lamp, Temple saw a big man both high and wide. Yet he stood like a guilty kid, neck bent forward and blue eyes peering out from under a forelock of thick white hair.

"We wouldn't be in a 'rough neighborhood'," Electra said, hands on hips, "if *you* weren't in one, or in Vegas at all, for God's sake."

"You're looking…festive," Jay said.

Temple bit off a laugh. Electra, with her colorfully patchwork white hair that predated the fad for purple and indigo chalk streaks, was her own eccentric self. Festive was the perfect word.

It did not appease. "Festive? I am furious, fellow. You show up in Vegas just as some scumbag is fixing on building an extreme strip club a rhinestone's throw from my residential building and its attached wedding chapel. There goes the neighborhood."

"I'm sorry about that, Electra." Had Jay owned a hat, he'd have been holding it in front of his generous belly and turning it around and around. *Aw, shucks.*

"You swore I'd have first crack at the land. It's in our divorce settlement."

"Weel, I need the money."

"So Diane told me. So you sold me out."

"I didn't know about the strip club, honest."

"Oh, *now* you're being honest." Electra looked over her shoulder. "Better take notes on your phone, Temple. Jay Edgar Dyson is being honest."

The name made Temple blink, but Electra seemed to think nothing of it.

CAT IN A ZEBRA ZOOT SUIT 89

"This is a red-letter day," Electra said. "Or night, rather. Honest as a…carnival barker. So my livelihood has to go down because yours crashed?"

"Folks aren't much into big recliners, except old people, Electra." He shrugged. "I didn't want to do it, but these big-time Vegas investors are real persuasive. I actually got comped at Harrah's when I arrived, and I thought I could win the money to tell them to go fly a Fokker 100."

"That's an early airplane, isn't it?" Temple wanted to know. "And who comped you?"

"This rep for the buyers. Nemo is his name."

"Wait." Temple's suspicions were confirmed, but she wanted to make sure. "Leon Nemo isn't the buyer?"

"Naw. Some other parties, I guess. Real estate investors."

"Buyer-schmuyer," Electra said. "What I need to know…is it a done deal?"

"I signed something."

"What?" she demanded. "An intent to purchase? A deed?"

Jay's wrinkled brow just aggravated her more. "You always had the business head of a turnip," she told him. "I don't. I do have the divorce agreement, and it states I have a right to buy the property first."

"Maybe." Jay shrugged again. "But the property's in my name and our divorce papers are what you might call a gentlemen's agreement."

"No gentleman involved," Electra shot back.

"Anyway, these people got the money to get their way. They are made of money down to their undies, I'd bet."

"How much did they offer?"

"That's private," Jay said. "And so's my room. I'm thinking you and your pint-size deputy better leave."

He shuffled forward, a wall of high and wide, but not handsome, bulk. Electra retreated in revulsion, pushing Temple into the doorway.

"You…cheap, thieving jerk," Electra accused as she backed away into the noisy night. "Some people aren't fit to occupy space on the planet. How much did they pay you? I want my money from our deal."

"None of your beeswax, hon." Jay grabbed the door edge to shut them out.

"You can't run away from me. I know people you don't want to mess with in Vegas," Electra fussed. "You'll be sorry—"

"I'm betting my people are nastier than your people, Electra," Jay said as he slammed the door closed in her face.

Behind her, Temple teetered on the edge of the concrete walkway, even though her sneaker soles were flatter than a morning-after wallet.

Electra backed right into her. "Sorry, hon! *Hon.* He called *me* 'hon', can you believe it?"

Temple edged around to Electra's side. "We better leave."

They stepped forward into a waiting circle of women. Black, white, Asian women, and one maybe-woman, all on six-inch hooker heels.

"That old guy cold cock you, sistas?" asked a black woman in a blonde wig.

"It's all right," Electra said. "I have some persuasive bill collectors." She pulled a bit of gun butt out of her shoulder bag.

"Some kink you must have on," another Sister of the Night commented. "What is it, grade-school girl and nun clown?"

Temple just wanted to be away from there. "You got it. We *are* a sister act," she said, citing some TV show icons of the past forty years. "*The Flying Nun* and Betty White. Red-hot act. We have a tight schedule. Gotta go." She grabbed Electra's elbow and propelled them both toward the car.

"Weird. Must be doing well with that," a last comment drifted after them.

"Oh, my Lord," Temple said as she buckled her passenger seatbelt. "That was a weird, useless outing. I thought for a moment you were going to pull out your gat and shoot him."

Electra's profile was grim as she turned the Probe under a streetlight and into the traffic flow. "That was a useless ex-spouse. What a louse. What a coward."

"Maybe," Temple said. "Maybe not."

"You're standing up for him?"

"No. I'm saying maybe he's been dealing with some local Big Bad Wolf worth being scared of. I don't like the vibe I'm getting off the people associated with this strip club project."

"Me neither. It sounds like they're putting pressure on Jay Edgar, but, believe me, baby. Nobody can do that better than I can, and I have just begun to fight."

14
Ride and Seek

When I spot Miss Electra Lark pulling out her old Probe car from behind the storage shed that houses Mr. Max's Hesketh Vampire motorcycle, all the Sensing Something Strange hairs on my hackles rise.

I then spy my own Miss Temple exiting the Circle Ritz wearing sunglasses after dark, stopping to perch on the top step while our esteemed landlady gets her car. Why is Miss Electra not driving her usual Elvis Blue Suede Shoes edition Volkswagen Beetle?

I race over to the oleanders ringing the parking lot. A certain stand of the hedge they form always harbors a guard cat or two from Ma Barker's clowder. I have ensured this handy presence by dragging down excess bounty from my despised stock of Free-to-Be-Feline for the feral community. My act of charity was almost outed last night by the mysterious intruder.

This is an excellent exchange program. Inside, I get kudos and head pats from Miss Temple for "doing so much better on eating your healthy food". Outside I get shoulder rubs for providing gourmet inside-cat food to the feral crew.

This is known in international diplomatic circles as a win-win situation.

Luckily, my business partner and aspiring daughter, Miss Midnight Louise, happens to be on Free-to-Be Feline patrol tonight. She eats up that trendy tasteless kibble that resembles rabbit turds. I keep silent on the matter, since it is handy to have her in my debt, but I would like to believe that no blood relative of mine would eat that stuff if not forced.

"Quick, Louise!" I say. "I need some impromptu tailing."

Her pointed little face with the harvest-moon-golden eyes pokes through a makeshift bonnet of spiky green oleander leaves. I must admit she is enough of a looker to be a relative, but I am not copping to that rap. They can sue guys for illegal littering these days, you know.

"Is Mr. Max back?" she asks eagerly.

"We have just determined he is gone, so no." He is her favorite tailing assignment, but she has been put on the Mr. Matt Devine detail in recent weeks and is none to happy about it, given the nightly round trip to outlying radio station *WCOO*.

"And," I add, "no silver Jaguar detail for you tonight, Mr. Matt is already at the radio station. Miss Electra's getting out the old Probe. Something Is Up."

Miss Louise boxes her airy eyebrow hairs. "That is a very rough ride. Perhaps they are just going out for a Dairy Queen."

"Whatever! I want you undercover and with them. Hurry. You'll have only a minute to eel into the backseat when Miss Temple enters the front one."

"At least she does so slowly, so as not to scuff her precious shoes. Although they are oddly ordinary sneakers tonight. Now *that* is suspicious."

"You cannot judge her on that. Poor people! They are forced to cover their very insufficient lower feet. They do not have our elegant retractable shiv design. At least my Miss Temple paints her pathetic toenails a vibrant Predator Red to make up for it."

Louise has tired of me defending my roomie. Her black coat melts into the asphalt as she hastens away, avoiding overhead lights. She is lurking beside the doorstep as the white Probe appears and stops.

Miss Temple enters the passenger seat, and slams it shut more speedily than is her wont. I cringe.

Yet when the Probe pulls away, Miss Midnight Louise is nowhere in sight, not even a hair of her luxurious rear member caught against the white car door.

What a relief! I would never hear the end of it if her precious "train" had suffered a fender bender. And so to bed.

With the flurry of Miss Temple and Mr. Matt leaving to catch a plane early the next morning, I do not expect a report from Louise for a while.

After they depart, I am enjoying a morning snooze from my undercover position beneath the oleander bushes, imagining my lost love, the Divine Yvette, cosseting my ears and purring pretty little French nothings into them. You might wonder how a French purr differs from a plain American one. There is a world of difference, believe you me.

"*Phffft.*" I awake spitting. Miss Midnight Louise is looming over me, cleaning her toe hairs right under my nose. I sneeze again. "You will never pass as French with that kind of public grooming," I warn her.

"When I want to pass as French, I will eat some *pâté de fois gras.*"

"Goose liver is not my favorite appetizer. Neither is it the goose's. So you accompanied the Circle Ritz ladies home last night?"

"I accompanied them home early this morning. They barely missed coming through the parking lot ahead of Mr. Matt Devine."

"Why, that would be almost three a.m."

"I am stunned by your adept math skills, Daddy Densest."

"What would the ladies be doing out at such an hour?"

"What ladies of the night do."

"What? Not my Miss Temple."

"And your Miss Electra. They visited a party who was checked into the Araby Motel."

Now I am sitting up, nursing my indignation. "That is a low-brow haunt of lowlifes and the ladies of the night they attract."

"Or the ladies of the night attract them. It is not fashionable, and especially not French, to bad-mouth ladies of the night nowadays. That is a lifestyle choice."

"Not for my Circle Ritz ladies."

"Chill, dude. From what I heard, they were there to admonish a certain resident named Jay Edgar Dyson."

"So this human was of the male persuasion?"

"In a very understated way."

"Huh?" Louise can get on her high horse to the point of vagueness.

"Like you, only in human terms. Old, fat, and apologetic. A good role model for you."

"Most amusing, Louise, but untrue. I am merely middle-aged, solidly muscled, and *never* apologize. That way lies the low road to cringing and whining like the inferior canine species."

Louise fans her fore-scimitars to show off their exquisitely curved points. "You are right that this Jay person alternated between whining and bluster. I had to listen at a steel door, so some comments were slightly garbled. Jay Edgar is a former mate of Miss Electra Lark and is allowing shady characters about Vegas to buy property of his that adjoins your landlady's holdings."

"I knew she was upset about neighborhood interlopers, but am surprised Miss Electra owns enough real estate to have it considered 'holdings'. This is beginning to sound like a game of Monopoly. That should be fun."

"Not for Jay Edgar. Miss Electra cussed him out worse than a rabid wolverine. She was mad enough to end his leash on life, and as much as said so."

"That does sound like no chance of a reconciliation."

"Both of your Circle Ritz lady friends gave him the two a.m. shuffle, and left him flat. He came out shortly after to try his luck with the lurking ladies of the evening, but they said his tastes were too peculiar and moved their business operations to the motel down the street."

"Well, that is a whole lot of nothing to report."

"It would be, if that was all I observed." She flicks a crumb of Free-to-Be-Feline from one long whisker. (Why has Miss Midnight Louise bought the party line on that putrid excuse for kibble? Sometimes I think she does things just to annoy me.)

"Okay. Spill," I tell her.

An elegant mitt-sweep sends an anthill of army-green pellets tumbling around my toes.

"Consider it spilled," she says. "And here's my last nugget of information. A weasely dude with ungroomed long hair and a soul patch came slinking along as soon as the ladies of the night left. He knocks and is admitted after Jay Edgar says something about getting out a bottle. I figure they will jabber until dawn, which is already paling the night sky, so I ankle out of there."

"How did you get back to civilization?"

"I hopped a ride in a seventies Cadillac Eldorado with a custom pearlized white and metallic magenta paint job, padded gold vinyl top, gold hubcaps on Gangsta whitewalls and interior black shag so long the three lady and two guy riders did not even notice me."

"Louise," I say, "you hitchhiked in a pimpmobile. Not classy. How close to home did that ride get you? You must have had to hoof it from the Strip."

"Not to worry. The Eldo stopped in our own backyard and I slipped out with the occupants."

"Our backyard? Where?"

"Right by that big old deserted building that has your favorite Circle Ritz ladies in such a tizzy."

15
Cat Track Fever

"It's a good thing," Max mused from under the face-shading brim of a tweed hat tilted low over his eyes, presumably to aid sleep, "that airlines banned the use of metal knives after 9/11."

His six-foot-four frame was stretched almost full-length as his torso leaned back on maximum recline in the plane seat, but his knees were folded so his feet were braced on the bulkhead wall dead ahead.

Thinking of "dead", he opened one eye to take in his seat partner by the window. "Otherwise," he added, "I might have a miniature table knife between my ribs by now."

"Don't flatter yourself," she answered without turning to look at him. "I would never use a weapon on you that had touched airline food."

She pointedly gazed out and down through the small window, which Max knew showed only darkness lit by the tiny, lonely lights of big ships now and then. Max had made this flight many times and found the drone of a trans-Atlantic plane's engines a lullaby. Not that he would sleep a wink on this flight, no matter how lazy and laid-back he appeared to be.

Unlike Max, who'd shed his trademark black designer turtlenecks and slacks for blue jeans, a disgustingly casual plaid flannel shirt, and the narrow-brimmed Trilby hat that was often seen on elderly male Brit pub-goers, Kathleen O'Connor had only semi-reclined her seat for the sixteen-hour flight from Las Vegas to JFK to Dublin, Ireland.

She wore a microfiber emerald pantsuit. A purple velvet beret tilted to the right haloed the panther-black hair that made her delicate pale profile into an exquisite cameo The flagrant hat somewhat distracted from the still-enflamed scratches flaring on her left cheek. Her schoolgirl-stiff posture made the dramatic outfit seem a costume, Max thought, and the injury a piece of stage makeup. Max had always told Temple that naked was the best disguise, and Kathleen, a.k.a. Kitty the Cutter, was the perfect example of that.

As for Max, he was perfectly content to let Kathleen's boldness distract from him. Besides her, there were plenty of people in Ireland, north and south, who wanted to kill him.

"I'm disappointed," she commented, almost as lazily as he'd been speaking.

He waited.

"No private jet? No shadowy international counterterrorism sponsor? Not even First Class?"

"Bulkhead seats, though," he said, proudly.

"A perk for *you*. I don't need that." She was five-three, tops, and her feet in kitten-heeled black patent leather shoes were propped on a huge black tote bag.

Max smiled again. Kathleen dressed as innovatively as his ex-fiancée, Temple Barr, except Temple was shorter and would have worn three-inch heels. Temple had also come up with the "Kitty the Cutter" nickname, and Max had to school himself to use the formal version now.

"Killing *you*," Kathleen said, "was never my intention."

"Yes, that would have interfered with my ability to suffer for loving you and leaving you right after, but seventeen-year-old guys are fickle."

"Did you?" she asked sharply.

"What?" *Love me* would always go unspoken with her.

Her jaw muscles tightened. "He said you said you had."

"Matt Devine the radio shrink, you mean?"

Your fiancée's new fiancé."

"He's a pretty good shrink," Max admitted.

Kathleen licked her bright fuchsia color lipstick, a rare nervous gesture. "He said because I'd lacked 'all positive social connections' growing up I couldn't understand close bonds. Or the guilt and responsibility you owed your cousin when he was blown up in the pub bombing while we were...in Sir Thomas and Lady Dixon Park."

"You know, Kathleen, my memory is still really screwed up. Belfast was almost twenty years ago. The answer you want may never come to me. What about *my* answers? Were you behind sabotaging my bungee cord act at the Neon Nightmare club?"

"No."

"Did you ever don a Darth Vader mask and cloak to join your longtime IRA ally, Santiago, then threaten those disgruntled unemployed magicians who owned Neon Nightmare?"

"Is it truly serious you're being?" She sounded indignant. "Santiago liked over-the-top stunts, and those Synth freakos were meddling with old IRA business in North America, but me, indulge in any such fakery? If I threaten, I act."

"There were two Vaders. Both were attacked and marked by a pack of cats. You know the ones I mean. Santiago's body bore the track marks down his back and legs when he was autopsied." Max's forefinger drew a soft line under Kathleen cheek scars. "Are you marked someplace other than this?"

"Is it possible you'd like to find out for yourself?" Her words were part taunt, part seduction.

"It's more than possible you'd like to find that out for yourself. No one human scarred you, in that instance."

"Those feral cats! They pack and attack like dogs. I've seen them hunting that way in the barrios of the major South American cities, more so than in the U.S. You saw it. Your girlfriend's housecat can don the 'mask' of a carnivore and the cloak of darkness and be as feral as a black panther. And if you want to see my scars, you'll pay dearly for the privilege."

Strong emotion had pinked her marked cheek, her small, strong body had tensed even more, and Max felt it, the adjacency, the intimacy, the mind's-eye photographic still of them lying almost side-by-side and, more than a memory, a feral desire to embrace heat and danger and sin and maybe even death.

"Your three a.m. shrink," Max said to change the subject, the emotional rush, ASAP. "He said you were cat-track free."

She frowned, distracted. "So that's what he was up to that night? Trying to see my backside without committing a mortal sin?" Her small cascade of laughter startled Max as much as a machine gun spray of bullets, but he kept still. "Father Straight-and-Narrow broke a sweat going undercover, all right. My God, he'd almost got me to admitting there had been some good priests, but he had to ruin it by going off and leaving. All men are alike."

Max found himself smiling along with her, mentally clinging to the fact she was a psychopath made not born, but still a psychopath. Going off and leaving her was a cardinal sin in her mind.

Kathleen shifted her seat to the recline position so abruptly that Max jerked upright by reflex, every muscle tensed.

"Relax, Max," she purred, turning her face so close to his he smelled the lemon from the Atlantic cod on the dinner menu. "We're going home, to where 'our hearts have ever been'. Or, rather, to where our young hopes have been left dead and buried, like Danny Boy's abandoned love. You think you hold my daughter's name and location hostage. I certainly hold your sainted cousin Sean's location hostage. All these years, and kin still separates us, and joins us. I'll take you home as no set of ruby red slippers could, not even on the munchkin feet of Temple Barr."

He leaned back and tilted the hat brim lower over his eyes, done with jousting. "Where do you wish to go first, my wild Irish rose? To meet my lost kin or your own?"

"To Hell, where Jack the Ripper claimed he was from."

"Fair enough," Max said. And yawned.

He knew the next step now.

He hoped those he'd left behind in Vegas were making the right moves too.

16
Off, Off and Away

"This certainly is a...squat...main terminal," Matt said.

He turned in the car's passenger seat to view Minneapolis-St. Paul airport through the rent-a-Ford's rear window. Temple kept her eyes on the road as she drove around continually curving exit lanes.

"Don't look back," Temple said. "And I'm pleased you're not nervous with me driving."

"Why should I be? Glad we got some sleep on the flight, though. Even you, who doesn't work nights."

Temple swallowed an urge to lie and over-explain why she'd been shy of sleep the night before. In daylight, that midnight Araby Motel expedition with Electra looked even more loopy than it had at the time.

Matt turned to face front and the passing freeway flora. "I like the coolness, but it sure is hairy here, like in Chicago."

He was right. Minnesota greenery was aggressive. Temple had forgotten that after living a couple years in a desert community like Las Vegas. Still, she was pleased. Most guys, even the best of them, had trouble relinquishing the steering wheel to a mere girl. Her brothers had been the worst at that.

"Don't diss the terminal, Chicago boy," Temple said. "My mother was an extra there when they filmed *Airport*."

"*Airport*?" Matt repeated.

Temple sighed. *Airport*, yes, *the* major motion picture of 1970. The Twin Cities of Minneapolis and St. Paul had gone crazy at being the film's site. For Temple's mom, it was the highlight of her college life. One day she'd spent the afternoon hours until dawn "milling" left and right in the main concourse area, depending on whether her birth date was an odd or even year. Repeated examinations of the final film's stopped frames had revealed no glimpse of her telltale fire-engine-red hair.

"Being an extra sounds hard on the feet," Matt said after Temple explained.

"My mom felt no pain. She glimpsed star Burt Lancaster and even saw a scene-stealing cameo by the 'First Lady of the American Theater', Helen Hayes." Temple cranked the steering wheel hard left as they glided under an underpass. "That terminal has been built onto since then. Back in that day it was considered ultramodern and exciting."

Matt shook his head and faced forward. "All this greenery seems claustrophobic after doing time in Las Vegas."

"It *is* pretty hairy around here." Temple grinned as she spurted the rental car into the pulsing westward traffic flow.

"Do you mean 'hairy' as in masses of flowing leaves or scary 'hairy' as in what meeting your extended family will be like for me?"

"Both." She spared him a glance from the crowded lanes. "Don't worry. Your blond coloring will fit right in with all the Swedes and Norskys in Minnesota."

"Your brothers too?"

"Kinda."

"Where did your red hair come in?"

"Must be some Scots-Irish in the mix." Temple smiled. "You don't look too edgy for a prospective son-in-law. We're on the Interstate and you're *still* not nervous about me driving."

"Why should I be nervous *or* driving? You know the terrain, and I don't."

"You're just too logical for the average guy. I love it, but I warn you that logic won't work with the Barr family Front Four."

"Your...brothers," Matt guessed. "I know they're all older, but why do you call them the Front Four?"

"Football nuts." Temple sighed. "Then they go to lakes and do horrible things to innocent fish. Even in the dead of winter. They've been teasing me since I was born and haven't stopped yet." Temple recalled the joke emails from her brothers popping up occasionally on her cell phone. She knew they missed her, but, being boys, didn't dare admit it.

"So you escaped."

Temple nodded, not taking her eyes off the road. "It was all 'harmless' stuff, but I was grown, moved out, and on my second great job before I left the Twin Cities, and I still never was able to shed their 'Little Sister' attitude. Their *really* little sister." She made a face.

"So you're more nervous than I am about what our reception will be?"

"You shouldn't worry. Mom's on our side. Or yours, rather. And Dad's automatically for anyone who is *not* tall, dark, and Max."

"Max isn't so bad."

"*You* say that?"

Matt shrugged. "Your dad only met me once in passing. How do I get a free pass?"

"He knows Mom watches *The Amanda Show*, and will probably run off with you if I don't."

Matt laughed. "I had no idea of the kind of pressure I escaped by being a blissfully ignorant of family matters during my sixteen years as a seminarian and priest."

"Or you escaped by not meeting my whole family until now."

"That Vegas hit-and-run dinner did its job in making me a 'better than' instead of an 'also-ran'. Apparently the great and powerful Max Kinsella didn't score too high with your parents and brothers."

"Putting it mildly."

Matt turned his head to view the neighborhood and hide a grin. Temple knew Matt, her Current and Committed, would always want to one-up Max, her Ex and...Exiled.

It was surreal to wonder if Max was in Ireland dodging stalker Kathleen O'Connor while she and Matt made a Romcom movie-like journey to her parents' home to pave the way for their wedding.

"Pleasant neighborhood," Matt commented.

Surprised, Temple surveyed the long and low sixties split-level homes that had always seemed bland to her as they glided past. "Compared to the close-packed two-story, nineteen-twenties brick two-flats your Chicago relatives live in, this is Super Suburbia," she agreed.

Seen with new eyes, the expansive lawns were gently rolling and as green as envy. In fact, Minnesota's lush emerald lawns were a prize asset. What a pain to mow all summer long! Temple wondered if her brothers helped Dad out these days, even though they were all married with children and lawns of their own to mow.

Oh, God. Children. She hoped that topic would not come up when her many nephews showed up tomorrow for Sunday dinner. Too much too soon.

A familiar string of brass numbers on a wrought-iron lamppost by the curb had her turning into the driveway in front of a two-car garage. Concrete stairs flanked by yew trees were now hosting a stream of large, looming, descending adults.

"The big question is," Temple said, popping the trunk lid, tightening the combs on her zebra-print pillbox hat, and leaning in to give Matt a last, private comment as five tall male shadows surrounded the car.

"What sleeping arrangements will they assign us?"

17
The Midnight Louie Boogie

Now that the lovebirds are hundreds of miles out of my way, I can thoroughly investigate the midnight incident of slot machine madness without fear of my Miss Temple showing up.

Luckily, as night falls and maybe even knocks itself out, I find Miss Midnight Louise at the nearby police substation where Ma Barker's clowder is based.

"Why are you sticking so close?" I ask.

"I fear," she says, "we need to investigate the underground gambling hell from which those antiquated slot machines were imported and exported in a matter of only hours last night."

"Maybe you have hit on it, Louise. We witnessed some sort of traffic in antique gaming machines."

"Whatever was going on is crazy," she concludes.

I cannot disagree, so we trot the few blocks to the old building and slip through the broken slat in the padlocked rear basement doors that allowed the slot machines in and out hours ago. It is hard to imagine the stomp of work boots up from the dark regions below on these deteriorated stairs, but is maybe why they are in such bad shape. The slot-machine parties have been held here before.

The night is ours, in its customary still, dark condition. This is when we creatures of darkness—bats, cats, rats, owls and opossums—come forth to explore. Or hunt.

I must admit that my long domestic routine with Miss Temple Barr has made me a bit weary in the middle of the night. Since both of her suitors had night jobs, we all had to stay on the same page, as they say, and retire in the wee hours.

I let Miss Midnight Louise lead on our path down into the lower depths, now that the slot machines have been returned to the obscurity they had so long ago earned.

We slink down the shambling stairs at the building's rear, step by step, stealthy pad by stealthy pad. We are a moving whisper in the night. Unseen and unthought of.

Such lesser lights as Punch and Katt and the moneyman Leon Nemo would never linger here, with dawn only an hour away.

Yet the very ebb of night is prime time for our kind. Louise pauses to let me lead now. Earlier, I explored the slot-machine-spewing basement briefly, and noted that many locked storage rooms line the space. I had assumed the most recent residents, antique mall purveyors, each had possessed a basement storage facility. I had not realized that vintage Las Vegas slot machines would be a major collectable.

Three steps down, Louise puts her chin on my shoulder and curls her shivs into my manly flank. Such an affectionate pose is highly unlikely from her. I detect a subtle shiver of anxiety. "Louie. I sense something is not right."

She almost always calls me some scathing derivation of "Pop" or "Dad".

"What?" I ask.

"I do not think we are alone down here."

"Of course we are not alone. There are random rats and mice eating away at any of the storage room contents that are edible. Or not."

"*Hmm*," says Louise, "perhaps *we* could eat away at the rats and mice."

She cannot fool me. She is totally addicted to the Asian sushi offerings of Chef Song at the Crystal Phoenix Hotel. I am the Great Black Hunter, who once subsisted and feasted on the chef's prized koi pond residents. Now I am planet friendly. I dine on kibble and people food, which is getting more politically correct by the month. Soon I will be surviving on moth and marigold.

Still, my whiskers tremble to a waft of insubstantial air, the mere murmur of other times and other faces. Karma is not the only feline phenomenon who can channel past hauntings.

My ears pick up a tinny, fragile sound. Am I hearing the circular shimmy of an old record spinning on an antique gramophone? My shivs begin to twitch in an intoxicating rhythm. My pads begin to tap dance down the stairs.

Have you seen some of those Disney cartoons from the thirties, where every character from Goofy to Mickey Mouse steps to a syncopating beat? It is like I am back in one of my À la Cat commercials, with the Fontana brothers in their zoot-suited sartorial rainbow backing me up. Me, the hep black cat leading the jazz-baby, swing-time parade.

I am looking around, and my trusty night vision is broadcasting in black-and-white.

Hi-de ho.

Thirties nightclub and film black entertainer Cab Calloway is swinging out in his pale zoot suit and pancake hat, singing "Minnie the Moocher".

That was caught on film. This is Vegas, baby. where the ghosts go to jive. I spot Josephine Baker, the black Venus of Paris, as long and loose and lovely as an exiled black American performer on the Continent has ever been. She has the liquid moves of the Black Ninja Brigade in Ma Barker's clowder.

Here she is again, in a magic basement, conjuring thoughts of Count Basie, bein' told by the Strip hotels black folks cannot come into Miss Josephine's Vegas show. So she sits on the stage doin' nothing. *Hi-de-ho.* Us black cats rush the aisles when we are finally let in. Then she cuts loose.

So do I. I spin Louise into a ragtime do-si-do. And the faster we spin, the more we see of the phantom basement and its ghostly cavalcade amid cries of "Go, voodoo daddy"!

I am watching the film clips from a black-and-white forties' film, *Hellzapoppin* featuring black performers doing a heckuva lotta jazztime, swingtime, and lindy hopping. These folks are as fluid in motion as my kind is. They are doing back flips, under twists, every spine-bending, mind-bending move we black cats can make.

All the dancers are dressed in old-fashioned service roles uniforms of that era, frilly white maids' aprons and caps over black uniforms, and as white-capped and white-clad cooks and nurses, white-coated waiters and train conductors, or jumpsuit-capped service uniforms all wearin' black-and-white spectator shoes and bobby sox. Everybody, every hep cat who has got rhythm is mopping up the floor with more moves than even a movie camera can record. It is past the birth of jazz and swing, it is an infectious sound and beat and joy of breakin' out of an uptight time.

I am doin' a rear-leg risin' solo, swinging Louise around by her fast-tappin' tail and the whole place is jumpin' with jive.

The quick-timing feet in their bobby sox and shoes retreat to the edges, the lines of storage units padlocked shut, to leave Louise and me doing our spotlight solo.

I am five again, doin' jive again, serenading the ladies from the backyard fence with Hi-de-ho. I make a classic cool daddy-o with a cat-chain down to my ankles. I am the cat's pajamas with a harem of crazy little mamas.

"The lyrics are politically incorrect, Daddy-o, but I did not know you could cut a rug," Louise says, turning a tight circle on her tippy toes. "You are the RKO-radio Daddy-o."

I know this is a dream, or a hallucination, but it seems all the pent-up, long-gone pizzazz in Vegas's secret past has survived in this old building and its basement.

And then everything unwinds to slow motion, and the movie folk dances slow until they are almost at a standstill, like a photographic still.

And in the still, still of the night, I hear the "Memphis Cat" Himself, wailing out "Heartbreak Hotel" like he did it his first time in Vegas at the New Frontier Hotel.

I see Elvis in his prime. Nineteen fifty-six. A black-and-white figure from an era photographed in black-and-white.

I see the storage lockers as cells, and Elvis sliding down a fireman's pole and rocking out like a crazy-limbed Siamese in mating season.

"Look, Louise," I say. "The King is here."

"Kitty Kong?" she asks, looking around for the rumored King of Cats. But she cannot see Elvis. Only I can.

This is not the first time I have seen Elvis in Vegas. He and I go back a long way, thanks to my nine lives. He knows I will keep quiet about his ghostly gigs. He knows I pick up and amplify his vibe. And now he is the absentee star of a new Vegas attraction. The Elvis Experience offers Graceland artifacts, theater shows… and the obligatory wedding chapel.

Poor Miss Electra is getting a lot of competition. I hope she will be allowed to keep her soft sculpture tribute to Elvis in her Lovers'

Knot wedding chapel pew. He has the best lap of the lot and likes the company.

The EE is Everything Elvis, but no Elvis tribute performers need apply. It opened April 23—Shakespeare's birthday, I happen to know, thanks to Ingram—at Westgate Las Vegas. The Westgate was previously the Las Vegas Hilton and earlier the International when Elvis performed there. Many of the current staff knew Elvis, including an eighty-two-year-old cocktail waitress who worked during Elvis's first show there. I find it amusing that Elvis will be occupying 28,000 square feet of the former *Star Trek*: The Exhibit attraction. Perhaps Elvis will transport in some night and we can boogie.

Back in the fifties, Elvis bombed with the New Frontier's audience of Midwestern married couples more into Lawrence Welk than the Memphis Cat. But that is all right, mama, that is all right with me. We hep cats are accustomed to being misunderstood by unenlighted generations before and after us. He came back and owned the town.

All this YouTube nostalgia reminds me of the Moulin Rouge, Vegas's first hotel-casino with all-black entertainment. All the Strip's white show-stoppers went there to stage their own integrated late, late show: Frank Sinatra, Judy Garland, Sammy Davis, Jr. After that, the Strip had to integrate because of the competition, so the need was gone and the Moulin Rouge only lasted eight months in nineteen fifty-five.

It occurs to me, as I rock and roll with Louise and all these ghosts of times past, that there might be a very important footnote to the Moulin Rouge saga, something seriously relevant to the memories and cycles of life and death, but personal and institutional in this forgotten venue.

But now that I have listened to "Get Happy" singer Judy Garland tell me to "come on get happy" (although she never did, poor woman) and watched Elvis walk down Lonely Street to Heartbreak Hotel, I cannot quite recall what that is.

That is a pity. I yawn as the music and motion grows faint and feeble and fades, as do we all. Miss Midnight Louise and I lose our rhythm and find ourselves waking up from conking out on a pile of plastic garbage bags for a bed in the dark, empty basement. We leave to walk through the Vegas dawn to get a little peace and quiet.

18
Family Matters

Suburbia was a new landscape for Matt...not to mention how strange being officially viewed as a prospective son-in-law was. He wondered how an essentially irreligious family of Unitarians would regard a formerly celibate priest as Temple's future husband. At least, like stage magician Max Kinsella, Matt was slightly famous because of his radio talk show.

As he stood and shook hands with the strapping Barr family men, he saw that Temple's relatives were less bombastic than his large Polish family clan, but they were bigger people. They seemed like bodyguards as they escorted him and Temple up the exterior stairs and into the house's main living area that stretched above the garage below. A sliding glass door in the living room overlooked a deck.

The low, eight-foot ceilings made Matt uneasy, like being a sandwich meat everybody was examining for two much fat. He was used to and loved the Circle Ritz's high, barrel ceilings. His family's venerable Chicago row houses and two-flats boasted ten-foot ceilings.

Matt relaxed with a tiny sigh when Temple's beefy dad released her from a bone-squeezing hug, pumped Matt's hand with an accompanying backslap, and then suggested they all go out on the deck for barbecue and beer. That seemed familiar.

Ah, air as fresh as the great outdoors. The cedar wood deck was expansive enough to hold a picnic table for twelve and overlooked a sea of mowed grass that lilted in gentle swells to a row of untrimmed bushes and trees. Minnesota tamed and Minnesota wild.

"Grew up in Chicago, I hear." Roger Barr confirmed with a grin. "City boy. This grass here is heaven. Until you have to mow it."

"Can't argue," Matt said, enjoying the breathing room so he could take in…four chunky guys all older than he, all wearing loose khaki shorts and well-filled-out T-shirts celebrating the Vikings, the Timberwolves, the Swarm and the Wild. The St. Paul Saints on Daddy Barr's chest gave Matt hope. *God help me*, Matt thought quite sincerely. He did not speak Sports. He was a stranger, yes. And in a strange land, even more so.

Temple was disappearing into each brother's embrace in turn, but emerging uncrushed. "Gee, guys," she said, "I'm glad to see you again, too, and your full heads of Hair Club for Men."

That was a joke. Keith, David, Tom and Hank were in various forms of transition to forty and middle age, which meant more middle and less luxuriant hair topping.

Matt duly shook their hands, which ended with a final slap each time. Good thing his job didn't rely on using a computer keyboard, like Temple's. His shoulders would be out for a week if this continued.

"Say, Matt," said Keith, the apparent eldest. "We don't generally watch daytime TV, but Mom insisted we eyeball a tape of *The Amanda Show*, and you are one cool talker, guy."

By then Temple had arrived at Matt's side to slip an arm through his.

Bad move, Matt thought. The boys didn't want to see he had a sponsor.

"It's a living," Matt said with a shrug.

Temple opened her mouth to (unfortunately) sing his praises and future talk show prospects, but suddenly all attention turned to the sliding glass doors from the house behind them.

Matt, who'd wondered since he'd briefly met her in the chaos of a major Vegas banquet, what womanly steel had borne and put up with this lusty male throng—saw Temple's mother in her element at last and stood still in shock and awe.

She was a true "slip of a thing". Her girlishly slim frame curved like a leaf about to be blown away, yet belied by those ample sixty-something laugh lines. Her short-cropped hair still flashed a glint of fiery red among the iron gray. Now he knew the gene pool Temple and her aunt, Kit Carlson Fontana, had sprung from, the fey side of the northern European spring, not the Viking one. It was insane to think this wiry elf could have carried and borne all these big-headed brothers, although Karen Barr broadcast the calm control of a woman who had managed child-bearing with amazing ease, like everything else in her life.

"Matt Devine." She paused in the open doorway to the deck, her extended arms holding a tray of muffins. "Put these out on the picnic table, sweetie, and we can all get eating." She cocked an eye at her sons. "Yes, boys, you can safe-crack the ice chest for the Hamm's beer now."

Matt was actually relieved to have some heavy lifting to do—Minnesota muffins weren't wimpy. They were as big as his fist and darkly dotted with nuts and berries.

Temple joined him at the redwood buffet table. "The worst is over," she whispered. "Nephews tomorrow. They're smaller and have slightly better manners. So far."

"Hamm's beer?" Matt had never heard the brand name.

"Founded here, and once the glory of Minnesota. Now owned by CoorsMiller, and just a select brand for oldsters. 'From the land of sky-blue wah-ah-ters'," she sang. "'Hamm's, the beer refreshing.'"

Matt had never heard Temple sing and raised his eyebrows at her on-key soprano. "We could make beautiful music together on Electra's Lowery organ at the Lovers' Knot," he said.

She gave him a sassy hip bump. "We already have that covered at the Circle Ritz. As for home-grown products here, Land-o-Lakes butter is still a going concern," Temple added with a smile. "Minnesota and heavy-duty dairy products keep on trucking."

"And your brothers." Matt watched them grabbing hamburgers and heaping hot dog buns with tablespoons from a slimy pile of apparent bean spouts.

"Sauerkraut," Temple murmured under her breath.

"Where are their wives?"

"Saved for the visit's second day. All those women and kids were deemed too overwhelming for you right off."

"I was a pastor at a Catholic parish, Temple," Matt told her. "Large families are not a stress factor for me."

"This one will be. Whatever you do, don't let my brothers talk you into a friendly game of touch football after lunch."

Matt eyed the huge, grassy yard. "I can do that."

"Not with my brothers."

Matt noticed Temple's grip on her lowball glass had grown white-knuckled. "Where'd you get a cocktail?" he asked. "I could use one."

"In the kitchen with Mom. Out here, it's only beer for boys. You do not want to look like an effete intellectual who knocks back Gilbey's gin with that crowd."

"Gilbey's?" Matt wrinkled his nose. "Not my brand of gin."

"Vegas spoils you. Toast the Hamm's bear like a good boy."

"Bear? Aren't the Bears a Chicago team?"

"And you say you don't speak Sports. Very good. A cartoon bear was the Hamm's beer mascot." Temple glanced over her shoulder. "Tom is heading our way. That can't be good after three bears. I mean, beers."

"Temple, how much Gilbey's is in that glass?"

"Enough for what's next, I hope." Temple edged around to stand beside him.

"How's about we take a stroll on the lawn," Tom suggested to Matt. He was the Timberwolf T-shirt guy.

Matt nodded at the shirt logo. "The Wolves going the distance?"

"Basketball season is over," Tom said with a frown.

"Uh, right. I meant next season."

Keith turned to Temple. "Can we borrow your guy for a while?" His arm made a sweeping gesture to the backyard. "Introduce him to the great Minnesota outdoors."

Temple frowned. "I don't want any grass stains on those khaki pants of his."

Tom hitched up his roomy knee-length shorts. "No problem, lil' sis. We'll take care of your guy."

"Do not call me 'lil' sis'," Temple warned. "And your guts are an endangered species if you yobos get out of line with my guy."

Tom of the Timberwolves turned to shrug at his grinning three brothers in their equally aggressive team T-shirts.

They surrounded Matt with collegial backslaps. "Just a little touch football to settle the sauerkraut." Keith, the Viking, said that. Tom the Timberwolf nodded with cheesy sadistic glee.

Matt let Temple's super-sized big brothers swarm him in a pack down the deck stairs onto the yard. If touch football was the rite of passage here, he could manage it.

Temple placed her hands on the deck rail, like Juliet on her balcony, and shouted down in a Kate the Shrew voice, "If you guys tear out the stitches from his bullet wound, I'll see that you'll be drinking your Hamm's out of your shoes."

"Bullet wound?" Keith reared back to regard Matt with astonishment. "You have a bullet wound?"

"Nothing major," Matt said. "It was a while back."

"Bullet wound," Tom of the Timberwolves repeated. "How on earth that'd happen, man?"

"From a semiautomatic. Actually a Walther PPK."

"A James Bond gun. Cool," Hank of the Wild said.

"What's a talk show host doing catching a bullet wound?" Bruce of the Swarm asked.

"It's complicated. Your sister is overreacting."

"Tell us about it, Matt," Keith said. "No kidding. Somebody shot you? Why the hell?"

Matt was amused he could make points with them without uttering a single lie. "I do my radio shrink gig at a Vegas radio station, *WCOO.* You know crazies abound in Vegas. And on live media if you do call-ins, you can attract the occasional fringe person. A stalker. It's all in the ethernet…but occasionally a crazy gets through the security and breaks in."

"At the radio station? Someone came in and got a shot off?"

"Like I said, rare. And the shot went wide of doing permanent damage, by an inch, I'm told. Crazy-proof security has now gone in. Not to worry, guys. I'll survive to marry your"—he thought for a second—"your little sister."

Temple booed him from the deck, but her brothers grinned.

"What the heck?" Tom rubbed his balding buzz-cut. "*WCCO* is our big radio station. Kinda weird coincidence."

"World's full of them," Matt said.

"You seem pretty tough about getting shot," Hank mused.

"What's tough is being a celibate priest," Keith said. "I just don't see that going with our little sister and a bullet wound."

Matt got inspired. "You've seen movies with martial arts monks, haven't you, guys? Shaolin kung fu monks?" They nodded, puzzled by his drift. "The Catholic church has had monks and brothers for centuries too. 'Brothers', that's what they're called in the West. So. Nobody asks questions about their private lifestyle; nobody who lives." Matt lifted his hands in a praying position and then separated them as he took a throwing stance. "We gonna toss a football around or not?"

"Yeah, sure. Brother," Tom said just before the football slapped Matt's open palms and he took off running, ducking, and shouldering anyone in his way.

Matt had played enough basketball and touch football with the parish high school teams to know how to keep it interesting, but not injuring. The Barr boys kept their moves at the same level now that they knew he was playing hurt. And that Temple was watching.

So everybody worked up a light sweat and looked good and they all were soon relieved to hit the deck for a second round of food and drink. Or mostly drink for the brothers.

"That ring is breathtaking." Temple's mother came to sit beside Temple and Matt on the long traditional sofa in the living room while Roger and the boys finished off the cooler contents from the deck. *Hamm's, the beer refreshing.*

Temple formally presented the ring on her left hand to Karen. "It's vintage. I don't think you had a chance to really study it at that large, noisy dinner table in Vegas."

The "boys" hadn't even noticed the rubies and diamonds glittering on their sister's knuckle. And now they were downstairs watching ESPN on the recreation room's sixty-inch TV.

"Of course, it's vintage," Karen said. "You were begging for dress-up clothes since you were three." Karen smiled at her husband, who'd taken the big brown leather recliner after depositing three crystal lowball glasses of straight Wild Turkey Kentucky Spirit on the coffee table. Sipping whiskey. "Who picked it out?"

"Guilty," Matt said.

"I'm impressed." Karen glanced at her husband.

Roger Barr grunted, a content paterfamilias at the moment. "That's a large bunch of bling for my baby girl's tiny finger."

"Dad, if my finger is strong enough to hold my always overloaded tote bag by one strap, it sure can support a high-carat bunch of Art Deco."

"As you can support yourself," he said. "We get it." He glanced at Matt. "You know, these liberated days there isn't anything for parents to do anymore but foot the bill."

"Dad, I'm a big girl. I'll foot the bill for my own wedding."

"We will," Matt said.

"Then the only question is where and how," Karen said, blue eyes glittering like sapphires.

"My family is in Chicago. And very extended." Matt shrugged his resignation. "They're threatening the Polish cathedral."

"The cathedral is magnificent and its aisle is endless. I could have a train, a long, long train," Temple told her mother. "I've always wanted to wear taller clothing."

"Remember, dear," Karen countered, "we have a lovely woman minister at our Universal Unitarian congregation, and you could hold it anywhere, at the Historical Society in St. Paul or the American Swedish Institute in Minneapolis."

"The Swedish Institute mansion is gorgeous," Temple told Matt.

"You could have a train here too," her mother mentioned, adding a tempting point.

"What about Las Vegas?" Roger suggested. "Tons of fancy places."

"Possibly the best solution." Karen sat forward. "Destination weddings are the thing these days, and the sports bars and casinos would keep your brothers busy and out of our hair."

"To us, Vegas is…" Temple sounded hesitant.

So Matt finished her dropped sentence. "Old hat when you live there. Although Temple's hotel client there would be sure put on the Ritz for us."

"Oh, the Crystal Phoenix is spectacular," Karen agreed.

"And," Temple said, "we live at the Circle Ritz condos and our terrific landlady is a Justice of the Peace and has a wedding chapel on-site. Electra would be in Seventieth Heaven if we got married there." She looked at Matt. "You played a Bob Dylan wedding march on Electra's organ when we first met, remember?"

"A Bob Dylan wedding march?" Karen was dubious.

"You'd have to hear it on an organ to see what Temple means," Matt said. "It's 'Love Minus Zero, No Limit'."

Karen shuddered. "Sounds hippy-ish."

The conversation lapsed into a generation gap silence.

"I know!" Temple said, revving up PR sell-mode and sitting taller to present her pitch. "They used to have progressive dinners in the seventies, each course at a different house. We could have progressive weddings."

"Not a bad idea," said Karen. "First, the bridal shower here in Minneapolis with your old girlfriends, then a simple UU wedding—"

Temple took up the narrative. "And then the groom's dinner in Chicago with Matt's family and a full-regalia Catholic ceremony so we're not living in sin in the eyes of the church."

"And then—" Karen was getting as carried away as Temple, "we all go to a lavish reception at your hotel in Las Vegas."

"After," Temple says, "a brief civil ceremony in Electra's Lovers' Knot wedding chapel so her feelings wouldn't be hurt. And it's not 'my' hotel," she said modestly, "although the owners make me feel like that."

"Oh," her mother cooed. "Aldo's brothers," she told Roger. "The Fontanas are the large Italian family that ran to boys, too, and they look out for Temple. I'd love to meet and thank each and every one of them."

The mental picture of a flock of courtly Fontana brothers gathering around her elfin mother stopped Temple's fantasy scenario cold.

Matt hoped he didn't look as dazed and white-faced as Roger Barr did at the moment. Both men sipped bourbon and kept their mouths shut.

"Too expensive," Temple said with a sigh.

"Too exhausting," her mother added.

The women sat silent also, mulling over reality.

After Temple's brothers left at 7:30 p.m., Karen and Temple cleared up the picnic table while Matt and his future father-in-law tidied the popcorn and beer-can strewn recreation room on the lower level.

"I suppose we're expected to have a man-to-man talk," Roger said, shoveling the mess into a huge garbage bag.

"Do you have any questions?" Matt said.

"Nope. I know what you do for a living, what you're maybe gonna do. What you did do." The already well-marked furrows on Rogers's forehead deepened. "I'm a little uneasy about this stalker thing."

"That's a fluke. That person is now out of the country and in the hands of the law." *Well,* Matt thought, *Max Kinsella was certainly a law unto himself.*

Roger nodded. "Then I don't need to know anything else, except getting to know you better. And finding out what kind of folderol the women will be putting us through."

He dragged the trash bag through a door to the garage and then led Matt up the stairs, where Temple and Karen were back on the couch, curled up with their shoes off.

Karen rose. "We'll all need our rest for tomorrow with the entire crew, guys, and then you take off, too soon. Our master is thataway, but you're going thisaway." She pointed to a hall leading left off the living room. "Tom put your luggage in the foyer."

Temple and Matt nodded without comment.

"We did somehow manage to have four boys and one girl," Karen said, "so there are now three empty bedrooms and two baths in that part of the house. Take your pick of the accommodations."

Whew, Matt thought, *diplomat Karen saved us all from the awkward moment of anyone declaring to sleep together or apart.*

"Maybe," said Temple with a wicked eyebrow lift, "we'll just do progressive bedrooms."

Of course, Matt knew, negotiating the sleeping arrangements at the old homestead with Karen's daughter would be a lot trickier.

19
In Dublin's Fair City

It may have been a long way to Tipperary in the old Irish song, but Belfast was only a two-hour drive from "Dublin's fair city, where girls are so pretty". In terms of "the Troubles" time, it was a centuries-long journey of political and personal pain and suffering.

Max hankered for the drive through tranquil green countryside to lull him, to make up for the sleep he'd lost while traveling with Kathleen. He must have learned his current self-hypnotic drone state during his counterterrorism work. With it, he could function automatically, yet snap out of it at the first sign of a threat.

Kathleen's toe nervously tapped the floorboard as their rented Honda maneuvered the city's eternal gridlock and narrow streets. He knew where he was going and hoped to find a precious parking space. Then a jolt of adrenaline zinged his senses like an inhalation of Chinese mustard as he spotted a blot of familiar bright red ahead, near the river Liffey.

At the same instant, Kathleen finally broke the silence. "So is a visitation to my daughter the first step in your Pilgrim's Progress program?"

"It would seem logical."

Kathleen burst into laughter. "You sounded like the late, great Mr. Spock just then. If you're expecting me to provide you with a weepy reunion, you can forget it. I excised her and my abuser's DNA from my life when she was an infant. This is pointless. You should book yourself a flight back to the U.S."

"And leave you 'a lone wolf' ticking time bomb out there somewhere?"

"How are you going to ensure that I'll not be that no matter what you do? Ah, such an unexpected sentimentalist you turned out to be. What convinces you that seeing my grown daughter will make me a changed woman?"

"Nothing," Max said, fully engaged now that they were quarreling and because he'd been driving through the Dublin streets with Garry Randolph's ghost fighting for possession of the left passenger seat. He faced Kathleen square on for an instant. "I'm curious to see how she turned out."

"You seem to share that abnormal curiosity about other people with the Cinderella-footed Temple Barr, she of the whole wardrobe of tiny glass slippers. God, she wears a size five! Even I need a six. Was that what drew you to her?"

"How do you know her shoe size?"

"The Circle Ritz is easy to break into. Poor little Cinderella. I made a contribution to your rival's mother's wedding at that attached chapel weeks ago. You know the drill. Brides require something old, something new, something borrowed, something blue. 'Something stolen' was an amusing addition to the list. I "borrowed" the mate to one of tiny Miss Temple's intended wedding shoes."

"I heard about the wedding, but really, Kathleen. Petite shoe-size envy? Women compete over the most trivial things."

"Like you?" She slid him a knowing glance. "No. I just let her know I'd been the culprit and gave that shoe back. I wasn't as stupid as the wicked stepsisters, to maim myself over her shoes, or her. You haven't answered what the attraction was."

"These things aren't programmable, Kathleen. That's why they're natural wonders, unless we ruin it by too much analysis. Maybe, mostly her...energy and honesty."

"I'm energetic."

He laughed. "Yes, you are. Tireless, I'd say."

"I was born amid lies."

"Yes, you were."

"Do you think I can become honest, an 'honest woman'?"

"Only if you become honest with yourself."

"Bollocks!"

"Then don't ask me. I will note you're wearing aqua today. That hardly matches the 'honest' color of your eyes, blue."

"Your color as well. A magician is the most dishonest creature on the planet."

"More of a juggler of the truth."

"You used colored contact lenses in your performances and posters. 'The Mystifying Max', green-eyed huckster selling illusion for more than a hundred dollars a ticket. Where were your blue eyes then?"

"I was on the run too." He pursed his lips. "If I gave you a hundred thousand dollars as a delayed donation to the IRA, would it be used for victim reparations?"

"*This* victim would keep it as reparation. Besides, you never paid for our rendezvous in Sir Thomas and Lady Dixon Park."

His look was chiding. "You never asked. But I think I've paid plenty."

Driving on the left was an easy switch for Max. His brain had retained automatic reflexes, he noticed, better than memory of emotions.

"We're parking here?" Kathleen sounded a bit panicky. "What's here?"

He went around to the left side to let her out. "Tourist overload. We walk from here." He took her arm, firmly, and guided her over the rough cobblestones until she jerked her arm away.

And spied a bright red façade labeled in bold gold letters, crammed with patrons.

"'Temple Bar,'" she sneered. "You are so predictable. You fly in the face of irony. That's where your local spy got the photos of Iris. It's a tourist trap."

"She's currently visiting Dublin."

"And drinks there like a tourist?"

"It's a world-famous pub. Your daughter takes advantage of the local watering holes."

"She's a drunk."

He shook his head, laughing. "Come and see."

He took her arm in custody again, but she resisted. "She's a barmaid."

He shook his head again. "Come see and then speculate."

They had to fight a constant flow of people coming and going. Soon Max, with his unusual height and a bit of maneuvering, had them standing by a just vacated table, being swabbed down for new customers.

"Two Belfast Blonde pints," Max ordered before the girl could whisk away. She nodded.

"You didn't consult me," Kathleen complained.

"All craft beers here are superb, and Belfast is where we're headed."

"It's back to the beginning, I see. Meanwhile, this place is so crowded, so noisy on the inside, so luridly red on the outside," Kathleen groused.

She looked prim and proper among the overwhelmingly young and casual crowd. And annoyed.

"Your resemblance to your occasionally visiting daughter is less likely to be remarked on in a crowd," Max pointed out. "Unless you want a public outing."

"Lord, no."

Their pint glasses landed like UFOs in their midst, and Max handed over a generous ransom to make for a quick exit, if necessary.

"Thank *you*, sir." The serving girl flashed a smile with a brightness that made up for its brevity.

"I hate ale." Kathleen stared at the honey-dark brew with knitted eyebrows.

"You're here to look, not drink. So look." He nodded to the stand-up bar.

The girl's blue-black hair among mostly ruddy and brown heads was hard to miss.

Iris provided plenty of side and three-quarter glimpses of her face. She was standing sandwiched between two men also in their mid-twenties. Obviously just good mates, to Max's trained eye. This was a post-work meet. Likely more men and women would join the party. Crumpled bills lay on the bartop, ready for a second round.

Meanwhile, Iris tossed her head and hair and cracked jokes and smiled, delivering what the Irish call "good craick"—bar talk that creates fellowship and jolly exchanges…and alcoholics. In a green land under a gray sky and veils of rain and mist, indoor warmth of any kind was a necessary boon.

"I hate ale," Kathleen repeated, "and the little bitch may look like me, but I see traces of the bastard who fathered her."

Max wasn't surprised. Remnants of paternal genes were bound to show in Iris's face and body, even in a gesture or a certain angle of the head. Yet, to him or someone's casual glance, she was a remarkable "twin" to Kathleen. Anyone who saw them together would think them sisters, rather than mother and daughter.

He was surprised to realize that Kathleen's right hand was curled into his forearm like a claw.

"Who are those men with her?" she asked. "They are going nowhere. She's not even flirting with them. She has nothing to gain there."

"I hope not," Max said. "My sources say she's seriously seeing a law student at Trinity College. She works as a copy editor for a small publishing house that specializes in poetry."

"Poetry!"

"It's a famous Irish export," he said mildly. "Like politics."

"Not married at twenty-six," she muttered.

"Smart, no doubt," he said.

"I presume you researched her foster parents, spy that you are."

He nodded. "They are still 'free-thinkers' and still firmly atheist. Iris went through a rebellious stage when she investigated the Catholic Church because of a boyfriend—"

"What—?"

"The parents were upset, but Iris became more interested in hot yoga instead. Sensible child. Useful exercise, if hard to find in a chill climate like Ireland."

"She'll marry this Trinity man?"

"Looks like it. I can't say if she's contemplating having children."

"At least your intelligence gathering has limits."

"But…she's filed an inquiry with her adopted parents for permission to find her Magdalene birth mother."

The nails of Kathleen's hand cut through his tweed jacket like Freddy Kreuger's razor gloves in a horror movie. "I'll kill you if that succeeds."

"Fair warning," he said, eyeing her untouched glass. "Drink up anyway. You wanted to leave. We've got a long way to go and a short time to get there."

Oddly, she did just as he said.

The car CD player happened to hit a classic Irish folk song from ugly olden 18th-century times, that Max had played on both recent trips to Ireland, a favorite of his, and hadn't songs like this heard young inflamed his and Sean's desire to visit Northern Ireland?

He and Sean could have been the "lone wolf" fanatics of an earlier day instead of just the romantic deceptive phenomenon's victims.

The minstrel boy to the war is gone
In the ranks of death you'll find him.

His father's sword he has girded on,
And his wild harp slung behind him;

"Land of Song!" said the warrior bard,
"Though all the world betrays thee,

One sword, at least, thy rights shall guard,
One faithful harp shall praise thee!"

The Minstrel fell! But the foeman's chain
Could not bring his proud soul under;

The harp he loved ne'er spoke again,
For he tore its chords asunder;

And said "No chains shall sully thee,
Thou soul of love and bravery!

Thy songs were made for the pure and free
They shall never sound in slavery!"

20
Driven to Murder

Matt watched the luggage spit out from the carousal and snake past on the McCarran Airport conveyer belt.

"That trip to Minnesota was easier than I thought," he said, "but I'll never come back for 'ice fishing' season."

Temple smiled. The yellow-and-magenta yarn she'd tied to their checked luggage handles certainly stood out among the lime green and orange pompons decorating the other bags.

"An invitation to ice fishing is the highest compliment from my brothers," she explained. "It's the ultimate macho male tribute. That means you rank up there with the Greats, like Wayne Gretsky."

"Wayne who?"

"Hockey star."

"I'm ready to swear off all things Minnesota until the next family visit up north. Tell me that will be a while."

"You sure were great with my nephews on Sunday, all sixteen of them."

"I was assigned to a parish with an attached grade school, remember? Mass quantities of 'tweens and teens don't scare me."

"So that's why you get along so well with Molina's daughter, Mariah."

"Too well. I feel really awkward about taking her to the Dad-Daughter Dance she's counting on. I understand a single mother's dilemma with those type of events, but isn't that Detective Alch closer to the family?"

"He's Molina's go-to guy at work," Temple said, "but he isn't as cute as you are."

"Dads aren't supposed to be 'cute'. They're supposed to be comfy and lived-in, like a recliner chair." He didn't want to mention he was no rooting for Rafi Nadir.

"Like *my* dad?" Matt leaned forward to snag the biggest bag as it glided past.

"Right."

"Oh, look, here's mine." Temple grabbed the end handle of the smaller bag and slung it off the conveyer belt before Matt could play Galahad and do it for her.

"I could have gotten that," he said.

"I may be small, but I don't want to lose my tote bag-toting muscles."

Matt shook his head. "You must carry twelve pounds in those things. Not good for your back."

"But they are my trademark."

"Along with the high heels." Matt smiled down at her current pair, a relatively tame zebra-print pump. "I must admit they showcase your sexy ankles."

"Sexy. We better get home."

They pulled up their rolling handles and turned in tandem to head for ground transportation.

Three Fontana brothers materialized as a pastel-suited wall in front of them. They were disturbingly developing Mystifying Max habits now that the original was off the Vegas scene and possibly out of Matt and Temple's private lives forever.

"We'll take those." Bracketing brothers snapped down the roller handles on Temple's and Matt's luggage and hefted the bags. Fontana brothers would never be seen dragging luggage behind them like dog-walkers.

Bag-grabbing passengers paused to crane their necks to catch a glimpse of Temple, the one small woman at the center of a crowd of six-feet-tall hot guys. Cell phones lifted into action. She felt like a movie star…until she heard Matt's name being whispered.

He shrugged at the attention. "So much for sneaking back into town."

"The Ghost Limo awaits," said the central brother. "It is a sedan repro of the custom convertible car created for the movie *Topper*, based on a 1936 Buick Series 80 Roadmaster, with Buck Rogers-style body and fins. It could be operated with no visible driver, because the young high-flying couple who died in it come back as ghosts."

Temple, the vintage film fan, was knocked out. "No! Cary Grant was at the wheel of that amazing car."

"Alas, he is no longer with us. Julio will drive."

Temple felt like a pampered movie star anyway.

Gangsters limo service was only one of the Fontana brothers' businesses, and they created the most dreamy custom limo jobs around. If you visited Vegas and weren't "taken for a ride" in a Gangsters' limo, you hadn't lived. If you stayed at the Fontana family hotels, the Crystal Phoenix or Gangsters, the airport rides were free. Otherwise Gangsters' rides were costly, but always made a safe round trip, unlike the fabled bumpy rides with real mobsters.

"Thank you...Ernesto," Temple ventured.

Tall, dark, handsome men may be a cliché, but in Las Vegas and with the Fontana Family, they were also a conundrum in triplicate. Temple was getting better at telling apart the remaining eight bachelors of the Fontana pack now that the eldest, Aldo, had married her aunt Kit. That made him her uncle-in-law, Temple guessed. Oh, my God! That made her feel *old*, to regard Vegas's most eligible bachelors as all...in-laws, rather than out-laws.

Travelers were turning to watch what seemed like a celebrity parade of some kind. Heads turned even more when the party reached the ground transportation curb and a long cream-colored car that had all the futuristic curves of a Dairy Queen top-fillip throbbed there in idle.

"This is swell, boys," Temple said, "but Electra said she'd pick us up in her old Probe. It's roomier and more suitable for luggage-loading dings than my Miata or Matt's Jaguar."

Ernesto fiddled with his rose-gold tie clip. "Miss Electra has encountered an unfortunate impediment to coming here to pick you up."

Meanwhile their three pieces of luggage were disappearing into a trunk so huge it made them look like Barbie doll accessories.

"I can do that, guys," Matt was saying to no avail.

Ernesto leaned down to murmur in Temple's ear, broadcasting a faint scent of male cologne she had never been able to detect in any samples in dozens of *Vanity Fair* magazines. So post-Ralph Lauren.

"Miss Electra is, um, tied up right now," he whispered.

"Why do I think you mean that literally?"

He shrugged, which adjusted the fall of his designer suit jacket, then shot the sleeves to reveal rose-gold cufflinks. "She is being entertained at Metro Police headquarters."

"Entertained? You mean *detained*, don't you?"

"Some might put it that way."

"Enough with the evasive charm. Tell me what's going on."

"Not to worry. The Fontana family lawyer is right beside her."

"My God! Where?"

"Possibly still in an interrogation room, I believe. Shoddy places, even in the magnificent new building. I only presume. I have not yet been honored to be a guest there."

"Interrogated? By whom? For what?"

"By our friendly neighborhood chanteuse and cop, Lieutenant Molina."

"She's a homicide cop."

"This seems to be a case of homicide."

"And Electra is a suspect?"

"Many are called in these cases, but few are nailed."

"The victim isn't—?"

"An ex-husband of our dear landlady? I fear he is an 'ex' in the most, er, permanent fashion."

"Not… Jay Edgar Dyson?"

"Not anymore."

Temple's jaw and shoulders slumped with shock. Her tote bag handles started slipping through her nerveless fingers, but Ernesto caught the bag and ushered Temple into the limo's cavernous white leather interior.

He leaned in after her, a living example of Scent Surround. "You also are on the interrogation list, dear lady."

"Me?"

"Not to worry. Gangsters is providing complementary limo service for all involved. And a getaway car, if needed."

Matt had overheard the news and invited Ernesto to join them in the horseshoe of luxuriously padded seats.

"Normally I ride shotgun." Ernesto patted the subtly padded shoulder of his Emanogildo Zegna suit coat. The firearm in the hidden holster was a Beretta, of course. The Fontanas patronized all things Italian. Ernesto ducked to take a seat opposite them and turned to the glittering façade of the bar.

"Better not," Matt said. "We're going straight to police headquarters and I don't want high-end booze on our breaths. When did this happen?"

"Yesterday. Miss Electra was invited to headquarters for an interrogation today. I happened to be dropping by the Circle Ritz to give her a saltimbocca recipe and was able to offer her the same, calming white-glove Gangsters transportation service you experience now."

"Couldn't someone have called us in Minnesota?" Temple asked.

"Miss Electra wouldn't hear of interrupting your family reunion, Miss Temple. We promised to drive you direct from the airport to the interrogation room." Ernesto made a sour face. "The lady lieutenant was most unbecomingly fierce about that. Not even Julio could dissuade her to wait until you'd settled back home at the Circle Ritz."

"What awful news," Matt said. "It's crazy that Electra Lark would need to be anywhere near a police headquarters, but what can Temple know about this? Molina has a lot of nerve issuing a command appearance. We've been traveling all day. Temple is tired. Are they interviewing all Circle Ritz residents? If so, I can do it today and give Temple a break."

"You are not on the list," Ernesto said.

"That's even crazier. What could Temple know about some crime that happened while we were out of town?" Matt looked at her, with a firm nod. And then frowned.

Temple knew she looked guilty.

"Wait a minute." Matt eyed Ernesto. "Temple asked if the victim was—then broke the sentence off…and you mentioned this Jay Edgar guy." He turned to Temple. "You can't have known him, an ex-husband of Electra?"

"Not known him, no." Temple made an apologetic shrug. "But I could have met him."

"Where? Not at the Circle Ritz, surely?"

"No. Not there."

"Then where?"

"At the Araby Motel."

"The—" Matt was speechless.

"I think," Ernesto said, leaning forward to look them each in the eye, "that the gentleman, since he's not called upon to answer questions, should have a nice stiff Scotch. And the lady should sit back in silence and compose her thoughts for the forthcoming chat with the police. At least she is known to them as a solid citizen."

"So is Electra," Temple complained. "All of this is just plain bogus. And since when does Gangsters chauffeur people to police headquarters instead of to the nearest underground nightclub?"

Ernesto could only shrug his impeccably Emanogildo Zegna-tailored shoulders. Some mysteries even Fontana brothers forebear to question. Temple wondered if Julio's recent attentions to Molina had made things better, or worse.

Matt had insisted on accompanying Temple into the Crimes Against Persons offices, although Ernesto also insisted he alone was needed as escort.

Temple was further unnerved when she learned that Electra had been interrogated and released, and likely she would be too. She was relieved Electra hadn't been arrested after seeing the police, but wondered if her account, coming after Electra's, could inadvertently make things worse, not better.

Even with Matt and Ernesto as escorts, Temple would have felt a lot calmer with Midnight Louie by her side.

21
Vegas Blues

When Matt and Temple heard Lieutenant Molina paged, she appeared so fast that both Matt and Temple started...guiltily, some might say. Especially Temple.

"Wait here," the tall police officer told Matt, indicating a spare modern chair among a long row of mostly empty ones. "With that."

He took custody of Temple's tote bag, as instructed, and sat.

"Excuse me, Lieutenant," Ernesto said with a rueful smile, "before you rush off, you should know that Miss Barr has legal representation."

Temple was shocked, but Molina coolly cocked a strongly dubious eyebrow.

"The Fontana family law firm is getting a workout recently." Molina sighed and stepped away to confer with a colleague.

"I have a lawyer?" Temple leaned up to whisper Ernesto. "I don't have, like, a lawyer that I know of."

"No problem." Ernesto patted the top of her forearm. "We always keep several at hand." He turned to a person sitting farther down the line of chairs, whom Temple had taken for a bookie about town, like Nostradamus, the rhyming odds maker.

At Ernesto's nod, a roly-poly balding man with tortoiseshell-framed glasses and a lot of white shirt frontage showing beneath a snugly rumpled suit coat hastened their way.

Temple was even more shocked. How could the fashionably slick Fontana males employ a lawyer who looked like a dropout from mail-order law degree school? And his equally shoddy and bulging briefcase was festooned with untidy paper corners sticking out every which way.

"Lester Savoy," Ernesto introduced him to Temple. "Our longtime legal eagle."

He looked more like an adult ugly duckling. He didn't quack like a duck, though, and rolled out a short introduction-instruction spiel.

"Miss Barr, I've also been honored to represent Mrs. Lark and am acquainted with the facts of this situation. Just relax in the interrogation room, but convey the least information possible to answer any questions. I'll be the Invisible Man unless you are asked a question it would be in our better interests to let go unanswered."

Invisible? No one was going to miss that Hawaiian-themed tie, which barely reached the fourth button on his wrinkled shirt. An aroma of cigar—not a pleasant vanilla-scented one, but the burned alfalfa-fertilizer kind—screamed "shyster".

Matt was looking appalled, but Ernesto quickly shepherded this new odd couple of Barr and Savoy into Molina's custody. "All bright and shining and ready for you, Lieutenant."

Molina's eyelids shuddered shut for half a second.

Waving a hand holding a slim file, she gestured Temple and Savoy to precede her farther into the bowels of the building, Actually, everything here was too new and modern to qualify as the usual seedy bowels of a police station. Temple knew that from having witnessed an interrogation here during the recent Black & White rock band murder case.

Now, out of the blue rather than the black-and-white, Temple was going to be facing the other side of the one-way mirror. The wrong side. As the interviewee.

Even an interrogation room that smells as pristine as a new car can't disguise its unpleasant purpose. Molina gestured her inside to a seat at the familiar bare table.

Somewhere during their progress to the room, Detective Alch had turned into a tail and brought up the rear. The veteran detective, with his salt-and-pepper shock of hair and laid-back manner, reminded her of TV's Lt. Columbo, Peter Falk. He spun to shut the door behind him while Lester Savoy pulled out the chair next to his and…left Temple to seat herself.

As Savoy sat, he slapped the briefcase to the tabletop, a small mountain of scuffed calf-excrement-color brown leather. It stank of cigars too.

Molina recited the date and names of all present for the recording device. Her voice was as flat and factual as her wardrobe of solid-color pant suits were monotone and her working shoes were loafers to spare the egos of shorter male colleagues or superiors.

Temple wondered how Electra had fared when she had sat in this same room earlier today? Temple wished she'd been able to consult with Electra beforehand. No chance when she'd been whisked from airport to police headquarters, and the Fontana brothers had played accessories before the fact.

Temple also wondered if Molina's new rapport with Julio Fontana was a cynical plan to use them to her advantage…or the start of a real romance for the relationship-averse single mother pushing forty.

Right now, Molina was all cop and started the session. "To begin, Miss Barr, you've just arrived back in Las Vegas after a two-day trip to Minnesota?"

"Yes."

"The purpose?"

"To see family."

"Did Mrs. Lark call you or communicate with you in any way during that time?"

"No."

"Were you aware that she had been questioned in connection with a murder?"

"No."

"Did you communicate or try to communicate with her when you landed in Las Vegas?"

"No. I hadn't heard anything—" Temple glanced at the warm hand with hairy knuckles resting on her forearm and stopped her answer with a simple, "No."

"Before you left town, you accompanied Electra Lark to the Araby Motel last Friday night?"

"Yes."

"Why?"

"Because it's in a bad neighborhood. Safer for two."

"So you knowingly went into a 'bad neighborhood' in the middle of the night?"

"Yes."

"Again why?"

"Electra needed to go there."

"For what purpose?"

"To see a man about a property sale."

"This man was known to Mrs. Lark?"

"He…she said he was her ex-husband."

"Did Mrs. Lark give you a name?"

"She called him Jay, and later, Jay Edgar."

Molina rolled her eyes at the name. "Was she afraid of him?"

Temple wanted to squirm for the first time. She was starting to wonder what kind of case the police were building against Electra. And what she might say that would seem harmless and could be damning instead. How could Molina ever believe Electra capable of murder, a nice elderly lady like Electra—with a kooky youthful spirit, granted. Darn.

"More afraid of the neighborhood he was in," she said.

"What property was involved?"

"Some land near Electra's residential building."

Molina consulted the contents of the file. "Property that Jay—not an initial, J-a-y—Edgar Dyson had promised to offer to Mrs. Lark before he sold it to anyone else?"

"Yes. That's what she said." Temple winced to hear Molina being as precise as a coroner like Grizzly Bahr doing an autopsy in recording information for the casebook. This was super serious.

"But he *had* sold it to someone else?" Molina asked.

"It looked like that, but he was vague about how far the deal had progressed."

"He said that in his motel room?"

Temple nodded.

"Respond vocally please," Molina instructed.

"Yes."

"What was the tone of the discussion between them?"

"Tone? Um, mixed."

"Mixed?"

Temple eyed Savoy, who'd been scribbling illegible notes on a yellow legal pad with an edge soaked in brown liquid, either coffee or tobacco spit. He didn't look up, so she committed truth.

"Electra wanted him to live up to his promise—"

"So she was angry."

"More…adamant."

"And Dyson?"

"He was apologetic. He complained that the people interested in the land had flown him into town, put him up at hotel, and then, when he lost at the gaming tables, started pressuring him to sign over the property to cover his losses."

"*His* tone as he revealed this?"

"Whiney," Temple answered promptly. She saw Alch stifle a smile.

"And Mrs. Lark's reaction?"

"She was…upset."

"Angry."

"Yeah."

"She threatened him?"

"Not exactly."

"How inexactly was it?"

Temple sighed. "It was sort of a political correctness thing."

"Political correctness?"

"She implied he was taking up too much space on the planet."

"Well, it's worse now."

"How?" Temple asked, startled.

"The space Mr. Dyson's taking up now is horizontal, not vertical."

"Oh." Temple imagined Jay Edgar laid out on Grizzly Bahr's autopsy table and shuddered. A much too ugly mental visual.

Molina turned over some papers. "You left the victim's room at the Araby Motel at…?"

"Two twenty a.m."

"How did you know the time?"

Temple thrust her left wrist forward to display her unusually large analog watch. "My job depends on good timing. No LEDs for me. I keep my eye and trust on the big hand and the little hand at all times, and I was eager to get home. Back to the Circle Ritz."

"Because?"

"It was late, the area was shaky…and my fiancé was due home from work at a night job."

"So you told him—it is a him? One never knows these days."

"That you very well know, Lieutenant."

"So you told him about your offbeat expedition."

"No." Temple shut her mouth, irritated. Molina's ridiculous last comment had been calculated to needle her into giving a knee-jerk answer. And she had. The truth.

Temple glanced at Savoy. He held a shading hand over his eyes, and she couldn't read his expression.

Molina had tuned out his presence. "So you didn't mention this midnight outing to anyone."

"No."

"Not your fiancé, and not even when you and he flew off the very next day for Minnesota?"

"No."

"Not even when you spent five hours captive in airplane seats with plenty of time to converse."

"No."

"What did you talk about during the flight?"

Temple sighed. "I don't know. The latest national news. Who was going to drive the rental car. My various relatives' names and ages."

Molina leaned forward, narrowed her eyes. "Who *did* drive the rental car?"

"I did," Temple snapped. "I knew the area. I didn't need a GPS."

"And you're sure Mrs. Lark never said anything that threatened Jay Dyson?"

"I, ah, didn't say that."

"Oh, she did?"

"He was reneging on a deal made when they were divorced. She wanted him to know she expected him to keep his word."

"Someone's word is not legally binding."

Temple turned to the Fontana family lawyer, who'd been irritatingly silent. "I don't know. We have a lawyer in the room. Is it legally binding, Mr. Savoy?"

"Depends," he said.

"And I should probably put *you* in some of them for all the good you're doing here," Temple answered, immediately realizing Molina had pushed her into making an irritated response again.

The lieutenant smiled like a shark. "Never mind, Miss Barr. We have witnesses who heard Mrs. Lark being very specific in her plans for Mr. Dyson if he didn't do as she wanted."

"Witnesses?" Temple remembered the hookers. How much had they seen or heard that was damaging?

"I also understand that you claimed to be a member of the Sisterhood of the Streets, that you and Mrs. Lark were a 'sister act'. Is that something Vice might be interested in? Or perhaps your evidently long-suffering, kept-in-the-dark fiancé?"

"You know that was a joke."

"Maybe, but you'd gone way out of your normal fields of operation to tell it, and this follow-up situation is definitely not a joke. Even if it's because you gave me a rare opportunity to use a classic line.

"Don't leave town again, Miss Barr."

22
Off Duty

Ernesto, the expert chauffeur-psychiatrist by virtue of his job shepherding limo-loads of tourists around Las Vegas, reversed his recommendations on the next leg of the long, long trip from the airport in a long, long custom car.

The dimness behind the dark tinted windows soothed unsettled nerves and Ernesto did more to achieve that by getting to work again as mixologist at the glittering bar. Temple leaned back in the channeled red leather upholstery and sighed deeply.

Ernesto smiled. "For the sophisticated lady recovering from a wearing interrogation, I recommend the Daiquiri, a drink created to soothe the vintage soul." He handed Temple a delicate, footed cocktail glass.

"For the dyspeptic, displeased gentleman, I suggest a Peppermint Schnapps."

"I've got reason to be dyspeptic," the usually affable Matt snapped, accepting the Schnapps.

Temple hid her amused expression behind a sip of the Daiquiri, fearing it was far too ladylike to soothe the savage soul of a dishonest hussy like her.

"Ernesto," she asked, "how did Electra's husband die? I hope it wasn't by gunshot, because Electra brought one in her purse to the Araby Motel. I'm afraid the ladies of the night saw it."

The limo slipped smoothly into motion with Julio at the wheel, but the emotions inside decidedly did not match the ride.

Matt turned into Molina and started interrogating Temple. "You went out in the dead of night with Electra to a notorious local motel and didn't tell me? Makes me wonder what else you didn't tell me."

"It was Electra's secret, and *her* ex-husband. She couldn't sleep not knowing if he was selling his interest in the land adjacent to hers."

"Excuse me," Ernesto said, "your discussion should be private. The police are not giving out details of the killing because they are rather bizarre." He had their rapt attention. "However, there is not a detail, no matter how closely guarded, that a Fontana brother somewhere will not find out some part of it. Between us and the color-coordinated cat lying on the black carpeting—"

"Louie's here?" Temple interrupted, inspecting the pooling dark at her feet.

One slitted green eye opened near the door.

Nodding, Ernesto went on. "The late Mr. Dyson was not killed at the Araby Motel that night, as one would think, which is good for Miss Electra. He was found dead the next morning, in that old building near the Circle Ritz he owned, or perhaps had just sold, which I'm afraid is *not* good for Miss E."

"How…truly strange," Temple said.

"No matter how he died," Matt said, "the fact is you and Electra put yourselves in the middle of a murder case by running off like hotheaded teenagers to an unsavory place at an unsafe time. Who'd you think you were? Max Kinsella and his cousin Sean?"

"Matt, that's not fair!"

"It's a pretty fair summary of the situation."

"*Piano, Piano,*" Ernesto urged, fanning his fingers in a quieting gesture. He then excused himself to ride with the driver and left them to it.

"And this took a nighttime visit?" Matt asked as the limo proceeded after a pause.

"Electra needed to know what Jay had really done. We'd seen the people who were planning on putting in a strip club just down the street—"

"Must have been a classy crew."

"Hardly. And the exterior of the Lovers' Knot chapel had been vandalized—"

"Even worse if there were vandals about. How did you get to the Araby Motel?"

"Electra drove."

"The Elvis edition Beetle I won and gave her?"

"No, she'd never risk that. Her old white Probe."

"But she'd risk herself. And you."

"She was the only person who could make her ex tell her the truth, and make him feel guilty enough about it to spoil any deal he had going. With, perhaps, mob elements."

Matt threw back some peppermint schnapps and nearly choked. Schnapps was potent stuff. "How'd Electra even find out about this fishy deal?"

"Bits here and there. Diane, Jay's most recent ex-wife, warned Electra Jay was in her neighborhood.

Temple went on. "When the Circle Ritz had the Incident of the Cat in the Night-time—you may recognize that the animal in question was a dog, not a cat, in the Sherlock Holmes story, but Midnight Louie gives it a whole new twist—when that intruder showed up in my bedroom, I thought maybe Stalker Kathleen was still around. Electra said, maybe not, and then showed me the defaced front of the chapel. Vandals had already been attacking the building. I can't see Kitty the Cutter wasting her venom on architectural details when there are live people around to harass."

Matt nodded, ruefully. "The only inanimate object Kathleen O'Connor had it in for was stealing your one shoe of the pair you planned to wear to my mother's wedding in the chapel, and Kathleen actually gave that back to you."

"Yeah. Dangled it off my balcony. So," Temple said. "I wondered who would attack the building. Electra surprised me with a tour of some of her other properties surrounding the Circle Ritz. I then wondered if the vandalism was more general."

"Was it?"

"No. Her tenants are having a hard time, though, being mom-and-pop businesses post-Great Recession. At the end of our walkabout, we found the empty building down the block that Electra *doesn't* own was looking ready for revamping into a raunchy strip club."

"Is there any other kind than raunchy?" Matt asked.

"Uh, there are traditional strip clubs and nowadays there are nudie bars," she told him gingerly. "You would not believe what they are like."

Temple hated to disillusion Matt about how low Las Vegas could go, but she could tell her last comment had given him pause. He had a funny look on his face, and it couldn't all be the peppermint Schnapps.

She pushed her advantage. "You can see that would devastate Electra's livelihood at the wedding chapel, not to mention the quality of future Circle Ritz tenants and possible condo investors. *We* may leave, you know, but she'll always be there."

"Yeah." Matt was looking even sicker. "I see you were trying to help her out. How did you know where the old rogue—what's-his-name—was holing up?"

"Ex-wife Diane again. She kept tabs on him. I'm sorry I didn't tell you where I was going. I know *you*'d never sneak around investigating stuff without telling me, but this came up, and Electra's livelihood was at stake, and I owe her. And…I was afraid she'd go alone. At least I can alibi her now for that time."

Matt nodded slowly. "You probably don't know this. I wouldn't want to upset you, but the Araby Motel is one of the places I looked for Cliff Effinger when I first came to Vegas. I hate thinking of you visiting such a scuzzy dive."

"Oh. Yeah, that joint so totally has 'Cliff Effinger' written all over it. No wonder it gave me the creeps. The hookers were nice, though."

"Temple!"

"Sisterly solidarity overcomes all lifestyle biases." She drained the Daiquiri as the limo oozed to a stop so smooth and slow it felt like slipping into a bath of warm molasses.

She put Matt's empty glass back in the bar, then laid a penitential hand over his. "I know *you*'d never go out somewhere scuzzy alone at night without telling me, Matt. Not *now*. Not now that Kathleen's not around to blackmail you into secret rendezvous with her poisonous self. Oh, maybe back in the day when you were hunting Effinger too, but that's over now." She tried a smile.

Matt looked embarrassed and something else Temple couldn't name before he swept her into an encompassing hug. "You are much too good for me, Temple Barr," he said.

"Not really, but I'm working on it." She grinned. "I'm sorry I left you out of the loop. I just had a relapse of Nancy Drew-itis and was so curious to see what Electra's ex was like. She can't have murdered him, not morally or physically. Anything we can do to help clear up that mess, we should do."

"Amen." Matt nodded to the unseen chauffeur and his sibling behind the dark-tinted privacy window. "And those guys up front are just the dudes to help out."

"So Vanilla—as in Fontana brothers' ice-cream suits—is the New Black. And...the Fontana brothers are New Max?"

Matt nodded slowly. "Never thought of it that way, but probably."

"Well, I happen to know that Julio is on Lieutenant Molina's cell phone speed dial."

"We might need an inside man at the Circle Ritz," Matt said, exiting the dim, cavernous cabin for the sizzling sunshine in the building's parking lot outside.

Temple blinked as she was caught between the cool dark inside the limo and glaring daylight. The wink of Louie's single eye gleamed like an emerald ear stud on the inky-black floor carpeting. Apparently, he was riding shotgun for the Fontanas now.

23
Just Hanging Around

As the saying goes, "A cat may look at a queen".

I get a bit confused by that. A pedigreed lady-cat who is breeding stock is called "a queen". And then there are England's Elizabeth the First and Elizabeth the Second, queens of England. And though one was and one was *not* breeding stock, they are called queens too.

I mention this to Miss Midnight Louise when I drop by the Crystal Phoenix Hotel and Casino to look her up.

I had slipped back into the Gangsters limo when we passengers were unloaded at the Circle Ritz. The lovebirds were distracted by "discussing" Miss Temple's Unsanctioned Midnight Adventure. When I followed Ernesto into the driver's compartment, he and Julio just shrugged at my presence. They know me well from my Crystal Phoenix days of old and have learned to accept that my druthers are the equal of theirs.

"We would not want to continue in the middle of that lovers' spat either, Louie," Julio said, chuckling.

And there I am back on my chauffeured way to the Crystal Phoenix and Miss Midnight Louise, as planned. I was unofficial house detective there before she showed up—from who-knows-what no-name littering and dismal alley—so I have no trouble locating her office in the lavish indoor flowering greenery surrounding the Crystal Court eatery.

I am thankful Louise scorned my old outdoor stand beside the hotel pool's canna lily and koi pond for office use. I can visit it to commune with my old pals, the koi, and see if they require any services, like population control, I might be happy to provide.

"What," Miss Midnight Louise inquires, "has bestirred you to make the long hike from the Circle Ritz to here?"

"Hike, *hah*! I was chauffeured here, but I am seeking a companion for a long hike back to the Circle Ritz."

"You are as out of luck as any empty-pocket gambler, Daddy-o. Why should I wear out pad leather on your impulsive say-so. An elderly screen queen traveling with a pair of afghan hounds has just checked in, and I must ensure her high-strung canines do not disturb the other guests."

This is when I bring up the queen/queen conundrum.

"Well, that is off-topic to both our jobs. The definitions of 'queen' have nothing to do with our firm, Midnight Investigations, Inc."

"I beg to differ. I am keeping in mind that whereas crime scene tape prevents all curious humans from crossing invisible thresholds, we as a species have a particular free pass."

"I have responsibilities. I cannot go gadding about just because you have found some Crime Scene tape to violate."

"Ah, well. I suppose I will have to clear Miss Electra Lark of murder by myself. I work better alone anyway."

I have already turned away, and would have been out of hearing range, except that I have spotted a bit of Shrimp Diablo a guest has dropped on the floor. Such culinary carelessness is not tolerated at the Crystal Phoenix, and would not be allowed to lie undealt with for a second during my administration.

While I am *tsk*ing over this sad state of affairs, Louise catches up to me, snags the tidbit with one front shiv and pops it into her mouth. "What do you mean 'clear' Miss Electra. I was not aware that she was cloudy."

"What? I cannot understand you when you talk with your mouth full. And Miss Electra is indeed under a cloud, a cloud of suspicion. Of murder."

"Ridiculous," she comments. I am not sure to what precisely she is referring. Usually it is me. "Of course we must observe the crime scene, but we need not walk. I just saw a Fontana brother passing... There is sure to be another around."

She bounds off, expertly threading through milling tourist feet and ducking behind hotel floral displays and luggage carts until we near the main entrance. There we slip out on a trolley, hidden behind piles of leather-scented luggage ripe for a thorough and joint shiv sharpening. I even leave my initials on one. Customizing indicates the finest brands.

We go public at the curb, where Miss Louise blatantly sits at the valet's desk, curling her long black train around her dainty front feet. Normally, I prefer to come and go undercover, but now am forced to join her. Luckily, people are concentrating on wrestling tips and baggage and we go unnoticed.

When a low black sports car pulls up, Louise trots across to the closed passenger door. "Come, Louie," she calls me (like a dog). I follow with a feline slink in time to see a Fontana brother unpretzel his long, pale-attired legs and stand. It is the Crystal Phoenix Hotel boss man himself, Mr. Nicky Fontana.

Miss Midnight Louise looks up at him, and blinks her round gold eyes. I back her up with an unblinking green stare.

"What is this?" Mr. Nicky asks.

The driver comes around and turns out to be Mr. Julio Fontana. My Miss Temple seems to have some difficulty telling the ten suave brothers apart, but it is no problem for me and Louise. Every human has a different scent, including traces of recent meals. *Umm.* Sea bass in a white wine and herbed butter sauce. I could do without the white wine, but it is nice to see adult litter-brothers socialize—whether in Ma Barker's clowder by the police substation or on two legs along the Strip.

"Louie and Louise," Julio says. "Seeing them making the scene together would sure get Carmen Molina's hackles up. Have you had a recent murder at the hotel?" He chuckles.

"None, thank God," Mr. Nicky says.

"Are you sure?"

Mr. Nicky is looking a little worried, but not too worried to jibe his brother. "And…'Carmen' Molina, huh? She does not give out that first name for public consumption, bro. Is the Iron Maiden of the Vegas police force moving from Mexican to Italian cuisine?"

"Not drastically, but she is definitely weary of black cats cluttering up her crime scenes. Why are these two together? The big guy usually hangs at the Circle Ritz."

"And our dainty house cat does not leave the premises."

(Little does he know.)

We listen to the brotherly byplay and keep mum. We are the strong, silent types.

Unlike dogs, we do not have to yip, gurgle, scratch, whine or paw to make our druthers known. We just stare straight at them until the people figure it out. Maybe it is some secret power known only to Bast, but if we wait long enough, and stare long enough, we will get what we need or want.

"You know," Julio says, nervously jiggling his car keys. "Maybe I better get Midnight Louie back to the Circle Ritz."

Midnight Louise finally stirs. She nestles her shoulder against mine—*ugh*, and blinks her short black lashes.

"She wants to go with?" Julio asks his brother. "I thought she was fixed."

"Sure is, so no harm done. Just make sure you bring her back after the visit."

"So I am chauffeuring a cat? Crazier things have happened in Vegas."

"And stayed in Vegas," Mr. Nicky adds. "I wonder what got into these two? They nailed a pickpocket at the hotel recently, so we better let them do what they seem to want."

Louise and I have minded our manners and ridden on the Tesla Roadster's black floor carpeting, not the leather seats, in case a claw should snag. When released in the Circle Ritz parking lot, we scamper for the surrounding oleander bushes, leaving Julio scratching his head as Miss Electra, happening to exit her own car, jumps as if she had just seen a ghost. (The electric-powered Tesla arrives as silently as a stalking lion and tends to startle people, which the Fontana brothers appear to enjoy doing.)

Among the oleanders, Ma Barker awaits us with a voice as sharp as her claws.

"About time," she growls. "I have stationed all the shades and patterns of brown and gray from the clowder around the building in question. That's the best camouflage color inside and out, and the police seem to have it in for us black cats lately."

"So no Black Cat Ninja Brigade?" I ask. Browns and grays are, well, pedestrian.

"This is a dead scene," Ma answers. "The crime has been committed and the forensic team has recorded and dusted and scanned the place from asphalt to attic. As you suggested, Louie, people have come lurking around. Perhaps word of suspicion falling on your clowder leader at the Circle Ritz has disturbed her charges."

(I should point out here that Ma Barker is feral to her fingernails and not attuned to human social structures. Since she is the female leader of the pack, she considers Miss Electra Lark as an equal, and considers Miss Electra's human residents as both Miss Electra's underlings and responsibility.

That is not much different from my position inside the Circle Ritz, or indeed, any of our breed's. We all have underlings and thus responsibilities.)

Louise and I hustle around to the other side of the Circle Ritz, strolling by the half-occupied shopfronts to the huge abandoned building where Jay Edgar's body was found. The police are keeping the COD top secret. That means Cause of Death, not Cash On Delivery. Although, it could have been a hired hit, who knows?

Even now Ma is pacing toward the banned building, strutting under the yellow crime scene tape like she was queen. It is a cakewalk for us to survey and sniff the perimeter, then slink inside through a sloppily boarded-up back door.

"*Hmm*," Ma pauses to note, wiggling her skimpy black whiskers. "A rodent-rich environment. I see why people find this a desirable property."

Louise and I exchange head rolls. Ma is a product of her times. She even thinks the cages of the Trap, Neuter, Return groups are alien UFOs landing to abduct our kind and her gang to some distant planet. She will complain about not seeing a clowder member for a day or so. Then sniffing alcohol on him or her (or should I say, the new "It" cat?)—after said abductee returns dazed and unsteady, she will accuse the poor soul of cozying up to a human out on a binge.

Still, no one has better scouting instincts than Ma Barker. We follow her somewhat bent tail. Ma has paced far down the long corridor between the first floor stalls. The place is reminiscent, if not redolent, of a horse stable.

At last we reach a point where the floor grunge has changed from a patina of dust into a carpet of actual refuse and dirt.

"*Hmm*," Ma opines. "Some homeless humans had a clambake here." She sniffs the area, between sneezes. "Only the usual street filth ground into shoe soles. Unfortunately, humans do not lick those clean."

"*Meeuw,*" Louise comments in disgust. She follows the disturbed filth to the edge.

I have an idea inspired by my out-of-body mind experience here. "These marks in the grit. Reminds me of old-time ballrooms, when humans shuffled around on soap powder they dribbled on the floor."

"You are an old-style gigolo, all right," she accuses me. "You know what I mean."

"This could just be the usual *CSI: Las Vegas* shuffle, Louise, but what puzzles me is that I detect no smell of blood."

"But why is the floor disturbed here in the middle of things?" Louise has moved to the first step of the central staircase. She gazes farther up. "Was the victim pushed down these stairs, and therefore the fatal injuries were internal?"

"This mountain is made of steps." Ma Barker sounds puzzled.

I have forgotten the only Vegas structure Ma has ever entered was when I recently smuggled her into the Crystal Phoenix. As a life-long feral, she has encountered curbs, and even perhaps a back step or two, but an entire one-story flight is utterly foreign.

"You want to watch yourself, Ma," I warn. "Those boards may be shaky."

"*Hah.* I have excavated Dumpsters the size of boxcars in my day, sonny."

I still worry, because she is creeping up the outer edges of the steps, quite a balancing act for one of her years.

"Louise," I hiss under my breath. "Go up and shadow the old dame so she does not fall."

"Fall?" Louise's burning look singes me. "She is preserving the crime scene evidence. Even from here I can see that many footsteps have been dancing up and down those stairs."

I take another squint and am shocked. My standing as primo private eye is about to be eradicated by dames of two different generations. How could I miss the faint disturbances on the steps? Rats! I mean, I took them for rat and mouse scratchings.

After giving a backwards sneer, Louise has obeyed me and is following Ma's trail. I take the other far side of the stairs and shoot up it like a rocket, arriving up top first, at least.

Looking down, I notice ladders leaning against some deserted cubicle walls. *S*-shaped trails through the dust show they have been moved and replaced.

Meanwhile, Ma and Louise contemplate the ragged ski slide to death from their perches atop the stairs.

"My Bast-blessed side whiskers," Ma mutters under her breath, "this manufactured mountain deathtrap has my head whirling worse than playing on the giant Jungle Jim at the Neon Graveyard museum. No wonder this Jay Edgar person with his pathetic, useless, slippery soles skidded right into the Clark County Morgue. I could strike the killing blow myself with one good leap at the back of his knees with all claws out."

"He must have been inspecting the property," I muse as I circle the disturbed dust at the top of the stairs. A jerking plunge to one's death should produce some blood, though, even if it is only the artistic dribble out the side of mouth TV crime shows excel at creating. And I smell no blood at all, which means I smell a rat.

I must admit that my girl assistants have treaded carefully around any human traces, leaving plain imprints of their neat little feet.

Then I spy a strange symmetry in the stair-top markings. Parallel lines here and there, some brushed across, others clear as ice skate blades. Skates up here? Was some daredevil human so stupid as to attempt to skateboard down the staircase of an abandoned building?

I leap atop the newel post at the top of the stairs, confident I am disturbing no evidence.

"Louie!" two yowls reprimand me.

It does not matter. From my higher perch I have spied evidence for my unique and undoubtedly correct theory.

Poor Ma. Poor Louise. Their vision is limited by their born-feral perspectives.

Mr. Jay Edgar Dyson did not fall to his death.

He was not pushed to his death.

I nod my head at the dull, dust-coated glass chandelier hanging above us and disappearing into the high cathedral ceiling above. Random glints on one of the chandelier's giant, strong, curved branching arms indicate where a rope or heavy drapery cord rubbed the glass clean.

Mr. Jay Edgar was hung. Hanged? Whatever. He was strangled, ergo no blood. And ergo the several straight marks of a ladder's feet, made by the killer to string him up...and made by the authorities to bring him down.

"Our guy," I tell the ladies, "was turned into a human chandelier pendant."

"Then your keeper's clowder chief cannot have done it," Ma says.

"For once and for all, Ma, get it right. My *roommate,* Miss Temple Barr, is a client of my detective business. Miss Electra Lark is a landlady for the Circle Ritz residents. I deign to live there and also to provide personal protection for Miss Temple. For the last time, I am not a kept cat. I rule my own roost. And I am an independent private investigator. I will not compromise any investigation. As for Miss Electra, I must consider she could have done this killing if she had a coconspirator."

"She could have made someone do it if she had a gun," Louise says. "And by the way, Ma, I am a full partner in Midnight Investigations, Inc."

"Junior partner," I say.

She huffs and puffs. "A female cannot be a 'Jr.', although you certainly are a senior citizen."

"No quite yet, you little ingrate."

"How I put up with your senile maunderings, I do not know."

She waps me across the nose. I wap her across the nose.

Wait. That nose-wapping was not us. It was Ma Barker doing a one-two rowdy-kitten slap-down. I have not felt the like in years.

"Sit down and shut up," Ma growls in a disciplinary basso that lives up to her canine name. "If this is the way you two run your business, you will soon be pulling guard duty for those pesky alien abductors. I suggest if these so-called abettors to a hanging are a real possibility, you start looking for, and finding them."

I fear that Ma Barker is right. With Miss Temple's private life all in a lovers' knot wad lately, I fear she has forgotten me and my crime-solving prowess. Hopefully, her affairs will get much simpler post haste and finding the murderer will be number one on the menu.

24
Counting Sheep

"I've been in a bar, now I want to go into the convent." Kathleen announced as Max steered the Honda out of Dublin on the busy M1. "Is that what you're hoping, Michael? That I'll finally 'find religion', as you put it in the States?"

"No, but you badly need to find a new mania, a new cause," he said.

"Do I? I don't need to find anything you might think I would." She sure knew how to pout, looking kittenish with her chin pointed down and her unearthly aqua eyes gazing up at him. The fading pink scar tracks looked like she'd run a pale lipstick tip over her cheek for some punk-style look. "I know about That Damn Movie."

"'That Damn Movie' doesn't ring a bell."

"Phil-o-*meen*-a." Her bitter, twisted lips mocked the title and herself.

Max nodded. "The Little Indie Film That Could. Dame Judi Dench playing the title character got the film a lot of notice for a biopic. Oscar nominations."

"I'm amazed you and the Circle Ritz crowd are so *au courant* about films. Particularly that one. Always thinking of me and my sad orphaned history."

Max shrugged. "And it's a great detective story."

"Not solved by Philomena. That woman was a sheep. Her toddler was taken from her, sold to American adoptive parents for two grand, and the Magdalene 'asylum' for fallen women would never tell her where he was sent. She only found where he was after he was middle-aged and dead, and after he'd had himself buried at that damnable place in case his birth mother ever came looking for him. The nuns knew they were searching for each other and kept them apart. Philomena did nothing but accept that she deserved the disdain and pain the Church handed out to her and her despised unwed mother cellmates. Sheep. Meek sheep."

"I see Philomena's quest as one of being reconciled with the past," Max said. "A horrible past, but she accepted that she couldn't have changed it."

"She could have taken the baby and run."

"You did that, Kathleen. You owe your plucky past self more than rage and bitterness in the present."

"And what about your past? You clutch your guilt like a talisman. It's a way to ward off people from getting close, isn't it? Father Matt would say that. Poor Michael. You can't leave your young self behind either."

"Don't call me Michael."

"I'll call you what I want to call you. Is Michael the Martyr any better or saner than Kitty the Cutter?"

"No," he said. "The punishing world you fled now has been exposed and has changed, but women and children are still being treated as badly, or worse, in much of the world elsewhere today."

"Screw foreign atrocities. I only care about *my* world. My IRA work helped end the daily brutal rule of the English over the Irish in Northern Ireland."

"And it was for the Irish Catholics you fought."

"Sheep, but now that they're not distracted by centuries of ethnic discrimination, perhaps they'll become more critical of their goddam religion."

"Or, their religion will become more critical of itself."

"Religion causes strife and suffering because it encourages people to despise those not of the 'true' faith. Look at the Mideast."

"Not my field of operation."

"What is, now?" she asked.

"I'm retired, although some folks won't accept that."

"And your last mission is to find dear lost—but alive if I'm not lying—Cousin Sean."

"Not quite my last mission."

"Right. You want to find the grave of your partner in undercover work."

He nodded.

"And you wanted to introduce me to my now-grown surrendered daughter, whereupon I would supposedly melt into a bloody, woolly, ill-smelling, bleating *sheep* of sweetness and light upon a first glimpse of her."

"Never expected that."

"So. We have a rental car. You are licensed and able to drive on the left side of the road. Where do we go next?"

"To church, I think."

"I won't cover my head. I won't kneel. And I may spit in the baptismal fount."

Max laughed. "You're finding your inner brat. I'm glad you're making up for lost time."

And he was.

"This is the place where I was kept," Kathleen said as Max pulled the Honda up to the convent church. He'd made sure to rent a car model different from the one he'd shared with Garry a mere two months ago. Yet, every time he glanced left at Kathleen in the passenger seat, he saw a gray ghost with a slack neck and bloody temple in the curve of closed window glass behind her.

"It's also the place I visited on my last trip." Max closed that conversation by going around to open her door.

She swung her narrow legs to the ground, looking up at him in that same disturbing way he only identified now: like the preternaturally knowing evil child in a horror movie. He pulled her up by the icy hand. She seemed to take perverse satisfaction in his courtesy.

The old brown brick building with red-brick bordered windows looked as ancient and abandoned as before when he'd visited with Garry. Against troubled gray clouds a crucifix stood in relief atop the rambling building's only peaked roof.

As before, when they walked around the church to enter the rectory door, an old nun met them there. Even though her inexpensive gray-and-black clothing weren't part of a habit, a simple headdress and lace-up black oxford shoes all screamed "nun".

Max braced himself for fits from Kathleen, but she merely looked the woman up and down. "Not from my day."

"You were here?" the nun asked. "What's your name?"

"O'Connor," Kathleen said almost passively, as if used to answering on command.

"Sinéad O'Connor?" The nun named a famously troubled Irish singer.

"*She* was in one of these places?" Kathleen's laugh was corrosive. "I should have recognized her as a soul sister. Should I shave my head like Sinéad in penance for that sin of omission, Mother? Is my black hair still too long, too thick, too inciting?" She thrust her hands roughly through it, like a madwoman.

The old nun just shook her oddly clad head. "We are not what we were."

"Too bad. I am." Kathleen pushed past her, but she didn't head for the church out front, or the brick two-story building behind it. She went around to the back, her stylish suede pumps following a broken path of grown-over inlaid stones that made her lurch from time to time like one drunk or drugged.

"You can't—" the nun began.

"Wait here. I'll accompany her." Max followed, avoiding the path for the thick, more even grass.

Despite her gait, he saw Kathleen was purposefully trodding only on the old and rough stones. He remembered a child's game from snow-bound Wisconsin. Pie. One kid pushed booted feet along to plow a circle in the deep, untouched snow, and divided it into slices. Every kid who came after had to follow his or her footsteps without falling into the unmarked portions of snow.

Max slowed, not wanting to overtake Kathleen. She was the trailblazer on old ground, plowing back in time in her own wayward fashion.

He followed her into an overgrown garden, fenced by a stone wall that tumbled down to the earth in places. On the distant rolling green hills, sheep grazed. Kathleen, looking that way, gave one disgusted bark of laughter.

Then she began lurching among the wildflowers. "I'm walking on the dead," she said over her shoulder, not looking back to acknowledge him.

Max looked down. The inset stones were random now, inscribed with words and dates. Some were only first names. The dates all spanned young lives, as young as fourteen. Some had an inscription. *Lamb of God.*

Lamb to the slaughter, more like, Max thought, infected by Kathleen's fury. A million Irish had died in the Great Famine of the 1840s. A million emigrated. Almost 5.000 had died in the Troubles between British overlords and Irish underlings since. And Irish families and authorities had disowned, shamed and condemned to hard labor in both birth and work 30,000 of their daughters, some of whom lay at last among the wildflowers, able to feel exile and pain no more.

"If I had all that IRA money you think I have," Kathleen said. "I would buy this place. I would turn this church into the brothel it was and let the sheep in to graze on these graves. Well?" She turned to fix him with a fiery defiance.

"Your cause is just," he said. "Your solution is a revenge fantasy. You and the world deserve more than fantasy."

She looked away, over the fields of green. "It's beautiful here. All this greenery is a whited sepulcher, as is the grass beneath our feet. The Church still won't admit it was as much about money as morality. And what is the 'morality' of a church shaming and punishing the girls they kept ignorant of the facts of life in convent schools? Philomena was eighteen when she got out and didn't know where babies came from. Of course they got pregnant, and then parents sent them to the nuns, who were paid by the state for each mother and child, as well as the labor the mothers had to do six days a week for pay they never got. Our names were changed, toddlers were ripped away without notice. They robbed of us of our children and we had to bow and scrape and call our brutal childless captors 'Mother'."

"Inhuman," Max murmured. "So you do know something of the book or film *Philomena.*"

"You really can't stay here," came a voice. The old nun had followed them.

Kathleen's laughter was maniacal. She took a step toward the nun, who stepped back.

"'*I can't stay here.*' Here, where I was imprisoned from birth with my imprisoned mother."

Another step. "'*I can't stay here.*' Here, where I was never adopted out because I had become the good Father's 'favorite'."

Another step. "'*I can't stay here.*' Here, where he began 'interfering' with me at the age of four and every nun looked away, or her eyes narrowed as she berated me for having such lavish hair, for being too pretty, like my mother before me, dead and buried beneath our feet by then."

Another step. The elderly nun was stumbling backward. Max didn't interfere.

"'*I can't stay here.*' But I had to, didn't I, when I was pregnant at fourteen? Many of the other girls had been impregnated by their fathers or brothers or cousins, but I was like Mary, my most un-immaculate conception was courtesy of the head guy. And he would soon have another pretty little bastard of his own. That's the only time I talked to God. I told Him to damn you all to Hell, and escaped with my infant daughter."

"I wasn't here then," the nun said. "I was raised in a later generation. The institutions are gone. We're more aware."

"So you would have been a kinder, gentler keeper, then." Kathleen stopped her advance and looked the woman up and down with contempt. "You still wear the uniform, as did the guards at Auschwitz."

"Oh, that awful movie, *Philomena*," the nun cried out. "Everyone knows it's full of lies, inaccuracies and exaggerations."

"You forget. I *was* here. The man who found Philomena's lost son, Martin Sixsmith? Nuns and the church blocked him at every stage. Thousands of records had been burned. Oh, that *lying* movie, *Philomena*. The United Nations investigation ruled what the Magdalene institutions did to girls and women and their babies was *torture*. And the church has yet to admit responsibility.

"You had better hope there's truth in a heavenly reunion for those mothers and babies, because I'll send you all there to see for yourselves before I'm done."

"You're crazy," the nun cried, turning to retreat into the dark, hulking church buildings behind her.

"That was quite insanely mad of you," Max said.

Kathleen's breath heaved out of her chest. Her hands were bloodless and so was her face, white marble with the pink veins of the fading cat scratches etched across it. Her expression was as twisted as she was, her beauty gone.

"Well done," he added. "You have certainly done your homework on *Philomena*, but I think you've spit in the baptismal font enough for today."

He took her arm to lead her back to the car. She stumbled beside him, silent.

25
A Valentine Surprise

Jay Edgar Dyson, killed in the very building that threatened Electra's financial survival. What a shock. Temple had assumed someone had killed him at the Araby Motel after she and Electra left.

Temple paced in her living room, alone. Louie had disappeared.

Just back from their happy, successful visit to her Minnesota family home, and she and Matt had parted on the elevator, both a bit disappointed. One couldn't see the other's point of view about Temple's risky Araby Motel outing.

She picked up her cell phone and speed-dialed Matt's apartment to make up.

There was no answer. She closed her eyes. Such a stupid thing to quarrel over. With all that had happened, of course Matt was hypersensitive about her staying safe. With Electra fearing for her livelihood, of course Temple felt obliged to be there for her.

Now maybe Matt wouldn't be there for Temple. She had to admit it was an impulsive outing that courted bad outcomes. She'd apologize, if only…

Her doorbell rang. She ran to open the door, phone in hand.

"Matt! I was just calling you."

He had his cell phone in hand. "Me too."

"I'm sorry," they said together, then laughed.

They bumped the wrists of their cell phone-holding hands and then hugged.

"I guess these smart phones are smarter than we are," Matt said. "I just worry about you."

"It was a stupid stunt. Electra was so upset and she would have gone alone. Now look at the mess we're all in. Dyson dead. Police interrogations. Us quarreling."

"We better drop these cell phones," Matt said, steering her to the sofa and pulling her down on it with him. "We communicate much better face-to-face."

"*Umm*," Temple agreed a couple minutes later, stretching her formerly stressed-out shoulders and neck.

Matt gave her a last kiss and picked up his cell phone.

"Hey, I thought a cell phone wasn't ever going to come between us again," Temple said.

"This one has to," Matt said with a smile. "While we were too worried and busy to check, Tony Valentine left a message. I just called him back. He wants a meeting as soon as possible, requesting your attendance."

"*My* attendance? Matt! An agent wouldn't ask a significant other along for a business meeting unless he had a huge offer. The network must have green-lighted your new talk show."

"You think?" He looked a bit dazed. "I haven't exactly encouraged them lately."

"No, you didn't. You had to drop your career plans to play the hero-decoy and make yourself a target for a psycho. Three a.m. 'counseling' sessions with Kitty the Cutter! I'm sure she pulled out all her seductive wiles."

"I'm temptress-proof. She threatened you, Temple. I'd do anything necessary to keep you from harm."

"Actually," Temple said, "your being so noncommittal with the Chicago suits probably was savvy negotiating. Now. Where are my lucky shoes? I think I'll be clicking my heels together and chanting 'There's no place like Water Tower Place' soon."

Matt picked her up and spun her around. "I'm ready to leave Las Vegas too," he said, "but which are your lucky shoes?" He set her down carefully on her three-inch-high heels.

"Anything that coordinates with what I'm wearing when I'm with you. You know what?"

"What?" Matt smiled down at her.

Temple was glad to see that recent faint wince of worry had vanished from his warm brown eyes. "I'm going to celebrate the big deal Tony has for you by getting some new shoes at the Stuart Weitzman boutique in the Caesars' shopping mall. Is that too extravagant?"

"Anything your big heart and tiny feet desire. Your stock of estate sale and resale shoes have earned some fresh high-design spikes."

"It's silly, but when you've spent your entire life staring into people's shoulder blades in crowds, a spiffy heel assist is so esteem-building."

"I'm sure Tony will be pleased to underwrite such a noble objective while collecting his percentage." Matt frowned.

"What?" Temple asked in her turn.

"I let Kathleen's taunts get to me, and upped the amount of my income via speaking engagements from Tony that goes to charity from ten to twenty percent. It occurs to me I don't have a right to reduce my income when I'm not just me, but a 'we'."

"Gosh, you are a saint in the making." Temple shook her head. "You can do what you want with your money, but including some animal causes among the charities would appease your shoe-hound fiancée. What a guy! Not only generous, but you want to *honor* your word made to an armed and dangerous psychopath."

"How'd you know Kathleen was armed?"

Temple felt her mouth go dry. "I didn't. I was speaking metaphorically. Armed with a gun even then? And you went back for more?"

"Not a gun. Straight razor. I only had to take it away from her once, when she got overwrought."

"Unbelievable. You are one cool guy, but it's time we got outa Dodge. Speaking metaphorically again."

"I understood Kathleen. She had absolutely no power until she escaped the Magdalene asylum. She needs to flaunt it now. And she's not here anymore. She's off in the wilds of Northern Ireland, playing tag with Max."

"Enough of that woman in our lives. I'm going to fetch my currently lucky shoes…the zebra-stripe numbers from the successful trip up north." Temple consulted the large-face watch on her wrist. "And then it'll be time to leave for Tony Valentine's office. Lord, that's a great surname for an agent. Every new gig is a Valentine gift."

Tall, with a full head of taffy-white hair, Tony Valentine looked more like a classics professor than what entertainment agents had been called for decades, a "ten-percenter"...although nowadays a package fee of three percent could be charged on top of it.

Temple didn't know how Matt had lucked out in getting a patrician-looking agent in a profession where agents were often regarded as crass, greedy and possibly crooked.

Then again, not looking like all of those things could be a license to steal.

As a PR person, Temple had met all kinds of people. As a sometime amateur detective she'd met plenty of the crass, greedy and crooked, and Tony Valentine passed her character test.

"Late-night talk-show shoes," he commented as she and Matt sat down, "but with class."

Correction: Tony passed with an A-plus. "Thanks. I'm so excited to hear what you've got to say. Matt is wonderful with people and on talk radio and on *The Amanda Show*. I may be prejudiced, but the network is going to be blown away."

While Matt looked properly abashed by her gushing, Temple noticed that Tony Valentine was growing more and more amused.

"Temple," Matt warned. "You're overdoing my virtues."

"No, I'm not. Guys can't have sissy things like 'virtues', they just have strong points."

Tony leaned back in his cushy leather chair. Behind him, through a billboard-size window-wall, the sunlit Vegas Strip glittered like a river with lane-to-lane lines of hot metal melted into liquid mercury.

"Yes, I've heard from the network," Tony agreed, "but Matt's future isn't the reason I called you here today." He tapped long tapered fingertips together.

While Tony enjoyed a dramatic silence, Temple exchanged a bewildered glance with Matt, who leaned forward.

"I know," Matt said, "I've maybe been a little indecisive with the network. Some personal issues have been a distraction. I wouldn't blame them for backing off."

Tony let his reclining seat snap upright. "You two aren't calling off the wedding?"

"There's nothing formally decided, like a date, if it would interfere," Temple explained, wondering whether the network had concluded it would prefer an eligible Matt.

"It's on, more than ever," Matt said, taking Temple's hand.

"Glad to hear it." Tony beamed like a presiding clergyman, ready to direct them to exchange vows and rings. "Actually, I have an unexpected offer from a client of the network's. It's a bit awkward, since I don't represent either of the entities in the deal."

"You mean you don't rep the network's client?" Temple said, puzzled. Agents represented individuals usually. If not Matt, who...?

"It's a big advertiser."

"Talk-show hosts don't do ads," Temple said.

"Usually not, no."

Temple eyed Matt again. Why was Tony acting so coy?

The agent cast a mock-rebuking glance at Matt. "You didn't tell me you were cohabiting with a TV personality."

Squeaky-clean Matt, ex-priest, had to set the record straight. "Temple worked for a couple years as a TV reporter in the Twin Cities, but that was her first job. Nothing anybody would remember."

"Thanks a lot," Temple said.

"Of course she was tops at her job," Matt told Tony, "but who would want...I mean, TV reporters don't usually move to the entertainment side of the camera."

"Neither do radio counselors," Temple said.

Tony jumped in fast. "The wedding may very well be off if you continue speaking, Matt," Tony said. "So I'll get to the punch line. The 'TV personality' I'm referring to is your cat, Miss Barr."

"Midnight Louie?"

"I believe that is the name. Why so incredulous? He has a certain rep in this town." Tony grinned. "A rap sheet? Or should I say a *track* record."

Temple leaned back in her chair. "So that's it. À La Cat pet food is back with an empty bowl, begging for Louie's services again. He was so much more personable than that yellow tabby they were using before, that Maurice."

Temple gave the French name, "Mau-reece", the British pronunciation, Morris.

"I swear that camera hog my roomie replaced tried to kill Louie when he was strutting down a long staircase wearing a flamingo pink fedora." She turned to Matt. "I swear Louie wanted to kill *me* for allowing them to fasten that headgear on him. He looked so dashing in vintage fifties black and pink, though."

"*I'd* want to kill you if you tried to fasten a flamingo-pink fedora on me," Matt told her.

"Well, the Fontana brothers wore fedoras matched with pastel zoot suits for that commercial and looked terrific."

"We can't all be Fontana brothers, thank God," Matt answered.

"Agreed," Temple said. "I'm a one-of-a-kind girl myself."

They smiled at each other like there was no tomorrow.

"Hello, young lovers," Tony interrupted. "I'm not through talking the deal." He rapped his knuckles on the glass desktop. "Apparently the network execs like what they saw of Miss Barr when you two had dinner with them. À La Cat wants to do a series of 'story' TV ads, which is a big deal."

"Oh," Temple was rapturous. "Like those Taster's Choice coffee ads back before I was born, with the cute courting couple."

"Before you were born." Tony sighed. "Depressing fact. Early eighties phenomenon. I remember them like they ran yesterday. How do you know about them?"

"Communications major. We had classes in advertising and TV. Besides, they're on YouTube. Louie's first round of commercials did a bit of that, using the Persian cat, Yvette. And Fancy Feast has used a smashing Yvette-type cat for years, and did a kitten/couple story segment recently. Oh," Temple said, her voice turning sour.

"What?" Matt asked. "If you don't want Louie doing commercials again, we can just say no."

Tony frowned. "What's the matter?"

"I hope they're not going to use Yvette again. I just remembered Yvette's owner is that unbearably overbearing B-movie actress, Savannah Ashleigh."

"'Oh' is right," Matt said. "I've met and dealt with her. She definitely is Ego à la mode."

"Well," Temple went on in her usual spritely tone. "She's more to be pitied than despised. Maybe they won't be using Yvette. That's an old approach."

"One thing I'm sure they'll be using, Miss Barr," Tony said. "And that's you."

"Me?"

"You. Their idea is all cat's-eye view. Well, your shoes and legs, and possibly your voice, if it passes muster. Mr. Midnight will be given an off-camera voice as well."

Temple turned to Matt. "That's a radical new approach. Too bad Humphrey Bogart died. He'd be perfect for Louie's voice."

"A voice actor can suggest anything," Tony said. "There'd also be podcasts and social media. For all of which you and Louie would be reimbursed. It could add up to a fat sum, and I'd stipulate that you'd get all the footwear you wore for the commercials gratis."

"Paid in Prada. Oh, my. That's worth clicking your heels together and having to relocate to Kansas."

"Temple." Matt was shaking his head. "Slow down. They may want to portray an ordinary woman with ordinary shoes."

"No woman wants to see ordinary shoes on TV. Well, maybe marathon runners and such do."

Tony responded to Temple's enthusiasm with a broad smile. "À la Cat is the producer, of course, but they've committed major funds to this campaign and want a top-notch creative director, so it'll be a slick project. In fact, they mentioned that 'fedora' commercial with the Fontana brothers chorus line of zoot suits, and wanted something similar, this time with Louie in a zoot suit."

"What's a zoot suit?" Matt asked, "as compared to a monkey suit?"

Temple and Tony exchanged glances. He was old enough to know, and Temple was hip enough to know, but no way would a Gen X Midwestern ex-seminarian and parish priest know.

She tried to explain. "A zoot suit can be a monkey suit, but it can't be the other way around."

"A monkey suit, my dear boy," Tony told Matt, "is something you'll be wearing at your upcoming wedding, unless your lovely fiancée gives you a pass. Usually it's formal white tie and tails getup, but it could be a dinner jacket ensemble. With side-satin-striped black trousers. On the other hand, a zoot suit—" Tony deferred to Temple with a glance.

"It's a hip man's entire outfit, from the time when baggy-pants Vaudeville entertainment gave way to Le Jazz Hot and a sleeker, more modern look. Picture Judy Garland in frumpy baggy clown suit singing 'Be a Clown' to Judy Garland in a man's black tuxedo jacket, fishnet tights, heels and fedora singing 'come on get happy'. Funky to sexy in a generation or two."

Matt frowned. "Can you get me some DVDs on that?"

"It's all on YouTube," she said. "Jazz came out of the black music scene. In the twenties and thirties black performers started showing up in movies. Cab Calloway got famous and wore exaggeratedly formal pale zoot suits, but it wasn't until swing dancing in the forties that the zoot suit culture took off."

"It was the first commercial 'teenage' fad," Tony said with nostalgia. "And it appeared in minority cultures, both black and Hispanic, before it went mainstream."

"That didn't end well," Temple took up the narrative. "It was punished at the time in both cultures. The high-waisted baggy pants with tight ankle cuffs and loose, knee-length Civil War general coats, along with extravagantly swagged watch chains called hipster cat-chains were socially threatening. Think gangsta rap, which I have major problems with. Can it convert to something less misogynistic? Time will tell."

"I think I've seen photos. 'Swagged watch chains'," Matt repeated. "Origin of 'swagger' and 'swag' today?"

"Good point," Temple said. "Hip dudes used to be called hep or hip 'cats'. Louie would love that, without the chain."

"I remember," Tony mused, "post-war zoot suit riots. We fifties teens of the James Dean era were hit with comparisons to 'hoodlums'. With zoot suits in the forties, the excuse for a teen rebel uniform with the many yards of material zoot suits required was considered 'unpatriotic' in a time of fabric shortages.

"What's expensive is faddish," Tony added. "Wealthy zoot suiters wore multiple gold 'watch chains' looped down to their ankles. Poor guys yanked toilet chains off old-style tanks and used them. The point was, WASPs didn't wear them. The underclasses did. And during World War Two sailors took offence and beat and stripped the zoot suiters."

"That's not faddish fun," Matt said. "That's a horrible footnote of history. How can people be dressing in zoot suits now and dancing down stairs in cat food commercials?"

"Because we've gotten over teen fads and outcast castes," Temple said. "Not totally, but the creativity and expressiveness of that time and those people has been integrated into our cultural fabric. So we can share the fun and enthusiasm without the negative connotations."

"This is way too deep for cat food commercials," Matt said.

"Maybe not," Temple said. "The zoot suit rebellion has been declawed by a lot of decades of social progress. The next step after belated acceptance is celebration."

"So you're saying cat food commercials can be relevant social commentary?" Matt sounded and looked dubious.

Temple shrugged. "I'm saying people just want to have fun. Don't overthink it and maybe they'll accidentally learn something. That top-notch director they want?" Temple asked Tony. "Danny Dove right here in town would be great at that."

Tony was surprised. "The choreographer?"

"Set designer too. Catch the Black & White rock-group show with French Vanilla at the Crystal Phoenix Hotel. Danny designed both the fixed and moving stage settings. *WOW*," Temple said. "Maybe the ads can start out in noir black-and-white, and then, *POW*, go to Technicolor, like *The Wizard of Oz* movie."

"That's a hot ticket," Tony agreed. "She's quite the idea girl," he told Matt before turning back to Temple. "It was your Zoe Chloe Ozone persona that inspired the network."

"That old blog and podcast stuff from the teen reality show?" Temple shook her head and sighed. "It's dead in the water and has been for months. Fads fade at warp speed in today's media world."

"And a good thing," Matt put in. He eyed Tony. "She went undercover with that persona and nearly got killed."

"As she said, nothing dies on the Internet. Matt. Zoe Chloe is still out there. There could be a TV tour in this and you're perfect for that," he told Temple.

"Would Louie have to travel?" Temple wondered.

"Perhaps. Is that a problem?"

"*Nooo*," Temple said. "He's got a brand-new zebra-print carrier for the job. He'd look fab in a zebra-print fedora. Or zoot suit."

"Whoa, Temple," Matt said. "He would not love wearing the suit, I bet, and do you really want to tote a twenty-pound cat on and off a plane? Airlines don't even provide room for under-seat shaving kits or feet these days."

"First class," Tony said, "would be in the contract. And media escorts. Don't worry, Matt. I'd see your fiancée is treated like a queen, or at least a bestselling author."

"Say," Temple sat up taller. "I could write a book about Louie!"

Tony made a note on his leather-bound legal notepad.

Matt groaned. "Tony, Temple and I need to think and we need to talk this over. It could be hell moving to Chicago with Temple starting such a multi-pronged media project."

"Of course." Tony eased back in his chair. "I see this as complex, yes, but fortuitous."

"The network hasn't been pestering me," Matt said, "or you, about my possible national TV talk show gig. Meanwhile, every celebrity and his and her siblings are starting new shows."

Tony grew serious. "True. You've played pretty hard to get."

"I'm not playing anything, Tony. My mother just remarried and Temple and I are thinking about scheduling a wedding. I don't want us to be rushed into something so demanding it'll ruin our private lives."

"Very sensible," he said, standing to end the visit. "Keep this top secret. Buzz blows deals as often as it hypes them. If you have any questions, let me know. This is only in the development stages. It's good to know about, because you both can still have a lot of input now."

Matt shook, and then Temple shook, Tony's soft manicured hand.

At the door Temple turned. "And I do have to ask Louie if he wants to do this."

"How would you know?" Tony asked.

"Oh, Louie knows how to make his druthers known, don't worry."

26
The Minstrel Boy

Max's heart was pounding. He felt he'd been making a pilgrimage commemorating the Stations of the Cross over all of Ireland, south and north, with Kathleen. The fourteen harsh images often hung on Catholic church walls, memorializing Jesus's suffering, crucifixion, and death...and, sometimes a last image, a happy ending, the resurrection.

Sometimes Max thought the Church fixated on darkness. Yet now, so did Max. This journey, he hoped, would end at the grave of the best man he'd ever known, but first he must deal with the unsuspected living. He hoped he was on the brink of witnessing a rising from the dead.

Kathleen, practicing the controlling cruelty that had dominated her childhood, had told Max nothing, nothing about his cousin. Only that Sean was alive. That Sean was alive and now they were here, in County Tyrone of Northern Ireland, where he and Sean had gone astray on a quest for their roots and "adventure" tourism.

He stood with Kathleen before a quaint white-washed cottage. Ireland was breathtakingly picturesque, but traditionally the land and people were poor, with a harsh and tragic history. The only thing the modern Emerald Isle had to sell was charm until the "Celtic Tiger" awakened in the '80s with a burst of high-tech businesses. Then a second Irish "famine" came with the global recession.

Max took in every feature of the simple building—the gravel driveway with a green iron gate. The house, clad in white stone, was shaped like an arc or a simple church, a long main floor with an A-shaped second story. The windows weren't in even rows. Simple narrow wood frames painted bright green dappled the white stone canvas here and there. Green window boxes on shallow stone sills spilled over with fuchsia, purple and white petunias, blooming as madly as any second-story pub window box in the British Isles.

This modest traditional home could be a whited sepulcher, hiding a blasted life behind its green-framed Irish charm.

Sean Kelly, Wisconsin boy by birth. Mourned and missed for almost twenty years. Max thought his thoughts sounded like an obituary. But, unless Kathleen had played the sadist again, Sean was somewhere behind that bright green-painted wooden door, breathing the same clean, earthy Irish air that had Max close to hyperventilating. He hoped Sean wasn't under a gravestone in the back garden. He wouldn't put it past Kathleen to "mirror" his past to match the tragedy of hers.

Max's training as a magician had made him seem eternally cool and collected and had served well onstage and under cover. And now…now he was a bipolar boy again, one moment agonizingly unsure and an instant later filled with a cocky conviction he would soon be master of his own life and druthers, he would know the truth fully and master his fears and guilt.

Maybe, Max thought, this was his moment for finally growing up.

Kathleen sighed, ruefully. "Ah, so green it is, so white the stone, so black the hearts. So charming the accents, so savage the hypocrisy."

"You're regaining your lost native Irish lilt," Max told her.

"I spoke mostly Spanish when I worked South America for the Cause. Sure, and I can sound as Irish as the cleaning lady when I want to. That encouraged Irish-Americans to donate to the IRA."

"You have a gift for languages, then."

"Gift? Perhaps. Why would you be interested in my 'gifts'?"

"No reason." He studied the house again. "The architecture is so pure and simple, timeless. You don't realize at first how big and well-situated the structure is. The roof has some skylights. That's not authentic 'Irish cottage'."

"So we're doing a review for *Architectural Digest*?" Kathleen's tart tone was at least an improvement on downright angry.

Max gazed out over a bright green rolling quilt of landscape, seamed by darker green hedgerows and brown stone walls. "Peaceful too," he added.

"Things may seem so long-distance lovely," Kathleen said, "but there's always dirt beneath the grass and shamrocks, soil beneath the soul."

Max eyed the worn stone sill underlining the aggressively green front door.

"Is he...are they, even home?" he asked, walking to the gate to view a parked car on the paved area behind the house and inhale the drift of roses from the charming garden.

Charm. That word again. Lucky charm. Max had always cultivated both luck and charm, but he had a feeling they had run out on him now.

Kathleen would never bring him to a picture-postcard ending. He again inhaled the scent of dozens of roses, amused by the intricate white wrought-iron garden table and chairs glaring against the everlasting green, and speculated about the owner of the parked Opel Zafira car.

He circled back to Kathleen. Her jade-green pantsuit and plain black pumps blended with the scenery. A designer scarf swathed her throat and shoulders, as vividly floral as the flower boxes and distracted attention from her facial scars. She had white skin, like the stone-clad cottage, black hair, like the dark and bloody history of the land beneath it, and...something very wrong about the eyes. He'd been avoiding direct glances, partly to quell his accelerating emotions as he neared a reunion with Sean. Hope. Fear. Guilt. Anger.

It took him a second to figure out what was wrong...different. She wasn't wearing her exotic aquamarine-tinted contact lenses. He was seeing the clear blue eyes of young Kathleen O'Connor, twenty-three and the prettiest girl in Northern Ireland, at least to two teenage American boys from Racine, Wisconsin.

Max knew then there was no way to escape this time machine, or the revelations and shock Kitty the Cutter was about to inflict on her two long-ago admirers.

27
Send Off

Temple was madly typing away at her laptop the next morning when the doorbell rang. She jumped up and Louie, startled, skittered off her desk, sending printouts flying.

"Louie!"

Her complaint was wasted. He was already at the door when she got there.

She loved that each unit at the Circle Ritz had a real, live nineteen-fifties doorbell. Temple was not the domestic type—in fact she happily bordered on incompetent—but answering a doorbell made her think she was the perfect, efficient fifties hausfrau in full skirts, high heels, and pearl necklace, as portrayed on TV series then.

"Electra," she greeted the landlady. "Come on in. I've got Crystal Lite and Pecan Sandies and have been jotting down ideas for a charmingly kick-ass urban village. That'll take your mind off current events of the criminal kind."

"I'm afraid not, dear."

Temple noticed then that only one tame swatch of yellow decorated Electra's hair, and it disappeared after two inches, like a fading sunbeam. Electra with almost all-white hair seemed older, frailer, and several gallons low on her natural zest.

"Come sit down. Something's happened. The police—?"

"Not them. Yet." Electra arranged the folds of her pale blue muumuu, which seemed to reflect her mood. Blue. "I wonder if you can go to a funeral with me today."

"*The* funeral? That's fast. Who would arrange to bury Jay Edgar here in Vegas? Wait. Are *you* doing it? At the wedding chapel?"

"Heavens, no!"

"Then who would, um, sponsor it? I don't think you mentioned having kids with him. And he hadn't been back in town for years."

"He had no kids by anybody. His other ex-wife, Diane, keeps in touch with me. The police contacted her by phone in Dayton. She gave them Jay's lawyer's name in Dayton. And she was invited to the funeral too."

"By whom?"

"A woman named Cathy Zevon. She claims to have been his fiancée."

"And she's here, in Vegas?"

"I guess so. She's using my friend Sam's funeral home, and I checked. She's paying for it. In cash."

"Curiouser and curiouser. Jay Edgar didn't mention anything about having a fiancée along or in town, when you gave him what-for at the motel?"

"You can get anything you want in terms of companionship in Vegas," Electra said with a sad smile, "including, I guess, a convenient fiancée."

"This is so fishy."

Louie, who'd been rubbing on their ankles during the conversation, paused and interjected a strong *merow* of agreement. Temple had observed that cats expressed emphasis in a progression from *mew* to *meow* to *merooow*.

"Of course I'll go with you," Temple told Electra. "For one thing, the police will probably have someone there watching who attends and I might be able to spot the observer."

"The police will be watching me?"

Temple nodded. "And Diane. She didn't know about a fiancée?"

"They both still lived in Dayton, Ohio, so she's pretty sure he didn't have one."

"What terms were Jay and Diane on?"

"Not close, but in touch now and again. She gave the police his lawyer's name. I guess they needed to know if Jay had a will."

"What do you think?"

"Sure. He was a businessman, even if his recliner store recently went belly-up. The Great Recession did a job on a lot of people. He'd have all the paperwork. Jay's the one who brought me to Las Vegas, like your Max, to get married."

"Uh, not like Max. We didn't come here specifically to get married."

"But Max left and you stayed. That's what happened with Jay and me. That's why I trusted him to honor our agreement that I'd have first dibs on his land adjacent to the Circle Ritz. That's what we did when we came to Vegas to get married. We were both starting over and investing our life savings in real estate. We weren't kids, so we kept our investments separate."

"What broke up the marriage?"

Electra made a face. "His gambling. You heard what he did here just now, got deeper in debt. It was criminal to get him comped at a casino."

"The people who wanted that building site knew how to play him. I bet they didn't know about you or your claims on the property."

"Which are nil. A promise is worth nothing when the promiser is dead. My 'claim' was paper-thin when he was alive." She sighed. "I guess worrying over the Circle Ritz and Lovers' Knot is pointless when I'm a suspect for murder."

"That is so lame, Electra. The murder hasn't even made the paper."

"They just don't want the way they found him to get out."

"Shot dead is big-time headline news?"

Electra bit her lip and shook her head. "Your Lieutenant Molina was more than stern about me not telling anybody this, especially you."

"She's not 'my' anything but a pain, and she specifically mentioned me?"

"They had to ask me specific questions." Electra's voice started to break. "So I know Jay was found hanging from that giant chandelier in the future Lust 'n' Lace building. It's not a way I'd want to see him go."

"Oh, my God. Why suspect you, then? It could have been suicide. Anyway, you couldn't haul a man up a ladder and hang him."

"They think I could have made him hang himself at gunpoint. They think I was mad enough to kill him. And I sorta was."

"Still bizarre."

"There's some evidence more than one person was involved."

"I see. You'd need a man to help you hang him. Who'd you get to do that? Matt? Or, holy moly Molina! She might be thinking Max would help you. She wouldn't know he's left Vegas. If he has. I hope so. You know what this murder method reminds me of?"

"Nothing good, I'm sure. What?"

The death of Matt's wicked stepfather, Clifford Effinger."

"*Euww*, that ship thing."

"Another elaborate killing. It's like someone is sending someone else a message."

Louie leaped up beside Temple on the couch and rubbed his chin against hers. "Louie! Your whiskers tickle."

She pulled her face away, still thinking despite the distraction. "It's like that darn building is attracting a nexus of evil." Louie began kneading his paws on her lap. "*Ouch*, Louie. That pricks." She tried to push him away. "I swear. You could almost film a horror movie there."

"Temple, it's creepy enough now as a murder site. You're right, though, a lot of ghosts of previous business incarnations haunt that place. I wonder if anyone associated with it lived at the Circle Ritz?"

"Maybe there *is* a connection. I'm going to investigate the place's history. It might have more than face value," Temple decided.

Louie stopped needling her lap and leaned up to nudge his furry face against her forehead and began purring up a storm.

"He's certainly gotten awfully affectionate all of a sudden," she told Electra.

"You can see from my marital history that a good man is hard to find," Electra said, stroking Louie's long black tail, "but a great cat will never let you down."

28
Laid Off

Appropriately for a man hung from a giant dusty crystal chandelier, Jay Edgar Dyson's funeral parlor reception room boasted a much more tasteful and petite and sparkling chandelier.

Ironically, the mysterious fiancée had chosen Sam's Funeral Parlor, with its white-pillared Tara façade, where Matt's stepfather had been "laid out". She had also sprung for a funeral announcement in the paper.

Temple studied the sparse group of people who'd signed the book and entered. Most were male senior citizens with bald or very low thread-count heads. Not likely mob-related. Gambling buddies, probably.

In fact, a short spry guy with black still streaking his gray hair approached her. She was mystified until she realized he always wore a snappy fedora around town, but had doffed it in respect for the place and occasion.

"Nostradamus," she greeted him. "Did you know Mr. Dyson?"

"Only to see and nod in passing. Or spend some time just gassing."

Yup, it was the rhyming bookie, all right.

"Is his death a surprise to you?"

"Rumor is it wasn't quite kosher. Me…" He shrugged. "I know better than to look for closure. There still are elements in this town that would bring an okay guy down."

Temple nodded. "Thanks."

He leaned close and lowered his voice. "If you're still doing the Nancy Drew act, you'll need someone to watch your back."

"I have someone to watch over me."

"More than one, I bet, at that. Say hello to my pal, the lucky black cat." Nostradamus winked at her and moved on to gaze into the casket.

Nostradamus knew everybody in town, and apparently, everything. And he suspected murder, even though it hadn't made the paper.

Temple sighed and looked around again. She hadn't realized until now that funeral parlors she had visited were so similar to Las Vegas wedding chapels. There was the same, hushed ceremonial air enhanced by thick carpets and banks of flowers. There was the fact of knowing it wasn't holy ground, yet that an event of great solemnity was underway in this over-luxurious setting.

And it was a setting the late pianist Liberace, the swami of glitter, would have loved. The soft, lavish upholstery of the coffin lid was propped as showily ajar as a Steinway grand piano's top board...the corpse's face looked as slightly painted as a stage actor's...or a mannequin's.

Seeing Electra here not wearing her Justice of the Peace robes seemed strange. She had added an artificial silver sheen to her white hair and wore dignified navy blue. Standing next to her was a tall, thin blonde woman of sixty-something wearing snazzy red glass frames. Definitely Diane, not the mystery fiancée.

Temple joined them, deciding she didn't need to gaze upon the not-so-dear departed ever again.

She was not surprised to see Detective Su present. Her usual, darkly sober mini-Molina pantsuit was funeral-appropriate. Temple lifted one eyebrow at Su in greeting, which was not returned.

After Electra introduced Temple to Diane, she murmured, "We were saying that an urn and a photograph would have done for us."

"At least the surprise fiancée, and not the estate, is paying for this," Diane said. "I'm here to eyeball the supposed fiancée, frankly."

"Me, too," Temple said with feeling. Everything about the murder reeked of a setup. "I bet the police are interested in her too. Is there a reading of the will?"

Electra nodded. "Temple, you can come with us when we leave. The police found the lawyer and he transferred that duty to an attorney here in town."

"Another waste of estate money."

"Diane," Electra warned. "The man was murdered. We don't want to sound like gold-diggers."

"Speak for yourself. I'm a retired clerk with a tiny pension. I'm sorry Jay died ahead of his time, but you and I earned some recompense for time put in."

"At least you were out of town when it happened," Electra said.

"I'm still a 'person of interest'."

"Hey. That's actually a good thing for women our age," Diane said with a wry smile.

"When did you get to Vegas?" Temple asked.

"Not until this morning, and I have the plane ticket to prove it." Diane narrowed her eyes. "Electra has mentioned her 'famous' tenants in the past, and I know you're an amateur detective."

"Well, not really. Not officially."

"Don't be modest. I'm sure you won't get anything on me. Just show me the hussy and the will, and I'm on the next plane home."

"Hussy at six o'clock high," Electra trilled under her breath, looking to the gold velvet curtains at the entry archway.

A tall, thin woman in black paused for an entrance moment. She was a walking cliché wearing a close-fitted suit with a pencil skirt, sheer black hose, and a brimmed black hat with a matching veil.

"*The Bride Wore Black*," Temple muttered, referencing a title by that very dark noir novelist, Cornell Woolrich. "She's like out of a really bad *Movie of the Week*. And I know her!" she added in surprise.

"You do?" Electra was shocked.

"You do, too," Temple answered.

"No...."

"Yes. Look at that black dyed hair."

"What would Lindy Lukas be doing here?"

"Visualize her in tight jeggings and boots," Temple urged.

"My Lord."

"Yes," Temple said, "Diane, meet Cathy Zevon, a.k.a. Katt Zydeco, strip club manager."

"Actually," Diane said, "I *would* like to meet her. Sounds like you and Electra can do the honors."

"No…" Electra began, but Diane was willful for a willowy blonde and apparently still felt a sense of possession about Jay.

Temple and Electra could only follow Diane as she marched forward to meet and greet the lady in black.

"I'm a former Mrs. Dyson. I understand you were the next Mrs. Dyson-in-training. A little young for a man in his seventies, weren't you?"

"Jay had a youthful spirit."

"How'd you meet?"

Temple watched Diane's interrogation with growing amazement. She'd never have had the nerve to confront a woman who'd paid for the visitation and burial even if she'd come out of the woodwork.

So Temple ventured a question of her own. "You met here in Vegas, didn't you?"

Cathy Zevon/Katt Zydeco's eye makeup had been in deep mourning even before Temple had heard of Jay Edgar Dyson or met him. Her "smoky eye" could have survived a five-alarm fire. Her dark pupils were inky black as she fixed Temple with a cold stare.

"You're the Miss Nosey from the Lust 'n' Lace site. It's none of your business, but we've been inseparable since Jaysy came to Vegas."

"And I'm sure Leon Nemo made the introduction," Temple said.

"It's Nemo's job to make introductions, but it isn't your job to question our actions."

"She's only acting for us," Diane said. "We widows. You're not claiming to be another one."

"Maybe I'm not, and maybe I will turn out to be one. You never know in Vegas, with its instant marriage industry. Now I'm going to pay my respects to the dear departed."

Every eye upon her, she cat-walked to the casket—one spike-clad foot crossing in front of the other—to place a black-gloved hand on the brass rail and gaze and sigh as if performing in a high school Shakespearian tragedy.

"Oh, Jay," Diane wailed as the trio walked away and out of the reception room, "did you go off the rails with one bad mama!"

"Maybe not," Temple said, noticing that Merry Su had snapped some shots of Ms. Zevon/Zydeco with her cell phone. "Maybe one bad mama *pushed* him off the rails."

29
To The War Has Gone

The solid green door required a knock. Max's fist produced three knuckle-tingling blows. Three was a fairytale number. Good things, and bad, came in three.

"A moment," a voice inside said. Male. Tinged with an Irish accent, so engaging and easy to pick up.

Max stepped back, almost into Kathleen behind him, Kathleen poised to impress this outdated Kodak moment on her vengeful brain.

"I'll get it," a woman's voice trilled, pure Irish to the vocal sway on the word "get".

The door opened immediately, slamming Max with the vision of a wide smile, a pale but freckled face, hair as crazy red-gold as Temple's, only curdled with curls haloing her head and shoulders. He couldn't even register what she wore, just that vivid, welcoming presence.

"May I help you?" she asked. "We're between engagements, but not for long."

Between engagements? Was this a show business couple? Here? How?

"I've...we've come from America," Max said inanely.

"Don't you all?" the woman remarked in good humor. "And it's happy we are to have you here. Come in to see the place."

Well, yeah. As Max stepped over the threshold, he heard rattling in another room.

"Is it just the two of you, then, sir?" the woman inquired, stretching her neck to see past Max's six-feet-four to the short woman in his wake. "You and your...lady."

How adroitly she'd avoided "marrying" them. Max was deeply grateful for her tact.

He was still too taken aback to register anything but shards of the room. Wide wood plank flooring, wavy white stone walls and a tall brick chimney with a rough beam mantelpiece. Age-blackened vertical wooden beams here and there.

The woman was perhaps forty, bare of makeup, her pale brows arched and her mouth humorous. Her nose was straight, but meant business. Cheery confidence would describe her. "I'm Deirdre," she said.

Yes, you are a dear woman, aren't you? The last thing Max had expected behind the green door was a warm welcome.

"And are you Irish-American, too?" Deirdre asked Kathleen.

Kathleen just nodded. Max chanced a deeper look at her. No, this was not the scene she had planned to stage-manage.

"Well," Deirdre said, "we can have tea, but as long as you're standing, would you like to look at the upstairs first?"

"Yes, indeed," Max said. "I'm Max. The architecture is... charming." He could sense Kathleen seething with frustrated expectations behind him. Max added to the civil social ritual unfolding. "The cottage looks so traditional, Deirdre, but the skylights are a perfect modern touch for this cloudy climate."

Deirdre led the way up a narrow set of stairs, a tall woman as solid as the front door. "The place is an old barn we've converted to a bed and breakfast. We've redone the upstairs to offer a bathroom and four guest bedrooms, one with an en suite, simple but comfortable."

She opened a door onto a spacious bedroom dominated by a large, elegant iron bedstead against a curtained window, flanked by tables. Above it, a slanted ceiling rose to meet two old beams in a ceiling pierced by a skylight and pocked by modern can lights.

A smaller, much older window on the side wall was flanked by a chair and a huge wall mirror.

"Wonderful," Max said, knowing the sheer social normality of every word and gesture of his interaction with Deirdre was driving

Kathleen crazy. Crazier. "How long have you run the bed and breakfast?"

"Fourteen years. We'd been daft to stay in the city any longer than that, and the Troubles were still bubbling along back then."

"In Antrim and Down counties?" Max asked.

She nodded. "In Belfast, the worst of it." Her lips hardened into a taut line. "Now that is mostly under control," she added briskly, the accommodating hostess again. "You Americans have no idea of the hard-hearted hatred that seared both sides during that time. Belfast requires 'peace walls' between sides and still seethes. Yet here we are delighted to provide stress-ridden vacationers with a piece of Irish peace, so to say, not only in the country, but in our rare bit of countryside."

Max was juggling two scenarios for his cousin. He was Deirdre's husband and a lucky man. Or, perhaps, a hired man. She'd need someone handy about the place. A head wound, Kathleen had said, if she could be trusted. The fact that Sean, if truly alive, had never gone home could mean severe brain damage, long medical stays, relearning to walk, talk, think.

But if he were here—Max wandered to the window behind the bed and gazed out on the serene countryside all rumpled in shades of green to the horizon. Green, the color of hope. If he was here, Sean had cornered a piece of heaven. Then why hadn't he ever gone home to his grieving family?

He turned to see Kathleen watching him intently. She knew why.

"The reason," Deirdre said, perhaps afraid Max was too enchanted by this cozy, modernized cottage, "we're vacant now is because of a cancellation. I can only offer you the one night."

"I'd like to go downstairs," Kathleen said, sharply.

Deirdre looked at Max. He shrugged, ever so slightly, then told her, "The lawn and garden below look stunning. Does it require a lot of upkeep?"

"My Lord, man," Deirdre said with a laugh. "Try to keep the greenery from growin' on our famous Emerald Isle. It requires constant 'groomin', wouldn't you know?"

On that they clambered back down the wooden stairs, sounding like a home invasion crew.

"Deirdre," came a man's voice with an Irish lilt, "there's a car in the drive, have you—?"

They collided at the bottom of the stairs, Deirdre still on the first step and taller than the man who looked up at her. Max higher still, looking down on a man's head of thinning rusted gray hair. "We have company," the man told Deirdre. "I didn't know." His hand waved a wrench apologetically.

Guests, Max guessed, weren't to meet the maintenance side of this rural paradise.

The man backed away to let them all descend, Max turned to take Kathleen's hand for the last steep step. Her fingers were ice cold. Her adrenaline had kicked in at peak performance. Max tried to look the newcomer in the eye, but the guy was looking down, pulling screws from his work belt.

"I'd best be back at it," he mumbled, moving around the corner to what must be the kitchen.

"Wait," Kathleen said. "Someone's here to meet you, Sean."

Deirdre's stance immediately stiffened. Max recognized a defender as surely as if she'd been a Doberman. His gut tightened. If this was Sean, he hadn't escaped the pub bombing without serious damage. Max felt like someone about to walk into a burn ward... bracing himself to face people who'd suffered horrible hurt and disfigurement, but desperately trying to see and show the humanity that could look past that to the person.

"Sean," he said, far sooner than he'd wanted to.

The man froze, giving Max time to recognize his right profile and rejoice at the slim slice of normality. The receding hairline itself was an amazing alteration. Then he remembered their uncle Dennis. Sean's appearance had always skewed to the Red Irish side of the family, while Max was a poster boy for the Black Irish model.

So different they had looked, so linked they had been. First cousins, blood brothers, best friends.

"You're Michael, aren't you?" Deirdre accused, stepping between Max and Sean. "You turned traitor and disappeared, and now you're back?"

There Max was, between Kathleen at his back and Sean's defender at his front. He sensed Kathleen relaxing as the gladiator games between family began.

"Sean," Max said. "All the evidence and witnesses said you hadn't survived. That's what the Ulster government cabled to your parents, our parents. We all believed it and grieved."

"This is one witness," Deirdre said, her yellow eyes blazing like topazes on fire, "who didn't stick around to testify. I'd seen him, an American boyo in the middle of a bloody war zone. He wouldn't leave," she told Max. "He wouldn't leave without *you*, although you'd had no such qualms. I had to drag him away from the pub bar, and wasn't fast enough."

She lifted her left arm and pulled up her cardigan sleeve, exposing burn scar tissue that resembled a Jackson Pollock painting.

"And you!" She turned on Kathleen before Max could react, black pupils overwhelming her pale-ale eyes as she recognized her. "You, acting like a true daughter of Ireland and then flirting like a whore to turn two naive boyhood friends into rivals. You, playing God, and luring one from the bombing site, and not the other, saving one and not the other. Well, I saved Sean, banshee witch! I got him away.

"They say you became a money machine for the IRA, but I always knew your kind. You were just a slut lookin' to ruin men for your own pride and pleasure. I should take your eyes out."

And she lunged to do just that.

Max reached out an arm to stop her a second earlier than Sean did the same. Their forearms crossed like swords, straight and tense, and Deirdre rebounded as the men's eyes met.

Right arm works, thank God, Max tallied. *Left side…iffy.*

The men stepped back as Deirdre did.

"We should talk," Max said.

Sean knew whom he was addressing. "Deirdre, watch the woman here in the front lounge. We'll be in the rear one."

Sean turned without revealing his full face, or his left side, and limped around the corner. Max evaluated Deirdre and Kathleen. Deirdre was standing with feet wide and braced, fists on hips. Kathleen had turned sideways to her, watching the woman, as poised to move in any direction as a snake.

Each stood tensed, broadcasting hate, showing the defensive fire of a bear defending her cub. He knew his she-bear wanted the opposite outcome for him. Kathleen wanted Max to be devastated, and welcomed any confessionals between the cousins that would drive the thumbscrews deeper.

Her motives didn't bother Max at all. The would-be bond-breaker had become an inadvertent matchmaker. It was down to a wrestling match between him and Sean with the angels of their better beings. Between the two careless, impulsive teenagers they had been and the wounded men their separate lives had made them. They needed to know how, and why, and why not.

And the women, however well or ill intentioned, couldn't affect or change a moment of that.

Sean kept his back turned as Max entered the room. "Close the door," he said.

His voice was deeper now, a reminder of how young they'd really been that Irish summer of long ago.

As Max complied he heard the two metallic *pings* in sequence. A paranoid would think of a gun being cocked, but Matt wasn't surprised to see two open bottles of beer standing on the kitchen counter. An under-counter cap remover explained the pings.

"We drink home-style," Sean said, holding out a brown bottle.

"Fine by me." He knew pouring beer into glasses would be clumsy for Sean.

"There." Sean pointed. "Take that stool. The kitchen's been redone with all-American bells and whistles, breakfast bar and stools."

"Impressive. It's a stunning location," Max said, leaning his hip on a stool.

"This valley is beyond pleasant, and handy for tourists, being equidistant from Belfast and either coast. How'd you hook up with Kathleen again? In America? How did you find me?" Sean sat on a stool near the kitchen's farmhouse sink.

"I can't say I've looked for you all this time. Some human remains left were powder and bone. Your DNA was found in the pub wreckage. I accompanied what seemed to be all that was left of you home to Racine for a funeral and burial."

"With Father Flynn officiating."

"The same."

"Must have gone on for hours."

Max shrugged. "Long enough. So. Why weren't you at your own funeral?"

"Deirdre's right. I stayed too long at the Fair. She did too, on account of me."

"On account of you waiting for me?"

Sean ignored Max's self-blaming interjection. "I didn't believe Deirdre at first, that it was so urgent I leave. I'd been drowning my sorrows at you waltzing off with Kathleen. Got stubborn and tipsy. Got Deirdre injured as well as my damn self."

"I'm sorry, Sean. I've been sorry for all these years."

"Your problem. I've got plenty enough of my own."

"Such as?"

"It's not pretty." He turned his full face toward Max finally, Max braced for his worst nightmare, a badly burned face, ear gone, eye perhaps damaged, with the familiar red-brown color floating within a skin and bone setting melted into a mask of scar tissue.

But, no, though the sight was bad enough. Max remembered high school guys bewailing the zits and pock marks of acne. He and Sean had escaped the curse, until the pub bombing. Sean's freckled cheek had become a minefield of black bits of shrapnel and pale scarring, far less devastating than third-degree burns, but severe enough to make startled people politely look away.

"I say I got it in service." Sean's weary smile was symmetrical, a better sight for Max. "I don't add it was in service to teenage stupidity."

"Which I heard about in quintuplet when I got home."

"Our parents, of course." Sean frowned. "Who else?"

"Father Flynn."

"I imagine your first confession after getting home would be giving the good father an opportunity to mete out a stiff amount of penance."

"My first mortal sin," Max agreed. "A month of daily rosaries. What about your arm?"

Max nodded at Sean's left arm, held cocked in the sweater sleeve is if in an invisible sling. A sling of scar tissue. The left hand

and fingers were untouched, looking artificial in their normality. A simple gold band on the third finger attested to Deirdre's loyalty that had become love.

Sean filled him in. "Besides the beauty mark, no hearing on the left side. Permanent limp. Bum arm. I'm used to it, and to people adjusting to it. Otherwise, I function quite well here. Deirdre's a wonder. Her own burns were of a lesser degree; at least I managed that. She's the 'front' for our operation. I don't often see the first-time guests, or rather, more importantly, they don't see me except at a distance in the traditional visored cap, mucking the grounds and gardens. Some repeaters I socialize with."

Max drank down a third of the beer. "That's why you never came home, Sean? Never told anyone you were alive? You didn't want them to share your pain?"

"Mike, it was over a year before I was even able to think straight. The IRA took me for one of their own. They'd wanted 'innocents' cleared out of the targeted pub, particularly American tourists."

"Particularly American donors," Max said bitterly.

"You knew their cause was just, Mike. That's why we came north to see for ourselves."

"We came north because we were punks. Teenage towers of bravado. We wanted to drink beer and score with girls. We wanted adventure, a last reckless summer before college and marriage and kids. And, yes, I believed the cause was right, but not the means, and I especially believed that after a pub bombing killed my best friend. Why the hell didn't you ever tell me? Or the damn family?"

"After taking my bearings from that long year of skin grafts and rehab, I thought it best they remember me as I was. I wasn't going to college, Mike. I wasn't getting married, or didn't think I was. And children? 'Twas against the church, but I'd not bring children into this intolerant, bomb-ridden world. And it's even worse now."

"'Twas," Max repeated. "A bit of a brogue sounds good on you, Sean."

"Are you going home and telling them about me, Mike?"

"Home? Telling them? I've been away almost as long as you."

"What? Why the hell?" Max hated seeing Sean's wonder expressed on his two-sided face. If he spent enough time with him, he knew the scars would fade in his consciousness and he'd see Sean as he was now without pain. As Deirdre saw him.

"Why didn't you stay at home, Mike?"

"Look at it. Two cherished sons beg for a solo trip to the Auld Sod as a high school graduation present," Max said. "Proud parents grant our wish to revisit the family roots. They give us tons of addresses in Ireland, but after a few obedient rounds, we hop up to Northern Ireland to see the 'Troubles' first-person. Only one son comes back, with a pile of presumed ashes to bury."

Sean bent his head. "I've always imagined a fine funeral mass."

"No doubt about the mass. But." Max waited until Sean raised his head to look him in the eyes. "One son is gone. The other son is hale and healthy and had avoided the bombing by the skin of his teeth. Why?

"Do I tell them I was busy committing mortal sin with a pretty Irish colleen, an act that made me a man now? No, I wasn't a man. I was the stupid young fool who chased a skirt to leave my cousin, my brother, to die in an IRA pub bombing.

"The dead boy's parents can't stand the sight of me. My own parents are deeply puzzled about why we weren't together, not that they wished me your fate. All my tap dancing and evasions didn't explain why I was the 'miracle' survivor and you were not. Why we inseparable friends would separate. I couldn't even seek absolution in confession for that part of it. Father Flynn was a meddling old fellow, all for good reason, as he would judge it."

Sean turned a bit more toward Max. "I heard later you'd come back. I know what you did. I found out after my year in hell. You went after the IRA agents who bombed the pub, IDed them and got them arrested and in jail."

"I thought they were executed." Max was relieved to learn he wasn't a murderer by proxy.

"No. Sentenced to life, and that was overturned with the Peace. You still got an IRA price put on your head for that. I figured you'd head for Wisconsin and safety and forget about me. Now you're telling me, after all that, you exiled yourself from home too?"

"Yup." Max leaned forward to clink bottles. "We went off the reservation together, and, apart, we stayed lost and loose and following our own stubborn courses. We are indeed two of a kind."

"Christ!" Sean's good hand slammed the beer bottle down on the butcher-block countertop. "Deirdre wanted to blame you, but I wouldn't let her. I stayed dead, stayed away, so that *you* could have a normal life with the family. And now you say you didn't take it? Why the hell not?"

"Tracking those pub bombers, I discovered a knack for undercover work. My youth and vengeful self-hate and fury were assets. I was recruited as a counterterrorism agent. My mentor was a magician who taught me the trade as a perfect cover for going anywhere in the world. I couldn't stand seeing the questions on the faces of our families, Sean. I stayed away out of cowardice."

"Me, too, maybe," he said with a weary laugh. "Aren't we a pair? Send in the clowns."

"Except, it's so good to see you, talk with you again. Clear this crap out of the cupboards."

"You pity me."

"Are you kidding? I've been a rolling stone. I had a girl and the sun was always shining, and then...my past caught up with me again. I had to go on the run. My mentor, the wisest man I've ever known, was shot dead during our last visit to Northern Ireland just weeks ago. And the lovely Kathleen has never forgotten or forgiven me for caring more about your so-called death than her life. After years of raising money for the IRA in the Americas even after the peace, she found out I performed in Las Vegas."

"You performed in Las Vegas and the family never knew?"

"I used a deliberately corny performance name, 'The Mystifying Max'."

"Max? Where'd that come from?"

Max pursed his lips in a smile and waited.

"Oh, no! Not those awful middle and confirmation names."

"Yup. Michael Aloysius Xavier."

"And I'm Sean Owen Turlough. MAX, huh? Way better than SOT."

Max started laughing. They'd get going on an absurdity as teens and laugh themselves silly. Some of that back and forth was coming back. "Owen *Turlough*, really? It sounds like Turdlough. Forgot about that. And who can pronounce Aloysius?"

"Al-low-ish-is. It has 'Ish' built in. 'The mystifying Alo-ee-see-us' does not have a ring to it, and you sound like a drunk when you say it."

"On the other hand, SOT is an apt set of initials for an Irishman," Max said.

"Then let's have another brew," Sean said, still laughing.

"What about the women in the other room?"

"Let 'em drink tea." Sean pried open two more bottles and handed him one.

"I mean, Sean, Kathleen is a loaded pistol. She led me to you only to hurt us both. She may have killed a bunch of people."

"Deirdre knew how to handle her then, and she can do it even better now. We noticed a strange rental car lurking in the neighborhood a few weeks ago. Now I realize it was her. Is this her way of punishing you for pursuing the terrorists instead of the Black Velvet Band?"

"Yes. You know that song?"

"Every Irishman does." Sean crinkled his eyes to regard Max. "'Her eyes they shone like the diamonds…' Damn, but they did."

Max heard the next lines in his head. *And her hair hung down to her shoulders, tied up with black velvet band.*

Sean was still smiling at the memory. "You literally left your home and your family, like the song said, to follow…not the Black Velvet Band, but a course in counterterrorism. In a contrary way, you fulfilled our teenage quest, to contribute to the Irish cause." He ticked bottles with Max. "Here's to peace and the only terrorism-resolved country in the world. Our beautiful love, Ireland. And I fulfilled our quest to find Irish roots and love of the Old Country."

Max nodded, too touched to speak. Sean's spirit and laughter had made his injuries fade already.

Sean clicked bottles again. "And to those who perished in the good fight to end all fights. "You've had quite the James Bond run, Mike. I mean, Max. I'm sorry about your mentor's death. Who killed him? Was it what's left of the IRA?"

"I don't know. Maybe 'retired' IRA members with long memories or the so-called 'Real IRA', which remains a paramilitary organization and attacks drug dealers and criminal gangs. 'The Troubles' of a thousand years of discrimination and oppression to the point of genocide doesn't end with a clean edge. I should warn you. Kathleen O'Conner found you and told me you were alive. She's been stalking me and anyone I can vaguely call mine for the last year or two. The IRA winning an age-old battle and the resulting member retirement comes hard for a psychopath."

"She's still lethal? Kathleen?" Sean started up from the stool.

"Nothing Deirdre can't handle, as you said," Max reassured him. "I made sure of that before I left them together."

"So. You nailed her that day of the pub bomb, really?"

"Sean, that's crude."

"Yes, but it what was we both wanted and you got it."

"It shouldn't have happened. She was terminally damaged, from long before we met her."

"Aren't we all?" He looked hard at Max, both sides of his face exposed. "You pity her."

Max lowered his head. Nodded. "Hers is one of the more horrendous stories from the hell that was the Magdalene laundries. Asylums, they called them, and those imprisoned there certainly courted madness. She's expecting our reunion to savage both our wounds. Can you imagine that kind of…anger and pain?"

"I've spent my time in hell asking why me and therefore why not my best friend? It took years to grow up and realize that was unworthy of me, and you, and the God we profess to follow, including in the Way of the Cross. That was the whole point, wasn't it? Humankind is capable both of uplifting and casting down and will suffer for either. Our job is to do better than expected. Let's disappoint the poor girl. I'm grateful she found me, and that you cared enough to find me. I'm grateful you see the me beneath life's scars. I'm grateful we're alive and can quit kicking our own asses for long-ago misconceptions."

Max got up to clink bottles together. "Nothing like some Irish beer to banish the crud of almost twenty years. To union and reunion."

Sean's grin was back, the one that made him look like Huck Finn. "To Deirdre and Ireland. I love it here, Max. I love maintaining the place and the land. The sunsets almost knock your eyes out. I wouldn't change anything."

They stood at the same time. Sean looked shocked. "My Gawd, I believe you've grown two or three inches since we were last together."

"Probably. Perhaps it's the rack Kathleen's had me on. What are we going to do about her?"

"Go and see if Deirdre has had to hog-tie her."

"Seriously?"

"We keep some sheep to shear. Sure, a bit of a thing like Kathleen is lighter than any ewe."

"As kids, we always longed for Ireland long distance, Sean." Max nodded. "And you've got it, in a time of more peace than ever before."

"In fact, I had a role in some of those discussions, but I'm retired now, and content."

"I envy you."

"Retirement?"

"Contentment." Max slapped his palms on his unlikely jeans, plain and strong, like the life Sean had made for himself.

They returned to the front lounge, where the big American "picture window" of the '50s made an Old-World barn into a modern *HGTV* viewing palace.

The landscape as dimming, the distant blue hills almost luminescent. Flowing waves of shades of green were darkening and melding together. A peachy glow edged Ireland's western land mass that served as the selvage edge of England and Europe. This was the bookend to Homer's "rosy-fingered dawn" described in his *Odyssey*, Max thought, only this was sunset. He felt that his own odyssey was almost coming to an end.

He caught himself glancing at Kathleen, whom he caught in the same act. The scenic beauty was too overpowering not to share. This embodied the "terrible beauty" of Ireland and the Irish cause to be free of England, as the poet Yeats had called it, thinking of the woman he'd loved, Maud Gonne, a patriot so fierce she declined his love.

Deirdre stood, her tall, sturdy, rounded form reminding Max of a mother goddess. "Sean is cooking dinner. I'll get him started and bring us all a glass of Madeira to toast the sunset. These are the most beautiful in the world."

In the picture window the white wrought-iron table and chair set glowed with an unearthly light-lavender shade, as white objects did in the black lights of a strip club stage. Kathleen's pale face shared the halo effect.

Max grinned at his own comparison. Strip club? Wild, Northern Ireland was the antithesis of pop culture sleaze. Everything...the air, the view, the light, the surrounding sea was so clean it could have been etched on the mind and emotions like a laser light, like the famous Waterford Irish crystal.

Deirdre had approached on silent feet over the rug and set delicate glasses on the large square coffee table in front of the modern sectional sofa.

"I'll be wi' you in a minum," she said, backing away like the clouds shrouding the horizon.

Alone together.

"You spoke the truth," Max told Kathleen. "You did find Sean. Alive."

"I heard you laughing in there. You and Sean. What do you have to laugh about? Him disfigured and toiling in a bed and breakfast on the back of beyond, you leaving the woman you loved behind to marry another man."

"Chill, Kathleen," Max told her. "You're back in the land of your birth, having accomplished your aims. I'm here, as you wanted, an exile again. I warn you. I won't prosecute you, I won't obsess over you. I won't be what you need any more than I was almost twenty years ago."

She kept silent.

"And I'm grateful to you," he added, savoring a sip of the sweet wine.

"Grateful! As well you should be. I got you out of the doomed pub. I lured you away to the park. *You*! I picked you. Of all the men and boys I could have had with a snap of my fingers and twitch of my ass, and did, proving it over and over, I had you that day while your cousin was suffering and almost dying. I had you."

"I had a girl and she had me," he said, "and the sun wasn't always shining. You were the thing I desired most in that moment, that I forsook my cousin-friend and my faith for, and well willing to do so. You were beautiful and brave and a fierce patriot, most of all."

"So you might have loved me. For the moment, I suppose. That ex-priest who tried to analyze me said so. Your rival."

"It's not all rivals and religion and truth or dare, Kathleen. My emotional memory is kaput, but I think I must have loved you, as much as a randy teenager understands that concept. I'm sorry the kind of love you needed wasn't what a boy could give you."

"I had no faith," she mumbled. "I had nothing but my anger and my nerve and my female assets. I was almost disappointed when you agreed to accompany me to the Sir Thomas and Lady Dixon Park so readily. I thought you were just like the rest. Until you touched me."

Max shut his eyes. Did a teasing itch of familiarity dredge up a memory, or a supposition? Yeah, it had to have been a moment a boy dreams of, fears, covets. And…he had shared it with a young woman who'd been an incredibly abused child from the Magdalene Asylums. He'd shared it with a hopeful soul, seeing something in him that wasn't harsh and dirty and corrupted. And he had not been worthy.

Mea culpa, mea culpa. My fault, my fault. I am not worthy.

Father Flynn would have been happy to hear that from him at last.

30
Paid Off

Breedlove, Conway and Gallagher, attorneys at law, weren't far from Sam Funeral Home's, so Temple and Electra shared Temple's two-seat red Miata while Diane drove her rental car to meet them there.

Temple had to wait in the expected mahogany and leather outer office while Electra and Diane, apparently the only heirs, went into the attorney's inner office. She tapped her toe impatiently on the forest-green plush carpeting while paging through *Newsweek* magazine. Thank God some magazines were still in print.

She wanted to *be* there, an eyewitness at this oft-filmed cinematic cliché, the second she'd viewed today, The Reading of the Will. The first had been the Black Widow from Central Casting.

Of course, with one lawyer who knew no one involved, including the deceased, and two fairly friendly ex-wives, the event was not likely to be drenched in drama.

Which was why Temple leaped out of her seat when a soprano "*No!*" boomed from behind the closed door to the inner office.

The outburst was followed by a bass male murmur and rapid breathless soprano arpeggios.

Temple paced the waiting room.

She neared the door, stopped, and listened with all her attention. She could hear nothing clearly, except the counterpoint of agitated high and low calming tones.

Then all sound stopped.

Temple waited and wondered, and was caught flat-footed in the figurative sense when the door burst open, emitting a dazed-looking Electra and Diane.

Ethan Gallagher, a thin man in a stuffy, dark three-piece suit that looked horribly hot for Vegas, followed them out, frowning at Temple's proximity. "Remember, ladies, you don't have to reveal the terms of the will to anyone except the police."

He glared at Temple. She glared back and followed the women into the hall. "Well, Mr. Gallagher's parting words were on the rude side," she said. "Unless you want to keep the terms private from snoops like me."

Diane hesitated, but Electra didn't. "I need a drink. I need to sit down. Ditto for Diane. Take us somewhere, Temple. We are too gobsmacked to think."

A PR person's main meeting places are in the community she covers, its restaurants and watering holes. In Las Vegas, there were enough of those to trip over every fifty feet, even at 10:00 a.m. in the morning. After giving Diane directions, in fifteen minutes she had them all installed at the Stratosphere's 108th-floor Air Bar, with Electra and Diane ordering four-dollar strawberry-lime frozen margaritas, set down on paper napkins that read: *AFRAID OF HEIGHTS.*

Temple's stomach quavered at so much alcoholic sweetness, especially at extreme heights, so she stuck to ice water. She was driving, after all.

The cool green neon interior was fairly deserted and the 360-degree view of Las Vegas looked dusty and distant, like any southwest desertscape.

"So what's the news?" Temple asked.

Diane and Electra noisily sucked up flavored crushed ice. Diane spoke first. "I got the house in Dayton, Ohio."

"Is that a good thing?" Temple asked.

"At my age, any house is an asset," Diane said. "I didn't expect him to leave me anything."

"And Electra?"

Electra was staring out at the drab landscape, slowly slurping the lurid drink in its lowly plastic glass in front of her. "I can't believe it."

"What you got in the will?"

Temple glanced at Diane, who nodded solemnly. "I can't believe it either. But the lawyer said the house is free and clear, no liens or anything. And Electra—"

"Jay had it in his will." Electra's eyes shone with tears. "He left me all his Vegas land and the buildings on it. So I've got your baby urban village going, Temple. And to think I cussed him out just before he died."

Temple couldn't reveal at this maudlin moment that she had a hugely hot idea for said urban village. Instead, she offered consolation.

"Jay made the bequest long before you yelled at him," Temple said with a smile. "That's fabulous. I wonder why he didn't tell you that?" She jumped down from her skimpy bar-height chair, her heels hitting the smooth floor with a clap like hands. "Let's find a window that overlooks your new empire."

She rushed to the slanted glass windows with *DO NOT LEAN ON* signs posted at regular intervals. Outside, clothed body parts and screaming faces flashed by as the Stratosphere's extreme thrill rides plunged willing riders up and down and around at fearsome heights and speed.

"We're right near the Pawn Stars village," Temple said.

"That looks like an ant hill," Diane exclaimed.

"Four thousand people a day," Electra quoted Temple.

But Temple's high heels were almost striking sparks off the shiny floor as she raced to another window view.

"Come on. This is the window we want. Look. Down there." Temple pointed. "There's the police substation roof and your penthouse atop the Circle Ritz and a little bit over and down, your new, big empty building and lot."

"Oh, my," Electra said. "It's more land than just that. I need to get home and look up my plat maps. I think I remember where Jay's parts began and ended, but we could probably get them from the city too." Her excitement ebbed. "I'll always remember that building as where Jay died, where he was killed."

"He wanted you to have it," Diane said quietly, slipping her arm through Electra's. "He provided for us both. That's an amazing thing for a divorced man to do. If he hadn't been addicted to gambling—"

"There you go," Electra said. "A phrase that could go on many a Vegas headstone."

Temple put an arm through Electra's free one and pulled both women back to the bar. "Let's finish our drinks with a toast to Jay Edgar and then go get our feet on the ground. *Your* new ground, Electra."

What she didn't say, and wasn't about to over the older women's strawberry-lime frozen margaritas, was that she hoped J. Edgar Dyson hadn't signed any irrevocable documents with the interested parties who'd seemed determined to fleece him, and maybe even had killed him after he'd signed on the dotted line. The bizarre manner of death and location sure wouldn't help authorities look farther than Electra or her friends.

Nor did Temple point out that Molina and company would consider Electra being Dyson's most significant heir made her an even more likely suspect for engineering his macabre murder.

31
Sleepless After Sunset

Mea culpa, mea *culpa. My fault, my fault, I am not worthy.*

Even with Sean and Deirdre looking on, Max thought a man who had come all this way with a woman to a remote Irish cottage ought do more than feel regret and move on.

"If I ran away after that intimate moment, Kathleen," he confessed, "I wasn't ready for the responsibility of such a pure and needful love. It was the worst mistake of my life. I've paid for it every day, and you've seen that I've paid for it every hour."

He laughed a little. "I wish there was something that would redeem the moment for you."

She shook her head. "You've won. You've forgotten, and I can't."

Before Max could answer, Deirdre spoke behind him. "See the glorious sunset you've brought with you, Michael Kinsella."

He and Kathleen automatically looked away from each other to the picture window again, where the sky was bleeding all the colors of a watercolor box into undiluted strands of peach and aqua and magenta and orange and purple and scarlet and iridescent mother-of-pearl blue.

"Mother of God," Deirdre's soft croon sounded like a lullaby, "'tis the loveliest spot on earth."

Max waited for Kathleen's raw outburst, but she remained silent.

Deirdre said briskly, "Sean has things under control at the stove. We'll sit outside. Will ye take out the settings?"

"Of course," Max said, collecting Kathleen's glass with his—broken glass was a weapon—and heading for the kitchen to deposit them on the table. Sean wasn't there.

Deidre indicated a cupboard with tableware in ceramic pots and the dinner plates on a high shelf. Deidre must stand five-eight, Max thought, almost Molina tall.

He smiled to think of no-nonsense, emotions-stowed Molina peeking in on the dramatis personae in this domestic scene with utter shock.

Max reached for the plates and turned, almost bumping into Kathleen collecting knives and spoons and forks. He could feel her entire body tense to have someone standing this close, especially him.

He looked down on her shining black hair, wearing no black velvet band, and stroked his palm over it.

She remained frozen, staring down at the silverware in her hands, minutely trembling, fighting the instinct to lash out.

He stepped away without incident, and saw Deirdre watching.

"Michael, be a love, and take the butter dish out as well? Ah! *Max*, I mean."

Hands full, luckily, Max and Kathleen elbowed themselves out the pantry door to be ambushed by a Cinemascope version of the sunset that suffused the entire sky.

While their eyes feasted, their nostrils inhaled the smoky aroma of grilled steak. Sean stood at a portable stainless steel barbecue setup against the cottage's textured stone wall.

"A high-end barbecue?" Max asked. "Not a common item of Irish charm."

"It charms the tourists," Sean said. "The brews are on ice in the washtub, if that's charmin' enough for an Ugly American like you. And the ladies might need shawls against the goin' of the light. Deirdre'll give you a couple inside." Sean stepped forward to pull the heavy wrought-iron chair out for Kathleen, who stared at the thing as if it'd bite her.

Max darted inside to take two big serving dishes from Deirdre and ask for the shawls.

Forty-five minutes later, the food was gone and the lingering sunset was nearly gone. Two lanterns moved from the side table now flickered on all their faces, almost like flames.

Sean had fetched a wine bottle for the women. Max had tired of the strong Irish ale and itched for three fingers of Jameson's, but drank what his host did, eager not to challenge the habits of the house in this peaceful place.

"Have you thought of adding a fire pit, Sean?" Max asked. "It'd take away the chill."

"Too American, Max. The tourists like their comforts, but also like a bit of the primitive. Except for the stainless steel barbie, a must for the Aussies."

"You're right. You don't want to make this into a suburban backyard in Racine." Max looked around. "St. Patrick banished the snakes from Ireland, it's said, but I believe he exiled the mosquitoes too."

"Aye, I don't miss the mosquitoes in Wisconsin, as big as butterflies," Sean told Deirdre.

"And now carrying exotic and lethal diseases," Max said.

"But you don't have mosquito problems in Las Vegas."

"No, drought though."

"I can't stand it!" Kathleen's voice shattered the peace. "Look at you. Two self-satisfied retiree ex-patriots reminiscing over your pints."

"We *are* ex-pats of a sort," Max told Sean, ignoring her outburst.

"I don't mean from America, you dunces!" Kathleen had stood, her cheeks ruddy with wine and fury, her shawl clutched around her. "From the Cause. Even Michael here once gave a tinker's damn about undermining the resistance's bombing plots, and you, Sean, you were taken in by the IRA and ended up at a negotiation table. All that I did for years to raise money for guns and gold is fading like the setting sun into futility."

"Because we've won the peace," Deirdre said quietly.

"It will never last. The Orangemen still march in Belfast."

"And," Max said, "there's still a price on my head, or else I wouldn't be going to Belfast to find where Garry Randolph's body has been buried."

"Once again," Kathleen said, "you set yourself on a quest for a dead man. I suppose the living aren't good enough for you. I can arrange more such quests."

"Sit down, Kathleen," Deirdre said.

"Why should I sit at table with you lot of traitors?"

"This is my table and you will sit down, Kathleen."

To Max's amazement, she obeyed. Deirdre's intense command must have echoed a nun's from the Magdalene asylum. A stern parental "No!" can sometimes make an attacker pause. Max had used that trick, but Deirdre had not shouted.

"Body?" Sean asked Max. "Buried? Who is Garry Randolph?"

"The counterterrorism mentor I told you about," Max said, "who performed as the magician Gandolph the Great. My bungee-based magic act was sabotaged in Vegas and I fell, broke both my legs and a good bit of my brain, the part that remembers. Garry took me to Europe to escape, heal and revisit my past. We were on the run and got tangled up with some IRA remnants in Belfast. Trying to outdrive a shooting spree, I…Garry got hit. I…do you have any whiskey?"

Sean nodded at Deirdre.

"I'll have some too," Kathleen said. Sullenly.

Deirdre paused beside her, and put a light hand on her shoulder. "I'll bring the whiskey and then later you and I will have our say."

The bottle wasn't Jameson's but a good brand, nevertheless. Deirdre brought Waterford lowball glasses and the lantern light made the whiskey into liquid orange sunsets in the bottom of their glasses.

So it came to this, Max thought, night coming on and the four of them all still alive and older and drinking together in Ireland. He wondered if he should check under the table for a bomb.

He told Sean how Garry had put him in a private Swiss sanitarium to recover, how assassins may have found him, and Max had to escape into the Alps with casts on both legs. He told how he survived to reach Zurich and contract Garry, omitting mention of the woman psychiatrist from the clinic who was his doctor and/or hostage or assigned assassin.

Reminding Kathleen of the dangerously bright and beautiful Revienne Schneider might trigger another jealous jihad. Seeing

Revienne leave his Las Vegas house probably had spurred Kathleen to burn down the place with him in it. She'd certainly seemed surprised to see him when he'd hijacked her on this flight to the Old Sod.

"So," Max concluded, "when I finally connected with Garry, we flew to Ireland. He hoped retracing the path you and I made many years ago, Sean, from Ireland to Northern Ireland, would help my memory. We interviewed all shades of former IRA members in Belfast, and irritated someone enough to try to kill me. Us."

Max glanced at Kathleen, her shoulders hunched in the softly woven shawl, her hands cupped around the glass, warming the crystal as the liquor warmed her.

"What did you do with Garry's body?" Sean asked.

Max shut his eyes. "I had to leave it with our abandoned car in Belfast, hoping that his friends among the old IRA people who made the peace would claim it for a decent burial."

"And so do I," Sean said, leaning forward to put his good right hand on Max's wrist. "I'll help you find your friend if you reach an impasse."

Max was too stressed to do more than nod.

"Did the that trip, and this, help your memory?" Deirdre asked.

Max sighed. "Somewhat."

Even with them there, he couldn't afford to let down his guard in front of Kathleen. She'd palmed a steak knife when the meal was cleared. He'd disarm her before beddy-bye time. She might have slipped her straight razor through airport security too.

He laughed to himself, thinking of Matt Devine trying to glimpse if she had any cat-scratch scars on her back and the back of her legs during one of their 3:00 a.m. hotel rendezvous. He would bet the ex-priest had sweated that assignment.

Come to think of it, he was glad that job was done and he didn't have to worry about it. Kathleen had definitely *not* been one of the two Darth Vader-masked figures who'd tried to threaten the cabal of magicians turned would-be heist operators, all in a search for Kathleen's collected but now lost hoard of money and guns for the IRA.

Even as Max savored the straight whiskey and the cool darkness, he realized this family-like atmosphere was priming Kathleen nerves.

"Cheers," Kathleen said, lifting her glass. "What was it we were to settle, Deirdre? Why are you so eager to embrace the man who left your husband there in the pub to be blown up, and you along with him?"

"Boys. They were boys, Kathleen."

"Ireland makes boys men at fourteen."

"Only because of the Troubles. And who was it hangin' around the IRA men like a rock star groupie, jumpin' on any fresh outsider comin' in?"

"They were foolish not to use women in the Cause, except to breed more of them and nurse them when they were hurt or dyin'."

"Sure, and you wanted to fight like a man, Kathleen, only you used woman's wiles. You weren't a patriot. You thrived on the anger and hatred for the British Protestants and army, well deserved, but you needed the high emotions and the dance of betrayal for your own selfish reasons. You lived to turn one against the other, and so you did. Oh, you knew how to flirt and tease and you ached to destroy. You craved the attention, but despised the men who gave it to you."

"Deirdre," Sean began.

"Stay out of it. This is woman's work." She turned to Kathleen again. "I saw you playing one American lad against the other. They were innocents wantin' a bit of sin. They knew nothing of the grinding oppression we Catholics felt. Sure, they feared most the confessional back home once they'd stepped over the so-sweet forbidden fruit line thousands of miles away, not the tinderbox that was Northern Ireland. You were three-and-twenty. They were randy virgins of seventeen, well reined in by the Church. Our home-grown boys and men knew to dodge your temptations. They feared the confessional too. Or, if hardened, were willing to engage with you in a contest of who was using whom. But these two, their rivalry was trivial. Neither would have long resented the other for 'winning the beauteous colleen'. And the winner would have felt duly guilty afterwards."

Deirdre leaned forward on her folded arms. "You knew the pub needed clearing of innocents. Yet you lured one away and left the other unwarned. Did you choose Michael, or was he just the most susceptible?"

"What does it matter, Deirdre? Here they are again, holding hands on the table. If I thrived on destruction, as you say, it didn't work."

"It matters to *me*." Deirdre's passionate intensity matched Kathleen's for the first time. "I risked my life to save the boy you left behind. What made him the expendable one, Kathleen? What were you thinking besides the need to see innocent emotions toyed with and innocent blood shed? Why Sean and not Michael?"

"No," Max said. "We don't need to know. I doubt even Kathleen knows or can be trusted to speak the truth of it."

"You were more daring," Sean told him. "I thought you were taking a risk, to your soul or even health, but certainly not your life, when you went off with her. The idea was exciting, but I could never have gone through with anything. I really didn't want to win the prize. And," he added, smiling that slightly off-kilter Huck Finn smile at Deirdre, "I got the real prize."

"I may be sick," Kathleen said.

"You *are*. Then and now." Deirdre's judgment was unsparing.

"She'd spent her time in hell three times over by the time she was twelve," Max told Deirdre.

"Don't you dare defend me," Kathleen told Max, flaring to hiss-and-spit life. "That's not what I needed from you."

"You needed it from someone, and didn't get it."

Deirdre wouldn't do it for sure. "So Sean and I should be put through Purgatory again, Max? I think not. You're asking me to have her under my roof? I say no to even one night."

"We can't chain her outside, like a dog, Deirdre," Sean said.

Deirdre looked pleased at the idea.

"We'll drive on." Max checked his watch. Cell phone reception in these rural areas was patchy, just as in congested Las Vegas.

"You'll not go off alone with her again," Sean said, "save in sober daylight."

"What will we do with her, then?" Deirdre asked. "'Tis like having a scorpion under one's pillow."

Kathleen had sat back, swirling the whiskey in her glass, dropping out of the conversation, probably reveling in being considered so dangerous.

Max eyed her. Thought of the razor. "I'm a risk-taker, as you say, Sean. I'll leave with her now."

"No, man. These unlit rural roads are treacherous for a stranger. I won't let you go," Sean said.

"Wished that had worked the first time." Max grinned ruefully. "All right, I'll take her away in the morning. Meanwhile, you can put her in the main bedroom with me and lock your door for the night."

"Be gone wi' ye!" Deirdre exclaimed. "Do ye never learn?"

"On the contrary, I learn too much."

Kathleen stood. "You expect me to accept such shabby hospitality? I'll see you in hell."

Sean nodded. "'Tis certain you know that terrain well." He looked at Max. "You're the super-agent man. Guard yourself well this night."

Sean led Kathleen inside, but Deirdre stayed to catch Max by the sweater-clad arm. "You'll not make the same mistake again with her. No shenanigans?"

"Not in a thousand years."

Kathleen was quiet, even lamb-like, her shawl clutched around her, going upstairs. At the bedroom door she turned to look up at him, the spitting image of Vivien Leigh as Scarlett O'Hara. "How noble of you to have sacrificed yourself again."

"Inside," he told her. "I know about the steak knife." He tested the pocket of her silk blazer and pulled out the suspected plum.

He stuck his head into the hall before anyone disappeared for the night. "Deirdre, a lost lamb from the tableware for your dishwasher." He flourished the knife.

"That'd be the chef's," Sean said. "You're crazy, man."

"Yup. But I enjoy a challenge. Do you mind taking custody of Kathleen's traveling bag for the night?"

He handed it out and locked the door.

Kathleen spread her arms wide, the shawl serving as wings. "Do you need to search me for a nail file? A dangerous hangnail?"

"As tempting as ever. No. We'll sleep in shifts. You in the bed first. I on the chair."

"You don't intend to sleep at all."

"No. Do you?"

"No."

"Luckily, it's nearly midnight and this bedroom is on the east side of the cottage," Max said. "The sun will bathe us in spotlights in no time."

"Luckily for you."

He took the chair and nudged the ottoman nearer with his foot. "Really, Kathleen? Can you never separate sex and homicide? You should be a cop."

"I'm not a murderer. At least, not directly."

"Perhaps yes, perhaps no. I suppose you could argue that you never intended your hired doubles to die for you. What you do excel at is seducing other people to do your dirty work. I understand why you have so little faith in humanity."

"Oh, shut up. You 'understand'. I'm sick in the head, and you're a long-suffering hero."

"I do like the sound of that, but I'm giving up the martyr thing. Can you give up the psychopath thing?"

She sat on the edge of the bed and kicked off her shoes. "I didn't think."

"About what? And when"

"At the pub. Who'd get blown up, who wouldn't...other than that it wouldn't be me, and, thanks to me, you. I knew Deirdre would take care of Sean. She'd been making cow's eyes at him for an hour, but all he could see was me."

"You were a sight to behold."

"You can't mean that."

"No. I can't mean that."

She stared at him, seeking truth. "Your memory's untrustworthy."

"Yes. But...I can see what I might have thought."

"And that was?"

"That was what those who'd worst abused you thought. That you had the passionate spirit of an innocent child bracketed in beauty. It inspired them to envy, and to commit torment and destruction. It must have inspired me with a need to capture it, but the only word the world knows for that is lust. Pity. I know why you had to become them to escape memories of the abuse, but it's a goddamn shame."

Kathleen leaned against the headboard, arms crossed, and shrugged.

"Did you know about Sean surviving right after the bombing, or find out later?" he asked.

"No. I left soon after you vanished. They'd been wanting me to go to the Americas to solicit money for the resistance, and it was better I lay low after having been at the pub before the explosion. In fact, I was listed as among the lost."

"Is that when you started using the name Rebecca sometimes?" Max asked. "And why Rebecca?"

"Because she was a bad girl," Kathleen said with sudden vehemence.

"In a book."

"I see Miss Temple Barr has been refining your literary tastes to potboilers."

"She mentioned the book, so I looked up a movie review. Rebecca was dead, but her selfish, manipulative spirit haunted everyone who'd been in her life. I suppose she was your role model? That's why you used the name?"

Kathleen crouched like a cat at the edge of the bed, while her lips spelled out the answer. "'Rebecca' was the name the nuns assigned me in the asylum."

"They didn't use your given name?"

"They always changed the inmates' names to show them what they had been and who they were meant to be...was nothing anymore. It also kept us hidden and unable to find even each other afterwards. I found the novel, though. The so-called heroine was a sheep."

"But you were born there, to an...inmate. She couldn't even name you?"

"My mother's name was Kathleen, but they called her Dolores because her beauty brought her so much sorrow. I took her birth name back after I escaped."

Max was confounded again by the endless cruelties piled on these young girls, innocents preyed upon by boys and men, some even in their own homes, all of them surrendered by their families with shame and rejection, and with no other place to go.

"Most of the records have been destroyed, the Church says," Max mused. "Changing given names would further confuse any oral history. Clever and cruel."

"The Church lies."

"Doubtless. So does the government. Those severe, strict Old World attitudes of punishing women for their sexuality live on in the third world and even in the U.S., all in the name of religion." Max paused. "Maybe not in Canada. Canada seems more civilized than most." The dry comment put her off guard. "I've tracked you. The records say you and your daughter died."

"They couldn't admit I was able to run away with her." Kathleen's smile was radiant. "I was always a bad girl."

"You were a formidable girl. And admitting you'd escaped might have caused an investigation into the pedophile priest who raped you." He paused. "Why did you name your daughter Iris?"

"You've found her every secret. Not mine." She smiled smugly. "Those I chose to take her to were atheists. I wouldn't burden my child with a saint's name or any variety the *un*Blessed Virgin's name. The flowers have no denomination."

"Well…Iris is the Greek goddess of the rainbow. You can't escape religion in world history."

"Do you say so? I didn't get much education in Greek, although I learned Spanish and Portuguese in my travels."

"Rebecca," Max repeated, returning to Kathleen's Magdalene name.

And then…he understood something more about her, something deep and devilish and unutterably sad. His feet pushed the ottoman away as he leaped up.

"Now I see it. *Rebecca*, the book and movie. That's why you burned down my house! The housekeeper who was insanely devoted to dead Rebecca burned down the manor house, Manderley, so

Rebecca's husband and new wife would never have a place to call home. *Maxim* de Winter was her husband, and murderer. That's why you torched Garry's and my house. You wanted to destroy my memories of someone, anyone who loved me."

"You're mad." Kathleen's laugh was forced. "I don't live my life by a *book*. You humiliated me there, in that house, for the first time since the Magdalene asylum. All of you people and even a pack of cats, as if one of you were a witch or warlock." Her fingertips smoothed the fading quartet of slashes on her cheek.

"You had the satisfaction of inflicting some damage and humiliation yourself that night." He rubbed the back of his neck.

"Did I knock some memory back into you?" She was sitting on the edge of the bed now, swinging her stocking-clad feet, which didn't reach the floor, like a child. She was only a couple inches taller than Temple, Max reminded himself.

And here they were, reminiscing like classmates, as if they shared an advanced degree in Abuse and Terrorism 101.

"No," he said. "No memories. And, I imagine, a lot of possible memories I could have resurrected died in the fire."

"I should have torched that hellhole while we all were there."

"You can't afford repercussions of failed mayhem now. Sean knows you're back. He was influential in the IRA in fairly recent years."

"Influential in giving up the battle." She narrowed her eyes. "Where do you think I hid my razor?"

"I'm hoping in the travel bag I sent away."

"You can't send *me* away." She looked to the locked door. "You promised to control me." She looked at the LED numbers on the bedside table. "We'll not sleep and we've already discussed the only two books we have in common, Mr. de Winter."

"Wait. But not the film."

"I never saw the film of *Rebecca.*"

"I'm talking about the film of another kind of woman entirely."

"Oh, that Philomena. Named after a girl martyred at fourteen in the early days of the Church."

"Lord," Max said. "That sounds like Malala Yousafzai and other schoolgirls attacked and even killed by a religion desperate to keep women controlled. When was this?"

"I learned my church history. In 304 Rome. She is the patron saint of babies, infants, and youth." Kathleen's voice reeked with irony.

"Oddly amazing."

"Why?"

"Think about it. The book the film is based on, *The Lost Child of Philomena Lee*, has inspired thousands of Magdalene-adopted children to seek their birth mothers and information. It isn't easy, as we've said, with the girls in the convent forced to use other names and they never knew each other's true identities."

"Philomena went by 'Marcella'—" Kathleen shook her head, her beautiful black hair as glossy as onyx. "It's Martin Sixsmith who's the hero, the detective, who followed the few clues there were. Philomena didn't have the nerve to question the nuns and the Church. But Sixsmith…he was a fallen-away Catholic enraged by what he found. He had balls. He found the truth and created the exposé, not her."

Max wanted to smile. Kathleen didn't see that he was now playing Sixsmith to her Philomena Lee. She didn't want to confront the reality of her grown daughter, as Philomena had. She wanted only to nurse past grievances. Max needed to keep her off-balance, blinded by the roles that had always worked for her in that past.

"I understand why your keepers gave you the name they did," he said. "Google says Rebecca means 'beautifully ensnaring'."

"Oh, don't think the nuns back then had Google to underline their evil, only a wrathful God. We shall see how true I am to that name on this trip," she said, softly, seductively.

What really was her endgame? he wondered. She had his exclusive attention at last…but did she hope or need to seduce him again, or did she intend to kill him or get him killed?

32
Show Off

It had become dismayingly evident, during my earlier walkabout of the home site with the Misses Temple and Electra, that something dark and dirty is transpiring too close for comfort.

All my fringe senses (those a bit beyond the usual five) tell me that the Circle Ritz residents have only scratched the surface of what criminal or even mystical schemes may be deploying under our very noses.

This is not something I can share with the ever-skeptical Miss Midnight Louise. She is a modern girl, and scoffs at my seasoned intuition.

So. The next step is clear. I must prepare to humble myself in pursuit of deeper intelligence. The only question is whether I begin this quest with the insufferable Karma, Queen of Metaphysical Mumbo-jumbo, or with the equally annoying Ingram, who sits literally atop books and books of information, and presumably has more private access to Google than I would ever dream of.

I decide that Ingram is the better bet.

I also decide that I will not boldly go via the bookstore front door, where Ingram can see me waiting and not make one attempt to attract Miss Maeveleen Pearl's attention to admit me. Arranging an audience with Ingram is always complex. So I hunker down at the building's side and wait for an opportune customer to appear, alongside of whose ankles I can slip within.

In my hunting days when I had to crouch in a prey-blind, I was prepared to wait patiently for hours upon a likely prospect. Alas, we are all now in an era of fast food, me included. Once I discovered

I could work at the Crystal Phoenix with a nearby fishing hole, the koi pond, and tourists spreading their bread upon the waters by dropping tidbits for my maintenance, patience flew out the window.

I had heard about the Great Bookstore Recession, whereby such enterprises large and small and independent and franchised faced terrible losses at the advent of digital books and online retailing, but until you have sat for four hours on a weekday waiting for a customer to come, you do not realize what a travesty all this is.

At last some soul with a late lunch hour walks by and straight for the front door. I am almost catatonic with boredom by then and barely shake myself into action in time to streak for a disappearing pair of ankles.

"Oh, my goodness," the woman says, spinning as I whisk past her and behind a table display. "Did you know," she asks the approaching Miss Maeveleen Pearl, "there is a cat in here?"

"Yes. He is sleeping in the window display. His name is Ingram. If you are allergic, I can remove him to the stockroom."

Stockroom? I visualize pairs of feline-size Old Salem penal stocks imprisoning Ingram, who already wears prison stripes. I see Ingram's fore-and-aft soft pink footpads (mine are Bad Boy black) sticking through the wooden manacles, for passing vermin to tickle with their feelers. A comforting picture.

"I love stores with resident cats," the woman customer is saying. "Ingram is a strong presence. I could swear I felt a welcoming fur-rub on my leg coming through the door."

"I do not doubt it," Miss Maeveleen says, leaning confidentially close. "I often think cats can astral-project."

"That is just what I am looking for, a fun mystery series. So there is one about a cat that astral projects?"

"If there is not, there soon will be," Miss Maeveleen assures her, guiding her to a shelf where every book cover features homebody tabbies surrounded by images of food, items from every imaginable domestic hobby, and things that go bump in the night.

Holy Sam Spade! I shake my head. These domestic slaves do not walk the walk (the mean streets) or talk the talk (though several seem to be more than somewhat chatty with their amateur sleuth owners). I am sworn not to talk to humans by my own druthers. I lead; they follow if they are smart.

Unfortunately, I can and do talk to the animal kingdom. A P.I. must have *some* reliable sources.

A low, slow, advanced-degree East Coast drawl unrolls behind me. "So, Louie, what brings you to my cozy nook?"

Ingram apparently resided with a Yale professor early in life. I turn and face the music, probably something maddeningly repetitive, like Bach.

"I did not realize we were neighbors now, Ingram. How long has this been going on?"

"Less than a year in this area. You stopped consulting me long before that. Apparently you joined the flight to All Things Internet, as my employer faced rising rents and dwindling brick-and-mortar customers."

"No, Ingram. Trust me. I interact with the Internet only when an errant toe activates it if my Miss Temple has left it on."

"*Hmm.* Now you need some live-and-in-person information and have come crawling back to me for free advice and research, I suppose."

"Er, I do not crawl."

"I would advise you to at least beseech if you want anything here."

"I only need important information about Las Vegas history that may result in a renaissance for the Thrill 'n' Quill and all its literary works."

"And you are going to accomplish this all by your large little self?"

"Can the oxymorons. Our two closest human associates will benefit, if we can prepare the ground for a fruitful future."

"You are saying a farmer's market will be joining this sorry little street of broken retail dreams?"

"Not necessarily, although it is not a bad idea. I was speaking metaphorically," I point out.

"That is too great a leap for a lowlife like you. Try plain English, if you can."

I hold my temper and shivs in check. "Someone vandalized the Lovers' Knot wedding chapel attached to the Circle Ritz and someone was killed in the old empty building down the street the other direction. You need to help me assist Miss Electra Lark, who owns the very floor your feet pad upon. If we can prove that this man named Dyson's killing is linked to an outfit that tried to force

Dyson, Miss Electra's ex-spouse, to sell his property in the area, the ladies can launch a new, improved retail concept."

"Human relationships are intricate and often deadly. You are saying Miss Maeveleen may be forced to move again otherwise?" Ingram's furrowed brown brow resembles corrugated cardboard. He sure is slow on the uptake.

"Yes! The purchasing party intends to turn the building into a huge strip-tease and sex salon club."

"Oh, my. What a sleazy twist of fate. Miss Maeveleen refused to carry *Fifty Shades of Gray* and now she would have its associated unmentionable products sold practically next door." Ingram shudders.

I lean close. "Then tell me about the building. I broke in to survey the crime scene and got a weird vibe there. I heard tell it has had many uses through the years before it ended up as an abandoned antique mall. There must be a reason someone was killed over it and the land it occupies."

I know I have Ingram in the center pad of my mitt when he curls his clipped nails against his chest and narrows his eyes. "This is not the first instance of homicidal violence on that site."

I am not a dunce when it comes to feline psychology. I assume a "mirroring" posture to further cement Ingram's decision to be my confidential informant once again. "You do not say. How do you know?"

"It was in a book. Everything is. It would not do you harm, Louie, to spend more time warming the covers of a good book than warming a TV remote between your tender pads."

My jet-black pads are way more street-seasoned than Ingram's effete paddies, but I nod without defensive comment, and go on. "Miss Electra says the building has had many previous tenants, back to its start as a nightclub."

"A nightclub?" Ingram sounds indignant. "Do you have any idea what kind of a nightclub?"

"I suppose the place offered the usual ho-hum human pursuits, strong drink and silly dances."

"*Hmm.* You are basically right for a change, but we are talking about the post-World War Two, pre-Strip Las Vegas, when Bugsy Siegel took over the creation of the Flamingo Hotel for the Chicago Outfit."

I am no scholar, but Vegas is my beat and I know its landmark moments. "That entire building is indeed a monument if it dates back that far. I also know a fragment of the original Flamingo is rumored to still exist in the current, many times remodeled version."

Ingram's front shivs mangle the needle-pointed pillow that bears his name. He must be auditioning for a cat cozy mystery cover.

"Imbecile," he murmurs with a French accent. "The nightclub here was a secret site."

"Secret?" All my PI instincts quiver.

"Underground."

"Literally, or figuratively?" I ask, giving an amused, intellectual sniff. Two can play at that game.

"Both," he ripostes, tapping the top of my mitt with a sharp nail. I guess you could call it a literal riposte.

I wait with bated, and baited breath. I would not want a whiff of my lunchtime tuna braised in shrimp sauce to distract Ingram from a revelation.

"You will recall," he goes on with a yawn, "that during Prohibition bathtub gin and other illegal quaffs were served in private clubs, often below-ground in basements."

"I recall, but not personally."

"Later, during World War Two another item of culture was forbidden."

"Marijuana?"

"Well, yes, that, but this was in the wearing apparel category."

"All right. I give up. The only wearing apparel I am up to date on are my Miss Temple's high-heeled shoes and the collars forced upon domestic dogs. And perhaps a certain flamingo-pink fedora once forced upon me during my À la Cat TV commercial days."

Ingram has ignored me. "The establishment I reference featured swing dancing and such popular new libations of the decade as the Martini, Manhattan, Gimlet. Whiskey Sour, Gin rickey, Sidecar, Brandy Alexander, Brandy Stinger, Pink Lady, Tom Collins, Rob Roy, Sloe gin fizz, Bloody Mary, and the Shirley Temple."

By the end of this recital I am doing a Slow Gin Fizz in anticipation of a possible slugging match between Tom and Rob, and Mary and Shirley.

"Rum," Ingram drones on, "was in more supply during the war years, so rum cocktails like the Hurricane and the Dark 'n' Stormy were invented then."

"Where do you pick up this stuff?"

"The museum of the American Cocktail in New Orleans was drowned out by hurricane Katrina and relocated to the late Aladdin Hotel Desert Passage for almost two years in the mid-2000s. Any true connoisseur of Las Vegas would know that." Ingram lifts three eyebrow whiskers and looks down his common pink nose at me.

"You are talking of a bunch of recent has-beens. What about this old-time underground joint in the building just a few pit stops up the street?"

Ingram rubs his pads together, preparing to deliver one of his endless lectures from which I will get a few measly nubs of useful information.

"The place was called Zoot Suit Choo-Choo. It was where hep cats and hipsters wearing zoot suits danced to swing music and tossed their lady friends and long, long watch chains around like dough in a Pizzeria. Miss Maeveleen keeps a poster of an old cartoon movie short called *Zoot Suit Cat* on her wall, if you can bestir yourself to pad over to her desk and look."

This will require a leap down, an amble among freestanding bookshelves, and a leap up.

"A picture is worth a thousand words, Louie," Ingram snickers.

So I make the trek and confront the strangest getup I have ever seen on a feline standing upright like a man. It makes my flaming flamingo fedora pale by comparison, from the flat wide-brimmed hat to the long coat with big shoulder pads over pantaloons starting under the forelimbs and bagging down until tight at the ankles. This literal "hep cat" is swinging a watch chain so long it could lasso a llama. This is the zoot-suit getup worn by the dudes I saw cavorting during my basement dream state.

I take all this in and return to Ingram without incident.

"Well?" he demands.

"I have seen people thusly costumed in films on the Retro TV channels. What is with the watch chain so long you could trip on it?"

"They were named after us, Louie. 'Cat chains.' Every hip young man wanted to be a 'cool cat'. Some hipsters wore real gold chains. The poorer sort used the pull chains from water closet appliances."

"You mean toilets? That does not sound 'cool', but crass."

"I am amazed that even you, Louie, would find your sensibilities challenged by that. Anyway, the government banned the Zoot Suit."

"That is unAmerican!"

"You are ignorant. You, as a black cat, should remember how your type was subjected to chromatic cleansing in the witch-hunt days."

"I am well aware of four centuries of rabid persecution and burning. It is amazing any of us are left, and we still are left behind at shelters when it comes to adoption time, because the ignorant still superstitiously avoid black cats. So the ignorance is all on the side of homo sapiens, thank you very much." I shudder. "Who gave this human species the right to rule the world?"

Ingram blinks his eyes but does not answer. He does however, continue his lecture. Since this is what I do not pay him for, I listen.

"The jazz music scene of the twenties mingled black and white musicians, defying segregation laws. Cab Calloway, the black jazz singer, wore flamboyant Zoot Suits onstage. When swing dance came along, the Zoot Suit was the day's street fashion, like baggy shorts and T-shirts are today among teens.

"In 1942, the war effort banned excessive fabric, so wearing them became "unpatriotic". Zoot Suit riots in Los Angeles were started by sailors in port taking swings at the hep cats as "unpatriotic". Zoot Suiters were beaten and stripped and Zoot Suits burned."

"Like a book-burning?" I ask, aghast. "The getup is laughable, but so are all human clothes. Except my Miss Temple's," I add loyally.

"The riots lasted ten days, Louie. Yet the Zoot Suit lives on. You were a cool cat in a Zoot Suit was the saying."

"Yeah, and sometimes dead meat too, given the chromatic cleansing against my particular coat color during the witch hunts in Europe and America."

Ingram produces a weary sigh. "At any rate, violence also closed the Zoot Suit Choo-Choo club. While the Mob liked its own sharp-lapelled, pin-striped suits and snappy fedoras, they saw troubles with Zoot Suit Choo-Choo attracting other ethnic guys who might organize. One hipster got hung there, by his toilet tank pull chain, and the club closed."

"Hanged?" This nugget of unexpected information sets me back on my tail. "Who and why?"

"I do not know."

"You do not know?"

"It is just a footnote in Las Vegas history."

"Not to the guy who was hanged. Where can I get information on this for Miss Temple?"

Ingram yawns. "My afternoon nap time nears. Lure her into the store and get her to buy a book on Las Vegas history." His eyes are half shut. I curl the tips of my shivs into his shoulder and shake it.

"*Me-owie!*" he complains. "Do that again, Louie, and I will never enlighten you in future."

"How did you learn of this Zoot Suit Choo-Choo place?"

"In a book, of course."

"Which book?"

"I forget, and if I do not get my nap, I may even forget everything I know the next time you come in scraping for clues and unpaid research assistance." This time his peepers close down completely.

I sit there, perplexed. First I must attract Miss Maeveleen's attention so I can be released to the wild. Then I must find some way to lead Miss Temple to Zoot Suits, the Zoot Suit Choo-Choo nightclub and an obscure seventy-year-old murder on the same premises where the former *Mr.* Electra Lark has bought the farm in the same fashion.

There are times I have been forced to resort to charades to convey important news and clues to Miss Temple, but this whole Zoot Suit puzzle takes the cupcake.

33
Thrill and Quill

When Temple heard Electra's voice on her phone just before noon, she felt her stomach swoop a bit. What now?

"We've got to have lunch," Electra said.

"Lunch...okay."

"I know this is sudden, Temple, and you have work to do, but it could be important."

"That's one of the perks of working from home, Electra. I can always make time for a friend." Temple reflected that was also a problem sometimes, as playing hooky often seemed more fun than fingers to the keyboard. "Anything new from the cops I should know about?"

"No, not them, thank goodness, but I told Maeveleen Pearl the good news that I inherited that that pile of desert sand under that abandoned building."

"Maeveleen Pearl. The name's familiar."

"She owns the Thrill 'n' Quill bookstore that relocated to my mini-shop street, which is soon to be elevated to an urban village, if you have your way and I'm not in the federal pen."

"Electra, don't worry. Everybody's working to clear you."

Midnight Louie had appeared from nowhere and was rubbing back and forth on Temple's bare calves, which was pleasant but tickled.

"Clearing me is taking a lot of work," Electra remarked, "which isn't encouraging. Anyway, we can meet on the site and lunch at a charming little catering café not far away."

"What's it called?"

"The Magic Muffin."

"Just what we need for the village." Temple had a second thought. "Uh, it doesn't sell marijuana, does it?"

Louie stretched his forepaws up her legs, as if trying to reach the cell phone at her ear, or to listen in.

"What a thought!" Electra laughed. "No, pot is not legal here in Nevada, though everything else is. Even medical marijuana is tightly controlled."

"Let's you and me walk to the Thrill 'n' Quill together," Temple suggested. "I'd love to see the bookstore when we pick up Maeveleen. I'll meet you at the wedding chapel side in an hour."

As she ended the call, Temple looked around.

Louie had vanished as suddenly as he had appeared and cozied up.

34
Cat and Mouse

I like my routines, especially at mealtime. If anything could be more aggravating than the human propensity for impulsive changes of routine it is realizing I must beat the Circle Ritz ladies to the Thrill 'n' Quill and get Ingram to set the stage there.

Since my unearthly experience at the abandoned building, I realize I must direct my charges' attention to the exciting but deeply obscure days of yesteryear in Las Vegas. That is the only way to put them on the path to solving the puzzling murder that occurred just last week.

"Zoot Suit Choo-Choo" is not a search term I can easily persuade Miss Temple to input into her computer. Although I have in the past shown some digital dexterity over the operation of a printer, answering machine, and even rather creative arrangements of the alphabet on a keyboard, I am not suited to conveying long written messages.

No, it is my curse and gift to find creative ways to prod these unobservant humans into making leaps of logic. As it happens, a bookstore in the neighborhood might turn out to be a boon.

I am on the sidewalk outside the Thrill 'n' Quill in five minutes. I expect it to take me at least fifteen to get inside and set about my business. Even then, I am counting on luck and Ingram's encyclopedic memory of every item on the store's shelves. Bast knows, he has slept on every book and shelf in his long (and lazy) pseudo-literary career.

Still, a mean-street walker like me can use a sedentary assistant to consult, a feline kind of Mycroft to my Sherlock Holmes.

Ingram is in his usual spot pursuing his usual occupation. He is sound asleep in the store window. I leap up to tap the window glass. One striped ear tip twitches. I leap again, using the points of my shivs to turn a dull tap into sharp rap. One yellow eye-slit opens.

And shuts. What you might call an open-and-shut case. I do not have time to waste. I shall have to appeal to the denser species.

I go to the glass door, where I am more visible. I sit, clear my mind (which is hard because much is on it) and pretend I am Miss Electra's cat, Karma, in one of her New Age trances. Then I look into the store where Miss Maeveleen Pearl is bustling about near a row of shelves, back to me, and concentrate on my best weapon, The Stare.

If you Stare, they will come.

Well, maybe not right away. And I do not have time to waste. I twitch my whiskers and Stare Harder. I Stare so hard I am going cross-eyed. My vision blurs and then resolves into the striped brown side of Ingram pacing back and forth in front of the door.

At least his change of position has spurred some inside action.

Miss Maeveleen is bearing down on us like a movie closeup, her face growing jolly pink giant huge as she bends over to study the bottom of the door.

"Ingram," she says, "you have not seen your friend from the old shop in months, poor fellow. I will let him in to visit, but *you* are not going out."

Small chance of that. Ingram does not like to get his white gloves and spats dirty.

I eel through the crack and greet my hostess with a single ankle rub and a small chirp. We are not on intimate terms and I do not want to overdo it. Doling out the demonstrations of affection keeps the mystique going.

Ingram pads over to an overstuffed armchair near a reading table and jumps onto one arm. I notice some fancy crockery on the floor near a wall, but am not here to cadge a meal or a drink, so I loft atop the other chair arm.

And pose.

"How precious." Miss Maeveleen is there with her cell phone camera and Ingram is quick to offer a practiced head tilt. Then we are rid of her for now as she goes off to Facebook us, and we can get down to business.

"She is right," Ingram growls. "A year ago you dropped me like a nickel down a slot."

"My case load turned in a direction not requiring your expert help and depth of knowledge."

"*Phhtt*," he says. "Flattery is the resource of the unimaginative."

"You are right. The information I need and any way of conveying it from one species to another is virtually impossible in this case. I was overconfident to disturb you for such a hopeless task." I gather myself to jump back to the floor.

"Wait. The least you can do is tell me what crazy tangent you are chasing now."

"It involves murder, of course, and strange, exotic human rituals that would make a cat laugh, were evil not involved."

"'Evil', you say. Evil under the Las Vegas sun?"

Now Ingram is paraphrasing an Agatha Christie title. He does not realize I know this and know it shows his weakness for a mystery.

"Yes, but extending back decades. Too old to be found."

"Historical, you say?"

"And far too obscure to convey, even with the photographic memory and wide resources you possess."

"Try me."

"And the time factor is...hopeless."

"Try me." He is almost begging now.

"If you insist. I hate to set you up to fail, and Miss Temple and Miss Electra will be taking Miss Maeveleen to lunch in less than twenty minutes."

"Tell me!" Ingram is now almost grinding his fangs.

I shrug and give my thick ruff an absent lick. "I need to find a book with a particular reference. The phrase in question is 'Zoot Suit Choo-Choo'."

"I thought-we had discussed that thoroughly. Oh. I suppose you are trying to relive your triumphs in the À la Cat commercials. The Fontana brothers 'made' that production number. They wore the zoot suits and you stumbled and tumbled down the stairs."

"I was tripped by my evil rival, the spokescat Maurice."

"If you say so. However, the zoot suit, unlike you, has an interesting history and may be represented in books in inventory. Let me think."

Ingram closes his eyes and rapidly drones, "Zoot Suit. Referencing the Zoot Suit Riots of the nineteen-forties. Not in Las Vegas, though. L.A. So. Nothing in Historical Las Vegas section. Two in Entertainment section. Not in Fiction. Three books in Fashion. Four in Sociology. One in Cat, the Forties. Three in World War Two. Nothing in Trains, History. And certainly nothing under 'Choo-Choo' but *The Little Engine That Could*, Children's Fiction."

He opens his eyes and blinks. "Anything sound useful?"

"I know most of that," I mutter. "I thought Miss Maeveleen Pearl ran a mystery bookstore. Her inventory is long on miscellanea and short on murder."

"An independent bookstore owner today has to be resourceful. We are hanging on by my dewclaws. You already know about the Zoot Suit and the riots, why come to me again?" Ingram asks.

"Because I need to get the Circle Ritz ladies to trip over something concrete that will get them thinking about the Zoot Suit Choo-Choo club that existed in that abandoned building back in the fifties. I am sure there are clues there to a contemporary crime."

"And how do you know this?"

"Uh, certain connections."

"What connections?"

"Okay, it is a hunch."

Ingram glares at me.

"I had a...dream."

Ingram shakes his head slowly.

"Call it Karma."

"That flake! I am talking documented history here, not woo-woo speculation. There is nothing concrete about that site down the block except it will be the end of all small businesses in the neighborhood."

Ingram is, sadly, correct. I cogitate. When I look up at Ingram again to declare defeat, I am mesmerized by his...feet. His right shivs are tapping his folded forelimbs in agitation.

"I am forgetting a prime sales category at the Thrill 'n' Quill, so to speak, Louie."

"Am I suppose to wax hopeful over the word 'prime' or 'category'?" I ask sourly.

"Both, my good sleuth. Miss Maeveleen has descended, er, expanded, into selling used videos."

"So? I can see all that on retro TV. Miss Temple does provide me with best in cable and recorded entertainment."

Ingram lifts an admonitory claw. On him it is not a weapon of mass deconstruction. "Tut, tut. You say the Circle Ritz headwoman and your paramour are arriving here soon?"

I do not quibble about his demeaning descriptions. He would not fare well by me either. "Yes. It is our last best chance to clue them in on the nefarious doings at the future Lust 'n' Lace strip club site."

Ingram shudders in distaste. "Ghastly name. Let them come, and I will build it. A stunning big 'reveal', as we say in reality TV, only this will be live and in furperson. just get them to follow me when they arrive."

Am I to pin all my hopes on Ingram as Pied Piper? I must say he is the brainy type. And, when it come to push versus shove, when it comes to Ingram versus my Miss Temple's keen investigative instincts, I must put my money on her making the giant leapt for human kind.

It has been a twenty-minute wait and I am nibbling on my toenails.

The clever gong of funeral bells reverberates when Miss Electra and Miss Temple enter the mystery bookstore. I was too intent to notice that small touch on my earlier visit.

The three women confer, tsking over the challenging economic climate for the small entrepreneur, the crassness of the Vegas Strip mentality, and the superiority of cats over men as boon companions. Sadly, my Miss Temple is silent on this key issue, but she always is the diplomat.

Then Ingram goes to work as an ankle massager of world-class moves. I am shocked, but have agreed to give him the lead role.

Within two minutes he has the trio cooing over the rack of plastic-covered recorded items. Within thirty seconds he has pried one loose. It tumbles to the floor.

"Oh, look," says Miss Electra Lark, "the clever boy has selected our latest home entertainment. What a fun fat cat on the cover."

I manage to catch a glimpse of Ingram's selection and am left speechless and barely able to wiggle a whisker, or whisk past a female ankle.

"Zoot Cat" is pictured on the cover. It is that loathsome Tom from the *Tom and Jerry* cartoons where the Jerry-mouse gets Tom-cat's goat every episode. These are artifacts from a politically incorrect age and I am shocked that they are still available in their old, unadulterated form.

"Maeveleen," Miss Temple says, fishing the odious portrayal up off the floor. "So you have a DVD player for this vintage cartoon?"

No, no! It is denigrating to cats everywhere. We are long past these dated depictions as dumb and gullible and manipulated by mice. We are the smooth operators these days.

I cringe as Miss Maeveleen produces a laptop computer and the tinny period music unfolds and we all see the dated cat action in cartoon view.

"Yoo-hoo! Hey, Toots!" yells Tom at the door of a lady-cat. "What's cookin', Toots?"

Tom peeks through the window and sees Toots listening to a radio while painting her claws. The radio airs a commercial for a zoot suit. Tom decides to make his own zoot suit from an orange-and-green hammock.

Tom cat goes awry right there with that awful color combination, I think with a shudder.

Toots loves the suit Tom models for her…the coat hanger that widens the jacket shoulders and the long pocket chain, which is actually a bathtub plug.

"Now you collar my jive," Toots says. "You are on the right side, you alligator."

They jive dance, but Jerry clips the hanger in Tom's jacket to a window shade, then kicks Tom. As Tom pursues the fleeing mouse, the shade unravels and rebounds, rolling up Tom and tossing him into a fishbowl, where his wet zoot suit slowly shrinks. It pops off his body and drifts to the floor. Jerry jumps into the shrunken suit, now a perfect fit and dances away.

Everybody laughs.

"You know," Miss Maeveleen says, "this reminds me of a fifties-era nightclub near here called Zoot Suit Choo-Choo. Isn't that funny?"

Very unfunny. This is a cartoon entertainment, but they have always been about violence.

Maybe even murder.

35
A Pool of Suspects

It is not usual police procedure to convene a meeting on a murder case poolside in Las Vegas, but this was decidedly not a police operation.

The pool area was the only space at the Circle Ritz that could hold all the friends and neighbors of Electra Lark. And all of these people present were concerned about her being a person of interest in a spectacular murder case with overtones of an elaborate mob hit.

"A 'mob' of Fontana brothers, all ten, were an awesome presence on their own, especially accessorizing their pastel-cool summer suits with hot, black-framed sunglasses that would put them at home with George Clooney (the new Cary Grant) in a new *Ocean*'s Las Vegas heist film.

In tune with its vintage perfection, the Circle Ritz had a quaint little pool house with a striped awning to provide deep shade for Electra, flanked by Temple and Matt.

The Fontana boys had arrived with a large portable screen and small laptop computer. They proclaimed they had a "most intriguing" Powerpoint presentation based into their research into the scene of the crime.

"Not to worry, Miss Electra," Aldo Fontana told the guest of honor, bowing like a prosecuting attorney about to put on trial the real "person or persons unknown" they were searching for. "If your custom falls off because of this cloud of unjustified suspicion, I assure you we Fontanas shall purchase and occupy any lost tenants' residences."

Temple sat boggled by the implications. Under Aldo's plan, the Circle Ritz could become the coolest Fontana Brothers upscale frat house in Vegas. Hip people would kill to rent or own there. And the security would be Fort Knox-class.

"Wouldn't it," Matt asked, "be simpler to finger the fraudsters and the murderer or murderers without a mass move-in?"

"Of course," Nicky said. "My bros don't need cribs and could always take over a floor at the Crystal Phoenix, if they want."

Temple was very glad Nicky's wife and the hotel manager, Van von Rhine, wasn't here to learn of her husband's grandiose hospitality. But then, every Fontana brother was grandiose, and that would be criminal to stamp out.

Ernesto presented Electra with a suspiciously rum-colored giant cocktail glass accessorized with paper umbrellas and drew up a bamboo ottoman.

"Now you just rest your feet and sit back, Miss Electra. Let us boys figure out who mighta done it—even better, who we'd all like to nail for doing it—and who our concerned close friends, Mr. Matt Devine and Miss Temple Barr, need more information about once we have laid out criminally suspect persons in this local cast of *Clue*."

Electra wiggled her toes in their carnival-colored cork sandals—once Ernesto had swept the ottoman under them—and sipped on the long, long straw in her umbrella drink. "I'm most intrigued to see your presentation, fellas."

Temple smiled at Electra's *joie de vivre*. Now that luxury brand Céline had made an octogenarian Joan Didion their ad icon and Yves Saint Laurent had done the same with septuagenarian singer-songwriter Joni Mitchell (who'd written a song on the Magdalene asylums), Temple could revel in the idea of someday being a hip little old lady. She hoped to live long enough to be seriously removed forever from the "small and cute" and young category, like a lapdog.

Darn those Fontana brothers, their antique gallantry somehow got women feeling empowered! Of course the entire family fortune was based on Grandmama Fontana's Italian sauce empire. Sauce equals sauciness.

"Now." Aldo was evidently the chief prosecutor. "We have consulted family archives back to a time in which the Fontana escutcheon was slightly tainted in the public knowledge by the aura of Family connections not quite within the strict confines of The Law." He turned, his double back-vented jacket swaying as gracefully as if on a Milano runway. "As some would say, not 'legit'."

Temple could hardly stop from laughing. Any minute now, she expected the assembled Fontana Brothers to form a Broadway musical chorus and break out singing the "Sit down, sit down, you're rockin' the boat" chorus from *Guys and Dolls*.

She conjured a paraphrased second line, tailor-made for Fontana, Inc.

"And the Devil will drag you under by sharp lapels of your Emanogildo Zegna coat. Stand up, stand up, you're shakin' the boat."

Meanwhile, Ralph Fontana, his single diamond ear stud twinkling like a wink, hurried around the roomy patio to ensure the laptop computer projected the right image, a photo of the forlorn empty building.

"First," Aldo said, "I wish to notify those not acquainted with police photos of crime scenes and the like, that some images may be hard to take. Happily, we start with an architectural long shot of the building in which the gruesome discovery, Mr. Jay Edgar Dyson's dead body, was found.

"We Fontanas have been asked to research some of the possible perpetrators who might have what is called 'mob' corrections. Of course, we all know—" he pushed his impossibly stylish Italian sunglasses atop his head so his face was an open book, "—the FBI drove out all mob factions from Las Vegas by the end of the nineteen-eighties."

Nicky Fontana cleared his throat. Loudly.

Temple knew mob activity remained alive and well in offbeat areas like controlling meat sales rather than the more glamorous gambling violations.

"Anyway," Aldo went on, "we have learned that Mr. Dyson owned, as did his ex-wife, Miss Electra Lark, quite a bit of land surrounding this, what I can only call an abandoned hulk, on a nameless side street. Mr. Dyson, we learn, was lured to Vegas to discuss selling this vintage edifice, most recently a purveyor..." Here images passed in succession. "...of wigged-out old dolls (nothing personal to the older lady among us), chipped metal-painted toys and Depression glass, which I believe is called that because it is so depressing to look at, being all moss green and yellow colors, and often chipped besides."

Temple cringed as the dolls with their balding wigs and cracked China faces passed by, looking like escapees from old horror movies.

"And," Aldo added, "several hundred amps of rhinestone jewelry that Miss Temple Barr no doubt would covet."

Since all the illustrated pieces were either G-strings or showgirl bras, Temple doubted that, particularly since she was a 32 AN. All Natural. Still, she was flattered Aldo thought she might be interested in something other than crime scenes.

"This building looks innocent of everything but urban blight," he said. "Now we will segue to the Unusual Suspects."

Aldo flipped the screen image to images from old photos to present film clip as easily as his suit jacket vents fluttered in a Vegas breeze.

"First, the understudies." He clicked to a jail intake photo of a tough-looking guy. "In these shots, the suspects' 'performance' names are noted," Aldo explained. "Punch Sullivan did just that—punch and get punched—until taking too many 'dives' in fixed fights ruined his profile. Kat with a *K* was 'Cathy' with a *C* when she was assisting Vegas's lowest-level con men and street magicians off the Strip, and hooking on the side. Naturally, they were soon ready for bigger money-making ventures. After they got together and shifted their focus, they became a Team around Town. We are looking at a pair of known adult entertainment figures, two of dozens in Las Vegas. You gonna open a strip club, you need sexperienced overseers to keep strippers and patrons in order."

"Those two sound like something out of pulp novel," Matt whispered to Temple. "You actually met this odious pair?"

"Sort of."

Aldo went on. "In the Most Interesting Personality Involved category…" he said, bringing up a mug-shot photo. "The one, the only Leon Nemo," he finished with a flourish.

"My money is on that guy." Electra sat up and dumped her soggy paper umbrellas on a side table. "He's a bad 'un. He could railroad a weakling like Jay Edgar. I'd bet my instincts about my last, and late, husband on that."

Ernesto grabbed some copies of Nemo's photo and marched around the assemblage to pass them out. The letters and numbers under Nemo's photo were impressive, too, especially since they were in black and white.

"This jailhouse portrait was taken before nineteen sixty," Temple said. "Nemo is old enough to have been active in the heydays of the Vegas mobs."

Aldo's long, buffed forefinger nail pointed to Temple. "A dollar to the little lady on the money! His dyed black hair aside, Nemo is as old as the dessert dirt that hid Ten Binion's multimillion-dollar buried safe. He knows where the bodies as well as the booty in Vegas are buried, and if he's involved in the Lust 'n' Lace takeover, it ain't for the G-string dollar bills."

Temple smiled modestly as he confirmed her suspicions. "Then what?" she asked.

Fontana brother padded shoulders lifted in unison. "To be determined later."

"Having hit an impasse with the cast of crooks," Nicky said. "I suggested we look into the strange scene of the crime."

"And the bizarre manner of death, I hope," Temple said.

"Our sources on the Vegas scene are impeccable," Ralph stepped up to say. "For one thing, we have a bit of living history in our Uncle Macho Mario."

"A bit? He is the entire Old Testament," Julio said. "Problem is, he is a bit reluctant to testify against his old acquaintances. A matter of honor."

"Surely," Matt said, "such upstanding nephews can persuade an uncle to clear his conscience? If not, I could step in as a confessor. I still have the purple stole."

"My blushes," Aldo said. "We cannot have you assuming the mantel of a man of the cloth when you are so close to committing marriage. And also, by my admittedly old-fashioned uncle's lights, if you would hear his confession, you would need to be committed to eternal silence, or death."

Matt sighed. "Those are both pretty eternal. Temple might have objections."

"I would," she said. "If the dramatis personae are missing links on some fronts, what about the building in question? It's as old as Las Vegas, apparently, and had a racy history before ending up as an antique mall."

"That is easier to trace," Nicky said. "On my request, Van sat Uncle Mario down with a bottle of Tia Maria liqueur and his bouncing baby youngest grandniece, Cinnamon Angela Fontana. Maria, I should mention," Nicky addressed the company, "was the first name of our sainted and saucy matriarch and Mucho Macho Mario's sainted mama, Maria Guadalupe Fontana. And 'Angela', of course, speaks for itself."

"Between the oldest and the youngest of our Vegas line," Aldo said, "Uncle Mario was soon teary-eyed and reminiscing for a concealed recorder about his arrival in Vegas as a lad, when Bugsy Siegel was losing sight of the 'take' and getting the visionary stars in his eyes blasted to smithereens."

"Before someone shot out one," Ralph added.

"Poor Bugsy." Temple shook her head, sadly. "He had it right. Vegas was a pre-Disneyland theme park for adults and ahead of its time, but mob bosses tend to get so impatient."

Julio had small sympathy for Bugsy. "Mob bosses are primitive, like sharks. They bite first and think about it later, while digesting."

"So," said Temple, "while Uncle Macho Mario Fontana was digesting Tia Maria, what did he come up with?" She was hoping this Fontana progressive fairy tale was soon going to produce a high-octane ogre. "Vegas grew apace after Siegel's death," Aldo said. "In the early days it was crude frontier-themed motels and attractions. It was wide open, like a town in a fifties TV Western. There were still injuns around, and Chinese from the railroad-building days and other folk that would not be tolerated in an expanding Vegas for red-blooded Americans."

"Omitting red-blooded Indians, of course," Matt said.

"Native Americans," Nicky corrected. "Who are doing damn well in the casino business, better than Vegas or even Macao now. Leave 'em nothing and drive 'em out of anywhere desirable in the country and they end up getting future hot spots like the Oklahoma oil wells and the East Coast barrier tourist islands and, yup, casinos."

"Back then they weren't a mote in the mob's eye," Aldo said. "But there was one pesky type that hankered to come to Vegas like everyone else and had the numbers to be profitable." He hit the control and a logo familiar only to dedicated Las Vegas historians appeared on-screen.

If what happened in Vegas, stayed in Vegas, à la the classic advertising motto, Temple knew that episodes of shameful history in Vegas also stayed buried in Vegas.

"I gotcha," Temple said. "You're referring to the Moulin Rouge hotel-casino, founded in nineteen fifty-five for an underserved clientele ignored by the burgeoning Strip enterprises."

"Man," Eduardo said. "I've seen pictures of those cursive neon letters, Moulin Rouge. Looked snazzy with those long, low, finned convertibles sitting out front of it like tethered Detroit automotive manta rays. The place didn't last long, though."

Matt quirked an interrogatory eyebrow at Temple, who'd now become lead presenter.

"It had the lifespan of a mayfly." She shook her head. "I researched it recently in connection with the Crystal Phoenix Black & White band show. Black clientele, and even some performers, were frozen out of Vegas in those early days, when there were still national and local laws against 'mixed' accommodations and associations. There was no black mob, but a group created an all-black staffed hotel-casino across the tracks from the Strip, near the black neighborhood. Its major black performers made it so popular as an after-Strip-show hours joint for major white Strip performers who wanted to jam with the legends, that the Strip had to integrate its clientele in self-defense."

"That's a wonderful, ironic twist of history," Matt said. "Why is the place so unknown?"

Temple shrugged. "The Moulin Rouge only lasted eight months once the Strip imitated it. All attempts to repurpose the building or designate it as a historical site over the decades seemed to be jinxed. Eventually it was torn down."

"Sounds a lot like the old building near Electra's place," Matt said. "You'd think they'd salute the black and white mega-entertainers leading the pack in those days."

"The Rat Pack itself was a game-changer," Temple said. "I hate to say it, given Frank Sinatra's mob connections and his huge case of little-people-crushing ego, but the Rat Pack's Strip act— including a Brit actor who was a future Kennedy presidency in-law, Peter Lawford; a black super-entertainer, Sammy Davis, Jr.; a Jewish comedian, Joey Bishop, originally Joseph Gottlieb; and some young actresses the Rat Pack named 'Mascots'—Shirley Maclaine, Judy Garland, Angie Dickenson, Juliet Prowse, and Marilyn Monroe—broke the racial and bigotry barrier in this town, all the while it remained sexist. Women always come last."

"Not with we Fontanas," Aldo said. "We know we owe it all to Mama."

"And now Italians are the chic retro-villains in town," Aldo pointed out, buffing his nails on his expensive lapels. *Sit down, sit down, you're rockin' the boat.*

"I get it," Temple said. "You're saying that abandoned building also rocked the boat in its day back in the fifties, like the Moulin Rouge. How?"

Aldo clicked to another image. Another neon-smooth cursive sign appeared. *Zoot Suit Choo-Choo.*

"*Huh?*" Temple said.

"I will be passing around black-and-white photos," Aldo noted, "because negatives are all that remain of that building when it was first built, just like with the Moulin Rouge. However, you can see photos and films of similar joints' interiors on Internet boogie-woogie and jive sites and from Hollywood musical film clips."

"And last but not least. Here is Jumpin' Jack Robinson, Zoot Suit Choo-Choo star, maybe black, maybe Hispanic, maybe southern Italian. Founder, performer, the first freelance, un-mob affiliated entrepreneur near the Strip."

"That's not going to end well," Matt whispered to Temple before she could say the same thing.

Still, Aldo wanted to finish his presentation with a bang.

"Jumpin' Jack Robbinson, Zoot Suit dancing king and Sin City wild card."

Up popped a black-and-white photo. A broadly smiling entertainer was caught in an expansive dance mode. He was balancing on the outstretched heels of his black-and white spectator loafers, his baggy pants stretched to the limit, three swagging watch chains swayed from hip to ankle, and arms spread wide to embrace the world and the audience.

Temple guessed the performer's outfit and pose was an icon for the age of Zoot Suitery swag and swing. She remembered Fred Astaire doing a Bo Jangles tribute act that captured that black entertainment icon too.

"Found hung," Aldo said.

The discrepancy between the frozen-life image and the bare, dead fact had everyone shocked and speechless.

Aldo took a prosecutor's circular stroll around the assembly to come back front and hit the jury in the face with the facts. "Hung from an onstage light pole by the sturdy chain of a cheap toilet pull of the day, in nineteen fifty-six. In the basement of the building in question. The case was never solved."

Temple was desperately seeking that ogre who was the key to it all. "Don't tell me there were no suspects."

"Dozens back in that day," Aldo said. He adjusted his shirt cuffs. "One of the most colorful was capo of the Italian mob, naturally. Crude but effective. The cops called him 'Jack the Hammer'."

"That sounds like some shyster TV-ad lawyer's nickname," Temple objected. "That's not even an Italian name."

"Aldo was sparing the ladies' sensibilities," Ernesto said. "The mob boss was noted for taking guys out into the dessert and using a jackhammer to encourage them to talk, or keep quiet forever. Name of Giaccomo Petrocelli. Giaccomo. Italian for 'James', but in English it shortens to just plain 'Jack'. Giacc the Hammer."

Matt, beside her, shifted on his chair and coughed, as repelled as she by brutal mob execution styles.

Temple shuddered in the benign sunlight. "Not so plain," she told Ernesto. "An ogre like Giacco Petrocelli would be capable of hanging a man by his own Zoot suit chain. What happened to him?"

Aldo shrugged. "Somebody offed him after the millennium. Most of his power was gone. He never adapted."

More than fifty years ago a macabre message had been sent in a building a couple blocks from where she laid her head every night, Temple realized.

How on earth had Electra's ineffective, ordinary-Joe ex-spouse's body become the vehicle of another, undecoded message today? And who had sent messages by murder then and now? Obviously, two different killers. So who wanted to echo Vegas's Bad Old Days of Italian, Irish and Jewish mob control and violence, and maybe even the ethnic unrest? And why?

36
In the Ranks of Death

"This is my last quest, as you call it, of this trip, Kathleen, and it's sorry I am to drag you along, but I can't cut you loose until I leave Ireland in case you might kill me or in case someone else might want to kill you."

"Oh, cut the music-hall Irish palaver, Max Kinsella. It's tired I am of your endless do-goodin' and breast-beatin'. I might rather be killed. So what am I expected to suffer through now?"

"I confess it's all too easy to walk the walk and talk the talk in Ireland. I need to find the remains of Gandolph the Great, or be sure he was given a proper burial or cremation. I was forced to abandon his body in the car."

"Is it a church burial in Belfast you're after?"

"No. He wasn't Catholic, just a damn good man. I promise my intentions are purely secular, Kathleen."

"Despite the grandiose performing name, he sounds a right old fellow," she admitted, "and a far more decent father figure than I had." She shook her head and the glory of her flagrant thick hair the nuns had cropped. "Maybe you'll less regret following the black velvet band if we find him."

That "we" was revolutionary, so he didn't mention it.

The car's GPS guided Max over the curving hills to the M1 and a straight shot into Belfast in less than an hour. As Max and Garry had found on the previous visit, Americans were startled by how short distances and very little time could cross borders in the British Isles and Europe.

Belfast's population was almost 700,000. As they drove into the city, its views were dominated by Belfast Castle high on a hill and other large and stately red brick and white marble ministerial buildings dating back to earlier centuries, but also new, striking simple and clean modern office complexes.

The "Peace walls" meandered like scars through city, bunkerlike dividers between Catholic and Protestant neighborhoods painted with colorful urban graffiti six feet up, then bare concrete expanses topped by high wire fences.

"Where are we to sleep tonight?" Kathleen asked, her eyes fixed on the passing buildings and cars.

Hours of their mutual wariness gave her tone the same weariness he felt.

"We'll not be doing much of that, I'm thinking, with various factions sure to have an eye on me or you."

"You *want* them to find us."

"How else will I discover what happened to Garry's body?" Max had Googled a hotel on the fringe of the city center. "We can rest at a decent hotel, have a leisurely dinner, and then go walking."

"The perfect Max Kinsella night out. Feed the prey, then it's on foot, looking for trouble to find you. You sure know how to wine and dine a woman."

"I'm not going to get caught in another car chase."

Max pulled the Honda into an interior parking garage. They left their luggage inside, with Kathleen pulling out a loose-knit dark sweater and Max a light black leather jacket for the evening chill.

"This is a cheap American chain hotel," Kathleen said, sounding surprised and a bit indignant.

"We're not newlyweds, Kathleen. It's a solid, unassuming three-star hotel that's been redone inside and will keep us invisible and off the street until dusk, when we go hunting."

"Or being hunted."

"What's the matter? Home ground not a big enough advantage for you?" Max asked. "I'm the one who's the target."

In the dim parking garage, her posture and expression shifted. Max couldn't quite read how. Perhaps she'd arranged earlier to hand him over to the Real IRA. Their reserved double/double bedroom with en suite would be a prison cell for them until a late dinner would have a walk through Belfast for a chaser.

Dinner had been decent—salmon filet for her and for him the interesting Irish-prepared barbecued ribs, corn on the cob, cole slaw, and chips. Kathleen mocked his all-American menu choice.

Max didn't want to waste his time reading a long wine list, or drink much of it. He ordered a Bailey's Irish coffee with whiskey, his favorite after-dinner drink with Garry Randolph.

Kathleen ordered hot chocolate with whipped cream, marshmallows and a shot of sweet syrup. He mocked her all-American soda fountain dessert..

Then they got up, hooked their outer clothes off the chair backs and went into the cool, dark streets.

Max took Kathleen's sweater-clad arm. He didn't want her either ahead or behind him. He veered for the narrower and darker streets, for the oldest cobblestoned ways, graffiti-lined walls of abandoned public housing buildings into trash-occupied alleys, where the smell of urine ebbed and flowed like rank incense.

Lounging knit-capped gangsta youths on corners straightened at the sight of Kathleen, but Max pushed her between him and the wall side and gave them a long wolfish lowered-head glare.

He knew where he wanted to go, but not if he was exactly in the right place. This time, he wasn't still limping from his broken legs. He was more formidable, although he and Gandolph had fought their way out of the place he was hoping to find last time. The last time for Gandolph, by so few minutes.

A single man from behind took Kathleen's arm on the wall side into his custody. Max didn't turn to react, but spun to put his back the wall to confront the man coming toward them.

The men, wearing black knit caps pulled down to their eyebrows, were twenty to thirty years older than he, like Garry, but toughened by years of passionate, merciless urban warfare.

The advancing man spoke in a voice as soft and smooth and soothing as the best Irish whiskey.

"D'ye have such an ache to commit suicide, Michael Kinsella? Is that what brings you back to the Auld Sod again in so little time after suffering such a heavy loss your last time back?"

Max felt a swirl of triumph. *Bull's eye.* This was same bunch he and Garry had encountered during the previous trip. They had bargained before; they could bargain again.

He let Kathleen drift behind him, cursing him under her breath as the second man brought her along behind like excess baggage.

Shoved down narrow, steep stone steps into a cellar, they inhaled a crude potpourri of stale ale and smoke.

A man stayed guarding the bottom of the stairs. A lone man behind a long bar stared up as they entered. The place was empty except for a half-dozen men wearing peacoats and sweaters and the ubiquitous knitted or billed tweed caps lounging at wooden tables and chairs against a smoke-blackened brick wall. Pint glasses filled with dark amber liquid topped by a dispirited frill of foam circled their tables.

Max felt suddenly thirsty.

Above them all, hanging tin kettles and bellows dripped from blackened oak beams. The dark walls held rough oil portraits of long-dead Irish Republican heroes.

Max and Kathleen were released and left standing in the middle, the main man moving to lean against the bar and confront them. Him. The light above the bar revealed his features. Max recalled his name and would use it.

"D'ye have such an ache to commit suicide, Michael Kinsella?" he repeated. "Is that what brings you back to the Auld Sod again in so little time after suffering such a heavy loss your last time back?"

"That's just it, Liam. I'm here to find Garry Randolph's burial place."

The man nodded. "You two did a damn fine job of disrupting the IRA's agenda to drive out English rule years ago. The peace was hard-bought, but it finally came and is many years old. And so did the penalty for your actions then come due at last here on our common soil. We are not inclined to exact further punishment on ye at this late date."

"Apparently there are hold-outs," Max noted.

Kathleen smiled. "Like rock 'n' roll, the IRA never forgets."

Liam shook his head and paid her attention for the first time. "Kathleen, Kathleen, Kathleen, your nerve is as storied as your beauty, but we are all older now and cherishing different goals, different means. I can't say which is the greater shock for my old eyes. The sight of you again, or the sight of you accompanied by this misguided American traitor to our cause."

"He forced me back here," she said.

Liam nodded. "Politics does indeed make strange bedfellows, although I believe you and he are not new to this truth. I have never known in that case whether you were following your IRA head or your cold, cold heart, Kathleen, sleeping with the enemy, but the result was to make us a formidable foe for years and cost us dearly before the peace."

"I didn't come to Northern Ireland an enemy," Max said. "I was a sympathizer. And the dearly won peace now," he added, "means nothing if the lingering past is not forgiven, although not forgotten."

"Eloquent," Liam said, then again repeated himself. "D'ye have an ache to commit suicide, Michael Kinsella? We still have old business with you and will do it privately."

Liam nodded at his men. Two rose and swept Kathleen into a private room. Both she and Max started to object, but the movement was so swift that dissent was an afterthought.

Max wondered if the former IRA members wanted to spare Kathleen witnessing any brutal revenge they had planned, little knowing how much she'd rejoice in his maltreatment and bad luck.

Liam sighed and kept center stage, pacing in front of his patch of bar.

"Yes, the peace is here and holding, with exceptions. Too much blood has been shed," he said. "We don't hold a grudge against Randolph. He was a professional agent, he operated in Germany and Spain as well as Northern Ireland. You, on the other hand, Michael Kinsella, were a tourist and a turncoat, an Irish lad from America who betrayed us. At least you learned the taste for revenge we Irish have cultivated after centuries of brutal English rule."

"So this is a kangaroo court," Max said, looking around.

"Are you not going to plead mercy because of the stupidity of your youth?" Liam asked.

Max shook his head. "I did what I did to the best of my lights then and would do it again."

"Yet now you know your cousin did not die in the bombing, did in fact join us later."

"So you've been following us. Sean joined you in making the peace. And even though Deirdre saved Sean's life, other innocents perished in that explosion. They deserved justice too."

"We called in a warning. Whoever answered at O'Toole's pub couldn't hear in the hub-bub, put down the receiver and forgot it, thus tied up the line."

"You had cars."

"The time was tight and the traffic heavy."

"You had feet, as some in the pub probably lost."

"We were too late. During the peace negotiations, it was recognized the warning was intended and went awry. The men you and Randolph fingered for the job had their life sentences commuted at that time."

"So they're free, Sean is alive, and Garry is dead."

"Yes, Garry Randolph is dead."

Liam stood aside from his place against the polished wood bar.

Max stared past him, confused to see two empty pint glasses and a tall brass vase.

Not a vase, an urn.

"We've been expecting you. You're not one to let go, that's for sure."

"You cremated him out of revenge?"

"Respect. His death was not intended. Yet he was an agent who acted against a free Ireland. We'd never put him in Irish soil for eternity."

Max bit the inside of his cheek to keep from saying, doing something foolhardy, but regret for leaving Gandolph's body behind still burned his soul like rock salt would sear the raw place inside his mouth.

Liam narrowed his unsmiling Irish eyes. "Swear his ashes will go anywhere except the soil below and the air above Ireland, and you can take them away."

"I swear," Max said.

"Then your work here is done."

Max stepped to the bar, picked up the urn. It was lighter than he expected. Holding it gave him no self-defense moves.

The man guarding the door stepped aside. Max could carry Gandolph into the misty Irish night and back to...wherever a homeless man from Las Vegas would go.

"Hotheads remain among us," Liam said. "We intended to get information, not to take a life, even yours."

Max laughed wearily. "Sorry not to oblige you."

"That could be rescinded at any time. We still want information."

"About what? I'm retired. At least I am when I'm left alone. The two thugs you sent to find me in Las Vegas a couple of years ago forced me to leave for a while and then they beat up my girlfriend, a true threat to noble Irish manhood weighing in at one hundred pounds."

"She must not have said anything."

"She didn't know where I was." Max thought. "I don't think she'd have said anything if she did. Stubborn as a Skye terrier and as good at rooting out vermin."

Liam chuckled. "Her I'd like to meet. Sorry to inform you that *you* are not the high-value target you'd like to think yourself. We sent no men to find you, or to Las Vegas, although we may send some now."

"What about the rogue branch?"

"Too lazy. They like to vent a bit o' venom locally. We have a new benevolent mission."

"I'll believe that when I see it."

"You don't want to stay," said a man from the fringes. Flanagan, Max remembered.

Liam nodded. "This is a kangaroo court, as you call it. Only you're not the one on trial."

"Maybe I don't want to go," Max said slowly.

"Watch and pray, then," Liam said, consciously quoting Jesus's instructions to his disciples in the Garden of Gethsemane, where Judas would shortly finger him for the Romans.

Max grew even more uneasy. That reference evoked brutality, betrayal and destiny. He eyed the handsome urn. Someone had respected Garry.

Would he be forced to choose between getting Gandolph or Kathleen out of here before the night was over?

37
Ghost Stalking

Matt looked with loathing at the worn baseball cap on the Probe's passenger seat, then picked it up and pulled the grimy sweatband down over his clean blond hair.

The right "wrong" hat was the quickest and best disguise a man could manage. Matt had figured that out since he'd started tailing the guy from the Lucky Stars nudie bar. The hat and a beater car.

So far it had worked, but he needed to keep Woodrow Wetherly ignorant of his plans. When he'd started driving the Probe exclusively, Woody immediately had accepted Matt's explanation that the Jag was "in the shop".

"Knew a guy once, Matt. Mobster. Drove the pettiest Jaguar in Mafia-black you ever would see. Like a grand piano on wheels. Had two of 'em. Exact year, exact model. You know why?"

Matt had waited for the old guy's punch line. "One to drive while the other one was in the shop."

Matt then had added some rueful ha-ha's to Woody's wheezing laughter. "I tell you, Matt. Next time someone offers you a gift horse, hold out for a spare."

"Great advice," Matt had said, bracing for the sure shoulder clap. You'd think Wetherly had lived in Minnesota.

Now he wished the Probe hadn't been repainted white. Driving it in daylight was like bareback-riding Moby Dick. He'd never let Woody see him with the cap on. That might set Wetherly's retired cop instincts on edge. *What did Matt have to hide?*

Plenty, now that he'd glimpsed a ghost at the nudie bar. And now Matt was wondering if *Woody* had something to hide. He hung back far down the block, watching the beater of a different color he'd tailed to Woody's doorstep. He'd backed into an empty driveway with a screen of yuccas and waited for the beater car to leave.

The ancient Chevy was ugly enough to be a stand-out, yet a common sight. The dry Las Vegas climate allowed cars to cruise its streets for decades, even automotive dinosaurs just past the tail-fin stage, huge and wallowing, with trunks big enough to convey the cast of *Le Miz*. This seventies beauty had originally been a deep moss green, but the sun had bleached the car's paint job into a dull pea green pocked with dark gray, psoriatic spots.

Although Matt was too far away to see the driver, his features were burned into Matt's retinas. He was wearing the same ubiquitous baseball cap so useful for shading features and concealing hair, only this one had a greasy, graying ponytail trailing through the circle at the back.

Matt might have glimpsed a sparse soul patch above his chin. Or not. Either way, he was unshaven in a way that said "lazy" rather than trying for a fashionable stubbled look.

Age? Hard to tell. He had the slouching lope of an idler, but it could have as easily been an adolescent affectation as a sixtyish spinal curve. Something about him said "smoker", although Matt had never gotten close enough to tell or smell…hadn't dared to get that close in case he was recognized back.

Now, it was getting dark and that scabrous car had been parked outside Woody's house for a couple hours.

No less a law enforcement power than homicide lieutenant C. R. Molina had referred Matt to Wetherly as a possible source of information on old-time Vegas crime figures. Had she been helping him out, as Matt expected? Or setting him up in some way?

Molina had been pretty grim about something. She'd warned him against obstructing the law, at the same time as she'd sent him on a path that led to a nudie bar, of all places for an ex-priest to "frequent". Vegas entertainment venues equated getting "naughtier" with getting "nakeder". Even now the Circle Ritz population was reeling in deep legal trouble with an adult entertainment venture moving into the neighborhood, along with a truly nasty murder.

Matt spotted a shadow moving off Woody's old porch and around to the car's street side. Matt's prey was on the move. Matt started the Probe and drove a block over before taking the same direction. This older neighborhood didn't have confusing curved streets and cul-de-sacs, like the newer suburb of Henderson.

The familiar grid structure would allow Matt to avoid cruising past Wetherly's house in his own distinctive ride. Matt shook his head. Now that his prey had turned up at his recent mentor's home, Matt needed a second tailing car...or maybe a partner in tailing. Rafi Nadir came to mind. Someone had sicced Nadir on Matt, probably "for his own good". Could have been Molina. Or Max Kinsella before he'd left town, and probably the country.

Matt checked his rearview mirror. No vehicle was remotely near in this sleepy neighborhood occupied by aging people who'd paid off their modest mortgages years ago.

At the next cross street he spotted the Chevy's broad, undistinguished rear. The seventies sure manufactured ugly cars. Now that the sky was growing dim, Matt realized a white vehicle was a liability for nighttime tailing too.

Ninety minutes later Matt found himself back in Las Vegas, scratching his head. The Chevy had made a round trip almost to where it had started in Wetherly's neighborhood.

The driver had headed toward Red Rock Canyon, a popular tourist area north of Summerlin housing development, what was left of Howard Hughes-owned land in the valley. The canyon was thirty minutes outside of Vegas, so Matt had no trouble fading into the bus and SUV traffic.

Then the Chevy jolted off-road east into the desert just before the canyon, on a rough ranch road like many nameless paths branching off. The slow sunset in the west painted what was naturally orange-red by day a deep blood-red scarlet.

Matt could hardly stop watching the *National Geographic*-quality panoramic scene to keep an eye on his quarry. He had to bring Temple out here some evening as a surprise. Not long after they met, as he was fumbling toward his first romantic relationship after years of priestly celibacy, Temple had brought him out into the desert for a make-up "prom date". There'd been champagne and appetizers and some great CD music she'd selected.

"We've Got Tonight" by Bob Seger was now his favorite song. They'd "danced" and then they'd "made out" in the innocent fifties version of the phrase.

The memory had Matt's libido sizzling. He'd hardly known what to do then, but now he could imagine a pre-wedding dessert rendezvous at this same hour that would match the sunset for beauty and heat and seal their love for eternity.

Matt shook off the potent combo of scenic overdose, romance and lust. Sam Spade wouldn't be plotting to sweep "some dame" off her feet on a stakeout.

There was just enough light for him to see the driver bent over near a camel-shaped rock, digging something up.

A body?

Whatever it was required heaving into the seventies Chevy's huge trunk. The heavy steel frame did the car equivalent of "grunting". It swayed low for a moment.

Matt sensed departure and drove farther down the road. Tourist time was over so he did a Uey on the empty main road, pulled the Probe onto the southbound shoulder, and crouched by the front wheel well.

He stood up, gimme cap low over his bowed face as the Chevy turned south on the main road and headed back to Vegas. Even a white car was shadowy in this deep a dusk, and a driver who'd changed a tire or had a bit of trouble would be expected to limp back into town after one of the few vehicles heading that way.

It played like Matt had laid it down in his mind.

Until…

The Chevy ended up, not at Wetherly's place, but in an empty parking lot very near…the Circle Ritz.

The big dark car pulled up cozy-close to the semipermanent construction RV near the building. And didn't exit the car.

Matt parked the Probe down the street, noticing a faint light from the building's second-story windows. The murder scene.

Holy Christ. What was going on here? Well, he'd just have to do what Jesus had told his Disciples. Wait and watch.

He had a feeling he'd be glad the Lord was with him before this night was over.

38
Psychrisis

Most of us guys do not go in for this psychosomatic stuff—you know, supposed sixth sense abilities like precognition, clairvoyance, astral projection, telekinesis, telepathy and the like.

I must say my breed is more sensitive than most to unseen things, but that is because our vision operates on multiple focus, our spidery vibrissae sense every little stir in the atmosphere, and our spines are so agile that we are noted for always landing on our feet, which results in the belief of some that we have nine lives. I admit that we do seem to possess a mystical mojo.

However, I pooh-pooh "woo-woo" on principle. I do not wish to be taken for a ditsy dame of any species. Although I will admit to having plenty of telegenesis...that is not a real word, just a wee bit of word-play on my once and future career as an ace TV commercial personality.

Yet there comes a time and tide in the rational skeptic's life when certain eyewitness events call for an interpretation from more than the ordinary sources, such as the paranormal.

With light step but heavy heart, I prepare myself to bound up the Circle Ritz palm tree to the fifth-floor penthouse and into the paws of Miss Electra Lark's reclusive Birman, Karma, professional Sacred Cat of Burma who, yes, takes herself just that seriously.

You can imagine how unseriously she takes an earthy guy like me.

Still, I am haunted by a vague worry about the past and present manifestations I have experienced in the large abandoned building Miss Electra just inherited. It sniffs too much like big trouble much too close to the Circle Ritz and my protégés there, Miss Temple Barr and, by extension, Miss Electra Lark.

I land on Miss Electra's balcony and prepare to make abeyance to the sole feline presence. Karma is usually reluctant to admit me through the glass French doors and makes condescending comments about the state of my intelligence and even soul when I do get in.

Only my reflection greets me in the lowest pane of glass. Ordinarily, Karma has to assert her psychic superiority by being there to greet me, like a crazy mirror apparition.

I am expert at operating the lever handles on these Circle Ritz balcony doors, but when I leap up to begin my athletic second-story man contortions, my weight pushes the entire door open as if...as if a spectral hand had aided my efforts.

The sudden opening has my tender pads thumping hard to the floor, and I almost take it on the chin as well before I can pretzel myself into a relatively graceful four-point landing.

Once again Karma has put me off my paces.

Speaking of paces, I hear agitated shuffling within the dim landscape. Would you believe Miss Electra keeps the lights low for her visitor-shy companion? I have visited Karma before, and know the so-called psychically "sensitive" Birman requires a dim environment supplied with large upholstered furniture she can retreat under so as to "meditate".

Frankly, I believe Karma has a special condition, all right. She is agoraphobic. Miss Electra Lark has always catered to Karma's self-centered needs, to the point that almost no one even knows Karma is a resident. I have to admire our landlady's dedication to her needy roommate. Luckily, I am no strain on mine.

Besides shuffling, I also hear sighs.

Following these ghostly sounds into the main room, I come upon Miss Electra herself. She is holding a cell phone in her hand, and pacing back and forth, muttering. "I do not *have* what you want."

As my eyes swiftly adjust to the even dimmer darkness, I see the neatly ordered furnishings are littered with white pieces of paper tossed hither and yon.

"I do not have it! I do not even know what it *is*, much less where." Miss Electra's hand riffles her freshly zebra-striped hair (perhaps in honor of my new carrier of that pattern) and stops to admonish the phone screen in her hand. "Yes, you have what I want, you monsters! My poor, shy, sensitive, sweet Karma."

Uh...here I must interject—in the interest of full disclosure—that certain Asian dishes are sweet and sour, but I have only experienced the sour from Karma. However, an act against one of my kind is an act against all of my kind. And I suppose Her Tibetan Specialness is not a bad looker with her vivid blue eyes, brown mascara, and dainty white gloves and socks.

"I cannot find anything remotely like what they demand," Miss Electra is saying, biting her lip. "What shall I do?"

I have noticed that elderly individuals talk to themselves more than young ones, which comes in handy for an investigator like me who is all ears...they being very sharp and pointed and flexible ears. You might even say they had something in common with the Big Bad Wolf, except that I do not eat grandmothers like Miss Electra.

She is now shaking her head. "I cannot tell Temple, get her involved, dear girl, with her wedding plans and all. Nor Matt, that would be as bad. Who to call? Oh, dear. Going alone to that building where Jay died...I *told* them, I do not know. I do not have anything like that. And now they have taken my dearest companion. Such an ancient, gentle soul, in the hands of murderers."

Oh my Goddess! Karma has been kidnapped. Is it possible *I* was the object of a kidnapping when Miss Temple's place was broken into?

"'Tell no one,'" Miss Electra reads off the phone screen. "Oh, dear. Anyone coming to my rescue will give away the fact that I told. Maybe... If only I could make one tiny call..."

I can come to the rescue and no one will suspect me of being "told" a thing. Consider me Toto. Yes, comparison to a canine is demeaning, but that mincing little black dustmop was always one step ahead of Dorothy. Think about it. True. So it shall be with me.

I agree with Miss Electra. This time my Miss Temple must be kept well out of it. I retreat soundlessly, then catapult down the palm tree, rushing through the parking lot and bordering oleander bushes.

"No time to say hello-goodbye," I tell the clowder watch-cats as I streak through the bushes and past them.

A dog might "bark out" orders, but I use a mostly silent shorthand of strangled mews and guttural low growls that amount to: "Summon the Gray Ghost scouts and the Black Ninja Brigade. Cat in peril. I have a date with a gang of murderers under a lethal lighting fixture." ("Chandelier" is French and only the Divine Yvette, my lost love, and I know French.) "Tell Ma Barker to lead you under the mountain. She'll know where."

39
Gloves Off

Temple's faithful analog watch showed she had spent forty minutes typing down ideas for the new PR campaigns. The first project was for her and Louie's commercial future, and then— goofing off—plans for Electra's mythical, magical new marketing potential now that she had officially inherited the Lust 'n' Lace land and no one with a signed deed had shown up.

Urban planning was a kick. One hot new idea that might help Maeveleen Pearl's Thrill 'n' Quill bookstore…food and drink next door, as Barnes and Noble offered inside their stores. That was how the chain bookstores had "eaten up" the independents back in the day.

The Magic Muffin wasn't close enough and had a one-note menu, though deliciously varied. Maeveleen needed a full café right next door, and Temple had just the idea that might fly. She grabbed her cell phone to run the idea past Electra. No answer.

Darn. Hot ideas demand instant broadcast and feedback. And copious praise.

Temple tapped her toes. Her feet (in their shoes) often broadcast the clickety-clack of an old-time telegrapher's Morse code instrument. They kept her brain on simmer. If she were writing poetry, they'd be the meter that kept the words flowing. Thrill and Quill. The Mystery Menu. Café Poe. Amontillado Grill. Café Poetry. Café Coffee and Crooks. Crookery Nook. Nookery

Doc. *Getting out of hand.* Um, Coffee Noir. Café Noir. Café Noir Bar and Amontillado Grill.

Nothing was compelling. She tried Electra's phone again. Being invited to leave a message was not inspiring.

Temple checked her watch. Like many small businesses, Maeveleen's shop opened at eleven a.m. and closed at nine, hours that uniquely suited the location. Las Vegas's 24/7 operating schedule heated up in the afternoon and exploded in the evening hours. Her busy tapping feet kept the words spinning. Tempo. Tempo *Bar. Temple* Bar. Uh-oh, there already was one of those in Dublin. *Hmph.* No reason there couldn't be another. Las Vegas had once advertised it was "like no place else", but it had become like *every* place else—Venice, Egypt, Monte Carlo, Paris—why not have an Irish pub? Yeah, sure, and Max could run it.

Or, wait. A Chicago Bar, based on the hit musical, and Matt could run it.

Or...*you are getting really punchy, Temple.*

She shook her head free of outrageous ideas, and printed her note pages. She looked around one last time for Louie, then decided to head for the Thrill 'n' Quill. Louie had plenty of Free-to-Be-Feline in his bowl, Electra was out, and Maeveleen had to be on duty until nine. It was just eight thirty. Maeveleen was the perfect sounding board for Electra's new urban village concept, since hers would be a founding shop.

Temple was truly happy and hyped. Everything was rosy. Matt's career was back on track; so was Louie's. She had an exciting new career opportunity herself. Electra had dodged an economic bullet, and Temple could help her build a whole new retail world from the bottom up. High time to share her ideas.

"This is wonderful!" Maeveleen said after scanning Temple's two pages.

The shop was empty at the moment, except for two browsing women and Ingram snuggled in the window. He slept like Louie did, Temple noticed, always on duty. One ear down flat and the other perked.

"I particularly like the food places," Maeveleen said. "Local regulations have become so strict on banning animals where food is available, I can barely sneak in fast food for my lunch. What a difference a separating wall makes."

"This is all just blue-sky speculation," Temple said. "I haven't run it past Electra."

"Why not?"

"She's not answering her cell. Must not be around the Circle Ritz."

"No, of course not. A while back I saw her rushing past so fast she didn't even wave. I figured she was checking out her new building."

"When was this?

Maeveleen eyed the big clock on her wall.

"What a great cuckoo clock," Temple exclaimed. "I never noticed it."

"It's not a cuckoo-bird clock," Maeveleen said. "It's ravens baked in a pie. They pop out in appropriate numbers."

"Ravens? Weren't four and twenty blackbirds baked in a pie? Oh. Twenty-four hours. I get it. Ravens. Poe."

Maeveleen's broad smile showed her dimples. "Poe's poem, 'The Raven', is a mystery classic. Mystery is about the dark side of everything."

"Speaking of the dark side," Temple said, "it's getting late. Why would Electra be examining that building now? Its interior is darker than a bank vault even in daylight. I doubt any electricity is available."

"I'm sure Electra has her own plans for the space."

"Yes, but it helps to *see* the layout. Do you keep a decent flashlight here?"

"I park around the side, so no need."

Temple looked over her shoulder to the door. The shop was so cheerily lit, especially the front window in which Ingram basked, that you forgot the time. The sun set about eight thirty. That old building would be as dim as King Tut's tomb by now.

While Temple fretted, Maeveleen bustled away.

She returned and handed Temple something black plastic and bulky. "The Hardy Boys anniversary edition Junior Detective flashlight. I did put batteries in it so customers could try it out."

"I'm being silly," Temple said. "Let me call Electra again." She did.

"Well?" Maeveleen asked as Temple tapped the cell phone screen and set one impatient toe tapping.

"No luck. 'Leave a message.' Electra always keeps her cell on, given the things that can come up at an apartment building." Temple took the boxy flashlight. "I'll check the building, in case. She could have fallen on that rickety staircase."

Maeveleen looked dismayed. "I'd go with you, but I can't leave until closing."

"I've got a magic cell phone." Temple waved her (yes) *new* zebra-pattern Austrian crystal case before returning it to her tote bag with the printouts. Vegas hotel shops sold tons of crystal-embellished phone cases in every pattern under the sun, moon, and stars. "It should only take a few minutes to check this out, and I'll call you. I already entered your shop number in my contact list."

"Wonderful, dear." Maeveleen looked down. "Now don't you trip in those high heels."

Temple glanced down. "These are my pitons, like a cat's claws."

Even as she said it, she felt a small shiver of anxiety and rushed to get out the door.

The soft passage of air as it closed brought out goose bumps on her calves. That was odd, because the night air was as thick and temperate as lukewarm potato soup—maybe a baked potato with exotic toppings eatery, she envisioned—but the street was already darker than expected. Her imagined shops might show window lights or headlining neon at this hour, but once past the Thrill 'n' Quill only the occasional street lamp was on.

Temple phoned Matt. He wasn't answering either, although he often used the later hours before his show to do errands, Vegas being a 24/7 town. This was starting to feel ominous.

She looked back to see Maeveleen working at her computer and lit up like a sitting duck inside. Ingram had deserted the window.

He probably had been lured away by the bright, copy-reading lamp next to Maeveleen's computer, like Louie was on her desk. And if there were papers nearby, he'd be lying on them.

Temple looked up the dark street. Maeveleen had been right. Navigating the empty lot in heels would require a flashlight. *Thank you, Hardy Boys.* Luckily, she knew the terrain from daylight. She needed more than the Hardy Boys, though.

One call she knew would be answered. "Nicky! Hi. I'm worried about Electra. No. nothing concrete enough to call the police. I think she's in the abandoned building she inherited, and the female owner of the Thrill 'n' Quill bookshop near the Circle Ritz is alone in her shop nearby. Got some spare brothers for Maeveleen? Discreet backup would be welcome. Thanks."

Temple disconnected on his agreement and found herself in an unfamiliar state. Indecisive. Should she wait here for a flock of Fontanas to surround the Thrill 'n' Quill and the building just down the street with their black Tesla sport cars? Go inside with Maeveleen until she was sure the storekeeper had a bodyguard? There could be nothing good about where Electra was last seen going and her not answering her cell phone. Her muumuus all had pockets.

The sound of flip-flops hitting sidewalk made Temple turn to see the newcomer, a college-age girl in a hurry. "This place still open? I need some books for my creative writing class."

Books, plural. Good news for Maeveleen.

"Open until nine," Temple said.

"Great." The young woman blasted through the door, setting off the funeral bells.

She looked over her shoulder at Temple. "Cool effect. Thanks."

Temple wasn't so sure. Funeral bells could be an omen. She turned again to the bit of the empty lot she could glimpse ahead. Yikes. Dark came on fast in the desert and it seemed to be breaking records tonight. The Fontanas were en route. Meanwhile, anything could be happening to Electra, or nothing.

Temple saw movement near the lot, and took in a breath. Just a black cat, legs going as fast a centipede's, silently running out of view. More of a blur than a moving body.

Louie had been out before she left the condo. Apparently he'd been en route here too.

Temple trotted after him, her heels making a racket with no one around to hear them. That she noticed.

40
You Will Find Him

Max paused before taking the stairs up into that last step into the Irish air. "Kathleen?"

"We thank you for bringing her home again."

"You should know, she's—"

"We know what she is. For years her female fury made her the Cause's most profitable fundraiser."

Liam stood waiting, almost politely, for Max to leave. Max was getting an uneasy feeling. "That sounds like a testimonial."

Liam nodded.

"Like an obituary almost," Max added.

"Go on, man, you've got what you came for."

"She's worse now that the money-raising is done. She burned down my house."

"'Tis a shame, but 'tis none of your business now."

"I might not be done with her."

"We are not either."

Max sighed and turned back to face the room. "That woman tried to kill me more than once, the house fire being the latest attempt, which you'd no doubt applaud. She also threatened and stalked my innocent friends and acquaintances. Because of her, more than one of her hired associates has died. She seduces men because she hates them almost as much as she hates herself. She survived abuse from a childhood in a Magdalene institution that most men in this room would not. I brought her here to find Sean and Garry Randolph and rid my life of Kathleen O'Connor."

"Mission accomplished." Liam remained tip-lipped.

"But, ass that I am and you know me for, I can't abandon her to a situation that stinks to high heaven. What's going on?"

"At least you admit your serious assery. For an Irishman you certainly talk like a Spaniard." Liam sounded amused, rather than the expected angry.

"Spaniard?"

"Don Quixote, tilting at windmills, only something is in the wind here, you're right. This *is* a kangaroo court, but it's not for you. It's for Kathleen O'Connor."

Max swore. "There goes my Catholic conscience complicating my life again."

"If you want to sit yourself and your friend there at the bar and stay a while, you can have the satisfaction of witnessing it."

Pints were poured all around. Max couldn't decide if being handed one was a good or a bad omen. A last glass, or a last gasp. He couldn't drink here, and think as fast as he guessed he needed to.

Lingering in this place where every wall and table and face stirred memories of what would become his final adventure and moments with Gandolph was a kind of torture, and every man here knew and relished that. Add the smell of damp footwear and wool and yeasty beers...and he felt sick.

The men turned their heads as the door to the back room opened. Max slid the full pint glass to the back of the bar.

Kathleen came in, with the two men who'd escorted her inside. One dragged a chair from a nearby table, and took her arm to seat her at it. No beer or ale for her.

Her pale face looked even paler, eyes black with fear stared defiantly at Max, as if he were the only man in the room. Then she looked around, a bit wildly.

"What's this about? Don't I win a round of applause? I've brought you the traitor, haven't I?"

Max winced, not because she'd admitted her underlying motive all along, but because it wasn't sufficient.

"He was a rogue outlander, no doubt," Liam said, "and plagued us mightily back in the day, but he was never pledged to our cause, as you were."

"I've worked to aid the cause for almost twenty years," she answered. "Is it my fault you all ended it with a peace treaty?"

"We do, that," Liam said. "We do have a peace treaty. But you, my dear Kathleen, have a huge piece of the very lucrative booty pledged by all the faithful homeland exiles in South America. We've never seen so much as a *peso* of that. You yourself promised a 'mother lode'."

As Kathleen's interrogator spoke, the other men rose and came to take seats or stand in a circle around her.

Max recognized he'd been reduced to a mere witness to what looked like a witch hunt. He realized the accounting that could have been taken out of his hide, had he not been forgiven…had turned, with far more patriotic fury, on Kathleen.

His throat had gone so dry, he stretched out a long arm and reclaimed the pint glass for several swallows. Kathleen had mounted a vengeful crusade against him and his associates for more than a year. Were the IRA remnants showing him how they dealt with turncoats? Did they think he deserved, or even wanted to see their kangaroo court in action?

Kathleen crossed her legs, smartly clad in the blue-green pantsuit, and tossed her long black hair. "Sure, and is this recess on the playground, the boys ganging up on the girl?"

"For years you promised us the stockpiled results of your South American operations. That money is ours, donated to us. We'll use it for reparations for the families of soldiers who perished in our wars."

"A noble cause still," Kathleen said. Max noticed she had exaggerated the amount of Irish lilt in her voice. "The takings were in a…diffuse state, over time and distance. Some was left in wills to myself personally, or came from die-hards who wanted to stir the pot of resistance anew," she said. "Some had been collected earlier and…stored until it was easier to smuggle out of the various countries."

"And is some of it still there?"

"In South America? No."

"Then where in bloody hell is it?"

"Over the years my main South American associate managed to smuggle bits of it into the U.S. and get it safely hidden."

"Wonderful. Your associate can now make arrangements to get it to us."

"He's dead."

"What kind of a lame excuse is this?"

"Ask him." Her head gestured in Max's direction.

Every angry, disbelieving face in the room turned his way.

"Santiago," he said to Kathleen. "He'd been smuggling in some of the loot every time he had a U.S. gig?"

"Yes."

"Gig? Santiago, the city?" a man Max remembered as Mulroney asked.

"Santiago," Max explained to the group, "was a noted South American architect and concept designer. He'd never be suspected of smuggling, and would have had myriad ways to conceal almost anything in his project materials."

"'Was', past tense." Liam strode to loom directly before the seated Kathleen. "Then she's telling the truth. The man is dead."

"Not only dead. Murdered." Max emphasized the last word.

"Murdered. When?"

"Only weeks ago."

"By whom?"

"Unsolved," Max said with a sigh. "It could have been someone from the association of magicians called the Synth, which I mentioned to you on my last visit."

He had an offbeat and very secret suspicion who might have killed the flamboyant architect-designer, but that was unrelated to IRA issues. Or…was it? Was Santiago's death part of a political conspiracy instead of a planned sleight-of-hand treasure hunt and heist? Maybe the disgruntled magicians with their "Synth" secret society hadn't been as ineffective as everyone thought.

Liam remained dubious. "What were these 'projects' this Santiago created? And what was the bloke's surname?"

Max only now remembered that Temple had discovered Santiago's antecedents in South America had been Irish. Nothing these guys need know. "He never used a surname. Just the one name. Like Cher or…Bono."

"And what did he design, exactly?"

"Recreational fantasy attractions and rides, Disney for adults. His latest project presented Las Vegas's mobster past with an underground vintage car ride and holographic gangland figures."

"Like we would build a theme park based on the Troubles," Liam said, looking around at the shaking heads of his compadres. "Crazy. Americans are crazy, man."

"We are," Max said with a crooked grin. He was crazy for sure, volunteering to act as a buffer between the IRA has-beens and Kathleen.

The lead interrogator turned back to Kathleen. "So this man died and all the IRA money is lost in Las Vegas? You expect me to believe that?"

"Vegas got famous on people losing money there," Kathleen quipped.

The man behind her suddenly lifted up the back legs of her chair and slammed them down, jolting her.

"This is serious, woman," Flanagan said. "If we don't like your answers, we'll stop askin' questions and just take you out and shoot you as a traitor."

"You wouldn't do that to a woman," Max objected, shocked.

Kathleen ran a hand through her shaken locks and rounded on him with disbelief.

"Oh, Max Kinsella, you're still as naive as you were fresh out of American high school. They already have. Look up on your phone Jean McConville, widowed mother of ten, quite an accomplishment by the age of thirty-seven. Accused of spying for the British, she was abducted, shot in the back of the head execution style, and secretly buried. Only in the same year as your sainted film, *Philomena* came out, twenty fourteen, was a seventy-seven-year-old man arrested for the crime. Women who worked with the IRA knew her story by heart. And all of us approved."

Kathleen turned her head to look every man in the room in the eye. "Say here, this is me, that you've known since I was a girl. I was always for Ireland and the IRA. I raised millions for you in the Americas."

"And lost a couple million more," Flanagan muttered. "Yeah, you had the gift of partin' men from their money for the cause, but I've always suspected what you were doin' off there alone in Boston or São Paulo or Santiago, say. I told the brothers, you can't trust a whoring wacko."

In the silence, Max watched Kathleen's face. For the first time he saw color suffuse it, a flush that painted a measle-scape of color on her cheeks, like blotchy rouge.

Her knuckles as white as baroque pearls, her hands tightened on the chair's wooden arms, as if they were bound there, and Max worried they soon would be.

Kathleen would not go quietly.

"And who among ye held back and refused such tainted money? Who ran off to Confession or asked the priest to baptize the thirty pieces of tainted silver? How were my methods worse than to go secretly begging for pence to the good Catholic parishes of Chicago and Boston and St. Paul while I was being showered with pounds from the bad and the beautiful of Miami and New Orleans and Palm Springs and Rio and, yes, Santiago. But no, all along you didn't approve of the way I got it. What a stinking kegful of hypocrites! You're worse than pedophile priests murmuring rosaries while abusing altar boys."

Max held his breath.

Some element of the men's long silence suggested guilt.

"What we think of your bedding habits is not the point, Kathleen," Liam said. "The trouble is we have no reason to believe you're not a thief who's held back the last fruits of her recruiting. Who has cheated the widows and orphans. 'Tis maybe natural you'd want a retirement allotment, now that your assets are aging, but we can't let you cheat us. We couldn't let that happen before the peace, nor after it. Either tell us where that fabulous horde is, or you'll go to your grave with the secret."

She set her jaw and stared straight ahead, silent.

She was too proud to tell them she didn't know.

Max kicked himself again. "She doesn't know."

"If we wanted to hear from you, Yank, we'd have told you so."

"Listen. She did screw up. She'd been searching for me for years and finally found me in Las Vegas. She's been bedeviling the hell out of me and mine there ever since. I didn't ask to be the object of her obsession, but a stalker doesn't have time to mastermind a delicate smuggling operation."

"You sound like a fellow who could."

Max shrugged. "I'm a magician by trade, a secret agent by circumstance. Las Vegas is one of the surveillance capitols of the world. Better than Dubai, perhaps. It's not easy to hide, or move, or *remove*, money and guns there."

"Guns?" Liam was startled.

"Yes, and guns."

"So," he narrowed his eyes. "Who do you think that treasure trove should go to?"

"The money to the IRA for those widows and orphans, if you mean that."

"We do. What about the guns?"

Max shrugged. "To someone responsible, or be destroyed."

"Like the resistance?

"Depends which resistance."

"The Kurds?"

"God, yes."

"Good." Liam picked up his glass and walked to the bar. He hoisted the virtually untouched pint and handed it to Max, then touched the rolled glass lips in a toast. "You get us that money." He looked back to Kathleen. "We'll keep Mata Hari here on ice, so you're not distracted by a stalker. If you fail, she pays the price."

"No!" Kathleen sprang up, but strong hands pushed back down onto the chair. "He hates me! He doesn't know anything about what you call the 'hoard', I won't have my life depending on a turncoat to the IRA since the day I met him."

"Oh, you two have a tangled history, don't you?" Flanagan smirked. "Be interestin' to see what he does, won't it, Kathleen? Will he walk away again and leave you angry and alone?"

She started cursing in Gaelic.

Max's cool tones and stage projection overrode her. "I may have some serious personal business for a couple days after I get back to Vegas, but then I promise to search for and claim that undelivered IRA cash hoard. Can I go now?" Max asked.

Liam stepped back and spread his hands. "You know where to find us. As we know where to find you."

Max downed the beer, picked up Garry's urn, and left.

He paused outside the closed pub door to let the cold sweat shiver down his spine. He'd be interested to see what he did, too.

The last verse of the "The Minstrel Boy", added by an optimistic American after the Civil War, sounded in his mind has it had on the car CD system, from memory. It seemed written for Sean, for Garry, and even for Kathleen. Surely Ireland had always had its minstrel girls.

The Minstrel Boy will return we pray
When we hear the news we all will cheer it,
The minstrel boy will return one day,
Torn perhaps in body, not in spirit.

Then may he play on his harp in peace,
In a world such as heaven intended,
For all the bitterness of man must cease,
And ev'ry battle must be ended.

41
Face Off

Temple was not going through the building's front double doors...to end up in the dark with a flashlight, staring up at the huge, dirt-crusted chandelier that had served as a hanging tree for a man she'd seen alive, if only briefly. She remembered seeing Louie sniffing around the rear.

She skittered past the deserted-looking RV that served as an office and around to the back. She found a shabby door with some boards kicked out. Vagrants might have used the basement for shelter. The door to the outside had been caved in at one side.

She leaned against the building to strip off her heels and replace them with the foldable slippers she always carried in her tote bag. In doing so, she found a forgotten asset, the tiny, high-intensity flashlight on her keychain. So she stored the bulky Hardy Boys version in the tote, fished out the petite version and twisted it on. Better to make a smaller target.

The door opened on a small landing between rickety steps going up into the dark and sturdier ones going down. The air felt dry and had no particular smell, unlike damp, moldy Midwestern basements.

She glimpsed the black cat she'd ended up tailing dashing down the battered two-by-eight-board stair with the ease and energy of a creature who can climb a tree with Velcro-strong talons. This was starting to feel very White Rabbit, only with a Black Cat.

And maybe the cat was running with the verve of having been down here before, Temple thought.

"Louie," Temple called softly, teetering on the first wooden steps to the basement.

If Temple suffered from any one irrational fear, it would be claustrophobia rather than agoraphobia. She'd choose to be the cheese standing alone at the end of the nursery rhyme over the Ritz cracker crammed into a roll inside a wax wrapper and then sealed into a box.

She'd expected the basement to be a wide open space—dark, yes, but empty to its concrete block walls. What a decent Midwestern basement should be.

However the basement's exposed walls looked carved out of natural sandstone and caliche, a cement-hard soil compacted by the presence of lime. And the space wasn't as cavernous as she'd expected. Concrete block cubicles lined the outer walls, solid versions of the antique-mall display areas above, only closed in to the ceiling and locked with metal doors.

There must have been—well, count the doors on one side: twenty or so of them. Probably a storage unit for each of the upstairs sales booths in their heyday.

And the floor…it too was hard caliche, but the large central section had wooden floorboards, as if there'd been an interior room of some kind once. The condition screamed "long-abandoned". Broken-up concrete patches along some parts of the cubicle walls looked ripped up by a jackhammer, as if the Property Brothers crew from *HGTV* home network had passed through to bust up the old, but never came back to install the new and finish the makeover.

Hmm. She wondered about putting a funky fifties hippie nightclub down here, with poetry readings and candles in wine bottles. A scraping sound outside the flashlight's small beam made Temple sweep the edges of the area with pinpoints of light. No rats, no snakes. No cat either.

Great. She was hallucinating cats now. At least her soft slippers made her as silent as one.

Or maybe not. Her flashlight picked out a shadowy form. Midnight Louie pawing at a dark corner, nose to the ground, intent.

Cats only do that when there was something only they see, a crawling bug, maybe. Temple shivered. Vegas had lots of those. Scorpions, centipedes. Temple's toes curled in her slippers to avoid even the thought of stepping on creepy-crawlies.

"Louie! Don't bite anything that can possibly bite you back. Get away..." But Mr. Curious had to spot, sniff, paw, taste-test anything new that came into the condo, from a magazine to a centipede. And, if he could, take it apart. He could chew the metal off the top of lead pencils and then bat the extracted graphite rod around. She'd have to pursue him to recover the unsafe object.

No fast moves to be made here. The floor was deeply chipped away in places. She could sprain an ankle if she didn't watch out. She recalled the classic catchphrase from *Jaws*, "You need a bigger boat." She was pretty sure a Great White shark wasn't lurking on land, but she knew she needed her bigger flashlight. And maybe a Fontana brother or two.

"Louie! I'm not going to leave you alone down here. It's dangerous. Now, git. Go on!" She rushed him with a patter of steps going forward.

He wasn't fooled. This place was full of smells and nooks and crannies only he could detect and diagnose and dissect. He was like a mad scientist loose in a nasty, decrepit, dangerous playground.

"Louie, no!" she shouted. "Now quit that and get out." She flicked the flashlight fast toward the back stairs, wishing it was a red LED light no cat could resist, although Louie had gotten bored with an incorporeal toy that disappeared pretty fast.

Oh, boy. At times like these, when she was too committed to back out without going slowly, she wished she had a dog who would come when called.

Temple began to retreat. "Louie," she implored. She felt her flimsy flat-heel hit a hole and flailed to keep her balance. The tiny metal flashlight slipped out of her hand. Somewhere in the dimness a small metallic clink announced where it had fallen.

"Drat it!" No, that sounded too much like "rat". She shuffled a couple feet forward until she felt it and bent to retrieve it. Turning, she saw the steps had blackened and so had the door beyond them. Night had truly fallen.

She opened her mouth to call Louie...but heard a distant creak. Maybe from the far stairway. Temple found that sinister. If it had been caused by a footstep, had that stepper paused to listen?

Perhaps a passerby hearing her admonitions to Louie?

Someone who had come from vandalizing the Lovers' Knot front entrance again?

The unknown person who'd hung Jay Edgar Dyson.

Katt Zydeco, who was really a comics' super-villainess. *Oops.* She'd been watching too much *Gotham* on TV.

No, she was not going to yell or make noise again, not until she was safely out of here.

Something lifted her skirt edge. A mental *Eek!*

Then she felt a brush of velvet fur behind her knee. Louie! His erect tail was always getting fresh with her legs when she wore a skirt, as he moved back and forth around her ankles.

Great. He could trip her and she'd lie here unfound until global warming would have caused the Pacific to rise and swamp California and the Mojave desert...and a Great White shark would be found flailing in the tide and someone in the boat following would say, "You need a bigger flashlight."

Temple shook off her imaginative rerun of *Jaws*.

She took an unsteady step forward. A phantom tail brush saluted her other leg. She moved in hopes she could bend down and capture Louie, but another step brought only another unseen brush on her other leg.

Cats may not be able to see in the dark, but they do much better than a redhead with light-sensitive skin and blue-gray eyes. Temple knew. Carefully keeping her weight on a back foot before she slowly transferred it to a new step forward, she followed Louie's weaving path ahead of her.

Until her slippered toe stubbed something large and hard, in a totally creepy way. *Ouch!*

Was there now another abandoned dead body in Electra's inherited building?

The flashlight revealed a corpse, all right, a dead body of metal with a long narrow nose of shark-like saw-teeth. Why was she seeing sharks when she abhorred the species being demonized on "Shark Week" on cable TV? She recalled a *PBS* special that showed a sawshark, and then remembered something very insentient, something linked forever in the public mind with the word "massacre". A chainsaw. What was a chainsaw doing in a basement storage area? And a really nasty scissors-looking tool big enough to have pulled some real sharks' teeth?

She stepped carefully around the hardware and over the rough floor to examine one of the steel-doored storage units. Someone at some time had wanted to keep something very much under wraps in this building.

The flashlight revealed the door's big steel combination lock hooked over a thick latch...and showed the lock's curved neck had been cut through and was barely dangling from the latch. The flashlight beam glinted off the cut marks. They were the bright gleaming silver of new metal, unexposed to air and oxidation. She got out the big flashlight and illuminated the nearest door locks. All either had dangling cut locks, or broken locks lying on the floor below.

This damage was fresh, it was systematic, and the fact that all the doors had been breeched meant that the searcher or searchers had not found what was being sought. Temple parked the big flashlight in her tote bag again and used both hands to pull a door missing the lock entirely open enough to thrust her hand holding the tiny flashlight through.

She jumped. Huge metallic boxes taller than she stood in ranks like soldiers, light glinting off their steel silhouettes. The space seemed occupied by the mechanistic Borg from the *Star Trek* franchise. The "resistance is futile" aliens.

Temple backed away and was pulling out the big flashlight for a better view when she heard something from far above her, what would be a second story or attic in a house. A faint squeaking noise. Or, a desolate meow? Thumps, footsteps and maybe worse followed. Louie! She *had* seen Louie, only now he'd apparently gone *up* the back stairs. Why?

Another meow came from above, this time a puma's caterwaul, a long fierce growl changing into a wildcat scream, followed by a desperate feminine shriek. Electra! Then a man grunted and cursed.

Temple's imagination went wild. Following the big flashlight's broad beam, she backtracked to the stairs, then climbed the two flights of rickety steps to the top floor. Luckily, she weighed little and her flat slippers took her up the steps like a mountain goat.

She finally stepped onto the second story at the back of the building, switching to the tiny flashlight to be less noticeable, pointing it down to the floor, squinting down the hall between the abandoned antique mall cubicles, toward a black knot of figures gathered under the grotesque chandelier maybe two hundred feet away. The guttural buzz of lowered and threatening voices drifted back to her. And one higher, pleading voice. *Oh, Electra!*

She started forward, crazy, but she couldn't ignore the danger to Electra and Louie. Besides, reinforcements were coming.

As she walked on silent slipper soles, she detected motion on her left and froze, taking out Hardy Boys flashlight as a weapon. It didn't look like plastic at first glance.

About halfway to the figures ahead surrounding a light as if circling a campfire, she saw a dark, sitting cat, licking its paw.

Louie, that relaxed?

Then she squinted harder and saw…the dark color was brown, not black. This was Ingram! *That* was what…who…she'd felt grazing her calves and giving her goose bumps as she'd left the Thrill 'n' Quill. What would draw an ensconced, only-indoor cat like Ingram this far from home?

Ingram leveled a bored yellow gaze at her and switched to grooming his other paw. *What!* All she had on her side was this couch potato bookshop pussycat, who had probably only used its claws to work out an errant knot behind its ears?

She sighed and edged forward. Weirdly, the electrified chandelier was lit. Murky light filtered down through the dusty loops and faceted pendants of glass. It looked like a light fixture snatched from Mephistopheles in Hell.

The chandelier barely illuminated what resembled a stage set in a dark theater. Four standing men surrounding a simple worktable and chairs. Two women sat on the chairs, the most concentrated light from above falling on their pale-haired heads like the spotlights used in Film Noir police interrogation rooms. Temple recognized Electra's Bird of Paradise design muumuu, fading to pastel in the overhead light, as did her shadow-sunken features. Oh, Lord. The other woman was blonde. *Oh no, Diane!* Both of them, ex-wives of the dead man who'd dangled above this strange vignette at the top of the stairs only days ago…captives. Of whom? Why? What was happening here?

"I don't have it, I've said that over and over," Diane was telling the standing people, who must be the extortionists. Temple's fuzzy focus identified the silhouettes of the usual suspects, Punch and Judy, a.k.a. Punch Adcock and Katt Zydeco, Leon Nemo, and some other guy as tall and limber as Katt.

"Please let us go." Diane was whining, pleading now. "I went through every damn thing, paper or property, relating to Jay in Dayton and gave it to my lawyer to forward to the attorney here." Her blonde head swiveled toward Electra. "Tell them. They know you must have it. Don't be a hero. They mean to hurt us."

"I don't have whatever it is. I don't have anything from Jay," Electra said through gritted teeth. "I tore my place apart, looking for your damn paper. I brought anything you might want. It's all there. Let us go! Let us all go."

"All go"? Temple thought the usage strange. Only Electra and Diane were on the hot seats. And what "paper" was so valuable?

Then Temple saw that the table held a big box of some sort. Maybe something found in one of the violated storage units below. A few white sheets of paper lay atop it.

"This is a freaking marriage license, lady!" one of the men shouted as he grabbed one paper to shake in Electra's face. "Between you and the late Dyson. You think we give a damn about your marriage license?"

Leon Nemo's voice had lost its forced joviality and was all anger and threat.

"No," Electra answered, "but how would I know *what* you want? You won't say what it is, it's so secret. 'Just the paper', you said. Get me the right paper. It's a license.' What you're holding is the only 'license' I have, except for four others like it."

"We don't want your driver's license, that's for sure," Punch's deeper bass voice said.

"What 'four others' like it?" Katt Zydeco asked. "All *marriage* licenses?"

Temple barely saw Electra's shrug. "Yes. Marriage licenses. We can go and get the others. I had four other husbands."

"You?" Katt's jeering tone was not flattering.

"Forget jabbering with the old dame," Nemo said. "She's holding out on us. Let's get down to business." He slammed the palm of his hand against the box. It rattled and shook as Electra shouted, "Don't!"

It rattled. It was metal. Not as big as the machines downstairs, though.

Punch stuck the box with his fist and it slid a bit across the table. Electra whimpered.

Temple moved closer, unheard, unnoticed, but seeing more clearly. The box sides weren't solid. It was a metal fence.

Something in it moved. Something shadowy and alive.

A cat.

Temple felt sick. She'd always thought of Midnight Louie as her personal black panther with the street smarts of an undercover cop. His claws could disable a two hundred-pound man with instantly septic, six-inch long slashes that burned like the flames of hell. He'd come to her rescue more than once, smaller and underrated and fiercer than a Belgian Malinois used for K-9 duty. Heck, he'd take out the Malinois and his first cousin the German Shepherd too.

Now he'd been caught somehow, was caged and helpless while her friends were being brutalized by thugs. Temple had never felt the instant blind, unstoppable, defensive maternal rage that could lift cars off children, but she charged forward, immune to any personal danger, screaming, "Get away, you bastards!"

Her charge had the criminal crew turning wide eyes and mouths her way. Electra and Diane half rose from their chairs, their wrists visibly bound, but their shock and hope breaking the bonds of intimidation for an instant. The rope binding Electra's wrists was loosely tied—the fiends—to the chandelier. As the late Jay Dyson probably had been. Only that rope had been taut and around his neck, not securing his wrists.

The only sound for a few seconds was the weak slap of Temple's slipper soles on the wooden floor. Without her customary high heels, she sounded no more dangerous than a performing seal.

The captive cat in the cage produced another unearthly yowl. Louie used a spine-tingling Big Cat yowl when he attacked, but this cry ranged higher and higher into an ear-splitting banshee shriek.

The cat's eyes glared red in dimness. With its back hooped, tail straight up, and hair standing on end, it looked like it had been electrified by lightning, an iconic black "Halloween cat". Except it resembled a photographic *reverse* of a Halloween cat, for it was white, like a ghost.

The scene and sound were so unearthly three men and three women around the table were all frozen, as if posed. Everyone's eyes watched the cat and the cage. Everyone's hands but hers were clapped to their ears.

Temple wondered what exactly she was going to do when she reached them all, hit Nemo with her tote bag and kick Punch and Katt in the shins with her floppy slippers?

The caged cat howled again.

Temple could only stop her insane charge by throwing her arms around Electra on the nearest chair, pulling her down to the stability of the floor, both of them falling backwards, away from the scary down-slide of steps to the first floor. Diane crawled on her knees to join them.

Another noise, like the power tools Temple had seen in the basement grinding away added to the cacophony. The double wooden doors at the building's front shattered and burst open. Every eye focused there. Something big crashed through the opening in a blaze of light.

Temple made out the front grille of a car jerking up and down as the tires climbed the first few steps, the vehicle's body shaking and its bouncing, blinding headlights pinning everyone where they stood, or had fallen.

Its front wheels crashed through the steps a third of the way up.

Temple saw the driver's side door fanning open and a silhouette stepping out even as the motor died.

She sensed a silhouette, a shadow evading the gathering at the top of the stairs, sliding past her and slipping down the long dark hall behind her as she struggled to rise and help Electra up.

Below, a moving narrow black crack started between the headlights and snaked below the left headlight on the car's nose. The blot of black reared up and up in the figure of a hunched demon from a horror movie, an image projected and magnified by the light behind it, stretched up as a huge distorted shadow climbing the stairs. An image that resolved into the figure of a giant Halloween cat about to cast them all in shadow.

"What the hell?" Nemo yelled.

The caged cat shrieked again. "Punch, shut up that cat."

"Shoot the cat in the cage, boss?" Punch asked. "Those headlights. I can't focus—"

"Give me the gun," Katt said.

"Karma!" Electra wailed, gripping Temple's shoulders. "Karma."

Temple could only think they needed to call on more than fate.

But apparently it was effective.

She sensed or saw something in the absolute dark behind the invading car, like heat rising and distorting the air, a sort of visual storm surge along the floor that was dividing around the stalled car as the blurred mass and motion came racing toward the top of the stairs, multiplying into individuals as it neared.

Temple thought of the rats leaving Hamlin, but these were cats. A wind of cats, a tsunami of fur and claws and nerve-chilling howls swept up from the front stairs below. The first at the head of the pack to come into focus was black, but it wasn't Louie. It was a true scary Halloween cat from Hell with a raggedly coat and a mauled ear and one eye half shut.

It leaped straight for the table and the others came washing over everything behind it.

Washing like water or a strong wind, yes. Temple felt a chilling shiver of something cold passing through her even as running cats bumped her legs and arms as they leaped to the table and then up and over the shoulders and heads of Leon Nemo, Katt Zydeco, and Punch Adcock.

The chandelier above swung slowly like a possessed hangman's noose, its weak light flickering.

Temple looked up, horrified. She saw every thick crystal branch was occupied, ornamented, by cats. Black cats, white cats, gray cats, yellow cats, brown-striped tabby cats, calico cats, no doubt T.S. Eliot rum tum tugger cats, maybe even the Cheshire Cat.

And then all these cats with claws out dropped down like bats upon the flailing hands and shrugging shoulders and confused faces of Leon Nemo, Katt Zydeco, and Punch Adcock as they joined in the blurred flow of…entities down the long dark hall presumably to the back stairs and out into the warm Las Vegas night.

"What's going on with the air-conditioning?" Nemo demanded, frowning and batting away invisible webs. "Who let in that mangy pack of cats and spooked them?"

Temple realized then that nobody had seen the huge confluence of cats she had, but had certainly felt it.

"Get that guy," Nemo ordered, pointing.

Temple looked down the stairs and definitely saw, not a fading-away figure and not an oncoming mystical cat, but an energized man charging the stairs like a Navy SEAL. He leaped over the broken planks and his footsteps thundered up the remaining steps. The bill of a gimme cap kept his features shadowed despite the chandelier's milky light.

He pounced to kick Nemo's feet right out from under him. Leaning back from Punch's ham-sized fist, he delivered a roundhouse to the cheekbone that spun the hefty ex-boxer down a couple steps. Katt Zydeco, trying for a karate kick, had her suspended leg twisted and fell face-first to the floor.

The mystified threesome lay grunting, some from tiny fiery surface wounds inflicted by the claw-driven bounds the recent mass exodus of a few feral and many ghostly cats over their epidermis.

Was this Nine Lives moment a hallucination? Temple wondered. *Her* hallucination? Was she getting psychic as well as punchy?

Then the martial arts guy doffed the ugly cap, and grinned.

"Matt," Temple said, even more mystified. "How did you end up here?"

Everything in this murky scene was abruptly stage-lit as several twin orbs of bright light breeched the open doors and entered to hover eerily around the stalled white Probe, the black of night behind them. Then the blurred and light-bleached figures swarmed past the beached Probe as they too charged the stairs.

Were the debunked Las Vegas strip UFOs, laid to rest in the recent Area 54 affair, actually real and these newcomers the floating armada's crews? No. Temple remembered shiny black Tesla sport cars were electric and arrived as silently as gliding alien ships…or certain Vegas "Family" members turned into circling vultures.

Arriving Fontana brothers cooed Italian who-knows-what endearments as they dusted the ladies off, which was a bonus for suffering the night's terrors, and promised soothing limo rides to police headquarters.

They promised the same rides (without the soothing) as they helped Matt secure Nemo and his downed and dazed underlings. The brothers produced cool, matte-black steel handcuffs that matched the Family Fontana Berettas. They bound the cat-napping crew in uncomfortable, contorted positions on the dusty, gritty floor while Julio speed-dialed Lieutenant C. R. Molina.

Matt pulled Temple, then Electra and Diane, away from the dusty, gritty floor.

Temple grabbed Matt's hand and said one word. "Louie."

He turned to the table, then carefully righted and lifted the cage thrown to the floor in the assault.

Inside was…not Louie, but a serene cream-colored, long-haired cat with snow-white paws and a light brown mask that emphasized unearthly blue, blue eyes.

"Karma!" Electra bit her lip, her own eyes luminous with tears. She opened the cage door to stroke the silky fur. "I thought I'd lost you."

"Temple," Matt said softly, only to her, "I thought I'd lost you. That can never happen again."

His sentiment was wordlessly echoed by a velvety phantom brush around her ankles. She didn't need to look down. You-know-who had shown up at last.

So, say…Temple was a modern woman. Modern women deserve modern men. She could safely swoon now, knowing her boys, Matt and Louie, were safe. And knowing she'd take out anyone who'd threaten the life and loves she'd built for herself.

But she didn't feel like it. Not in the least.

42
Killer Karma

I must say that Karma has mighty potent…well, karma, but it was I who roused the cat clowder, which was the only physical force present. I could see my Miss Temple sensed Karma's invisible magnification of feline force. She may find her Inner Cat at that.

For once, I watched the action from the fringes.

When things have calmed down, I survey the situation. I showed up late because I had to give a high-five of the Front Four sheathed shivs to Ingram for leading my Miss Temple to the rendezvous while I was herding cats from the clowder to the scene. We all know how hard herding cats can be.

Ingram has headed home. He will be able to slip back into the Thrill 'n' Quill unnoticed when Eduardo visits to ensure Miss Maeveleen is undisturbed and closing up shop for the night. For "owners", people sure are dim about what their cat companions are thinking and doing.

Whatever Karma conjured, it was a first-class special effect befitting the most spiritual cat breed (excepting the Egyptian Mau).

The Sacred Cats of Burma are famed for defending a Tibetan monk when their temple was raided ages ago. Only two of their kind survived in Europe after World War II, one male and one female, luckily or unluckily, depending on one's interaction with Karma. She is of the revived Western branch of the breed, and mighty snooty about her exclusive line.

She does seem to have a smidge of astral projection talent, I confess. I suspect that Ma's clowder was enhanced by some such

Eastern out-of-body hocus pocus to produce the river of feline vengeance on Karma's behalf.

As for the cheesy "Cat signal" using the Probe's headlights to project a twenty-foot-high Halloween cat silhouette like the Batman signal in Gotham, I know the usual suspect for that.

What a drama queen! Females!

I realize Miss Midnight Louise, miffed because I assigned her to follow "dull" Mr. Matt, took advantage of the situation to grab the limelight as well as distract the villains at the top of the stairs. And what about Mr. Matt's NASCAR performance, huh?

I will still have to have a word with my junior partner when all the dander settles.

Whatever or however, tonight was a fine performance by all felines involved. For me, it was also good preparation for directing the new cat food commercials. Anonymously, of course. I do not need credit. Just control.

Julio is going to explain to Miss Lieutenant C. R. Molina that the captives were cut when they evicted resident vagrants and feral cats that had inhabited the abandoned building's basement.

Good luck with that story. It will not fly any better than the recent UFOs on the Las Vegas strip rumor.

When I show up after the main action, I cannot say I relish my little doll's saltwater on my relatively skimpy ruff, a poor thing, but my own. She should know by now I am her go-to guy, even when I do not put in a mind-rocking personal appearance.

With Mr. Matt there to hold and shelter and admonish Miss Temple for intemperate risk-taking behavior, I feel my role is—gasp—redundant. I am expecting to put up with a lot of that after the imminent nuptials.

It is at times, perhaps, the better part to be an invisible influence, which Karma well knows.

Miss Electra is repeatedly kissing Mr. Matt's cheek, calling him "my hero", and assuring him that her old Probe crashed upon her newly acquired stairs is of no account. In fact, both needed replacing and she will now save a bundle in demolition and hauling charges.

He is managing to accept her gratitude while hanging on even tighter to my Miss Temple. She is fretting about what Miss Lieutenant C. R. Molina will say. Or ask. Ask her and ask him.

Such sweetness and light gives me a tummy ache, so I withdraw unnoticed back to the fringes. Ma Barker and I sit together in the shadows, watching the mopping-up operations, which consist of patrol officers taking Nemo, Adcock, and Zydeco away.

The third man slipped away down the back stairs, but that being such a classic film noir title, *The Third Man*, I am okay with letting him go, especially as I know his size, gait, and scent. I will be ready for him next time if he is so foolish as to enter my territory again.

"I am surprised, Grasshopper," Ma muses, sounding contemplative. If you knew Ma, you would know how out of character contemplative musing is. "I am surprised you were content to merely sound the alarm and sat back to leave matters to your sponsors and my Las Vegas Cat Pack."

"If I help my clients too much and too often and too openly, they will not take pride in their own prowess. They will not believe they have such a thing. There are times when a guy-guy must step aside and let events happen for themselves. It is not about claiming credit, it is about the outcome."

Ma nods her scruffy head. Being a feral female is a tough—and usually not a long—life. Ma has held our gang together for longer than most, but it has taken a toll on her health and looks. Not her attitude, though.

"What do you make of that bit of folderol-spouting fluff? Karma Chameleon or whatever, some fancy purebred hokey name? She insisted on telling me I had used up eight-and-a-half of my lives and should think about retiring while I can."

"She fancies herself some kind of prophet, but she does not know Bast would not dare call you over the river Nile onto her own turf for at least a dozen more lives."

Ma gives a cat laugh, which sounds a bit like uncontrollable coughing to humans, who rush over and try to give us the Heimlich maneuver. So much for having a sense of humor.

"One thing I might consider," Ma says, looking sideways at me with her yellow eyes.

"Yeah?"

"I might let those UFO abductors catch me some night, with a full dish of sardines."

"Ma! Why?"

I know they are actually Trap, Neuter, Return do-gooders hoping to end the overpopulation and species cleansing afflicting our kind since forever, but I am not sure Ma cottons to the concept of "neuter".

"Sardines are hard to come by, and I am hoping to get what you did from a similar kidnapping," she confides out of the side of her mouth.

"What? A vasectomy?" I am horrified.

"Silly boy. Of course not, but I will have to get one of those unnecessary hysterectomy things humans go on about. I am hoping to get a tummy tuck thrown in, as you did. That improved your profile a lot." She winks. Or her one eyelid is habitually a little haywire.

There is no way to explain to Ma that only human miscommunication saved my, uh, assets. So I was not neutered, not by a long shot. I see I am going to have to somehow maneuver Ma into the hands of B-movie actress Savannah Ashleigh's equally dense plastic surgeon. That will be a very demanding operation in more ways than one.

To say the least.

So I do not say anything further. That is always an option and, with Ma, often the best one.

43
License to Lose

Temple sat back on her bare heels on Electra's Chinese rug. She'd neatened the papers Electra had flung every which way in a desperate search for anything that might placate Karma's catnappers.

Electra sat on her vintage cocoa-colored couch with the fringe border along the floor and Karma out of sight beneath it.

"Nothing resembling what the creeps wanted," Temple said. "Have you considered that we might have to search every storage locker for it, and never find it? Why didn't you tell me your cat was kidnapped?"

"I can't understand how anyone knew about her. I don't advertise I have her, really," Electra said, pleating her voluminous muumuu skirt into folds. "She's so shy. I provide her asylum."

"From what? Crooks like those nappers?"

"From overstimulation. I think she's a psychic magnet."

Temple gave up. "Well, she is beautiful. It's too bad the Lust 'n' Lace gang, when arrested, didn't fess up like crooks on TV and blab about what Jay Edgar had that was worth killing for." Temple moved another insurance document to its proper pile. "J. E. didn't seem so bad, from what I saw of him."

"He wasn't." Electra pursed her lips. "He just had a weakness other people liked to exploit. You know…" Her voice broke.

Temple got up to sit beside her. "What is it?"

"He didn't tell them what they wanted. He…died. I can't help but think, in some way, that paper he wanted to save, whatever it was, was meant for *me*, for my golden years. He'd already left me all the real estate he had, except the house for Diane, which was really sweet. Oh, Temple, I wish I hadn't cussed him out before he died. Why can't we know these things before we rant and rave?"

"We're not all Karma," Temple said, hugging Electra's plump shoulders. "And even the police can't always solve these cases. It's really not procedure for Molina to want to meet us at the building. Are you up to going back?"

"What about you, Temple? You nearly toppled down the stairs racing to my rescue. You were so cute in your little slippers with your curls and tote bag bouncing, coming on like Bruce Lee if he were a girl."

Temple shut her eyes. So much about that description was so wrong, but if Electra needed to think anything but crazy fear and rage had motivated her, fine.

"You know," Electra said, "watching Matt ram my old Probe into the doors and up the stairs like he was General Patton was worth the angst. Those would-be cat-torturing rats went white as sheets. We really taught them not to mess with the Circle Ritz."

"Right." Temple stood up and grinned. "Let's find out what Molina is doing to them dirty rats. She wouldn't have asked to meet us on site unless she has some info to torture us with."

In ten minutes they were standing inside the old building, gazing at the ruined lower stairs. The chandelier was gone after the police had photographed and fingerprinted it once again.

All five-foot-eleven of Molina came in through the open double doors, wearing one of her khaki pantsuits, loafers, with a badge on her belt, not around her neck, since this was not a "live" crime scene.

"Good morning, ladies. I hope, Mrs. Lark, revisiting this site is not too much of stressor for you."

That was Molina, Temple thought, using words like "stressor".

"I'm not a 'Mrs.' Lark. Lark is my maiden name. Luckily, I kept it all through my legal life."

"What's happening to the creeps who stressed her?" Temple asked.

Molina moved toward them in casual, sweeping strides that nearly matched her almost six-foot height. A smile kissed her lips and immediately left for the coast.

"Legally, we don't have much evidence besides kidnapping, extortion, and animal abuse to charge them with. The real question is what they wanted so badly that it involved so many for so little apparent profit."

Molina looked at the top of the stairs, to the absence of the shabby but spectacular chandelier. She regarded Electra with sympathy.

"Ms. Lark. I have to tell you that your ex-husband's murder is an open case. There's no doubt he was brought to Vegas by Nemo and his associates because they wanted to get something out of him."

Electra looked up, and sighed at the emptiness.

"There's no doubt," Molina said, "that they bound him, and later you, over the drop from the chandelier to threaten you both into divulging what they wanted. But. We can't prove it was murder in his case."

She came closer to Electra. "The threat to you was nasty, but hardly homicidal. As for Jay Dyson, they were rougher with him. I don't doubt the rope was around his neck. Poised over the staircase, he was a desperate man. He had not yet given them what they wanted."

Molina sighed. "Dyson dead was of no use to extortionists. He could have accidentally swung off the edge, by his struggles. Maybe he managed to do it himself, to stop them from getting what they wanted. From getting what he wanted to go to you."

"Oh, my Lord," Electra said. "I'd rather believe it was an accident by all parties present, than that Jay would sacrifice his life to keep something for me."

"That's very possible," Molina said. "Your ex-husband had lost his business. If he still had something of enormous value, perhaps the act of keeping it became an obsession and he *couldn't* give it up to anyone else. That would explain why you don't have any idea what it was and nothing significant is mentioned in the will. He was obsessively overprotective of it, and no one will ever find it."

Electra nodded. "Jay was stubborn."

"Well, darn it," Temple said, stretching to her full five-foot-three height in her heels, which made Molina look down at Temple's smartly shod feet and lift her eyebrows. "Then what are we meeting for?"

"That was just one speculative scenario." Molina's smile was broad. "Leave it to our fine Metro patrol officers. They recognized the call to this address and pointed us to their report about the same site a few days ago."

"Report?" Temple, uneasy, switched her weight from one foot to the other. "Just the other day or so?"

"Just the other night," Molina said. "Local residents complained of a large number of vehicles coming and going, using their on-street parking places and even No Parking zones. And making a lot of noise. Not a crucial call. By the time the patrol car got here, the block party was over, but there were signs a pop-up casino had been plugged onto the lot."

"A pop-up casino? Never heard of it." Temple couldn't help sounding dubious. Her job was to know Las Vegas venues pretty thoroughly.

Even Molina's sensible loafers must have hurt to stand on. She took a stroll around the area in front of the stairs and changed the subject. "This is a huge place, Ms. Lark. What are you going to do with it?"

Electra followed her, nervously. "I…we have plans. Something in the retail and restaurant line."

"Ambitious," Molina said, nodding. She turned suddenly to Temple. "What do you think a pop-up casino you've never heard of is?"

"Portable, of course. Temporary," Temple said. "Reminds me of the food truck movement. Would be like those parking-lot small circuses that churches sponsor for fund-raising. Would operate for a limited time. Would have to be nonprofit, though. Gaming is strictly regulated in Las Vegas."

"A-minus," Molina said, offering Temple a triple-folded website printout from her blazer pocket.

Temple scanned it. A company offered week-long insty-casinos where gamers were paid in prizes and any profits went to good causes. Portable booths and tents housed gaming equipment, so the experience "felt" like real casino gambling, but wasn't.

"What was the minus for?" Temple asked Molina.

"You were warm but not hot when you analyzed what a pop-up casino would be."

"Temple's ideas are always hot," Electra said, scanning the pages Temple handed her. "She was right on the money about this company."

"Not quite. There's another, much more serious kind of pop-up casino because of a quirk in Vegas gaming laws." She challenged Temple with another question. "Have you ever heard of a nightclub called the Zoot Suit Choo-Choo Club?"

Temple and Electra exchanged guilty looks.

"Um, yeah," Temple said. "Kinda."

Molina's foot stamped the floor. "Right here in this building, under us. That's where it was until it became the other murder site in this place, only it happened decades ago. Another outre hanging, this one by a zoot suit cat chain."

"The history of that time period," Temple said, her eyes narrowed, "has been quashed and forgotten. Past racist issues are unflattering to what the Strip was before it integrated for its own commercial good."

Molina looked contemplative. "The mob remembers." She took another turn around the huge area and looked up to where the ceiling was empty.

Every one of them pictured the murderous chandelier.

"*Someone* in the mob remembers," Molina said. "Remembers both the earlier murder by chandelier and the fact that the Zoot Suit Choo-Choo Club had a golden asset, a gambling license. A license that lasts forever, if every two years the site is used as a live gambling establishment."

"Is that's how the Moulin Rouge kept going for all the decades when it closed after eight months in nineteen fifty-five?" Temple asked.

Molina nodded. "So you *are* clued in. It changed hands, and the license with it. Nobody could make a go of the site because it was so far from the Strip. In order to keep its gaming license, the casino 'opens' once every two years with a temporary on-site trailer, like the one you've got parked outside." She glanced at Electra.

"I may not own that RV," Electra said.

"Nemo and company can reclaim it. They and others before them have kept that Zebra Zoot Suit Choo-Choo Club pop-up casino schedule going with the aid of 'unnamed' financial backers," Molina said. "They have photographic proof. If you could find the actual paper license in the next two years, Ms. Lark, you would own a prize the Strip conglomerates would love to snap up."

"And Nemo and company won't do jail time?" Temple asked. She wondered if the "others before them" had killed Jumping Jack Robinson over the gaming license too.

"Not much, unless I get more evidence in Dyson's death." Molina turned and walked out the new sturdy double doors. "New security doors installed in the back too?"

Electra nodded.

"Good." Molina grinned. "That ought to keep out 'the vagrants and feral cats' for a while. Ms. Barr sure knows how to spin a press release."

Temple managed to smile as sweetly as a good hostess escorting a guest to the door.

"By the way," Molina said before walking over to Detective Alch leaning against a white Crown Victoria in the parking lot. "You and Mr. Devine seem to have forged a more perfect partnership. You've even lured him into investigative action as well as an impressive martial arts display."

Temple wasn't sure what Molina meant, but there was some snark in there somewhere.

"Should I be looking for a wedding invitation?" the lieutenant inquired.

Temple snorted.

"Out-of-state trip to see the family, huh?" Molina said. "Speaking of which, it seems Mr. Kinsella has folded his tent and moved on."

Temple shrugged. "I really don't know where he is."

"I do know," Molina said, coming Great White Shark closer with her electric-blue eyes and white-toothed smile. "I know that the first time I interviewed you after you came to Vegas and Kinsella had gone missing at the same time a body turned up and fell down onto a craps table at the Goliath Hotel...I know you gave me that very same answer to the very same question.

"And look how that turned out."

44
Instant Redial

That night Temple hesitated over answering her bedside cell phone. She was wide awake at nearly midnight and thinking of tuning in to the first part of Matt's show. Maybe he'd give her a quick "good night" call before going on the air.

She glanced at the lit screen. No, not Matt calling. Not a familiar number. Foreign.

Her knuckles tightened on the nubbly crystal surface of the cell holder. "Yes?"

"I hope so." Max's voice.

Firm. Sardonic. More welcome than she wanted to admit.

"How did things go in Ireland? Are you all right? Is Sean really alive?"

"Yes."

"Yes, you're all right or yes, Sean's alive?"

"Both. Sort of."

"Oh, God, Max. I don't like 'sort ofs'."

"He's a bit the worse for wear, but the most contented man I've ever met. He survived the pub bombing with visible wounds, and the invisible one my generation of family is becoming known for."

Temple was confused. Then Max said, "Bomb explosion. Impact. Head wound. His memory is faulty."

"So, like you, Sean has been blessed with the multiple lives of a cat to have survived."

"Yeah. The IRA's call to clear the pub before the bomb blast went awry. An IRA sympathizer on site knew about the bomb, and was finally able to get him out of there, not quite soon enough. She was injured too, but he wouldn't leave because he was waiting for me to come back."

"Oh, Max!"

"A kick in the gut, yes. Sean was messed up on his left side, and was foggy about who he was and where he belonged for some time, so the IRA took him in as one of theirs until he healed. When Sean did remember his home and family, he learned I'd disappeared after getting the bombers IDed and arrested. He didn't want to go limping home after the dumbass moves we made on our own in Ireland, and by then he had an Irish wife. So he ended up working for the IRA, the peace not the terrorism. He and his wife run a bed and breakfast in County Tyrone."

"That's amazing. Even more amazing is the fact that Kitty the Cutter delivered. She didn't lie this time."

"She also didn't expect Sean and me to let bygones be bygones. She thought we'd spout recriminations and go for each other's throats."

"She found you once you went to Ireland?"

"Hell, Temple, I flew her over there. I wasn't trusting to luck with getting the likes of her out of all our lives in Vegas."

"You were *traveling* with her? How did you sleep?" Temple felt a blush teasing the edges of her cheeks. She'd hadn't meant "sleep", but just sleep.

"Not often. I'm exhausted. Look, I'm bringing Sean back with me."

"To Vegas?"

"Maybe, but principally to Racine, to reunite the family."

"Oh, my God. That'll be a three-act wrenching drama Eugene O'Neill couldn't live up to writing even if he were still alive. I can't imagine how shocked they'll be, and then angry at the two of you for cutting and running into new lives without them."

"You don't have to imagine," he said, "I'm hoping you'll round up your immense people skills and come along as a referee."

"What? No. I can't leave Vegas now."

"Last time I called from Ireland, you told me to come home."

"And I am telling you to 'go home' to Racine now. Everything is different. Matt and I are seriously committed. I can't leave my fiancé behind and go waltzing off to intercede between my ex and his cousin and their parents. I don't know these people, and I'm sure they don't want to know me."

"It's about *what* you know, not who you know."

"What do you mean?"

Max sighed. "There are holes in my recent memories. Holes in Sean's memory of the attack and why he decided to rebuild a life in Ireland, leaving everyone mourning when they didn't need to be. Including me. We need an outside negotiator, and I, I need the help only you can give, Temple. I need an ombudsman. I chose to be absent too. There are a lot of robbed lives in Racine."

"I can't ask Matt to step aside for you showing up in our lives again."

"Try. He's a compassionate guy."

"He's not a saint, and it would take the patience of one to stand for this."

"I'm emailing you a photo of Sean and Deirdre, his wife."

"I am not going to be emotionally blackmailed into going AWOL from Vegas to Racine, Wisconsin, of all places."

"Sure you will. You're a compassionate guy, too."

"I'm not looking at the photo if you send it. You cannot guilt me into putting Matt second again."

"Listen. Tell Matt that helping me settle the Kelly and Kinsella family matters is the surest way to get me out of the picture."

"Kelly and Kinsella. Sounds like a law firm."

"Or a string of Irish B and Bs."

"You retired? Impossible."

"You not curious? Impossible."

"Okay. I am curious. Where is Kitty the Cutter in all this?"

The pause was ominous. "She's confined to Ireland at the moment. We observed her grown daughter at a distance and then toured a Magdalene asylum so she could vent her spleen on an old nun, me, and God."

"Grown daughter? My God. You believe in living dangerously more than ever."

"Think about it, Temple. Racine won't be dangerous, just exhausting. The ends of stories always are. I need you."

And then he hung up.

Well, dang and a worse word for emphasis. She didn't need him. Not anymore. Last thing she needed. Her renegade thumb had brought up the photo. She'd expected Max Jr., but Sean Kelly's graying mahogany-red hair and freckled face spotted with specs of what must be shrapnel startled her.

Deirdre had a long, thick bushel of curly red-gold hair and a Sean O'Casey face, naturally strong and handsome. Temple had loved to recite the Irish playwright's dialogue in playwriting class in college. Had Temple's red hair been a main attraction for Max? Had Max's Irish heritage attracted her? Had both of them been drawn to unsuspected traces of their pasts, although Max's had been bred in the bone and the blood, and hers only in the imagination?

Temple looked at the phone screen, the photo. Time to turn the page. Close the book.

She'd ask Matt to write the last chapter. He deserved it.

45
Last Acts

The day after the night he'd stormed Electra's new building, been released by Molina to make his midnight radio show just in time, and had come home to Temple's place for a fervent and fevered reunion after they'd had a double dose of the aphrodisiac of danger, Matt stood in a small lot near a busy, cheesy Vegas corner staring at a motley assortment of older-model cars.

He'd lived such a straight and narrow life as a priest he had mounted up few regrets. Maybe not strangling Cliff Effinger was still one of them, given how deeply the man had impacted his, and also Temple's, life even after his nasty end.

Now he regretted sacrificing Electra's Probe to storming her new building's front doors. A sincere regret, but one also selfish. Now he had to buy a replacement car for undercover work, ASAP, and be discreet about it. He'd never had a father to teach him to drive or to buy a car.

There'd been nothing for it but to call the man standing next to him, a man less than ten years older. When he'd reached Rafi Nadir at the Goliath Hotel, he hadn't known how to describe what he needed.

"Hey," Rafi had responded jovially. "What you need, my man, is a Tote-the-Note place. What kind of credit can you come up with?"

"Solid."

"Or better yet. Cash?"

"How much?"

"You're the wheeler-dealer. Tell me."

"I was a priest for many years. I saved the little I earned."

"Priest? You're not doing badly with the redhead for all that." Before Matt could take offense, Rafi said, "Sorry. I've run into some Catholic chicks in my time. Okay. Grab a cool five grand cash in small enough bills to haggle with, and meet me where I tell you. Four p.m. I'm on night shift. I'll pick you up."

"Uh, thanks. I think. Last time you picked me up was kind of a downer."

Rafi chuckled. "Don't worry. We're going to enjoy this."

Rafi had been optimistic. Rafi had enjoyed it. They had played good cop/bad cop—guess who was which ?—and Matt left in a 2001 gray Chevy Impala LS, rear spoiler, dickered down to thirty-nine hundred and ninety-five.

"It's sort of dull," Matt had told Rafi while the papers were being processed.

"That's the idea. Be unnoticeable."

So Matt drove his new old car to Woodrow Wetherly's place, learning the vintage dashboard layout as he went.

This was a different encounter. Now Matt had seen what had been in the trunk of the beater car that had gone from Wetherly's place into the desert and back.

The car and the trunk that had been waiting outside Electra's hulking new building…

…while the lethal chandelier had emitted its last rays of electrified light before being later disconnected, disassembled, and taken away, like Leon Nemo, Punch Adcock and Katt Zydeco.

...while Matt had seen the driver he'd followed to Red Rock Canyon and back finally leave the Chevy and slip around to the back of the building.

...when Matt had left the Probe carrying its jack and sneaked up to the Chevy trunk to find out what buried desert treasure occupied its trunk. He'd hardly needed the jack to break in, the locking mechanism was so flimsy.

He had been braced for bones.

What he saw in the dim light from the street lamp was worse.

When he'd pulled off the bulky canvas covering, he'd found the bulky, battered old 35-pound jackhammer powering a long thick chisel spike, its angular steel pointed like a pencil that had been sharpened by a razor knife. The metal body was spotted with dark gouts of red paint.

A.k.a. blood.

Mobster Giaccomo Petrocelli. Jack the Hammer. So named for jack-hammering people to death.

A legend long dead, but not forgotten.

And his favorite murder weapon retrieved to murder again.

Then Matt saw the headlights of a fleet of silent oncoming cars, obviously Fontana Inc., and decided to bust the Probe into the building...now!

That was last night. This was tonight. So here was Matt, where he did not want to be, but had to be.

"You know," the old guy said, leaning back into his big, battered recliner. "The time has come to talk of many things."

Matt felt like the Walrus strolling down the path with the Carpenter toward some innocent oysters. Rightfully. Who would eat whom?

"Yes, my young friend. Kid. Sonny boy. I suspect you are on the verge of knowing too much. Your Midnight Hour may be closer than you think."

"I do think that myself," Matt said.

"And yet you came back. You're beginning to interest me again. I admit you could have your uses. 'Call me irresponsible'," he crooned in a raw croak. And cackled. "I always did love Sinatra. And I don't think your foolish alibis will bore me."

"Is that the next line of the song?" Matt asked.

"Maybe. Depends on you if there *is* a next line to the song."

Tailpiece
Midnight Louie Sounds Off

Call me Speechless. Which is my default setting anyway.

Who knew I was in for a career revival? When my Miss Temple comes home and falls on her knees before me and nuzzles my neck I know something fishy is up and it is not Chicken of the Sea.

I also know I am not Bast with a gender adjustment and do in no way merit bowing and scraping.

"Oh, Louie," she exclaims. "It is so exciting."

Yeah? Say Fancy Feast is importing sea scallops on the half-shell for my personal supply and that would be exciting.

She then unrolls this media deal and tells me what a star I will be and how we will work together again and be able to use the new zebra-stripe carrier I abhor while flitting from city to city to do talk shows.

At last! My previous on-camera brilliance has been identified. I have even been able to drag Miss Temple along in a bit role, obtaining her a certain fame and a slew of new high-heeled shoes for me to embrace in a little game of Kick and Bite the Leather. Plus she will get a payment almost as handsome as I am, and residuals. Perhaps a Pixar movie someday.

But then…she starts sweet-talking me into the infamous plan to conceal my svelte athletic form in a stupid zebra-striped zoot suit, not to mention a matching new version of the previously offending fedora hat. Using the Fontana brothers as a backup act in similar baggy pants and zebra-print lapels does nothing to assuage my sense of being presented as a figure of fun rather than of 007-level rakish charm. Is this proper attire for one who has been favorably compared to Sherlock Holmes (without the aversion to females), Columbo, and Mike Hammer?

Who does she think I am, Lord Peter Wimsey?

I turn my head and look at the ceiling, all disinterested like, so she will owe me. However, after my transcendent experience with Elvis and the gang at Zebra Zoot Suit Choo-Choo, I figure I owe it to my public to get out there again and cut a rug and earn my treats. Karma is not the only one who can channel the past.

Now on to the nitpicking. No good deed goes unpunished, it is said, and here all we of Las Vegas Cat Pack nation are indeed going unhailed and unheeded.

After running our footpads off on the piping-hot Vegas pavements from the edge of Downtown to the Lower Strip turf to track a murderer, tail sleazy purveyors of naughty entertainment and foil scheming mobsters, we have been left high and dry. With not even a little catnip to make the "high" part of the state pleasant.

And these are not the only sins Miss Temple has committed recently.

I can eavesdrop on a cell phone call. My burning ears tell me Miss Temple may be rushing off to an alien clime called Wisconsin, leaving Mr. Matt Devine in the lurch and surely miffed. I cannot blame him. My Miss Temple may mean well, but she can exhibit a shocking disregard for her nearest and dearest in her quest to solve everyone else's problems personally. I too suffer from this tendency.

I am mightily miffed myself, and have hied myself up a floor to Mr. Matt's residence, where we can hang out together as two wronged bachelors. Miss Midnight Louise argues that only Miss Temple can "compensate" for Mr. Max's memory issues on the momentous occasion of reuniting with his family and his newly found-alive cousin Sean. Miss Midnight Louise was always partial to Mr. Max, who has always been overrated in my opinion.

We shall see whether my candidate or hers will win out in the end.

Very Best Fishes,

Midnight Louie, Esq.

Want Midnight Louie's print or e-scribe
Scratching Post-Intelligencer newsletter or
information on his custom T-shirt?
Contact Louie and Carole at PO BOX 33155
Fort Worth TX 76163-1555
Or sign up at www.carolenelsondouglas.com.
E-mail: cdouglas@catwriter.com

Tailpiece
Carole Nelson Douglas on Where
Midnight Louie is Going...or Not

Some readers have been fretting in recent years that arriving at the *Z* book in Louie's Alphabetical adventures means saying "Goodbye". We were flattered. We were also worried about reassuring readers in a New Media world where book format, distribution, and sales has changed, changed utterly in just a few years.

First, the next book is *Cat in an Alphabet Endgame.*

Well, doesn't that mean "the End"?

It means the end of the alphabet titles, but not of Louie and his world. Now, because of *cata*clysmic changes in the publishing industry, books don't need title signals to the order in which they were written to be read.

After Louie debuted in *Catnap,* not wanting to imitate an established, hugely successful cat mystery series' title format, I used *Pussyfoot* for my next title. (This is admirable ethics, but very bad marketing.) In fact, I refused to use the publisher's proposed title sequence as "too close," but did come up with a format with "cat" in it. By then, I realized that the series would unreel like an ensemble-cast TV series that lasted several seasons. So when the publisher accepted *Cat on a Blue Monday,* I realized the titles could continue with an internal alphabet on the color (or pattern, later) word.

That solved a problem of book marketing then. Mysteries series couldn't be numbered, because if every title was not currently on the store shelf, readers wouldn't pick up a series at Book Four, say. And all books sold on shelves, not websites. For a lovely long while my Midnight Louie and Irene Adler series occupied two entire shelves at the chain bookstores. Then chain stores started stocking fewer books. (Independent bookstores offered book-savvy clerks to advise readers about book order, but began to suffer from the Big Box competition.)

As *Crimson Haze* and *Diamond Dazzle* came out, readers began noticing the internal alphabet, just another fun little "clue" they figured out. Meanwhile, I was constantly explaining that the alphabet started with the second letter on the third book, after *Catnap* and *Pussyfoot*. I suggested to the publisher that we combine the first two books under a new "A" title, *Cat in an Aqua* Something. They graciously took a hard look at doing that, but the combined "A" book would be too long to market at a low-enough cover price.

Then came ebooks and bookselling websites. All of an author's books were on virtual "shelves" together. Authors whose print books would have eventually moldered into forgotten dust now had a "literary legacy" with copyrights that would last for seventy years after their deaths.

I took this as time to tidy up the things that "can't be helped" in the way traditional publishing worked. *Catnap* in eBook became *Cat in an Alphabet Soup*. Taking that as a "foundation" title, I changed *Pussyfoot* to *Cat in an Aqua Storm*, after the car Temple drove when the series began. *Cat on a Blue Monday* now fit in place. And I had an extra "concluding" book after *Cat in a Zebra Zoot Suit* to wrap up the continuing personal storylines and crime plots, *Cat in an Alphabet Endgame*.

As for Louie and me, we're looking forward to exploring a reimagined world where the old remains in place but fascinating new characters and cases show up. Louie's a veteran at this, having debuted in the first category romance quartet (with mystery) and then moving to this mystery series when, as I found myself searching for a way to explain to a library audience recently, I came up with "he was violated by a romance editor". We all laughed hysterically. The fact is forty percent of his narration went to the cutting-room floor, without me being notified.

I used to say you can do that to me (because worse violations have happened in publishing), but you can't do that to a twenty-pound alley cat who thinks he's Sam Spade.

But even Louie can't reinvent himself single-handedly. Only readers can do that. Thank you all for your support of the long journey Louie and company have made. The four human protagonists have all been forced to reexamine their family origins and issues and their own misconceptions and flaws so they can reconcile their pasts with the present, and their futures. Louie's cat family has made the journey too. Few authors are permitted, given the ups and downs of a publishing career, to finish such a long series.

It you think this sounds like "Good-bye," it is really a way of saying, Hang on, the best is yet to be. In all of our lives.

The Bestselling MIDNIGHT LOUIE Feline PI series

"...just about everything you might want in a mystery; among other things, glitzy Las Vegas...real characters, suspense, a tough puzzle... On top of it all, a fine sense of humor and some illuminating social commentary."—*The Prime Suspect*

"Las Vegas' feline detective extraordinary returns...an excellent follow-up...and Louie is an irresistible combination of Nathan Detroit and Sam Spade. There is plenty of interest here for a lengthy, fun-filled series."—*Mostly Murder*

Cat in an Alphabet Soup (formerly *Catnap*)...*Cat in an Aqua Storm* (formerly *Pussyfoot*)...*Cat on a Blue Monday*...*Cat in a Crimson Haze*...*Cat in a Diamond Dazzle*...*Cat with an Emerald Eye*...*Cat in a Flamingo Fedora*...*Cat in a Golden Garland*...*Cat on a Hyacinth Hunt*...*Cat in an Indigo Mood*...*Cat in a Jeweled Jumpsuit*...*Cat in a Kiwi Con*...*Cat in a Leopard Spot*...*Cat in a Midnight Choir*...*Cat in a Neon Nightmare*...*Cat in an Orange Twist*...*Cat in a Hot Pink Pursuit*...*Cat in a Quicksilver Caper*... *Cat in a Red Hot Rage*...*Cat in a Sapphire Slipper*...*Cat in a Topaz Tango*...*Cat in an Ultramarine Scheme*... *Cat in a Vegas Gold Vendetta*...*Cat in a White Tie and Tails*...*Cat in an Alien X-Ray*...*Cat in a Yellow Spotlight*...*Cat in a Zebra Zoot Suit*... (forthcoming) *Cat in an Alphabet Endgame*

ABOUT THE AUTHOR

www.carolenelsondouglas.com
www.wishlistpublishing.com

CAROLE NELSON DOUGLAS is the award-winning author of sixty-two novels in the mystery/thriller, women's fiction, and science fiction/fantasy genres.

She is noted for the long-running Midnight Louie, feline PI, cozy-noir mystery series (*Cat in an Alphabet Soup, Cat in an Aqua Storm, Cat on a Blue Monday,* etc.) and the Delilah Street, Paranormal Investigator, noir urban fantasy series (*Dancing with Werewolves,* etc.). Midnight Louie prowls the "slightly surreal" Vegas of today, narrating interlarded chapters in his alley-cat noir voice. Delilah walks the mean streets of a paranormally post-apocalyptic Sin City, fighting supernatural mobsters with Louie's wile, wit and grit.

Douglas was the first author to make a Sherlockian female character, Irene Adler, a series protagonist, with the *New York Times* Notable Book of the Year, *Good Night, Mr. Holmes,* and the first woman to write a Holmes spin-off series. Her award nominations run from the Agatha to the Nebula, including Lifetime Achievement

CPSIA information can be obtained
at www.ICGtesting.com
Printed in the USA
FSOW02n1946041016
25760FS

Awards from *RT Book Reviews* for Mystery, Suspense, Versatility, and as a Pioneer of Publishing for her groundbreaking multi-genre work. She has won a clowder of Catwriters' Association first place Muse awards, and is a four-time finalist for the Romance Writers of America's Rita award in four different categories.

An award-winning daily newspaper reporter and editor in Minnesota, she moved south to write fiction full-time and was recently inducted into the Texas Literary Hall of Fame. She does a mean Marilyn Monroe impersonation, collects vintage clothing and homeless cats, and enjoys Zumba, but has never danced with werewolves. (That she knows of.)